RUDYARD KIPLING (1865–1936) wa⸺ ⸺ ⸺ ⸺Bombay in December 1865. He returned to India from England in the autumn of 1882, shortly before his seventeenth birthday, to work as a journalist first on the *Civil and Military Gazette* in Lahore, then on the *Pioneer* at Allahabad. The poems and stories he wrote over the next seven years laid the foundation of his literary reputation, and soon after his return to London in 1889 he found himself world-famous. Throughout his life his works enjoyed great acclaim and popularity, but he came to seem increasingly controversial because of his political opinions, and it has been difficult to reach literary judgements unclouded by partisan feeling. This series, published half a century after Kipling's death, provides the opportunity for reconsidering his remarkable achievement.

ISABEL QUIGLY has been a free-lance writer for nearly all her working life. She has written a novel and three critical books, and has translated about 50 books, mostly from Italian. Her last book, *The Heirs of Tom Brown: The English School Story*, dealt with, among many others, the best school story of all, *Stalky & Co*. She is writing a history of the Royal Society of Literature for publication in 1999.

OXFORD WORLD'S CLASSICS

*For over 100 years Oxford World's Classics have brought
readers closer to the world's great literature. Now with over 700
titles—from the 4,000-year-old myths of Mesopotamia to the
twentieth century's greatest novels—the series makes available
lesser-known as well as celebrated writing.*

*The pocket-sized hardbacks of the early years contained
introductions by Virginia Woolf, T. S. Eliot, Graham Greene,
and other literary figures which enriched the experience of reading.
Today the series is recognized for its fine scholarship and
reliability in texts that span world literature, drama and poetry,
religion, philosophy and politics. Each edition includes perceptive
commentary and essential background information to meet the
changing needs of readers.*

OXFORD WORLD'S CLASSICS

RUDYARD KIPLING

The Complete Stalky & Co.

Edited with an Introduction and Notes by
ISABEL QUIGLY

OXFORD
UNIVERSITY PRESS

OXFORD

UNIVERSITY PRESS

Great Clarendon Street, Oxford OX2 6DP

Oxford University Press is a department of the University of Oxford.
It furthers the University's objective of excellence in research, scholarship,
and education by publishing worldwide in

Oxford New York

Athens Auckland Bangkok Bogotá Buenos Aires Cape Town
Chennai Dar es Salaam Delhi Florence Hong Kong Istanbul Karachi
Kolkata Kuala Lumpur Madrid Melbourne Mexico City Mumbai Nairobi
Paris São Paulo Shanghai Singapore Taipei Tokyo Toronto Warsaw

with associated companies in Berlin Ibadan

Oxford is a registered trade mark of Oxford University Press
in the UK and in certain other countries

Published in the United States
by Oxford University Press Inc., New York

British Library Cataloguing in Publication Data

Data available

Library of Congress Cataloging in Publication Data
Kipling, Rudyard 1865–1936.
Stalky & Co.
(Oxford world's classics)
Bibliography: p.
I. Quigly, Isabel. II. Title. III. Series
Stalky and Company
PR4854.S68 1987 823'.8 86–16524

ISBN 978–0–19–955503–1

14

Printed in Great Britain by
Clays Ltd, Elcograf S.p.A.

CONTENTS

GENERAL PREFACE

RUDYARD KIPLING (1865–1936) was for the last decade of
the nineteenth century and at least the first two decades of the
twentieth the most popular writer in English, in both verse
and prose, throughout the English-speaking world. Widely
regarded as the greatest living English poet and story-teller,
winner of the Nobel Prize for Literature, recipient of honor-
ary degrees from the Universities of Oxford, Cambridge,
Edinburgh, Durham, McGill, Strasbourg, and the Sorbonne,
he also enjoyed popular acclaim that extended far beyond
academic and literary circles.

He stood, it can be argued, in a special relation to the age
in which he lived. He was primarily an artist, with his
individual vision and techniques, but his was also a
profoundly representative consciousness. He seems to give
expression to a whole phase of national experience,
symbolizing in appropriate forms (as Lascelles Abercrombie
said the epic poet must do) the 'sense of the significance of life
he [felt] acting as the unconscious metaphysic of the time'.[1]
He is in important ways a spokesman for his age, with its
sense of imperial destiny, its fascinated contemplation of the
unfamiliar world of soldiering, its confidence in engineering
and technology, its respect for craftsmanship, and its
dedication to Carlyle's gospel of work. That age is one about
which many Britons—and to a lesser extent Americans and
West Europeans—now feel an exaggerated sense of guilt; and
insofar as Kipling was its spokesman, he has become our
scapegoat. Hence, in part at least, the tendency in recent
decades to dismiss him so contemptuously, so unthinkingly,
and so mistakenly. Whereas if we approach him more
historically, less hysterically, we shall find in this very relation
to his age a cultural phenomenon of absorbing interest.

Here, after all, we have the last English author to appeal to
readers of all social classes and all cultural groups, from

[1] Cited in E. M. W. Tillyard, *The Epic Strain in the English Novel*,
London, 1958, p. 15.

lowbrow to highbrow; and the last poet to command a mass
audience. He was an author who could speak directly to the
man in the street, or for that matter in the barrack-room or
factory, more effectively than any left-wing writer of the
'thirties or the present day, but who spoke just as directly and
effectively to literary men like Edmund Gosse and Andrew
Lang; to academics like David Masson, George Saintsbury,
and Charles Eliot Norton; to the professional and service
classes (officers and other ranks alike) who took him to their
hearts; and to creative writers of the stature of Henry James,
who had some important reservations to record, but who
declared in 1892 that 'Kipling strikes me personally as the
most complete man of genius (as distinct from fine intelligence) that I have ever known', and who wrote an enthusiastic
introduction to *Mine Own People* in which he stressed
Kipling's remarkable appeal to the sophisticated critic as well
as to the common reader.[2]

An innovator and a virtuoso in the art of the short story,
Kipling does more than any of his predecessors to establish it
as a major genre. But within it he moves confidently between
the poles of sophisticated simplicity (in his earliest tales) and
the complex, closely organized, elliptical and symbolic mode
of his later works which reveal him as an unexpected
contributor to modernism.

He is a writer who extends the range of English literature
in both subject-matter and technique. He plunges readers into
new realms of imaginative experience which then become part
of our shared inheritance. His anthropological but warmly
human interest in mankind in all its varieties produces, for
example, sensitive, sympathetic vignettes of Indian life and
character which culminate in *Kim*. His sociolinguistic
experiments with proletarian speech as an artistic medium in
Barrack-Room Ballads and his rendering of the life of private
soldiers in all their unregenerate humanity gave a new
dimension to war literature. His portrayal of Anglo-Indian life

[2] See *Kipling: The Critical Heritage*, ed. Roger Lancelyn Green, London,
1971, pp. 159–60. *Mine Own People*, published in New York in 1891, was a
collection of stories nearly all of which were to be subsumed in *Life's
Handicap* later that year.

ranges from cynical triviality in some of the *Plain Tales from the Hills* to the stoical nobility of the best things in *Life's Handicap* and *The Day's Work*. Indeed Mrs Hauksbee's Simla, Mulvaney's barrack-rooms, Dravot and Carnehan's search for a kingdom in Kafiristan, Holden's illicit, star-crossed love, Stalky's apprenticeship, Kim's Grand Trunk Road, 'William''s famine relief expedition, and the Maltese Cat's game at Umballa, establish the vanished world of Empire for us (as they established the unknown world of Empire for an earlier generation), in all its pettiness and grandeur, its variety and energy, its miseries, its hardships, and its heroism.

In a completely different vein Kipling's genius for the animal fable as a means of inculcating human truths opens up a whole new world of joyous imagining in the two *Jungle Books*. In another vein again are the stories in which he records his delighted discovery of the English countryside, its people and traditions, after he had settled at Bateman's in Sussex: England, he told Rider Haggard in 1902, 'is the most wonderful foreign land I have ever been in';[3] and he made it peculiarly his own. Its past gripped his imagination as strongly as its present, and the two books of Puck stories show what Eliot describes as 'the development of the imperial . . . into the historical imagination.'[4] In another vein again he figures as the bard of engineering and technology. From the standpoint of world history, two of Britain's most important areas of activity in the nineteenth century were those of industrialism and imperialism, both of which had been neglected by literature prior to Kipling's advent. There is a substantial body of work on the Condition of England Question and the socio-economic effects of the Industrial Revolution; but there is comparatively little imaginative response in literature (as opposed to painting) to the extraordinary inventive energy, the dynamic creative power, which manifests itself in (say) the work of engineers like Telford, Rennie, Brunel, and the brothers Stephenson—men who revolutionized communications within Britain by their

[3] *Rudyard Kipling to Rider Haggard*, ed. Morton Cohen, London, 1965, p. 51.
[4] T. S. Eliot, *On Poetry and Poets*, London, 1957, p. 247.

road, rail and harbour systems, producing in the process masterpieces of industrial art, and who went on to revolutionize ocean travel as well. Such achievements are acknowledged on a sub-literary level by Samuel Smiles in his best-selling *Lives of the Engineers* (1861–2). They are acknowledged also by Carlyle, who celebrates the positive as well as denouncing the malign aspects of the transition from the feudal to the industrial world, insisting as he does that the true modern epic must be technological, not military: 'For we are to bethink us that the Epic verily is not *Arms and the Man*, but *Tools and the Man*,—an infinitely wider kind of Epic.'[5] That epic has never been written in its entirety, but Kipling came nearest to achieving its aims in verses like 'McAndrew's Hymn' (*The Seven Seas*) and stories like 'The Ship that Found Herself' and 'Bread upon the Waters' (*The Day's Work*) in which he shows imaginative sympathy with the machines themselves as well as sympathy with the men who serve them. He comes nearer, indeed, than any other author to fulfilling Wordsworth's prophecy that

If the labours of men of Science should ever create any material revolution, direct or indirect, in our condition, and in the impressions which we habitually receive, the Poet will sleep then no more than at present, but he will be ready to follow the steps of the Man of Science, not only in those general indirect effects, but he will be at his side, carrying sensation into the midst of the objects of the Science itself.[6]

This is one aspect of Kipling's commitment to the world of work, which, as C. S. Lewis observes, 'imaginative literature in the eighteenth and nineteenth centuries had [with a few exceptions] quietly omitted, or at least thrust into the background', though it occupies most of the waking hours of most men:

And this did not merely mean that certain technical aspects of life were unrepresented. A whole range of strong sentiments and emotions—for many men, the strongest of all—went with them. . . . It was Kipling who first reclaimed for literature this enormous territory.[7]

[5] *Past and Present* (1843), Book iv, ch.1. cf. ibid., Book iii, ch. 5.

[6] *Lyrical Ballads*, ed. R. L. Brett and A. R. Jones, London, 1963, pp. 253–4.

[7] 'Kipling's World', *Literature and Life: Addresses to the English Association*, London, 1948, pp. 59–60.

He repudiates the unspoken assumption of most novelists that the really interesting part of life takes place outside working hours: men at work or talking about their work are among his favourite subjects. The qualities men show in their work, and the achievements that result from it (bridges built, ships salvaged, pictures painted, famines relieved) are the very stuff of much of Kipling's fiction. Yet there also runs through his *œuvre*, like a figure in the carpet, a darker, more pessimistic vision of the impermanence, the transience—but not the worthlessness—of all achievement. This underlies his delighted engagement with contemporary reality and gives a deeper resonance to his finest work, in which human endeavour is celebrated none the less because it must ultimately yield to death and mutability.

ANDREW RUTHERFORD

INTRODUCTION

'An unpleasant book about unpleasant boys at an unpleasant school':[1] comments like this one of George Sampson's have dogged *Stalky & Co* since the stories first appeared in book form in 1899. And this was by no means the harshest. From Wells's condemnation of the heroes as self-righteous bullies and A. C. Benson's description of them as 'little beasts' to Maugham's magisterial 'a more odious picture of school life can seldom have been drawn',[2] the disapproval of Kipling's contemporaries was made thunderously clear. 'Mr Kipling obviously aims at verisimilitude; the picture he draws is at any rate repulsive and disgusting enough to be true,' wrote Robert Buchanan, his most virulent critic. 'Only the spoiled child of an utterly brutalised public could possibly have written *Stalky & Co* . . . It is simply impossible to show by mere quotation the horrible vileness of the book describing these three small fiends in human likeness; only a perusal of the whole work would convey to the reader its truly repulsive character . . . The vulgarity, the brutality, the savagery . . . reeks on every page.'[3] If at this point one feels like saying, with Stalky, something like 'Phew!', there are more recent comments in much the same vein—Edmund Wilson's, for instance: 'a hair-raising picture of the sadism of the English public-school system'[4]—and even today the book can arouse passionate feelings of dislike, resentment, even disgust.

Yet its supporters have been quite as fervent, and its popularity with the young, that only guarantee of a school story's longevity, has never waned. Intensity and exuberance in the hands of a writer like Kipling can hardly fail to arouse

[1] *Concise Cambridge History of English Literature* (Cambridge, 1942), p. 959.

[2] See *Kipling: The Critical Heritage*, ed. Roger Lancelyn Green (London, 1971), pp. 306–7, 318; *A Choice of Kipling's Prose* (London, 1952), p. vi.

[3] See *Kipling: The Critical Heritage*, pp. 244–5.

[4] See *Kipling's Mind and Art*, ed. Andrew Rutherford (Edinburgh and London, 1964), p. 21 (from 'The Kipling that Nobody Read' in *The Wound and the Bow*, 1941).

partisan attitudes, and the immediacy of *Stalky & Co* is one of the most remarkable things about it. That, and the fact that its outlook, its central characters, its ideals and ideas, still hold lessons for us today. The world it belonged to may have gone, but the points it makes still have relevance to ours, and the exuberance with which it makes them hammers this home.

Although it belongs to the school-story genre, it is unlike any other school story. *Tom Brown's School Days* started a literary industry which produced hundreds of school stories over the next century, all dealing with the self-contained, rule-ridden world of the Victorian—and later the Edwardian and Georgian—public school. Twenty-five years later Talbot Baines Reed with *The Fifth Form at St Dominic's* and other books gave the genre a recognizable popular form. His many followers were undistinguished and mostly indistinguishable, and stuck closely to the conventions he laid down. Parallel with their books went a more literary, more seriously intentioned brand of school story, aiming to give a more realistic or more romantic, sometimes a more adult, view of public-school life. Between the two and quite unlike either— the popular or the more individual, more ambitious stories— came *Stalky & Co*. It appeared exactly in the middle of the genre's century of life, several stories coming out at various dates after the early ones had appeared in book form, and the whole being collected as *The Complete Stalky & Co* as late as 1929.

The fact that Kipling was an incomparably better writer than the others (only P. G. Wodehouse, whose earliest books were school stories, can be mentioned beside him) makes *Stalky & Co* unlike the other school stories in quality, of course. When a writer of genius takes up a popular genre without condescension or casualness, indeed with the greatest commitment and (jokes notwithstanding) seriousness, and an enthusiasm for the task which is clear in every line, something happens to the genre, it shows possibilities and depths which, in the hands of others, it never seemed to possess. In Kipling's, the school story managed to cross the often uneasily described division between adult life and boyhood, and between the mature attitude of the writer and the unripe outlook of his heroes (a transition no other school-story writer coped with adequately). For all its 'commitedness' of mood, its sense of sharing totally the everyday life and outlook of fifteen-year-olds, looking back on them became not an exercise in nostalgia but a way of understanding and working out what was to come, what they were to grow into.

What happened to these boys? How did they apply the lessons learned at school to the world of warfare and imperial administration? These questions are implied throughout the book and answered explicitly in the final chapter. *Stalky & Co* is the only school story which shows school as a *direct* preparation for life. Most others actually make the world outside school seem irrelevant, an anticlimax, an unimaginable void. Kipling, for all his intense feeling for the school atmosphere and the moods of adolescence, shows school as the first stage of a much larger game, a pattern-maker for the experiences of life. This is mainly what makes it unlike the others, with their narrow, school-centred preoccupations and their belief, often implied and sometimes even stated, in the overwhelming importance of this preliminary stage of life, which was actually presumed to outdo the rest in importance. In Kipling, not only is a later life envisaged very clearly at school, but the divisions between school and the world outside are less clearly defined than they are in most other school stories; not just in the sense that the boys make free with the surrounding countryside and hobnob happily with the locals, bilingual in standard English and broad Devon, but in a metaphorical sense: school teaches lessons (obviously), but, less obviously, the lessons are much more than those of the classroom. It teaches the boys how to live; but above all, the boys teach one another.

But *Stalky & Co* was unlike the other school stories not merely in quality, or even in form. It was unlike them in kind. It dealt with an odd school, based on the United Services College where Kipling was sent, and it had few of the interests, accepted few of the conventions, of other school stories. The Coll, as it is called in the book, was a raw new foundation set up for boys destined for the army or the colonial service in some form, whose parents could not afford the smarter Haileybury, of which it was an offshoot. Those who came expecting the familiar features of school life barked their shins on the reality soon enough. 'The Head should have warned Mr Brownell of the College's outstanding peculiarity, instead of leaving him to discover it for himself the first day of term,' 'The United Idolators' begins, and this oddity is stressed again and again with a sort of sly pride. Difference, oddity, practicality, even poverty: these made for a certain truculence in Kipling and in the boys he describes, and brought a feeling of modernity and a sense of facing up to the facts of life and of careers that are noticeably absent from other school stories.

King, for instance, a master both disliked and reluctantly admired, keeps 'talking round and over the boys' heads, in a lofty and promiscuous style, of public-school spirit and the traditions of ancient seats'. But Flint, one of the prefects, puts this sort of thing into perspective. 'As I told King, we aren't a public school,' he says. 'We're a limited liability company payin' four per cent. My father's a shareholder too . . . We've got to get into the army or—get out, haven't we? King's hired by the Council to teach us. All the rest's flumdiddle. Can't you see?' To mention money, the importance of exams, the need for cramming ('King's the best classical cram we've got', and therefore must be borne), the non-public-school qualities and even status of one's own school—all this was heresy in the late nineteenth-century school story.

As for Kipling, who put himself into the book as the central character called Beetle, he was sent to the United Services College almost by chance, because the headmaster, Cormell Price, was a family friend. It was not really his sort of school. He was not really the sort of boy it catered for. As the only boy who wore glasses (and who was almost blind without them), he was the only one there physically unable to do what the others were being prepared for. However boyish and exuberant the mood of *Stalky & Co*, the future looms over all its action. This or that boy, we are told now and then, quite casually as he enters the story, will die in action in such-and-such a place, within the next three or four years. Danger, initiative, heroism, death: Kipling could write of them all but was not, unlike his schoolfellows, to be involved with them physically, factually. At sixteen he left school for a job on a newspaper in India, news of his remarkable gifts having gone ahead of him. If he was not to have the military glory of some of his friends (the model for Stalky himself ended as a general), he could at least be their chronicler.

Between his imaginative genius and their gifts as men of action—physical and psychological attributes he would never have himself—he was torn throughout his life and perhaps particularly at school; therefore even more so in writing about school, where the two collided most noticeably. The United Services College trained boys to become practical, efficient, brave and effective leaders throughout the Empire, and Kipling envied them their practicality and efficiency, admired their courage and competence (qualities he was to celebrate in all he wrote). His own time at the USC was successful, fulfilled, and apparently happy, his standing high with the other boys, his gifts recognized and encouraged by the headmaster and two other masters who had some influence on his early writing. But he did not and could not fully belong there. The ardour, vehemence, even aggressiveness and violence of his tone when he looked back to his school-days must surely have been a compensation for this, a sign of his wistfulness in the face of the privileged society of ingenious, daring, hardy future rulers in which he spent his curious early and middle teens.

I say 'curious' because he was curiously unlike the central schoolboy of fiction or of fact in those days; so odd, indeed, that it is surprising, and a sign of the school's open-mindedness, to find him accepted, even admired there. 'Anything that Gigger did "went" ', G. C. Beresford, the model for M'Turk, assures us;[5] also mentioning the 'Gigger regime' (Gigger was Kipling's school nickname, from gig-lamps, an allusion to the spectacles he wore). Kipling's high status at school was odd considering what an unlikely candidate for school importance he was. The public schools of the time were aggressively athletic, as book after book (memoirs as well as fiction) makes often wearisomely clear,

[5] *Schooldays with Kipling* (London, 1936), p. 202.

and Kipling was hopeless at games and made no pretence of enthusiasm for any sport but swimming. The intellectual or cultivated boy, the aesthete, the poet, the swot, was generally despised, whereas the school heroes, or 'bloods' as they were called, were almost invariably athletes, with the qualities that went or were thought to go with athleticism: physical strength, a masterful personality, and good looks. With them, even moral qualities were supposed to march, qualities of leadership, straightforwardness, a clean-cut presence and style of life. The boy the other boys admired and the masters respected was almost invariably a sportsman.

Whereas Kipling (who went so far in identifying with Beetle that he became 'I' in the final chapter, marked with that dark, unattractive and somehow scuttling, squashable name) was the very opposite of all this: brilliant and devious, intellectual and precocious, and very odd-looking indeed—which, in particular, counted at school. His difference from the rest lay not only, or not so much, in his poor eyesight (that on its own would have handicapped him, but made him a figure of pathos, perhaps likely to arouse sympathy) as in his presence and his looks. Small, plump, peering and furry, with a perceptible moustache when he arrived at twelve, a full-grown one in group photographs at fifteen, and a chest that had to be shaved for some minor operation at school, he was anything but familiar-looking or reassuring.

Obviously he was physically mature. He also seems to have been sexually forward, having fallen in love at fourteen and considering himself engaged to the girl for several years after leaving school. This never appears or is hinted at in the Stalky stories, but it does suggest his physical and emotional difference from the others. The patterns of school life in those days were homosexual in the literal sense that they were 'one-sexed', that women had no place there, the feminine and domestic qualities no importance. Not that Kipling ever goes into that—'beastliness' is the word he uses, as others did at the time, for any manifestation of homosexual feeling. But male looks and charm counted, in a single-sex community, and perhaps the monkey-like boy, so adultly furred, so distressingly plain, needed to put an almost hysterical enthusiasm into his memories of school to persuade himself that he belonged among the ordinary others, his cronies rather than lasting, lifelong friends.

*   *   *   *   *

As a series of stories, not a single novel with a continuous plot, *Stalky & Co* scores over most other school stories because it keeps up interest and emotional intensity in energetic bursts of narrative, each complete in itself, each worked out to make a satisfactory pattern. Most school stories sag because their plots are not interesting or convincing enough to keep up interest or conviction long enough. *Stalky & Co* has the same characters and situations throughout but very different things happen to them in each chapter. Each story, or nearly each one, is a carefully constructed tale of come-uppance, or who it is who gets it. It is about (on the whole lighthearted) revenge.

The first tale (of the *Complete Stalky*) is simple enough and serves to give Stalky his nickname. Officially he is Arthur Lionel Corkran, or Corky to his friends. But Corky becomes Stalky when he manages a particularly neat rescue of some silly boys who, unprepared, stumble into trouble with an angry farmer and his cattle; because in USC slang the word 'stalky' meant clever and cunning. In the stories it stands for survival, success against the enemy regardless of what means are used, a sense of power, joy, fun, even dignity in the achievement of victory. It stands for everything the schoolboy needs in order to keep his end up against authority and the school ethos. And this is perhaps mainly why *Stalky & Co* seemed a disruptive, subversive, and disturbing book to adults when it appeared, and why the young, girls as well as boys, so often find it exhilarating.

Most school stories, certainly the approved ones, were really on the side of the status quo and the conventions of school life. Their passionate devotion to athletics and the athlete, their championing of those with a roaring enthusiasm for what was then thought important at school—rivalries, house matches, matters of schoolboy honour and face-saving—showed that school-story writers (however much they might champion healthy high spirits, even 'wildness') were anxious to be on the winning side, the side that had adult approval. Whereas Kipling makes his *schoolboys* the winners, while the adults are often discomfitted. Mainly these adults are masters, but occasionally a local farmer or a priggish prefect (who in school terms counts almost as an adult) is spiked on the sheer stalkiness of Stalky.

Stalky is unlike other school-story heroes because he is indeed heroic, as the boyish Tom Brown and his imitators never are; he is outsize in cleverness, in leadership, in improvisation, and these qualities, which he learns and then hones with endless patience and practice at school, are going to stand him in good stead later, in amazing feats not just of dash and courage but of deviousness and ingenuity. 'Stalky stalked,' one of his friends says admiringly in the final chapter. 'That's all there is to it.'

When one of the book's critics[6] complained that the boys were 'not like boys at all, but like hideous little men', he had a point. Kipling's biographer Charles Carrington remarked that in *Stalky & Co* he shows 'a world of work like manhood, not a world of play like childhood'.[7] Stalky's school successes scored over others, although put across in the language of young uproariousness, are exactly like the imperial successes we hear of in the final chapter. In undermining the alliance between his two enemy groups, the Khye-Kheens and the Malôts, he uses exactly the same ruses that he used at school to undermine King or the prefects. Even the song from the house pantomime—'Arrah, Patsy, mind the baby'—is played on a bugle to rally troops and sort out allies from enemies. Details of school life and language are vivid after fifteen years and used with effect to describe, to make images of, the present. If this is adult life, working life, imperial life, then school life prefigures it exactly.

Stalky and his friends M'Turk and Beetle have few of the usual schoolboy interests—sporting success, the prestige of being prefects, cheering at house matches or even achieving (as Beetle is well able to achieve) academic success with the likes of King. (Unless, as happens in 'The Propagation of

---

[6] Robert Buchanan. See *Kipling: The Critical Heritage*, p. 245.
[7] *Rudyard Kipling: His Life and Work*, 3rd edn., 1978, p. 63.

Knowledge', they achieve it in a roundabout way by sharing the results of Beetle's wide reading among several boys, and thus teasing the unsuspecting King.) What concerns them is their private, even secret life, sometimes led in defiance of authority, as when they find a cliff-top hiding place where they read, smoke, and escape the pressures of communal life; sometimes in laudable or at least harmless pursuits, like writing poetry (in Beetle's case) or producing the house pantomime; but most often in keeping their end up and quietly—or not so quietly—gloating over the downfall of their adversaries.

No one discovers what ruses they use or even that they have used any at all, except their friend the chaplain, who sees round them all too well, and the headmaster, a great man who knows everything. The others merely know that, if Stalky is thwarted, something happens, someone else suffers for it. Stalky and Co always have alibis, unshakeable excuses, a look of injured innocence if accused. King's study is wrecked by a drunken villager, and no one can know that Stalky enraged him into wrecking it. When the three are turned out of their study, Prout's House is mysteriously disrupted (how? All anyone knows, except the chaplain, who guesses, is that it happens). Accused by King of being unwashed and smelly, they make his House stink to high heaven by sliding a dead cat in between attic floor boards and the ceiling below. In a notably nasty chapter two bullies are tortured as they tormented their young victim. A prefect too big for his boots is humiliated before his fellows by being accused of immoral conduct, Stalky and Co having got a village girl to kiss him in public. And so on. It is (though the word had not then been invented) purest oneupmanship in action.

Some of their ideas for these ruses come from books. Galton's *The Art of Travel* gives them 'the bleating of the kid excites the tiger', which suggests that bullies may be lured by the noise made by their victim. Mrs Oliphant's *Beleaguered City* gives them an idea for misleading Prout. Isaac D'Israeli's *Curiosities of Literature* is a mine of miscellaneous information which can be spread among his friends by Beetle for the confusion of King. Viollet-le-Duc shows him how a house is built and therefore where a dead cat may be stowed. But, as with Stalky's military manoeuvres in India, the best results come from the application of experience, the pattern of repeating something already done: in 'The Propagation of Knowledge', for instance, a boy tells how a sapper uncle of his discovered that the colonel examining him on field-fortification had a passion for the Lost Tribes of Israel, and by interested discussion on the subject with the old fellow got top marks in a subject he knew nothing about. The boys seize on the idea when they face an outside examiner in English Literature, who, they discover, is much taken with the Baconian heresy (that Bacon wrote the works of Shakespeare), which they have been swotting up to annoy King. When the examiner finds they can discuss it with him all goes smoothly, and they pass with flying colours.

Other themes are less dramatically but no less exuberantly introduced. In 'The United Idolators' an entire community is stirred almost to mass hysteria by a craze for a particular book,—*Uncle Remus*—its slang and oddities, its fetishes and characters. In 'Regulus', we learn what school stories very seldom tell us, that school work may be vigorously done and sometimes even enjoyed, that a little Latin may actually 'stick' and the master may therefore feel his uphill task is worth-while. In 'The Flag of their Country', we see adult falsity disgusting the young, when an MP the boys nickname the Jelly-bellied Flag-flapper talks of forbidden subjects like Honour and Patriotism, matters too close to their hearts and too delicately felt to bear talking about.

All this—the choice of theme, the intricacies of plot, the treatment—is so far from the form or content of most school stories that it seems another genre, certainly part of another world. Hardly surprising, when one considers that at Beetle's age of fifteen or so Kipling was already a prolific poet (published, albeit reluctantly) and an omnivorous reader in French as well as English, with the run of the headmaster's library. As nephew of two famous contemporary painters (Burne-Jones and Poynter), he had intellectual friends in London and a stimulating out-of-school life when he wanted it (including a cultural trip to Paris, much enjoyed) and was, as his biographer Charles Carrington puts it, 'a rebel and a progressive, which is to say, in 1882—paradoxically—that he was a decadent. His friends, his teachers, were liberals,' Carrington goes on; 'his tastes were "aesthetic", the writers he most admired were the fashionable pessimists.'[8] Then his headmaster and hero, Cormell Price, was anything but a mainstream Victorian pedagogue: not in orders, like most headmasters then, not even a strong churchman, and anti-Establishment enough to organize a Workmen's Neutrality demonstration in Islington to protest against Beaconsfield's imperialism. Kipling's study-sharers, too, were readers if not intellectuals like himself: 'Stalky' a fanatic for Surtees, 'M'Turk' for Ruskin, with the aesthetic interests this implied (he was the study decorator, the acknowledged expert on visual matters). L. C. Dunsterville, the original of Stalky, and G. C. Beresford, the original of M'Turk, both much later wrote books about their schooldays and their friendship with Kipling. Beresford's account is long-winded and uninspired and (although his drawings of 'Gigger' and others in the book are naturally interesting) adds little to what we know from Kipling. But Dunsterville's exploits in the army provided a remarkable example of stalkiness in real life and justified all that Kipling felt and said about the school's capacity to train boys for the future; in Dunsterville's case, a very particular future. Kipling himself wrote about the school—the 'real', not the fictional, school—six years before Stalky & Co first appeared, in an essay entitled 'An English School', first published in 1893 and later collected in Land and Sea Tales for Scouts and Guides; and in Something of Myself the chapter called 'The School Before its Time' has more to say about it. The discrepancies between 'real life' and fiction closely based on memories of it, and between Kipling's own memories and those of his friends, are, for the enthusiast, fascinating to follow in detail; and there is plenty of detail available. What is clear from both the real-life accounts and from Stalky & Co itself is that the atmosphere of this unusual school, or at least of Stalky and Co's Study No. 5, must have been remarkably unlike that of the average public school of the time. For one

[8] *Rudyard Kipling: His Life and Work*, p. 74.

thing, there were none of the usual compulsory parades, uniforms, bands, flags, and propaganda; there was no obvious militarism in spite of the school's army connections; and there was no fagging.

Nor was either school—the real one or the fictional Coll which, physically, was exactly the same—in size and shape and general appearance like the conventional public school. No elms or quadrangles or spaciousness, no ancient buildings or ivy-covered walls. 'Twelve bleak houses on the shore' Kipling called it in his dedicatory verses to the book; in other words, a row of seaside boarding houses, which had been adapted for this purpose. He seems to have enjoyed stressing its difference from other schools, its roughness and even scruffiness, the untamed boy material it was given to work on. In atmosphere and effect he made it tougher and coarser than it need have been, noisier, more violent, deliberately more excitable. Why was this, and what was Kipling trying to say by using what Andrew Rutherford has called 'a sophisticated Philistinism, a deliberate brutality of speech [which he suggests] is one of the most unpleasant features of *Stalky & Co*'?[9]

Partly, of course, it was for dramatic effect, the effect achieved with less artistry by children's comics, by all knockabout narrative. High spirits and excitement arouse a response in the reader and many readers of all ages and certainly both sexes have been moved, like the velvet-suited hero of a once-famous school story, *The Bending of a Twig*, to a partisan passion for Stalky's doings and to shouting 'Go it, Stalky!' as he does, if only to get back at authority. Partly it is an excuse to mock, not the boys Kipling approved of, who went through the system and came out on top in the Empire, but the prigs and conformers, those who lacked the aggressive, extrovert qualities he admired, who cheered at house-matches and behaved like the good boys of mainstream school stories. But partly, as I have suggested, it may have compensated for his own sense of inadequacy in a community where he could not belong, being psychologically an outsider, an artist in the wrong place, and physically incompetent: 'trained as an

[9] *Kipling's Mind and Art*, p. 183.

officer who could never have a regiment, a ruler with no one
to rule, an artist who must on no account betray his emotions,'
as Philip Mason puts it.[10]

And clearly, for all its loud-mouthed, even knockabout
qualities, the writing in *Stalky & Co* is on a very different
level from that of other school stories (as it could hardly fail
to be, coming from Kipling's hand). Edmund Wilson called
it 'from the artistic point of view, certainly the worst of
Kipling's books: crude in writing, trashy in feeling,
implausible in a series of contrivances that resemble moving-
picture "gags" '.[11] But his dislike of it made Wilson blind to
some of Kipling's finest descriptions of natural scenery (the
sea, above all) and a fluent, intensely observant style that is
anything but crude in its use of detail and of certain aspects
of boy behaviour, seen not exactly from boy-level but with a
persuasive understanding of boy nature.

Of course *Stalky & Co* was selective, as public school itself
was selective in taking boys out of their natural surroundings
and subjecting them to one of the most artificial disciplines
and rule-ridden systems ever devised as a training of the
young. It took, as school took, only certain parts of a boy's
nature, spirit, and personality. The domestic, the familial, the
feminine, the humdrum, everyday, uncompetitive aspects of
his being were all discarded and life was lived in dramatic,
highly charged, competitive circumstances where keeping
one's end up mattered supremely and the lonely,
uncomfortable eminence, the responsbilities and urgencies
and decisions that would be part of an administrative or
military life in the empire (or indeed anywhere else in the
world, away from home) were all foreshadowed. School was
like that, in Kipling's day, and *Stalky & Co* reflected the
reality. Self-respect, a proud reserve, a decent degree of
loyalty, keeping one's mouth shut when necessary: these
counted. 'If' put it all (and rather more, morally speaking) into
phrases that have been hated (because seized upon by the
wrong people) or loved (when they have no such barnacles of
feeling attached to them). The selectiveness of *Stalky & Co*,

[10] *Kipling: The Glass, The Shadow and The Fire* (London, 1975), p. 310.
[11] *Kipling's Mind and Art*, p. 23.

like the moral selectiveness of 'If', was a direct result of the age—its taboos, its restrictions, even its schools—but because Kipling's gifts always took him, sometimes despite himself, beyond these restrictions, his pin-hole view of the world from *Stalky & Co* opened out on to an immense panorama of life and experience beyond school: asking questions, giving answers. ' "Prove it," said the Infant. And I have!' These are the book's last words, Kipling's truculent, triumphant boast that he had made his point, that what he called rather oddly his 'tracts' and 'parables' (the words have religious overtones, of course) indeed proved all kinds of things about the nature of his society, even the future world as it was going to be.

* * * * *

Stalky himself is interesting as a period piece, though not attractive to modern readers; or rather, as heroic material, unacceptable today. It took an empire not just to contain him but to provide scope for his energy and qualities. When he first appeared, many people refused to accept the idea of such a man (for one has always to think of him as an adult, at least in importance and intention) being not merely useful but indispensible to the Empire. Hence some at least of the outcry. 'The Stalky ethos was raw, practical, and unsentimental,' Janet Adam Smith writes, 'and it shocked a good many patriots and loyal Old Boys.' Newbolt, she says, 'celebrates the solitary hero, honourable and brave . . . Kipling celebrates the ingenious and crafty hero, working with others in a vividly realised situation—to do his job. Newbolt's poetical heroes tend to die, nobly; Kipling's prose ones to survive, craftily. Kipling's were more use to the Empire.'[12]

Fictional or factual, Stalky also needed the imperial world to survive in, its ideas and attitudes to uphold his behaviour. The very adjective 'imperial' applies to him because to function at all such a man needs devoted followers, childlike admirers to whom he seems godlike, unquestionably right. At

[12] See her essay 'Boy of Letters', *Rudyard Kipling: the Man, his Work and his World*, ed. John Gross (London, 1972), pp. 16–17.

school, the study-sharers provide (as a rule, and on the whole) this ungrudging approval and obedience. Later, his Sikhs do the same: to them, he is 'an invulnerable Guru'. Now a guru is oracular and mysterious, a numinous presence with almost miraculous powers; he is not a power-sharer, a consulter of others. In other words—though the words are too modern for the context—he is in no way a democrat. Devious, circuitous, cunning Stalky may be, but he never really gives way. Impossible to imagine him in committee, with give and take, discussion, bargaining. Disliking authority, he is a sharp adversary to those above him, as well as an autocrat, kindly but immoveable, to those below. His nature is suited to war, or the occupation of a hostile country, or guerilla tactics; not to everyday life, peace, domesticity, the prosy, law-abiding present.

Perhaps T. E. Lawrence was the last full-scale Stalky, and to him as to other Stalkies retirement from violent action and leadership proved a pathetic anti-climax. Others, more obscure, were thrown up by the Second World War, and peacetime cramped, even crippled their spirits after it. Today such men have no place, no devoted followers or blind admirers, certainly no simple Other Ranks to idolize them. Just as the schoolboy hero declined from the attractive, merry, unintellectual Tom Brown to the thick-headed louts of the later school stories, who actively hated intellectual pursuits and debagged the aesthete or the artist whenever they had a chance to; so the exuberant Stalky characters of fiction declined into the ugly right-wing toughs who were Sapper's heroes, and in real life today's Stalkies have dwindled into the pathetic mercenaries who turn to dubious causes for adventure and gain. The century which began with so dashing a future for them, so broad a world in which they could operate, has no place for them now.

With Stalky, M'Turk and the others, Kipling-Beetle was at school over a hundred years ago. Clearly one cannot apply today's attitudes to ideas and behaviour of the eighteen-eighties, and because Stalky's attitudes may seem to foreshadow those of today's right, as those of his headmaster, Kipling's beloved 'Uncle Crom', foreshadowed those of the left (this should not be forgotten), it does not mean that either can be judged by modern criteria. Kipling was conjuring a world where many of our ideas had little place, and the qualities that world nurtured may seem largely irrelevant to ours. Yet in his day they seemed self-evidently valuable and desirable, and he put them forward without self-consciousness in 'If'. Light-heartedly though seriously, *Stalky & Co* put them forward as well, in a rather more indirect form, and festooned with a few others less admirable, more high-spirited (gloating, rough justice, and revenge). Steven Marcus has described well the modern reader's dilemma when faced with such a world, and such apparently superseded qualities:

The point to be grasped [he writes] is that among and alongside all these bad attitudes which seem calculated to outrage the values that most educated people today affirm—values which can be roughly summed up in the term liberal democracy—there exist other attitudes and values whose absence from contemporary life we all feel and are probably the worse for. The values are described by obsolete words like honor, truthfulness, loyalty, manliness, pride, straightforwardness, courage, self-sacrifice, and heroism. That these virtues exist as active and credible possibilities in the world of *Stalky & Co*, and that they seem not to in ours—or, if they do, appear almost solely in corrupted forms—must give us pause. Such a fact may serve to remind us that the moral benefits, conveniences, and superiorities of modern domestic societies have not been acquired without cost. Part of this cost seems pretty clearly to have been paid by a diminution in the older masculine virtues . . . In the moral life of history there are apparently no gains without losses. Few books urge us to confront this contradiction more barely and boldly than *Stalky & Co.*[13]

[13] Introduction to *Stalky & Co* (New York, 1962), reprinted in *Kipling and the Critics*, ed. Elliot L. Gilbert (New York, 1965), p. 152.

NOTE ON THE TEXT

The original publication dates of the stories in this volume were as follows:

Stalky & Co first appeared in book form in 1899, published by Macmillan in Great Britain, and by Doubleday and McClure in the USA. The following stories appeared in it:

'In Ambush'
'Slaves of the Lamp, Part I'
'An Unsavoury Interlude'
'The Impressionists'
'The Moral Reformers'
'A Little Prep.'
'The Flag of their Country'
'The Last Term'
'Slaves of the Lamp, Part II'

'Stalky' was collected in *Land and Sea Tales* (1923); 'Regulus' in *A Diversity of Creatures* (1917); 'The United Idolators' and 'The Propagation of Knowledge' in *Debits and Credits* (1926).

The Complete Stalky & Co appeared in 1929, and included the five stories which did not figure in the original *Stalky & Co*. The present edition follows the text and the arrangement of the stories in this volume.

SELECT BIBLIOGRAPHY

The standard bibliography is J. McG. Stewart's *Rudyard Kipling: A Bibliographical Catalogue*, ed. A. W. Yeats (1959). Reference may also be made to two earlier works: Flora V. Livingston's *Bibliography of the Works of Rudyard Kipling* (1927) with its *Supplement* (1938), and Lloyd H. Chandler's *Summary of the Work of Rudyard Kipling, Including Items ascribed to Him* (1930). We still await a bibliography which will take account of the findings of modern scholarship over the last quarter-century.

The official biography, authorized by Kipling's daughter Elsie, is Charles Carrington's *Rudyard Kipling: His Life and Work* (1955; 3rd edn., revised, 1978). Other full-scale biographies are Lord Birkenhead's *Rudyard Kipling* (1978) and Angus Wilson's *The Strange Ride of Rudyard Kipling* (1977). Briefer, copiously illustrated surveys are provided by Martin Fido's *Rudyard Kipling* (1974) and Kingsley Amis's *Rudyard Kipling and his World* (1975), which combine biography and criticism, as do the contributions to *Rudyard Kipling: the man, his work and his world* (also illustrated), ed. John Gross (1972). Information on particular periods of his life is also to be found in such works as A. W. Baldwin, *The Macdonald Sisters* (1960); Alice Macdonald Fleming (*née* Kipling), 'Some Childhood Memories of Rudyard Kipling' and 'More Childhood Memories of Rudyard Kipling', *Chambers Journal*, 8th series, vol. 8 (1939); L. C. Dunsterville, *Stalky's Reminiscences* (1928); G. C. Beresford, *Schooldays with Kipling* (1936); E. Kay Robinson, 'Kipling in India', *McClure's Magazine*, vol. 7 (1896); Edmonia Hill, 'The Young Kipling', *Atlantic Monthly*, vol. 157 (1936); *Kipling's Japan*, ed. Hugh Cortazzi and George Webb (1988); H. C. Rice, *Rudyard Kipling in New England* (1936); Frederic Van de Water, *Rudyard Kipling's Vermont Feud* (1937); Julian Ralph, *War's Brighter Side* (1901); Angela Thirkell, *Three Houses* (1931); *Rudyard Kipling to Rider Haggard: The Record of a Friendship*, ed. Morton Cohen (1965); and *'O Beloved Kids': Rudyard Kipling's Letters to his Children*, ed. Elliot L. Gilbert (1983). Useful background on the India he knew is provided by 'Philip Woodruff' (Philip Mason) in *The Men Who Ruled India* (1954), and by Pat Barr and Ray Desmond in their illustrated *Simla: A Hill Station in British India* (1978). Kipling's own autobiography, *Something of Myself* (1937), is idiosyncratic but indispensable.

The early reception of Kipling's work is usefully documented in

Kipling: The Critical Heritage, ed. Roger Lancelyn Green (1971). Richard Le Gallienne's *Rudyard Kipling: A Criticism* (1900), Cyril Falls's *Rudyard Kipling: A Critical Study* (1915), André Chevrillon's *Three Studies in English Literature* (1923) and *Rudyard Kipling* (1936), Edward Shanks's *Rudyard Kipling: A Study in Literature and Political Ideas* (1940), and Hilton Brown's *Rudyard Kipling: A New Appreciation* (1945) were all serious attempts at reassessment; while Ann M. Weygandt's study of *Kipling's Reading and Its Influence on His Poetry* (1939), and (in more old-fashioned vein) Ralph Durand's *Handbook to the Poetry of Rudyard Kipling* (1914) remain useful pieces of scholarship.

T. S. Eliot's introduction to *A Choice of Kipling's Verse* (1941; see *On Poetry and Poets*, 1957) began a period of more sophisticated reappraisal. There are influential essays by Edmund Wilson (1941; see *The Wound and the Bow*), George Orwell (1942; see his *Critical Essays*, 1946), Lionel Trilling (1943; see *The Liberal Imagination*, 1951), W. H. Auden (1943; see *New Republic*, vol. 109), and C. S. Lewis (1948; see *They Asked for a Paper*, 1962). These were followed by a series of important book-length studies which include J. M. S. Tompkins, *The Art of Rudyard Kipling* (1959); C. A. Bodelsen, *Aspects of Kipling's Art* (1964); Roger Lancelyn Green, *Kipling and the Children* (1965); Louis L. Cornell, *Kipling in India* (1966); and Bonamy Dobrée, *Rudyard Kipling: Realist and Fabulist* (1967), which follows on from his earlier studies in *The Lamp and the Lute* (1929) and *Rudyard Kipling* (1951). There were also two major collections of critical essays: *Kipling's Mind and Art*, ed. Andrew Rutherford (1964), with essays by W. L. Renwick, Edmund Wilson, George Orwell, Lionel Trilling, Noel Annan, George Shepperson, Alan Sandison, the editor himself, Mark Kinkead-Weekes, J. H. Fenwick, and W. W. Robson; and *Kipling and the Critics*, ed. Elliot L. Gilbert (1965), with essays, parodies, etc. by Andrew Lang, Oscar Wilde, Henry James, Robert Buchanan, Max Beerbohm, Bonamy Dobrée, Boris Ford, George Orwell, Lionel Trilling, C. S. Lewis, T. S. Eliot, J. M. S. Tompkins, Randall Jarrell, Steven Marcus, and the editor himself. Nirad C. Chaudhuri's essay on *Kim* as 'The Finest Story about India—in English' (1957) is reprinted in John Gross's collection (see above); and Andrew Rutherford's lecture 'Some Aspects of Kipling's Verse' (1965) appears in the *Proceedings of the British Academy* for that year.

Other recent studies devoted in whole or in part to Kipling include Richard Faber, *The Vision and the Need: Late Victorian Imperialist Aims* (1966); T. R. Henn, *Kipling* (1967); Alan Sandison, *The Wheel of Empire* (1967); Herbert L. Sussman, *Victorians and the Machine:*

The Literary Response to Technology (1968); P. J. Keating, *The Working Classes in Victorian Fiction* (1971); Elliot L. Gilbert, *The Good Kipling: Studies in the Short Story* (1972); Jeffrey Meyers, *Fiction and the Colonial Experience* (1972); Shamsul Islam, *Kipling's 'Law'* (1975); J. S. Bratton, *The Victorian Popular Ballad* (1975); Philip Mason, *Kipling: The Glass, The Shadow and The Fire* (1975); John Bayley, *The Uses of Division* (1976); M. Van Wyk Smith, *Drummer Hodge: The Poetry of the Anglo-Boer War 1899–1902* (1978); Stephen Prickett, *Victorian Fantasy* (1979); Martin Green, *Dreams of Adventure, Deeds of Empire* (1980); J. A. McClure, *Kipling and Conrad* (1981); R. F. Moss, *Rudyard Kipling and the Fiction of Adolescence* (1982); S. S. Azfar Husain, *The Indianness of Rudyard Kipling: A Study in Stylistics* (1983); Norman Page, *A Kipling Companion* (1984); B. J. Moore-Gilbert, *Kipling and 'Orientalism'* (1986); Sandra Kemp, *Kipling's Hidden Narratives* (1988); Norah Crook, *Kipling's Myths of Love and Death* (1989); and Ann Parry, *The Poetry of Rudyard Kipling* (1992); while further collections of essays include *Rudyard Kipling*, ed. Harold Bloom (1987); *Kipling Considered*, ed. Philip Mallett (1989); and *Critical Essays on Rudyard Kipling*, ed. Harold Orel (1989). Among the most important recent studies are Edward Said, *Culture and Imperialism* (1991); Sara Suleri, *The Rhetoric of English India* (1992); Zorah T. Sullivan, *Narratives of Empire: The Fictions of Rudyard Kipling* (1993); and Peter Keating, *Kipling the Poet* (1994).

Two important additions to the available corpus of Kipling's writings are *Kipling's India: Uncollected Sketches*, ed. Thomas Pinney (1986); and *Early Verse by Rudyard Kipling 1879–1889: Unpublished, Uncollected and Rarely Collected Poems*, ed. Andrew Rutherford (1986). Indispensable is Pinney's edition of *The Letters of Rudyard Kipling*, available in four volumes.

A CHRONOLOGY OF KIPLING'S LIFE AND WORKS

THE dates given here for Kipling's works are those of first authorized publication in volume form, whether this was in India, America, or England. (The dates of subsequent editions are not listed.) It should be noted that individual poems and stories collected in these volumes had in many cases appeared in newspapers or magazines of earlier dates. For full details see James McG. Stewart, *Rudyard Kipling: A Bibliographical Catalogue*, ed. A. W. Yeats, Toronto, 1959; but see also the editors' notes in this World's Classics series.

1865   Rudyard Kipling born at Bombay on 30 December, son of John Lockwood Kipling and Alice Kipling (*née* Macdonald).

1871   In December Rudyard and his sister Alice Macdonald Kipling ('Trix'), who was born in 1868, are left in the charge of Captain and Mrs Holloway at Lorne Lodge, Southsea ('The House of Desolation'), while their parents return to India.

1877   Alice Kipling returns from India in March/April and removes the children from Lorne Lodge, though Trix returns there subsequently.

1878   Kipling is admitted in January to the United Services College at Westward Ho! in Devon. First visit to France with his father that summer. (Many visits later in his life.)

1880   Meets and falls in love with Florence Garrard, a fellow-boarder of Trix's at Southsea and prototype of Maisie in *The Light that Failed*.

1881   Appointed editor of the *United Services College Chronicle*. *Schoolboy Lyrics* privately printed by his parents in Lahore, for limited circulation.

1882   Leaves school at end of summer term. Sails for India on 20 September; arrives Bombay on 18 October. Takes up post as assistant-editor of the *Civil and Military Gazette* in Lahore in the Punjab, where his father is now Principal of the Mayo College of Art and Curator of the Lahore Museum. Annual leaves from 1883 to 1888 are spent at Simla, except in 1884 when the family goes to Dalhousie.

1884   *Echoes* (by Rudyard and Trix, who has now rejoined the family in Lahore).

1885   *Quartette* (a Christmas Annual by Rudyard, Trix, and their parents).

1886   *Departmental Ditties.*

1887   Transferred in the autumn to the staff of the *Pioneer*, the *Civil and Military Gazette*'s sister-paper, in Allahabad in the North-West Provinces. As special correspondent in Rajputana he writes the articles later collected as 'Letters of Marque' in *From Sea to Sea*. Becomes friendly with Professor and Mrs Hill, and shares their bungalow.

1888   *Plain Tales from the Hills.* Takes on the additional responsibility of writing for the *Week's News*, a new publication sponsored by the *Pioneer*.

1888–9 *Soldiers Three; The Story of the Gadsbys; In Black and White; Under the Deodars; The Phantom Rickshaw; Wee Willie Winkie.*

1889   Leaves India on 9 March; travels to San Francisco with Professor and Mrs Hill via Rangoon, Singapore, Hong Kong, and Japan. Crosses the United States on his own, writing the articles later collected in *From Sea to Sea*. Falls in love with Mrs Hill's sister Caroline Taylor. Reaches Liverpool in October, and makes his début in the London literary world.

1890   Enjoys literary success, but suffers breakdown. Visits Italy. *The Light that Failed.*

1891   Visits South Africa, Australia, New Zealand, and (for the last time) India. Returns to England on hearing of the death of his American friend Wolcott Balestier. *Life's Handicap.*

1892   Marries Wolcott's sister Caroline Starr Balestier ('Carrie') in January. (The bride is given away by Henry James.) Their world tour is cut short by the loss of his savings in the collapse of the Oriental Banking Company. They establish their home at Brattleboro in Vermont, on the Balestier family estate. Daughter Josephine born in December. *The Naulahka* (written in collaboration with Wolcott Balestier). *Barrack-Room Ballads.*

1893   *Many Inventions.*

1894   *The Jungle Book.*

1895   *The Second Jungle Book.*

1896   Second daughter Elsie born in February. Quarrel with brother-in-law Beatty Balestier and subsequent court case end their stay in Brattleboro. Return to England (Torquay). *The Seven Seas.*

1897   Settles at Rottingdean in Sussex. Son John born in August. *Captains Courageous.*

1898   The first of many winters at Cape Town. Meets Sir Alfred Milner and Cecil Rhodes who becomes a close friend. Visits Rhodesia. *The Day's Work.*

1899   Disastrous visit to the United States. Nearly dies of pneumonia in New York. Death of Josephine. Never returns to USA. *Stalky and Co.; From Sea to Sea.*

1900   Helps for a time with army newspaper *The Friend* in South Africa during Boer War. Observes minor action at Karee Siding.

1901   *Kim.*

1902   Settles at 'Bateman's' at Burwash in Sussex. *Just So Stories.*

1903   *The Five Nations.*

1904   *Traffics and Discoveries.*

1906   *Puck of Pook's Hill.*

1907   Nobel Prize for Literature. Visit to Canada. *Collected Verse.*

1909   *Actions and Reactions; Abaft the Funnel.*

1910   *Rewards and Fairies.* Death of Kipling's mother.

1911   Death of Kipling's father.

1913   Visit to Egypt. *Songs from Books.*

1914–18 Visits to the Front and to the Fleet. *The New Army in Training, France at War, Sea Warfare,* and other war pamphlets.

1915   John Kipling reported missing on his first day in action with the Irish Guards in the Battle of Loos on 27 September. His body was never found.

1917   *A Diversity of Creatures.* Kipling becomes a member of the Imperial War Graves Commission.

1919   *The Years Between; Rudyard Kipling's Verse: Inclusive Edition.*

1920   *Letters of Travel.*

The Complete Stalky & Co.

TO THE MEMORY OF

CORMELL PRICE

HEADMASTER, UNITED SERVICES COLLEGE

WESTWARD HO! BIDEFORD, NORTH DEVON

1874–1894

'Let us now praise famous men'—
Men of little showing—
For their work continueth,
And their work continueth,
Broad and deep continueth,
Greater than their knowing!

Western wind and open surge
 Took us from our mothers;
Flung us on a naked shore
(Twelve bleak houses by the shore!
Seven summers by the shore!)
 'Mid two hundred brothers.

There we met with famous men
 Set in office o'er us;
And they beat on us with rods—
Faithfully with many rods—
Daily beat us on with rods,
 For the love they bore us.

Out of Egypt unto Troy—
 Over Himalaya—
Far and sure our bands have gone—
Hy-Brasil or Babylon,
Islands of the Southern Run,
 And cities of Cathaia!

And we all praise famous men—
 Ancients of the College;
For they taught us common sense—
Tried to teach us common sense—
Truth and God's Own Common Sense,
 Which is more than knowledge!

Each degree of Latitude
 Strung about Creation

Seeth one or more of us
(Of one muster all of us),
Diligent in that he does,
  Keen in his vocation.

This we learned from famous men,
  Knowing not its uses,
When they showed, in daily work,
Man must finish off his work—
Right or wrong, his daily work—
  And without excuses.

Servants of the Staff and chain,
  Mine and fuse and grapnel—
Some before the face of Kings,
Stand before the face of Kings;
Bearing gifts to divers Kings—
  Gifts of case and shrapnel.

This we learned from famous men
  Teaching in our borders,
Who declared it was best,
Safest, easiest, and best—
Expeditious, wise, and best—
  To obey your orders.

Some beneath the further stars
  Bear the greater burden:
Set to serve the lands they rule,
(Save he serve no man may rule),
Serve and love the lands they rule;
  Seeking praise nor guerdon.

This we learned from famous men,
  Knowing not we learned it.
Only, as the years went by—
Lonely, as the years went by—
Far from help as years went by,
  Plainer we discerned it.

Wherefore praise we famous men
  From whose bays we borrow—
They that put aside To-day—

All the joys of their To-day—
And with toil of their To-day
  Bought for us To-morrow!

Bless and praise we famous men—
  Men of little showing—
For their work continueth,
And their work continueth,
Broad and deep continueth,
  Great beyond their knowing!

CONTENTS

CONTENTS

'Stalky'

'AND then,' it was a boy's voice, curiously level and even, 'De Vitré said we were beastly funks not to help, and *I* said there were too many chaps in it to suit us. Besides, there's bound to be a mess somewhere or other, with old De Vitré in charge. Wasn't I right, Beetle?'

'And, anyhow, it's a silly biznai, bung through. What'll they *do* with the beastly cows when they've got 'em? You can milk a cow—if she'll stand still. That's all right, but drivin' 'em about—'

'You're a pig, Beetle.'

'No, I ain't. What *is* the sense of drivin' a lot of cows up from the Burrows to—to—where is it?'

'They're tryin' to drive 'em up to Toowey's farmyard at the top of the hill—the empty one, where we smoked last Tuesday. It's a revenge. Old Vidley chivied De Vitré twice last week for ridin' his ponies on the Burrows; and De Vitré's goin' to lift as many of old Vidley's cattle as he can and plant 'em up the hill. He'll muck it, though—with Parsons, Orrin and Howlett helpin' him. They'll only yell, an' shout, an' bunk if they see Vidley.'

'*We* might have managed it,' said M'Turk slowly, turning up his coat-collar against the rain that swept over the Burrows. His hair was of the dark mahogany red that goes with a certain temperament.

'We should,' Corkran replied with equal confidence. 'But they've gone into it as if it was a sort of spadger-hunt.* I've never done any cattle-liftin', but it seems to me-e-e that one might just as well be stalky* about a thing as not.'

The smoking vapours of the Atlantic drove in wreaths above the boys' heads. Out of the mist to windward, beyond the grey bar of the Pebble Ridge, came the unceasing roar of mile-long Atlantic rollers. To leeward, a few stray ponies and cattle, the property of the Northam potwallopers,* and the unwilling playthings of the boys in their leisure hours, showed through the haze. The three boys had halted by the Cattle-gate which marks the limit of cultivation, where the fields come down to the Burrows from Northam Hill. Beetle, shock-headed and spectacled, drew his nose to and fro along the wet top-bar; M'Turk shifted from one foot to the other, watching the water drain into either print; while Corkran whistled through his teeth as he leaned against a sod-bank, peering into the mist.

A grown or sane person might have called the weather vile; but the boys at that school had not yet learned the national interest in climate. It was a little damp, to be sure; but it was always damp in the Easter term, and sea-wet, they held, could not give one a cold under any circumstances. Mackintoshes were things to go to church in, but crippling if one had to run at short notice across heavy country. So they waited serenely in the downpour, clad as their mothers would not have cared to see.

'I say, Corky,'* said Beetle, wiping his spectacles for the twentieth time, 'if we aren't going to help De Vitré, what are we here for?'

'We're goin' to watch,' was the answer. 'Keep your eye on your Uncle and he'll pull you through.'

'It's an awful biznai, driving cattle—in open country,' said M'Turk, who , as the son of an Irish baronet, knew something of these operations. 'They'll have to run half over the Burrows after 'em. 'S'pose they're ridin' Vidley's ponies?'

'De Vitré's sure to be. He's a dab on a horse. Listen! What a filthy row they're making. They'll be heard for miles.'

The air filled with whoops and shouts, cries, words of command, the rattle of broken golf-clubs, and a clatter of hooves. Three cows with their calves came up to the Cattle-gate at a milch-canter, followed by four wild-eyed bullocks and two rough-coated ponies. A fat and freckled youth of fifteen trotted behind them, riding bareback and brandishing a hedge-stake. De Vitré, up to a certain point, was an inventive youth, with a passion for horse-exercise that the Northam farmers did not encourage. Farmer Vidley, who could not understand that a grazing pony likes being galloped about, had once called him a thief, and the insult rankled. Hence the raid.

'Come on,' he cried over his shoulder. 'Open the gate, Corkran, or they'll all cut back again. We've had no end of bother to get 'em. Oh, won't old Vidley be wild!'

Three boys on foot ran up, 'shooing' the cattle in excited and amateur fashion, till they headed them into the narrow, high-banked Devonshire lane that ran uphill.

'Come on, Corkran. It's no end of a lark,' pleaded De Vitré; but Corkran shook his head. The affair had been presented to him after dinner that day as a completed scheme, in which he might, by favour, play a minor part. And Arthur Lionel Corkran, No. 104, did not care for lieutenancies.

'You'll only be collared,' he cried, as he shut the gate. 'Parsons and Orrin are no good in a row. You'll be collared sure as a gun, De Vitré.'

'Oh, you're a beastly funk!' The speaker was already hidden by the fog.

'Hang it all,' said M'Turk. 'It's about the first time we've ever tried a cattle-lift at the Coll. Let's——'

'Not much,' said Corkran firmly; 'keep your eye on your Uncle.' His word was law in these matters, for experience had taught them that if they manœuvred without Corkran they fell into trouble.

'You're wrathy because you didn't think of it first,' said Beetle. Corkran kicked him thrice calmly, neither he nor Beetle changing a muscle the while.

'No, I ain't; but it isn't stalky enough for me.'

'Stalky,' in their school vocabulary, meant clever, well-considered and wily, as applied to plans of action; and 'stalkiness' was the one virtue Corkran toiled after.

''Same thing,' said M'Turk. 'You think you're the only stalky chap in the Coll.'

Corkran kicked him as he had kicked Beetle; and even as Beetle, M'Turk took not the faintest notice. By the etiquette of their friendship, this was no more than a formal notice of dissent from a proposition.

'They haven't thrown out any pickets,'* Corkran went on (that school prepared boys for the Army). 'You ought to do that—even for apples. Toowey's farmyard may be full of farm-chaps.'

''Twasn't last week,' said Beetle, 'when we smoked in that cart-shed place. It's a mile from any house, too.'

Up went one of Corkran's light eyebrows. 'Oh, Beetle, I *am* so tired o' kickin' you! Does that mean it's empty *now*? They ought to have sent a fellow ahead to look. They're simply bound to be collared. An' where'll they bunk to if they have to run for it? Parsons has only been here two terms. *He* don't know the lie of the country. Orrin's a fat ass, an' Howlett bunks from a guv'nor' [vernacular for any native of Devon engaged in agricultural pursuits] 'as far as he can see one. De Vitré's the only decent chap in the lot, an'—an' *I* put him up to usin' Toowey's farmyard.'

'Well, keep your hair on,' said Beetle. 'What are we going to do? It's hefty damp here.'

'Let's think a bit.' Corkran whistled between his teeth and presently broke into a swift, short double-shuffle. 'We'll go straight up the hill and see what happens to 'em. Cut across the fields; an' we'll lie up in the hedge where the lane comes in by the barn—where we found that dead hedgehog last term. Come on!'

He scrambled over the earth bank and dropped on to the rain-soaked plough. It was a steep slope to the brow of the hill where Toowey's barns stood. The boys took no account of stiles or footpaths, crossing field after field diagonally, and where they found a hedge, bursting through it like beagles. The lane lay on their right flank, and they heard much lowing and shouting in that direction.

'Well, if De Vitré isn't collared,' said M'Turk, kicking off a few pounds of loam against a gate-post, 'he jolly well ought to be.'

'We'll get collared, too, if you go on with your nose up like that. Duck, you ass, and stalk along under the hedge. We can get quite close up to the barn,' said Corkran. 'There's no sense in not doin' a thing stalkily while you're about it.'

They wriggled into the top of an old hollow double hedge less than thirty yards from the big black-timbered barn with its square outbuildings. Their ten-minutes' climb had lifted them a couple of hundred feet above the Burrows. As the mists parted here and there, they could see its great triangle of sodden green, tipped with yellow sand-dunes and fringed with white foam, laid out like a blurred map below. The surge along the Pebble Ridge made a background to the wild noises in the lane.

'What did I tell you?' said Corkran, peering through the stems of the quickset* which commanded a view of the farmyard. 'Three farm-chaps—getting out dung—with pitchforks. It's too late to head off De Vitré. We'd be collared if we showed up. Besides, they've heard 'em. They couldn't help hearing. What asses!'

The natives, brandishing their weapons, talked together, using many times the word 'Colleger.' As the tumult swelled, they disappeared into various pens and byres. The first of the cattle trotted up to the yard-gate, and De Vitré felicitated his band.

'That's all right,' he shouted. 'Oh, won't old Vidley be wild! Open the gate, Orrin, an' whack 'em through. They're pretty warm.'

'So'll you be in a minute,' muttered M'Turk as the raiders hurried into the yard behind the cattle. They heard a shout of triumph, shrill yells of despair; saw one Devonian guarding the gate with a pitchfork, while the others, alas! captured all four boys.

'Of all the infernal, idiotic, lower-second asses!' said Corkran. 'They haven't even taken off their House-caps.' These dainty confections of primary colours were not issued, as some believe, to encourage House-pride or *esprit de corps*, but for purposes of identification from afar, should the wearer break bounds or laws. That is why, in time of war, any one but an idiot wore his cap inside out.

'Aie! Yeou young rascals. We've got 'e! Whutt be doin' to Muster Vidley's bullocks?'

'Oh, we found 'em,' said De Vitré, who bore himself gallantly in defeat. 'Would you like 'em?'

'Found 'em! They bullocks drove like that—all heavin' an' penkin' an' hotted! Oh! Shaameful. Yeou've nigh to killed the cows—lat alone stealin' 'em. They sends pore boys to jail for half o' this.'

'That's a lie,' said Beetle to M'Turk, turning on the wet grass.

'I know; but they always say it. 'Member when they collared us at the Monkey Farm that Sunday, with the apples in your topper?'

'My Aunt! They're goin' to lock 'em up an' send for Vidley,' Corkran whispered, as one of the captors hurried downhill in the direction of Appledore, and the prisoners were led into the barn.

'But they haven't taken their names and numbers, anyhow,' said Corkran, who had fallen into the hands of the enemy more than once.

'But they're bottled! Rather sickly for De Vitré,' said Beetle. 'It's one lickin' anyhow, even if Vidley don't hammer him. The Head's rather hot about gate-liftin', and poachin', an' all that sort of thing. He won't care for cattle-liftin' much.'

'It's awfully bad for cows, too, to run 'em about in milk,' said M'Turk, lifting one knee from a sodden primrose-tuft. 'What's the next move, Corky?'

'We'll get into the old cart-shed where we smoked. It's next to the barn. We can cut across over while they're inside and climb in through the window.'

'S'pose we're collared?' said Beetle, cramming his House-cap into his pocket. Caps may tumble off; so one goes into action bare-headed.

'That's just it. They'd never dream of any more chaps walkin' bung into the trap. Besides, we can get out through the roof if they spot us. Keep your eye on your Uncle. Come on,' said Corkran.

A swift dash carried them to a huge clump of nettles, beneath the unglazed back window of the cart-shed. Its open front, of course, gave on to the barnyard.

They scrambled through, dropped among the carts, and climbed up into the rudely boarded upper floor that they had discovered a week before when in search of retirement. It covered a half of the building and ended in darkness at the barn wall. The roof-tiles were broken and displaced. Through the chinks they commanded a clear view of the barnyard, half filled with disconsolate cattle, steaming sadly in the rain.

'You see,' said Corkran, always careful to secure his line of retreat, 'if they bottle us up here, we can squeeze out between these rafters, slide down the roof, an' bunk. They couldn't even get out through the window. They'd have to run right round the barn. Now are you satisfied, you burbler?'

'Huh! You only said that to make quite sure yourself,' Beetle retorted.

'If the boards weren't all loose, I'd kick you,' growled Corkran. "No sense gettin' into a place you can't get out of. Shut up and listen.'

A murmur of voices reached them from the end of the attic. M'Turk tiptoed thither with caution.

'Hi! It leads through into the barn. You can get through. Come along!' He fingered the boarded wall.

'What's the other side?' said Corkran the cautious.

'Hay, you idiot.' They heard his boot-heels click on wood, and he had gone.

At some time or other sheep must have been folded in the cart-shed, and an inventive farmhand, sooner than take the hay round, had displaced a board in the barn-side to thrust fodder through. It was in no sense a lawful path, but twelve inches in the square is all that any boy needs.

'Look here!' said Beetle, as they waited for M'Turk's return. 'The cattle are coming in out of the wet.'

A brown, hairy back showed some three feet below the half-floor, as one by one the cattle shouldered in for shelter among the carts below, filling the shed with their sweet breath.

'That blocks our way out, unless we get out by the roof, an' that's rather too much of a drop, unless we have to,' said Corkran. 'They're all bung in front of the window, too. What a day we're havin'!'

'Corkran! Beetle!' M'Turk's whisper shook with delight. 'You can see 'em; I've seen 'em. They're in a blue funk in the barn, an' the two clods are makin' fun of 'em—horrid. Orrin's tryin' to bribe 'em an' Parsons is nearly blubbin'. Come an' look! I'm in the hayloft. Get through the hole. Don't make a row, Beetle.'

Lithely they wriggled between the displaced boards into the hay and crawled to the edge of the loft. Three years' skirmishing against a hard and unsympathetic peasantry had taught them the elements of strategy. For tactics they looked to

Corkran; but even Beetle, notoriously absent-minded, held a lock of hay before his head as he crawled. There was no haste, no betraying giggle, no squeak of excitement. They had learned, by stripes, the unwisdom of these things. But the conference by a root-cutter on the barn floor was deep in its own affairs; De Vitré's party promising, entreating, and cajoling, while the natives laughed like Inquisitors.

'Wait till Muster Vidley an' Muster Toowey—yis, an' the policemen come,' was their only answer. ''Tis about time to go to milkin'. What'ull us do?'

'Yeou go milk, Tom, an' I'll stay long o' the young gentlemen,' said the bigger of the two, who answered to the name of Abraham. 'Muster Toowey, he'm laike to charge yeou for usin' his yard so free. Iss fai! Yeou'll be wopped proper. 'Rackon yeou'll be askin' for junkets to set in this week o' Sundays to come. But Muster Vidley, he'll give 'ee the best leatherin' of all. He'm passionful, I tal 'ee.'

Tom stumped out to milk. The barn doors closed behind him, and in the fading light a great gloom fell on all but Abraham, who discoursed eloquently on Mr. Vidley, his temper and strong arm.

Corkran turned in the hay and retreated to the attic, followed by his army.

'No good,' was his verdict. 'I'm afraid it's all up with 'em. We'd better get out.'

'Yes, but look at these beastly cows,' said M'Turk, spitting on to a heifer's back. 'It'll take us a week to shove 'em away from the window, and that brute Tom'll hear us. He's just across the yard, milkin'.'

'Tweak 'em, then,' said Corkran. 'Hang it, I'm sorry to have to go, though. If we could get that other beast out of the barn for a minute we might make a rescue. Well, it's no good. Tweakons!'*

He drew forth a slim, well-worn home-made catapult—the 'tweaker' of those days—slipped a buckshot into its supple chamois leather pouch, and pulled to the full stretch of the elastic. The others followed his example. They only wished to get the cattle out of their way, but seeing the backs so near, they deemed it their duty each to choose his bird and to let fly with all their strength.

They were not prepared in the least for what followed. Three bullocks, trying to wheel amid six close-pressed companions, not to mention three calves, several carts, and all the lumber of a general-utility shed, do not turn end-for-end without confusion. It was lucky for the boys that they stood a little back on the floor, because one horned head, tossed in pain, flung up a loose board at the edge, and it came down lancewise on an amazed back. Another victim floundered bodily across the shafts of a decrepit gig, smashing these and oversetting the wheels. That was more than enough for the nerves of the assembly. With wild bellowings and a good deal of left-and-right butting they dashed into the barnyard, tails on end, and began a fine free fight on the midden. The last cow out hooked down an old set of harness; it flapped over one eye and trailed behind her. When a companion trod on it, which happened every few seconds, she naturally fell on her knees; and, being a Burrows cow, with the interests of her calf at heart, attacked the first passer-by. Half-awed, but wholly delighted, the boys watched the outburst. It was in full flower before they even dreamed of a second shot. Tom came out from a byre with a pitchfork, to be chased in again by the harnessed cow. A bullock floundered on the muck-heap, fell, rose and bedded himself to the belly, helpless and bellowing. The others took great interest in him.

Corkran, through the roof, scientifically 'tweaked' a frisky heifer on the nose, and it is no exaggeration to say that she danced on her hind legs for half a minute.

'Abram! Oh, Abram! They'm bewitched. They'm ragin'. 'Tes the milk fever. They've been drove mad. Oh, Abram! They'll horn the bullocks! They'll horn *me*! Abram!'

'Bide till I lock the door,' quoth Abraham, faithful to his trust. They heard him padlock the barn door; saw him come out with yet another pitchfork. A bullock lowered his head, Abraham ran to the nearest pig-pen, where loud squeakings told that he had disturbed the peace of a large family.

'Beetle,' snapped Corkran. 'Go in an' get those asses out. Quick! We'll keep the cows happy.'

A people sitting in darkness and the shadow* of monumental lickings, too depressed to be angry with De Vitré, heard a voice from on high saying, 'Come up here! Come on! Come up! There's a way out.'

They shinned up the loft-stanchions without a word; found a boot-heel which they were bidden to take for guide, and squeezed desperately through a hole in darkness, to be hauled out by Corkran.

'Have you got your caps? Did you give 'em your names and numbers?'

'Yes. No.'

'That's all right. Drop down here. Don't stop to jaw. Over the cart—through that window, and bunk! Get *out!*'

De Vitré needed no more. They heard him squeak as he dropped among the nettles, and through the roof-chinks they watched four slight figures disappear into the rain. Tom and Abraham, from byre and pig-pen, exhorted the cattle to keep quiet.

'By gum!' said Beetle; 'That *was* stalky! How did you think of it?'

'It was the only thing to do. Anybody could have seen that.'

'Hadn't we better bunk, too, now?' said M'Turk uneasily.

'Why? *We're* all right. *We* haven't done anything. I want to hear what old Vidley will say. Stop tweakin', Turkey. Let 'em cool off. Golly! how that heifer danced! I swear I didn't know cows could be so lively. We're only just in time.'

'My Hat! Here's Vidley—and Toowey,' said Beetle, as the two farmers strode into the yard.

'Gloats! oh, gloats! Fids! oh, fids! Hefty fids and gloats to us!' said Corkran.

These words, in their vocabulary, expressed the supreme of delight. 'Gloats' implied more or less of personal triumph, 'fids' was felicity in the abstract, and the boys were tasting both that day. Last joy of all, they had had the pleasure of Mr. Vidley's acquaintance, albeit he did not love them. Toowey was more of a stranger; his orchards lying over-near to the public road.

Tom and Abraham together told a tale of stolen cattle maddened by overdriving; of cows sure to die in calving, and of milk that would never return; that made Mr. Vidley swear for three consecutive minutes in the speech of north Devon.

''Tes tu bad. 'Tes tu bad,' said Toowey, consolingly; 'let's 'ope they 'aven't took no great 'arm. They be wonderful wild, though.'

''Tes all well for yeou, Toowey, that sells them dom Collegers seventy quart a week.'

'Eighty,' Toowey replied, with the meek triumph of one who has underbidden his neighbour on public tender; 'but that's no odds to *me*. Yeou'm free to leather 'em saame as if they was yeour own sons. On my barn-floor shall 'ee leather 'em.'

'Generous old swine!' said Beetle. 'De Vitré ought to have stayed for this.'

'They'm all safe an' to rights,' said the officious Abraham, producing the key. 'Rackon us'll come in an' hold 'em for yeou. Hey! The cows are fair ragin' still. Us'll have to run for it.'

The barn being next to the shed, the boys could not see that stately entry. But they heard.

'Gone an' hided in the hay. Aie! They'm proper afraid,' cried Abraham.

'Rout un out! Rout un out!' roared Vidley, rattling a stick impatiently on the root-cutter.

'Oh, my Aunt!' said Corkran, standing on one foot.

'Shut the door. Shut the door, I tal 'ee. Rackon us can find un in the dark. Us don't want un boltin' like rabbits under our elbows.' The big barn door closed with a clang.

'My Gum!' said Corkran, which was always his War Oath in time of action. He dropped down and was gone for perhaps twenty seconds.

'And *that's* all right,' he said, returning at a gentle saunter.

'Hwatt?' M'Turk almost shrieked, for Corkran, in the shed below, waved a large key.

'Stalks! Frabjous Stalks! Bottled 'em! all four!' was the reply, and Beetle fell on his bosom. 'Yiss. They'm so's to say, like, locked up. If you're goin' to laugh, Beetle, I shall have to kick you again.'

'But I must!' Beetle was blackening with suppressed mirth.

'You won't do it here, then.' He thrust the already limp Beetle through the cart-shed window. It sobered him; one cannot laugh on a bed of nettles. Then Corkran stepped on his prostrate carcass, and M'Turk followed, just as Beetle would have risen; so he was upset, and the nettles painted on his cheek a likeness of hideous eruptions.

"Thought that 'ud cure you,' said Corkran, with a sniff.

Beetle rubbed his face desperately with dock-leaves, and said nothing. All desire to laugh had gone from him. They entered the lane.

Then a clamour broke from the barn—a compound noise of horse-like kicks, shaking of door-panels, and various yells.

'They've found it out,' said Corkran. 'How strange!' He sniffed again.

'Let 'em,' said Beetle. 'No one can hear 'em. Come on up to Coll.'

'What a brute you are, Beetle! You only think of your beastly self. Those cows want milkin'. Poor dears! Hear 'em low,' said M'Turk.

'Go back and milk 'em yourself, then.' Beetle danced with pain. 'We shall miss call-over, hangin' about like this; an' I've got two black marks this week already.'

'Then you'll have fatigue-drill on Monday,' said Corkran. "Come to think of it, I've got two black marks *aussi*. Hm! This is serious. This is hefty serious.'

'I told you,' said Beetle, with vindictive triumph. 'An' we want to go out after that hawk's nest on Monday. We shall be swottin' dumb-bells,* though. *All* your fault. If we'd bunked with De Vitré at first——'

Corkran paused between the hedgerows. 'Hold on a shake an' don't burble. Keep your eye on Uncle. Do you know, *I* believe some one's shut up in that barn. I think we ought to go and see.'

'Don't be a giddy idiot. Come on up to Coll.' But Corkran took no notice of Beetle.

He retraced his steps to the head of the lane, and, lifting up his voice, cried as in bewilderment, 'Hullo? Who's there? What's that row about? Who are you?'

'Oh, Peter!' said Beetle, skipping, and forgetting his anguish in this new development.

'Hoi! Hoi! 'Ere! Let us out!' The answers came muffled and

hollow from the black bulk of the barn, with renewed thunders on the door.

'Now play up,' said Corkran. 'Turkey, you keep the cows busy. 'Member that we've just discovered 'em. *We* don't know anything. Be polite, Beetle.'

They picked their way over the muck and held speech through a crack by the door-hinge. Three more genuinely surprised boys the steady rain never fell upon. And they were so difficult to enlighten. They had to be told again and again by the captives within.

'We've been 'ere for hours an' hours.' That was Toowey. 'An' the cows to milk, an' all.' That was Vidley. 'The door she blewed against us an' jammed himself.' That was Abraham.

'Yes, we can see that. It's jammed on this side,' said Corkran. 'How careless you chaps are!'

'Oppen un. Oppen un. Bash her oppen with a rock, young gen'elmen! The cows are milk-heated an' ragin'. Haven't you boys no sense?'

Seeing that M'Turk from time to time tweaked the cattle into renewed caperings, it was quite possible that the boys had some knowledge of a sort. But Mr. Vidley was rude. They told him so through the door, professing only now to recognize his voice.

'Humour un if 'e can. I paid seven-an'-six for the padlock,' said Toowey. 'Niver mind *him*. 'Tes only old Vidley.'

'Be yeou gwaine to stay a prisoner an' captive for the sake of a lock, Toowey? I'm shaamed of 'ee. Rowt un oppen, young gen'elmen! 'Twas a God's own mercy yeou heard us. Toowey, yeou'm a borned miser.'

'It'll be a long job,' said Corkran. 'Look here. It's near our call-over. If we stay to help you we'll miss it. We've come miles out of our way already—after you.'

'Tell yeour master, then, what keeped 'ee—an arrand o' mercy, laike. I'll tal un tu when I bring the milk to-morrow,' said Toowey.

'That's no good,' said Corkran; 'we may be licked twice over by then. You'll have to give us a letter.' M'Turk, backed against the barn-wall, was firing steadily and accurately into the brown of the herd.

'Yiss, yiss. Come down to my house. My missus shall write 'ee a beauty, young gen'elmen. She makes out the bills. I'll give 'ee just such a letter o' racommendation as I'd give to my own son, if only yeou can humour the lock!'

'Niver mind the lock,' Vidley wailed. 'Let me get to me pore cows, 'fore they'm dead.'

They went to work with ostentatious rattlings and wrenchings, and a good deal of the by-play that Corkran always loved. At last—the noise of unlocking was covered by some fancy hammering with a young boulder—the door swung open and the captives marched out.

'Hurry up, Mister Toowey,' said Corkran; 'we ought to be getting back. Will you give us that note, please?'

'Some of yeou young gentlemen was drivin' my cattle off the Burrowses,' said Vidley. 'I give 'ee fair warnin', I'll tell yeour masters. I know *yeou!*' He glared at Corkran with malignant recognition.

M'Turk looked him over from head to foot. 'Oh, it's only old Vidley. Drunk again, I suppose. Well, we can't help that. Come on, *Mister* Toowey. We'll go to your house.'

'Drunk, am I? I'll drunk 'ee! How do I know yeou bain't the same lot? Abram, did 'ee take their names an' numbers?'

'What *is* he ravin' about?' said Beetle. 'Can't you see that if we'd taken your beastly cattle we shouldn't be hanging round your beastly barn. 'Pon my Sam,* you Burrows guv'nors haven't any sense——'

'Let alone gratitude,' said Corkran. 'I suppose he *was* drunk, Mister Toowey; an' you locked him in the barn to get sober. Shockin'! Oh, shockin'!'

Vidley denied the charge in language that the boys' mothers would have wept to hear.

'Well, go and look after your cows, then,' said M'Turk. 'Don't stand there cursin' us because we've been kind enough to help you out of a scrape. Why on earth weren't your cows milked before? *You*'re no farmer. It's long past milkin'. No wonder they're half crazy. 'Disreputable old bog-trotter, you are. Brush your hair, sir. . . . I *beg* your pardon, Mister Toowey. 'Hope we're not keeping you.'

They left Vidley dancing on the muck-heap, amid the cows,

and devoted themselves to propitiating Mr. Toowey on their way to his house. Exercise had made them hungry; hunger is the mother of good manners; and they won golden opinions from Mrs. Toowey.

* * * * *

'Three-quarters of an hour late for call-over, and fifteen minutes late for Lock-up,' said Foxy, the school Sergeant, crisply. He was waiting for them at the head of the corridor. 'Report to your House-master, please—an' a nice mess you're in, young gentlemen.'

'Quite right, Foxy. Strict attention to dooty does it,' said Corkran. 'Now where, if we asked you, would you say that his honour Mister Prout might, at this moment of time, be found prouting—eh?'

'In 'is study—as usual, Mister Corkran. He took call-over.'

'Hurrah! Luck's with us all the way. Don't blub, Foxy. I'm afraid you don't catch us this time.'

* * * * *

'We went up to change, sir, before comin' to you. That made us a little late, sir. We weren't really very late. We were detained—by a——'

'An errand of mercy,' said Beetle, and they laid Mrs. Toowey's laboriously written note before him. 'We thought you'd prefer a letter, sir. Toowey got himself locked into a barn, and we heard him shouting—it's Toowey who brings the Coll. milk, sir—and we went to let him out.'

'There were ever so many cows waiting to be milked,' said M'Turk; 'and of course, he couldn't get at them, sir. They said the door had jammed. There's his note, sir.'

Mr. Prout read it over thrice. It was perfectly unimpeachable; but it said nothing of a large tea supplied by Mrs. Toowey.

'Well, I don't like your getting mixed up with farmers and potwallopers. Of course you will not pay any more—er—visits to the Tooweys,' said he.

'Of course not, sir. It was really on account of the cows, sir,' replied M'Turk, glowing with philanthropy.

'And you came straight back?'

'We ran nearly all the way from the Cattle-gate,' said Corkran, carefully developing the unessential. 'That's one mile, sir. Of course, we had to get the note from Toowey first.'

'But it was because we went to change—we were rather wet, sir—that we were *really* late. After we'd reported ourselves to the Sergeant, sir, and he knew we were in Coll., we didn't like to come to your study all dirty.' Sweeter than honey* was the voice of Beetle.

'Very good. Don't let it happen again.' Their House-master learned to know them better in later years.

They entered—not to say swaggered—into Number Nine form-room, where De Vitré, Orrin, Parsons, and Howlett, before the fire, were still telling their adventures to admiring associates. The four rose as one boy.

'What happened to *you*? We just saved call-over. Did you stay on? Tell us! Tell us!'

The three smiled pensively. They were not distinguished for telling more than was necessary.

'Oh, we stayed on a bit and then we came away,' said M'Turk. 'That's all.'

'You scab! You might tell a chap anyhow.'

'"Think so? Well, that's awfully good of you, De Vitré. 'Pon my sainted Sam, that's awfully good of you,' said Corkran, shouldering into the centre of the warmth and toasting one slippered foot before the blaze. 'So you really think we might tell you?'

They stared at the coals and shook with deep, delicious chuckles.

'My Hat! We *were* stalky,' said M'Turk. 'I swear we were about as stalky as they make 'em. Weren't we.'

'It was a frabjous Stalk,' said Beetle. '"Much too good to tell you brutes, though.'

The form wriggled under the insult, but made no motion to avenge it. After all, on De Vitré's showing, the three had saved the raiders from at least a public licking.

'It wasn't half bad,' said Corkran. 'Stalky *is* the word.'

'*You* were the really stalky one,' said M'Turk, one con-

temptuous shoulder turned to a listening world. 'By Gum!
you *were* stalky.'

Corkran accepted the compliment and the name together.
'Yes,' said he; 'keep your eye on your Uncle Stalky an' he'll
pull you through.'

'Well, you needn't gloat so,' said De Vitré, viciously; 'you
look like a stuffed cat.'

Corkran, henceforth known as Stalky, took not the slightest
notice, but smiled dreamily.

'My Hat! Yes. Of course,' he murmured. 'Your Uncle
Stalky—a doocid good name. Your Uncle Stalky is no end of
a stalker. He's a Great Man. I swear he is. De Vitré, you're
an ass—a putrid ass.'

De Vitré would have denied this but for the assenting
murmurs from Parsons and Orrin.

'You needn't rub it in, then.'

'But I do. I does. You are such a woppin' ass. D'you know
it? Think over it a bit at prep. Think it up in bed. Oblige me
by thinkin' of it every half hour till further notice. Gummy!
What an ass you are! But your Uncle Stalky'—he picked up
the form-room poker and beat it against the mantlepiece—'is
a Great Man!'

'Hear, hear,' said Beetle and M'Turk, who had fought
under that general.

'Isn't your Uncle Stalky a great man, De Vitré? Speak the
truth, you fat-headed old impostor.'

'Yes,' said De Vitré, deserted by all his band. 'I—I suppose
he is.'

'"Mustn't suppose. *Is* he?'

'Well, he is.'

'A Great Man?'

'A Great Man. *Now* won't you tell us?' said De Vitré
pleadingly.

'Not by a heap,' said 'Stalky' Corkran.

Therefore the tale has stayed untold till to-day.

THE HOUR OF THE ANGEL

SOONER or late—in earnest or in jest—
(But the stakes are no jest) Ithuriel's Hour
Will spring on us, for the first time, the test
  Of our sole unbacked competence and power
  Up to the limit of our years and dower
Of judgment—or beyond. But here we have
Prepared long since our garland or our grave.
  For, at that hour, the sum of all our past,
  Act, habit, thought, and passion, shall be cast
  In one addition, be it more or less,
  And as that reading runs so shall we do;
  Meeting, astounded, victory at the last,
  Or, first and last, our own unworthiness.
And none can change us though they die to save!

'In Ambush'

IN summer all right-minded boys built huts in the furze-hill behind the College—little lairs whittled out of the heart of the prickly bushes, full of stumps, odd root-ends, and spikes, but, since they were strictly forbidden, palaces of delight. And for the fifth summer in succession, Stalky, M'Turk, and Beetle (this was before they reached the dignity of a study) had built, like beavers, a place of retreat and meditation, where they smoked.

Now there was nothing in their characters, as known to Mr. Prout, their House-master, at all commanding respect; nor did Foxy, the subtle red-haired school Sergeant, trust them. His business was to wear tennis-shoes, carry binoculars, and swoop hawk-like upon evil boys. Had he taken the field alone, that hut would have been raided, for Foxy knew the manners of his quarry; but Providence moved Mr. Prout, whose school-name, derived from the size of his feet, was Hoofer, to investigate on his own account; and it was the cautious Stalky who found the track of his pugs* on the very floor of their lair one peaceful afternoon when Stalky would fain have forgotten Prout and his works in a volume of Surtees and a new briar-wood pipe. Crusoe, at sight of the foot-print, did not act more swiftly than Stalky. He removed the pipes, swept up all loose match-ends, and departed to warn Beetle and M'Turk.

But it was characteristic of the boy that he did not approach his allies till he had met and conferred with little Hartopp, President of the Natural History Society, an institution which Stalky held in contempt. Hartopp was more than surprised when the boy meekly, as he knew how, begged to propose himself, Beetle, and M'Turk as candidates; confessed to a long-smothered interest in first-flowerings, early butterflies, and new arrivals, and volunteered, if Mr. Hartopp saw fit, to enter on the new life at once. Being a master, Hartopp was suspicious; but he was also an enthusiast, and his gentle little soul had been galled by chance-heard remarks from the three, and specially Beetle. So he was gracious to that repentant sinner, and entered the three names in his book.

Then, and not till then, did Stalky seek Beetle and M'Turk in their House form-room. They were stowing away books for a quiet afternoon in the furze, which they called the 'wuzzy.'

'All up!' said Stalky serenely. 'I spotted Heffy's fairy feet round our hut after dinner. 'Blessing they're so big.'

'Con-found! Did you hide our pipes?' said Beetle.

'Oh no. Left 'em in the middle of the hut, of course. What a blind ass you are, Beetle! D'you think nobody thinks but yourself? Well, we can't use the hut any more. Hoofer will be watchin' it.'

' "Bother! Likewise blow!"*' said M'Turk thoughtfully, unpacking the volumes with which his chest was cased. The boys carried their libraries between their belt and their collar. 'Nice job! This means we're under suspicion for the rest of the term.'

'Why? All that Heffy has found is *a* hut. He and Foxy will watch it. It's nothing to do with us; only we mustn't be seen that way for a bit.'

'Yes, and where else are we to go?' said Beetle. 'You chose that place, too—an'—an' I wanted to read this afternoon.'

Stalky sat on a desk drumming his heels on the form.

'You're a despondin' brute, Beetle. Sometimes I think I shall have to drop you altogether. Did you ever know your Uncle Stalky forget you yet? *His rebus infectis*—after I'd seen Heffy's man-tracks marchin' round our hut, I found little Hartopp—*destricto ense*—wavin' a butterfly-net. I conciliated Hartopp. 'Told him that you'd read papers to the Bug-hunters if he'd let you join, Beetle. 'Told him you liked butterflies, Turkey. Anyhow, I soothed the Hartoffles, and we're Bug-hunters now.'

'What's the good of that?' said Beetle.

'Oh, Turkey, kick him!'

In the interests of science, bounds were largely relaxed for the members of the Natural History Society. They could wander, if they kept clear of all houses, practically where they chose; Mr. Hartopp holding himself responsible for their good conduct.

Beetle began to see this as M'Turk began the kicking.

'I'm an ass, Stalky!' he said, guarding the afflicted part. '*Pax*,* Turkey! I'm an ass.'

'Don't stop, Turkey. Isn't your Uncle Stalky a great man?'

'Great man,' said Beetle.

'All the same, bug-huntin's a filthy business,' said M'Turk. 'How the deuce does one begin?'

'This way,' said Stalky, turning to some fags' lockers behind him. 'Fags are dabs at Natural History. Here's young Bray-brooke's botany-case.' He flung out a tangle of decayed roots and adjusted the slide. ''Gives one no end of a professional air, I think. Here's Clay Minor's geological hammer. Beetle can carry that. Turkey, you'd better covet a butterfly-net from somewhere.'

'I'm blowed if I do!' said M'Turk simply, with immense feeling. 'Beetle, give me the hammer.'

'All right. *I*'m not proud. Chuck us down that net on top of the lockers, Stalky.'

'That's all right. It's a collapsible jamboree, too. Beastly luxurious dogs these fags* are. Built like a fishin'-rod. 'Pon my sainted Sam, but we look the complete Bug-hunters! Now, listen to your Uncle Stalky! We're goin' along the cliffs after butterflies. Very few chaps come there. We're goin' to leg it, too. You'd better leave your book behind.'

'Not much!' said Beetle firmly. 'I'm not goin' to be done out of my fun for a lot of filthy butterflies.'

'Then you'll sweat horrid. You'd better carry my Jorrocks.* 'Twon't make you any hotter.'

They all sweated; for Stalky led them at a smart trot west away along the cliffs under the furze-hills, crossing combe after gorsy combe. They took no heed to flying rabbits or fluttering fritillaries, and all that Turkey said of geology was utterly unquotable.

'Are we going to Clovelly?' he puffed at last, and they flung themselves down on the short, springy turf between the drone of the sea below and the light summer wind among the inland trees. They were looking into a combe half full of old, high furze in gay bloom that ran up to a fringe of brambles and a dense wood of mixed timber and hollies. It was as though one-half the combe were filled with golden fire to the cliff's edge. The side nearest to them was open grass, and fairly bristled with notice-boards.

'Fee-rocious old cove, this,' said Stalky, reading the nearest. ' *"Prosecuted with the utmost rigour of the Law. G. M. Dabney, Col., J.P.,"* an' all the rest of it. 'Don't seem to me that any chap in his senses would trespass here, does it?'

'You've got to prove damage 'fore you can prosecute for anything! 'Can't prosecute for trespass,' said M'Turk, whose father held many acres in Ireland. 'That's all rot!'

''Glad of that, 'cause this looks like what we wanted. Not straight across, Beetle, you blind lunatic!* Any one could spot us half a mile off. This way; and furl up your beastly butterfly-net.'

Beetle disconnected the ring, thrust the net into a pocket, shut up the handle to a two-foot stave, and slid the cane-ring round his waist. Stalky led inland to the wood, which was, perhaps, a quarter of a mile from the sea, and reached the fringe of the brambles.

'*Now* we can get straight down through the furze, and never show up all,' said the tactician. 'Beetle, go ahead and explore. Snf! Snf! Beastly stink of fox somewhere!'

On all fours, save when he clung to his spectacles, Beetle wormed into the gorse, and presently announced between grunts of pain that he had found a very fair fox-track. This was well for Beetle, since Stalky pinched him *a tergo*.* Down that tunnel they crawled. It was evidently a highway for the inhabitants of the combe; and, to their inexpressible joy, ended, at the very edge of the cliff, in a few square feet of dry turf walled and roofed with impenetrable gorse.

'By gum! There isn't a single thing to do except lie down,' said Stalky, returning a knife to his pocket. 'Look here!'

He parted the tough stems before him, and it was as a window opened on a far view of Lundy, and the deep sea sluggishly nosing the pebbles a couple of hundred feet below. They could hear young jackdaws squawking on the ledges, the hiss and jabber of a nest of hawks somewhere out of sight; and, with great deliberation, Stalky spat on to the back of a young rabbit sunning himself far down where only a cliff-rabbit could have found foot-hold. Great gray and black gulls screamed against the jackdaws; the heavy-scented acres of bloom round them were alive with low-nesting birds, singing or silent as the shadow of the wheeling hawks passed and returned; and on the naked turf across the combe rabbits thumped and fro-licked.

'Whew! What a place! Talk of natural history; this is it,' said Stalky, filling himself a pipe. 'Isn't it scrumptious? Good old sea!' He spat again approvingly, and was silent.

M'Turk and Beetle had taken out their books and were lying on their stomachs, chin in hand. The sea snorted and gurgled; the birds, scattered for the moment by these new animals, returned to their businesses, and the boys read on in the rich, warm sleepy silence.

'Hullo, here's a keeper,' said Stalky, shutting *Handley Cross** cautiously, and peering through the jungle. A man with a gun appeared on the sky-line to the east. 'Confound him, he's going to sit down!'

'He'd swear we were poachin' too,' said Beetle. 'What's the good of pheasants' eggs? They're always addled.'

''Might as well get up to the wood, *I* think,' said Stalky. 'We don't want G. M. Dabney, Col., J.P., to be bothered about us so soon. Up the wuzzy and keep quiet! He may have followed us, you know.'

Beetle was already far up the tunnel. They heard him gasp indescribably: there was the crash of a heavy body leaping through the furze.

'Aie! yeou little red rascal. I see yeou!' The keeper threw the gun to his shoulder, and fired both barrels in their direction. The pellets dusted the dry stems round them as a big fox plunged between Stalky's legs and ran over the cliff-edge.

They said nothing till they reached the wood, torn, dishevelled, hot, but unseen.

'Narrow squeak,' said Stalky. 'I'll swear some of the pellets went through my hair.'

'Did you see him?' said Beetle. 'I almost put my hand on him. Wasn't he a wopper! Didn't he stink! Hullo, Turkey, what's the matter? Are you hit?'

M'Turk's lean face had turned pearly white; his mouth,

generally half open, was tight shut, and his eyes blazed. They had never seen him like this save once, in a sad time of civil war.

'Do you know that that was just as bad as murder?' he said, in a grating voice, as he brushed prickles from his head.

'Well, he didn't hit us,' said Stalky. 'I think it was rather a lark. Here, where are you going?'

'I'm going up to the house, if there is one,' said M'Turk, pushing through the hollies. 'I am going to tell this Colonel Dabney.'

'Are you crazy? He'll swear it served us jolly well right. He'll report us. It'll be a public lickin'. Oh, Turkey, don't be as ass! Think of us!'

'You fool!' said M'Turk, turning savagely. 'D'you suppose I'm thinkin' of *us*. It's the keeper.'

'He's cracked,' said Beetle miserably, as they followed. Indeed, this was a new Turkey—a haughty, angular, nose-lifted Turkey—whom they accompanied through a shrubbery on to a lawn, where a white-whiskered old gentleman with a cleek was alternately putting and blaspheming vigorously.

'Are you Colonel Dabney?' M'Turk began in this new creaking voice of his.

'I—I am, and'—his eyes travelled up and down the boy— 'who—what the devil d'you want? Ye've been disturbing my pheasants. Don't attempt to deny it. Ye needn't laugh at it. [M'Turk's not too lovely features had twisted themselves into a horrible sneer at the word 'pheasant.'] You've been bird's-nesting. You needn't hide your hat. I can see that you belong to the College. Don't attempt to deny it. Ye do! Your name and number at once, sir. Ye want to speak to me—Eh? You saw my notice-boards? 'Must have. Don't attempt to deny it. Ye did! Damnable! Oh, damnable!'

He choked with emotion. M'Turk's heel tapped the lawn and he stuttered a little—two sure signs that he was losing his temper. But why should he, the offender, be angry?

'Lo-look here, sir. Do—do you shoot foxes? Because, if you don't, your keeper does. We've seen him! I do-don't care what you call us—but it's an awful thing. It's the ruin of good feelin' among neighbours. A ma-man ought to say once and for all how he stands about preservin'. It's worse than murder, because there's no legal remedy.' M'Turk was quoting confusedly from his father, while the old gentleman made noises in his throat.

'Do you know who I am?' he gurgled at last; Stalky and Beetle quaking.

'No, sorr, nor do I care if ye belonged to the Castle* itself. Answer me now, as one gentleman to another. Do ye shoot foxes or do ye not?'

And four years before Stalky and Beetle had carefully kicked M'Turk out of his Irish dialect! Assuredly he had gone mad or taken a sunstroke, and as assuredly he would be slain—once by the old gentleman and once by the Head. A public licking for the three was the least they could expect. Yet—if their eyes and ears were to be trusted—the old gentleman had collapsed. It might be a lull before the storm, but—

'I do not.' He was still gurgling.

'Then you must sack your keeper. He's not fit to live in the same country with a God-fearin' fox. An' a vixen, too—at this time o' year!'

'Did ye come up on purpose to tell me this?'

'Of course I did, ye silly man,' with a stamp of the foot. 'Would you not have done as much for me if you'd seen that thing happen on my land, now?'

Forgotten—forgotten was the College and the decency due to elders! M'Turk was treading again the barren purple mountains of the rainy West coast, where in his holidays he was viceroy of four thousand naked acres, only son of a three-hundred-year-old house, lord of a crazy fishing-boat, and the idol of his father's shiftless tenantry. It was the landed man speaking to his equal—deep calling to deep*—and the old gentleman acknowledged the cry.

'I apologise,' said he. 'I apologise unreservedly—to you, and to the Old Country. Now, will you be good enough to tell me your story?'

'We were in your combe,' M'Turk began, and he told his tale alternately as a schoolboy, and, when the iniquity of the thing overcame him, as an indignant squire; concluding: 'So you see he must be in the habit of it. I—we—one never wants to accuse a neighbour's man; but I took the liberty in this case——'

'I see. Quite so. For a reason ye had. Infamous—oh, infamous!' The two had fallen into step beside each other on the lawn, and Colonel Dabney was talking as one man to another. 'This comes of promoting a fisherman—a fisherman—from his lobster-pots. It's enough to ruin the reputation of an archangel. Don't attempt to deny it. It is! Your father has brought you up well. He has. I'd much like the pleasure of his acquaintance. Very much, indeed. And these young gentlemen? English they are. Don't attempt to deny it. They came up with you, too? Extraordinary! Extraordinary, now! In the present state of education I shouldn't have thought any three boys would be well enough grounded. . . . But out of the mouths of——* No—no! Not that by any odds. Don't attempt to deny it. Ye're not! Sherry always catches me under the liver, but—beer, now? Eh? What d'you say to beer, and something to eat? It's long since I was a boy—abominable nuisances; but exceptions prove the rule. And a vixen, too!'

They were fed on the terrace by a gray-haired housekeeper. Stalky and Beetle merely ate, but M'Turk with bright eyes continued a free and lofty discourse; and ever the old gentleman treated him as a brother.

'My dear man, of *course* ye can come again. Did I not say exceptions prove the rule? The lower combe? Man, dear, anywhere ye please, so long as you do not disturb my pheasants. The two are not incompatible. Don't attempt to deny it. They're not! I'll never allow another gun, though. Come and go as ye please. I'll not see you, and ye needn't see me. Ye've been well brought up. Another glass of beer, now? I tell you a fisherman he was and a fisherman he shall be to-night again. He shall! 'Wish I could drown him. I'll convoy you to the Lodge. My people are not precisely—ah—broke to boy, but they'll know *you* again.'

He dismissed them with many compliments by the high Lodge gate in the split-oak park palings and they stood still; even Stalky, who had played second, not to say a dumb, fiddle, regarding M'Turk as one from another world. The two glasses of strong home-brewed had brought a melancholy upon the boy, for, slowly strolling with his hands in his pockets, he crooned:—

'Oh, Paddy dear, and did ye hear the news that's goin' round?'*

Under other circumstances Stalky and Beetle would have fallen upon him, for that song was barred utterly—anathema—the sin of witchcraft. But seeing what he had wrought, they danced round him in silence, waiting till it pleased him to touch earth.

The tea-bell rang when they were still half a mile from College. M'Turk shivered and came out of dreams. The glory of his holiday estate had left him. He was a Colleger of the College, speaking English once more.

'Turkey, it was immense!' said Stalky generously. 'I didn't know you had it in you. You've got us a hut for the rest of the term, where we simply can't be collared. Fids! Fids! Oh, fids! I gloat! Hear me gloat!'

They spun wildly on their heels, jodelling after the accepted manner of a 'gloat,' which is not unremotely allied to the primitive man's song of triumph, and dropped down the hill by the path from the gasometer just in time to meet their House-master, who had spent the afternoon watching their abandoned hut in the 'wuzzy.'

Unluckily, all Mr. Prout's imagination leaned to the darker side of life, and he looked on those young-eyed cherubims* most sourly. Boys that he understood attended House-matches and could be accounted for at any moment. But he had heard M'Turk openly deride cricket—even House-matches; Beetle's views on the honour of the House he knew were incendiary; and he could never tell when the soft and smiling Stalky was laughing at him. Consequently—since human nature is what it is—those boys had been doing wrong somewhere. He hoped it was nothing very serious, but . . .

'*Ti-ra-la-la-i-tu!* I gloat! Hear me!' Stalky, still on his heels, whirled like a dancing dervish to the dining-hall.

'*Ti-ra-la-la-i-tu!* I gloat! Hear me!' Beetle spun behind him with outstretched arms.

'*Ti-ra-la-la-i-tu!* I gloat! Hear me!' M'Turk's voice cracked.

Now was there or was there not a distinct flavour of beer as they shot past Mr. Prout?

He was unlucky in that his conscience as a House-master impelled him to consult his associates. Had he taken his pipe and his troubles to Little Hartopp's rooms he would, perhaps, have been saved confusion, for Hartopp believed in boys, and knew something about them. His fate led him to King a fellow House-master, no friend of his, but a zealous hater of Stalky & Co.

'Ah-haa!' said King, rubbing his hands when the tale was told. 'Curious! Now *my* House never dream of doing these things.'

'But you see I've no proof, exactly.'

'Proof? With the egregious Beetle! As if one wanted it? I suppose it is not impossible for the Sergeant to supply it? Foxy is considered at least a match for any evasive boy in my House. Of course they were smoking and drinking somewhere. That type of boy always does. They think it manly.'

'But they've no following in the school, and they are distinctly—er—brutal to their juniors,' said Prout, who had from a distance seen Beetle return, with interest, his butterfly-net to a tearful fag.

'Ah! They consider themselves superior to ordinary delights. Self-sufficient little animals! There's something in M'Turk's Hibernian sneer that would make me a little annoyed. And they are so careful to avoid all overt acts, too. It's sheer calculated insolence. I am strongly opposed, as you know, to interfering with another man's House; but they need a lesson, Prout. They need a sharp lesson, if only to bring down their overweening self-conceit. Were I you, I should devote myself for a week to their little performances. Boys of that order—I may flatter myself, but I think I know boys—don't join the Bug-hunters for love. Tell the Sergeant to keep his eye open; and, of course, in my peregrinations I may casually keep mine open too.'

'*Ti-ra-la-la-i-tu!* I gloat! Hear me!' far down the corridor.

'Disgusting!' said King. 'Where do they pick up these obscene noises? One sharp lesson is what they want.'

The boys did not concern themselves with lessons for the next few days. They had all Colonel Dabney's estate to play with, and they explored it with the stealth of Red Indians and the accuracy of burglars. They could enter either by the Lodge-gates on the upper road—they were careful to ingratiate themselves with the Lodge-keeper and his wife—drop down into the combe, and return along the cliffs; or they could begin at the combe, and climb up into the road.

They were careful not to cross the Colonel's path—he had served his turn, and they would not out-wear their welcome—nor did they show up on the sky-line when they could move in cover. The shelter of the gorse by the cliff-edge was their chosen retreat. Beetle christened it the Pleasant Isle of Aves,* for the peace and the shelter of it; and here, pipes and tobacco once cachéd in a convenient ledge an arm's length down the cliff, their position was legally unassailable.

For, observe, Colonel Dabney had not invited them to enter his house. Therefore, they did not need to ask specific leave to go visiting; and school rules were strict on that point. He had merely thrown open his grounds to them; and, since they were lawful Bug-hunters, their extended bounds ran up to his notice-boards in the combe and his Lodge-gates on the hill.

They were amazed at their own virtue.

'And even if it wasn't,' said Stalky, flat on his back, staring into the blue. 'Even suppose we were miles out of bounds, no one could get at us through this wuzzy, unless he knew the tunnel. Isn't this better than lyin' up just behind the Coll.—in a blue funk every time we had a smoke? Isn't your Uncle Stalky——?'

'No,' said Beetle—he was stretched at the edge of the cliff thoughtfully spitting. 'We've got to thank Turkey for this. Turkey is the Great Man. Turkey, dear, you're distressing Heffles.'

'Gloomy old ass!' said M'Turk, deep in a book.

'They've got us under suspicion,' said Stalky. 'Hoophats *is* so suspicious somehow; and Foxy always makes every stalk he does a sort of—sort of——'

'Scalp,' said Beetle. 'Foxy's a giddy Chingangook.'*

'Poor Foxy,' said Stalky. 'He's goin' to catch us one of these days. 'Said to me in the gym last night, "I've got my eye on you, Mister Corkran. I'm only warning you for your good." Then I said, "Well, you jolly well take it off again, or you'll get into trouble. I'm only warnin' you for your good." Foxy was wrath.'

'Yes, but it's only fair sport for Foxy,' said Beetle. 'It's Hefflelinga that has the evil mind. 'Shouldn't wonder if he thought we got tight.'

'I never got squiffy but once—that was in the holidays,' said Stalky reflectively; 'an' it made me horrid sick. 'Pon my sacred Sam, though, it's enough to drive a man to drink, havin' an animal like Hoof for House-master.'

'If we attended the matches an' yelled, "Well hit, sir," an' stood on one leg an' grinned every time Heffy said, "So ho, my sons. Is it thus?" an' said, "Yes, sir," an' "No, sir," an' "Oh, sir," an' "Please, sir," like a lot o' filthy fa-ags, Heffy 'ud think no end of us," said M'Turk, with a sneer.

"Too late to begin that.'

'It's all right. The Hefflelinga means well. *But* he is an ass. *And* we show him that we think he's an ass. An' *so* Heffy don't love us. 'Told me last night after prayers that he was *in loco parentis*,'* Beetle grunted.

'The deuce he did!' cried Stalky. 'That means he's maturin' something unusual dam' mean. 'Last time he told me that he gave me three hundred lines for dancin' the cachuca* in Number Ten dormitory. *Loco parentis*, by gum? But what's the odds, as long as you're 'appy?* We're all right.'

They were, and their very rightness puzzled Prout, King, and the Sergeant. Boys with bad consciences show it. They slink out past the Fives Court in haste, and smile nervously when questioned. They return, disordered, in bare time to save a call-over. They nod and wink and giggle one to the other, scattering at the approach of a master. But Stalky and his allies had long outlived these manifestations of youth. They strolled forth unconcernedly, and returned, in excellent shape, after a light refreshment of strawberries and cream at the Lodge.

The Lodge-keeper had been promoted to keeper, *vice** the

murderous fisherman, and his wife made much of the boys. The man, too, gave them a squirrel, which they presented to the Natural History Society; thereby checkmating little Hartopp, who wished to know what they were doing for Science. Foxy faithfully worked some deep Devon lanes behind a lonely cross-roads inn; and it was curious that Prout and King, members of Common-room seldom friendly, walked together in the same direction—that is to say, north-east. Now, the Pleasant Isle of Aves lay due south-west.

'They're deep—day-vilish deep,' said Stalky. 'Why are they drawin' those covers?'

'Me,' said Beetle sweetly. 'I asked Foxy if he had ever tasted the beer there. That was enough for Foxy, and it cheered him up a little. He and Heffy were sniffin' round our old hut so long I thought they'd like a change.'

'Well, it can't last for ever,' said Stalky. 'Heffy's bankin' up like a thunder-cloud, an' King goes rubbin' his beastly hands, an' grinnin' like a hyena. It's shockin' demoralisin' for King. He'll burst some day.'

That day came a little sooner than they expected—came when the Sergeant, whose duty it was to collect defaulters, did not attend an afternoon call-over.

'Tired of pubs, eh? He's gone up to the top of hill with his binoculars to spot us,' said Stalky. 'Wonder he didn't think of that before. Did you see old Heffy cock his eye at us when we answered our names? Heffy's in it, too. *Ti-ra-la-la-i-tu!* I gloat! Hear me! Come on!'

'Aves?' said Beetle.

'Of course, but I'm not smokin' *aujourd-hui. Parceque je* jolly well *pense* that we'll be *suivi.* We'll go along the cliffs, slow, an' give Foxy lots of time to parallel us up above.'

They strolled towards the swimming-baths, and presently overtook King.

'Oh, don't let *me* interrupt you,' he said. 'Engaged in scientific pursuits, of course? I trust you will enjoy yourselves, my young friends?'

'You see!' said Stalky, when they were out of ear-shot. 'He can't keep a secret. He's followin' to cut off our line of retreat. He'll wait at the Baths till Heffy comes along. They've tried every blessed place except along the cliffs, and now they think they've bottled us. No need to hurry.'

They walked leisurely over the combes till they reached the line of notice-boards.

'Listen a shake. Foxy's up wind comin' down hill like beans. When you hear him move in the bushes, go straight across to Aves. They want to catch us *flagrante delicto*.'*

They dived into the gorse at right angles to the tunnel, openly crossing the grass, and lay still in Aves.

'What did I tell you?' Stalky carefully put away the pipes and tobacco. The Sergeant, out of breath, was leaning against the fence, raking the furze with his binoculars, but he might as well have tried to see through a sand-bag. Anon, Prout and King appeared behind him. They conferred.

'Aha! Foxy don't like the notice-boards, and he don't like the prickles either. Now we'll cut up the tunnel and go to the Lodge. Hullo! They've sent Foxy into cover.'

The Sergeant was waist-deep in crackling, swaying furze, his ears filled with the noise of his own progress. The boys reached the shelter of the wood and looked down through a belt of hollies.

'Hellish noise!' said Stalky critically. "Don't think Colonel Dabney will like it. I move we go up to the Lodge and get something to eat. We might as well see the fun out.'

Suddenly the keeper passed them at a trot.

'Who'm they to combe-bottom for Lard's sake? Master'll be crazy,' he said.

'Poachers simly,' Stalky replied in the broad Devon that was the boy's *langue de guerre*.

'I'll poach 'em to raights!' He dropped into the funnel-like combe, which presently began to fill with noises, notably King's voice crying, 'Go on, Sergeant! Leave him alone, you, sir. He is executing my orders.'

'Who'm yeou to give arders here, gingy whiskers? Yeou come up to the master. Come out o' that wuzzy! [This is to the Sergeant.] Yiss, I reckon us knows the boys yeou'm after. They've tu long ears an' vuzzy bellies, an' you nippies they in yeour pockets when they'm dead. Come on up to master! He'll boy yeou all you'm a mind to. Yeou other folk bide your side fence.'

'Explain to the proprietor. You can explain, Sergeant,' shouted King. Evidently the Sergeant had surrendered to the major force.

Beetle lay at full length on the turf behind the Lodge literally biting the earth in spasms of joy.

Stalky kicked him upright. There was nothing of levity about Stalky or M'Turk save a stray muscle twitching on the cheek.

They tapped at the Lodge door, where they were always welcome.

'Come yeou right in an' set down, my little dearrs,' said the woman. 'They'll niver touch my man. He'll poach 'em to rights. Iss fai! Fresh berries an' cream. Us Dartymoor folk niver forget their friends. But them Ridevor poachers, they've no hem to their garments. Sugar? My man he've digged a badger for yeou, my dearrs. 'Tis in the linhay* in a box.'

'Us'll take un with us when we'm finished here. I reckon yeou'm busy. We'll bide here an'—'tis washin' day with yeou, simly,' said Stalky. 'We'm no company to make all vitty for. Niver yeou mind us. Yiss. There's plenty cream.'

The woman withdrew, wiping her pink hands on her apron, and left them in the parlour. There was a scuffle of feet on the gravel outside the heavily-leaded diamond panes, and then the voice of Colonel Dabney, something clearer than a bugle.

'Ye can read? You've eyes in your head? Don't attempt to deny it. Ye have!'

Beetle snatched a crochet-work antimacassar from the shiny horsehair sofa, stuffed it into his mouth, and rolled out of sight.

'You saw my notice-boards. Your duty? Curse your impudence, sir. Your duty was to keep off my grounds. Talk of duty to *me!* Why—why—why, ye misbegotten poacher, ye'll be teaching me my A B C next! Roarin' like a bull in the bushes down there! Boys? Boys? Boys? Keep your boys at home, then! I'm not responsible for your boys! But I don't believe it—I don't believe a word of it. Ye've a furtive look in your eye—a furtive, sneakin', poachin' look in your eye, that 'ud ruin the reputation of an archangel! Don't attempt to deny it! Ye have! A sergeant? More shame to you, then, an' the worst bargain Her Majesty ever made! A sergeant, to run about the country poachin'—on your pension! Damnable! Oh, damnable! But I'll be considerate. I'll be merciful. By gad, I'll be the very essince o' humanity! Did ye, or did ye not, see my notice-boards? Don't attempt to deny it! Ye did. Silence, Sergeant!'

Twenty-one years in the army had left their mark on Foxy. He obeyed.

'Now. March!'

The high Lodge-gate shut with a clang. 'My duty! A sergeant to tell me my duty!' puffed Colonel Dabney. 'Good Lard! more sergeants!'

'It's King! It's King!' gulped Stalky, his head on the horsehair pillow. M'Turk was eating the rag-carpet before the speckless hearth, and the sofa heaved to the emotions of Beetle. Through the thick glass the figures without showed blue, distorted, and menacing.

'I—I protest against this outrage.' King had evidently been running up hill. 'The man was entirely within his duty. Let—let me give you my card.'

'He's in flannels!' Stalky buried his head again.

'Unfortunately—*most* unfortunately—I have not one with me, but my name is King, sir, a House-master of the College, and you will find me prepared—fully prepared—to answer for this man's action. We've seen three——'

'Did ye see my notice-boards?'

'I admit we did; but under the circumstances——'

'I stand *in loco parentis*.' Prout's deep voice was added to the discussion. They could hear him pant.

'F'what?' Colonel Dabney was growing more and more Irish.

'I'm responsible for the boys under my charge.'

'Ye are, are ye? Then all I can say is that ye set them a very bad example—a dam' bad example, if I may say so. I do not own your boys. I've not seen your boys, an' I tell you that if there was a boy grinnin' in every bush on the place *still* ye've no shadow of a right here, comin' up from the combe that way, an' frightenin' everything in it. Don't attempt to deny it. Ye did. Ye should have come to the Lodge an' seen me like

Christians, instead of chasin' your dam' boys through the length and breadth of my covers. *In loco parentis* ye are? Well, I've not forgotten my Latin either, an' I'll say to you: "*Quis custodiet ipsos custodes?*"* If the masters trespass, how can we blame the boys?'

'But if I could speak to you privately,' said Prout.

'I'll have nothing private with you! Ye can be as private as ye please on the other side o' that gate, an'—I wish ye a very good afternoon.'

A second time the gate clanged. They waited till Colonel Dabney had returned to the house, and fell into one another's arms, crowing for breath.

'Oh, my Soul! Oh, my King! Oh, my Heffy! Oh, my Foxy! Zeal, all zeal, Mr. Easy.'* Stalky wiped his eyes. 'Oh! Oh! Oh!—"I *did* boil the exciseman!" We must get out of this or we'll be late for tea.'

'Ge—ge—get the badger and make little Hartopp happy. Ma—ma—make 'em all happy,' sobbed M'Turk, groping for the door and kicking the prostrate Beetle before him.

They found the beast in an evil-smelling box, left two half-crowns for payment, and staggered home. Only the badger grunted most marvellous like Colonel Dabney, and they dropped him twice or thrice with shrieks of helpless laughter. They were but imperfectly recovered when Foxy met them by the Fives Court with word that they were to go up to their dormitory and wait till sent for.

'Well, take this box to Mr. Hartopp's rooms, then. We've done something for the Natural History Society, at any rate,' said Beetle.

"Fraid that won't save you, young gen'elmen,' Foxy answered, in an awful voice. He was sorely ruffled in his mind.

'All sereno, Foxibus.' Stalky had reached the extreme stage of hiccups. 'We—we'll never desert you, Foxy. Hounds choppin' foxes in cover is more a proof of vice,* ain't it? . . . No, you're right. I'm—I'm not quite well.'

'They've gone a bit too far this time,' Foxy thought to himself. 'Very far gone, I'd say, excep' there was no smell of liquor. An' yet it isn't like 'em—somehow. King and Prout they 'ad their dressin'-down same as me. That's one comfort.'

'Now, we must pull up,' said Stalky, rising from the bed on which he had thrown himself. 'We're injured innocence—as usual. *We* don't know what we've been sent up here for, do we?'

'No explanation. Deprived of tea. Public disgrace before the House,' said M'Turk, whose eyes were running over. 'It's dam' serious.'

'Well, hold on, till King loses his temper,' said Beetle. 'He's a libellous old rip, an' he'll be in a ravin' paddy-wack.* Prout's too beastly cautious. Keep your eye on King, and, if he gives us a chance, appeal to the Head. That always makes 'em sick.'

They were summoned to their House-master's study, King and Foxy supporting Prout, and Foxy had three canes under his arm. King leered triumphantly, for there were tears, undried tears of mirth, on the boys' cheeks. Then the examination began.

Yes, they had walked along the cliffs. Yes, they had entered Colonel Dabney's grounds. Yes, they had seen the notice-boards (at this point Beetle sputtered hysterically). For what purpose had they entered Colonel Dabney's grounds? 'Well sir, there was a badger.'

Here King, who loathed the Natural History Society because he did not like Hartopp, could no longer be restrained. He begged them not to add mendacity to open insolence. 'But the badger is in Mr. Hartopp's rooms, sir.' The Sergeant had kindly taken it up for them. That disposed of the badger, and the temporary check brought King's temper to boiling-point. They could hear his foot on the floor while Prout prepared his lumbering inquiries. They had settled into their stride now. Their eyes ceased to sparkle; their faces were blank; their hands hung beside them without a twitch. They were learning, at the expense of a fellow-countryman, the lesson of their race, which is to put away all emotion and entrap the alien at the proper time.

So far good. King was importing himself more freely into the trial, being vengeful where Prout was grieved. They knew the penalties of trespassing? With a fine show of irresolution,

Stalky admitted that he had gathered some information vaguely bearing on this head, but he thought——The sentence was dragged out to the uttermost: Stalky did not wish to play his trump with such an opponent. Mr. King desired no buts, nor was he interested in Stalky's evasions. They, on the other hand, might be interested in his poor views. Boys who crept—who sneaked—who lurked—out of bounds, even the generous bounds of the Natural History Society, which they had falsely joined as a cloak for their misdeeds—their vices— their villainies—their immoralities——

'He'll break cover in a minute,' said Stalky to himself. 'Then we'll run into him before he gets away.'

Such boys, scabrous boys, moral lepers—the current of his words was carrying King off his feet—evil speakers, liars, slow-bellies*—yea, incipient drunkards. . . .

He was merely working up to a peroration, and the boys knew it; but M'Turk cut through the frothing sentence, the others echoing:

'I appeal to the Head, sir.'

'I appeal to the Head, sir.'

'I appeal to the Head, sir.'

It was their unquestioned right. Drunkenness meant expulsion after a public flogging. They had been accused of it. The case was the Head's, and the Head's alone.

'Thou hast appealed unto Cæsar: unto Cæsar shalt thou go.'* They had heard that sentence once or twice before in their careers. 'None the less,' said King uneasily, 'you would be better advised to abide by our decision, my young friends.'

'Are we allowed to associate with the rest of the school till we see the Head, sir?' said M'Turk to his House-master, disregarding King. This at once lifted the situation to its loftiest plane. Moreover it meant no work, for moral leprosy was strictly quarantined, and the Head never executed judgment till twenty-four cold hours later.

'Well—er—if you persist in your defiant attitude,' said King, with a loving look at the canes under Foxy's arm. 'There is no alternative.'

Ten minutes later the news was over the whole school. Stalky & Co. had fallen at last—fallen by drink. They had been drinking. They had returned blind-drunk from a hut. They were even now lying hopelessly intoxicated on the dormitory floor. A few bold spirits crept up to look, and received boots about the head.

'We've got him—got him on the Caudine Toasting-fork!'* said Stalky, after those hints were taken. 'King'll have to prove his charges up to the giddy hilt.'

' "Too much ticklee, him bust," '* Beetle quoted from a book of his reading. 'Didn't I say he'd go pop if we lat un bide?'

'No prep., either, O ye incipient drunkards,' said M'Turk, 'and it's trig night, too. Hullo! Here's our dear friend Foxy. More tortures, Foxibus?'

'I've brought you something to eat, young gentlemen,' said the Sergeant from behind a crowded tray. Their wars had ever been waged without malice, and a suspicion floated in Foxy's mind that boys who allowed themselves to be tracked so easily might, perhaps, hold something in reserve. Foxy had served through the Mutiny, when early and accurate information was worth much.

'I—I noticed you 'adn't 'ad anything to eat, an' I spoke to Gumbly, an' he said you wasn't exactly cut off from supplies. So I brought up this. It's your potted 'am tin, ain't it, Mr. Corkran?'

'Why, Foxibus, you're a brick,' said Stalky. 'I didn't think you had this much—what's the word, Beetle?'

'Bowels,' Beetle replied promptly. 'Thank you, Sergeant. That's young Carter's potted ham, though.'

'There was a C on it. I thought it was Mr. Corkran's. This is a very serious business, young gentlemen. That's what it is. I didn't know, perhaps, but there might be something on your side which you hadn't said to Mr. King or Mr. Prout, maybe.'

'There is. Heaps, Foxibus.' This from Stalky through a full mouth.

'Then you see, if that was the case, it seemed to me I might represent it, quiet so to say, to the 'Ead when he asks me about it. I've got to take 'im the charges to-night, an'—it looks bad on the face of it.'

''Trocious bad, Foxy. Twenty-seven cuts in the gym before

all the school, and public expulsion. "Wine is a mocker, strong drink is ragin'," '* quoth Beetle.

'Its nothin' to make fun of, young gentlemen. I 'ave to go to the 'Ead with the charges. An'—an' you mayn't be aware, per'aps, that I was followin' you this afternoon; havin' my suspicions.'

'Did ye see the notice-boards?' croaked M'Turk, in the very brogue of Colonel Dabney.

'Ye've eyes in your head. Don't attempt to deny it. Ye did!' said Beetle.

'A Sergeant! To run about poachin' on your pension! Damnable! Oh, damnable!' said Stalky, without pity.

'Good Lord!' said the Sergeant, sitting heavily upon a bed. 'Where—where the devil was you? I might ha' known it was a do—somewhere.'

'Oh, you clever maniac!' Stalky resumed. 'We mayn't be aware you were followin' us this afternoon, mayn't we? 'Thought you were stalkin' us, eh? Why, we led you bung into it, of course. Colonel Dabney—don't you think he's a nice man, Foxy?—Colonel Dabney's our pet particular friend. We've been goin' there for weeks and weeks. He invited us. You and your duty! Curse your duty, sir! Your duty was to keep off his covers.'

'You'll never be able to hold up your head again, Foxy. The fags 'll hoot at you,' said Beetle. 'Think of your giddy prestige!'

The Sergeant was thinking—hard.

'Look 'ere, young gentlemen,' he said earnestly. 'You aren't surely ever goin' to tell, are you? Wasn't Mr. Prout and Mr. King in—in it too?'

'Foxibusculus, they was. They was—singular horrid. 'Caught it worse than you. We heard every word of it. You got off easy, considerin'. If I'd been Dabney I swear I'd ha' quodded* you. I think I'll suggest it to him to-morrow.'

'An' it's all goin' up to the 'Ead. Oh, Good Lord!'

'Every giddy word of it, my Chingangook,'* said Beetle, dancing. 'Why shouldn't it? We've done nothing wrong. We ain't poachers. We didn't cut about blastin' the characters of poor, innocent boys—saying they were drunk.'

'That I didn't,' said Foxy. 'I—I only said that you be'aved uncommon odd when you come back with that badger. Mr. King may have taken the wrong hint from that.'

''Course he did; an' he'll jolly well shove all the blame on you when he finds out he's wrong. We know King, if you don't. I'm ashamed of you. You ain't fit to be a Sergeant,' said M'Turk.

'Not with three thorough-goin' young devils like you, I ain't. I've been had. I've been ambuscaded. Horse, foot, an' guns, I've been had, an'—an' there'll be no holdin' the junior forms after this. M'r'over, the 'Ead will send me with a note to Colonel Dabney to ask if what you say about bein' invited was true.'

'Then you'd better go in by the Lodge-gates this time, instead of chasin' your dam' boys—oh, that was the Epistle to King—so it was. We-ell, Foxy?' Stalky put his chin on his hands and regarded the victim with deep delight.

'*Ti-ra-la-la-i-tu!* I gloat! Hear me!' said M'Turk. 'Foxy brought us tea when we were moral lepers. Foxy has a heart. Foxy has been in the Army, too.'

'I wish I'd ha' had you in my company, young gentlemen,' said the Sergeant from the depths of his heart; 'I'd ha' given you something.'

'Silence at drum-head court-martial,' M'Turk went on. 'I'm advocate for the prisoner; and, besides, this is much too good to tell all the other brutes in the Coll. They'd *never* understand. They play cricket, and say, "Yes, sir," and "Oh, sir," and "No, sir."'

'Never mind that. Go ahead,' said Stalky.

'Well, Foxy's a good little chap when he does not esteem himself so as to be clever.'

' "Take not out your 'ounds on a werry windy day," '* Stalky struck in. '*I* don't care if you let him off.'

'Nor me,' said Beetle. 'Heffy is my only joy*—Heffy and King.'

'I 'ad to do it,' said the Sergeant plaintively.

'Right O! Led away by bad companions in the execution of his duty, or—or words to that effect. You're dismissed with a reprimand, Foxy. We won't tell about you. I swear we won't,'

M'Turk concluded. 'Bad for the discipline of the school. Horrid bad.'

'Well,' said the Sergeant, gathering up the tea-things, 'knowin' what I know o' the young dev—gentlemen of the College, I'm very glad to 'ear it. But what am I to tell the 'Ead?'

'Anything you jolly well please, Foxy. *We* aren't the criminals.'

To say that the Head was annoyed when the Sergeant appeared after dinner with the day's crime-sheet would be putting it mildly.

'Corkran, M'Turk, & Co., I see. Bounds as usual. Hullo! What the deuce is this? Suspicion of drinking. Whose charge?'

'Mr. King's, sir. I caught 'em out of bounds, sir: at least that was 'ow it looked. But there's a lot be'ind, sir.' The Sergeant was evidently troubled.

'Go on,' said the Head. 'Let us have your version.'

He and the Sergeant had dealt with each other for some seven years; while the Head knew that Mr. King's statements depended very largely on Mr. King's temper.

'I thought they were out of bounds along the cliffs. But it come out they wasn't, sir. I saw them go into Colonel Dabney's woods, and—Mr. King and Mr. Prout come along—and—the fact was, sir, we was mistook for poachers by Colonel Dabney's people—Mr. King and Mr. Prout and me. There were some words, sir, on both sides. The young gentlemen slipped 'ome somehow, and they seemed 'ighly humorous, sir. Mr. King was mistook by Colonel Dabney himself—Colonel Dabney bein' strict. Then they preferred to come straight to you, sir, on account of what—what Mr. King may 'ave said about their 'abits afterwards in Mr. Prout's study. I only said they was 'ighly humorous, laughin' an' gigglin', an' a bit above 'emselves. They've since told me, sir, in a humorous way, that they was invited by Colonel Dabney to go into 'is woods.'

'I see. They didn't tell their House-master that, of course.'

'They took up Mr. King on appeal just as soon as he spoke about their—'abits. Put in the appeal at once, sir, an' asked to be sent to the dormitory waitin' for you. I've since gathered, sir, in their humorous way, sir, that some'ow or other they've 'eard about every word Colonel Dabney said to Mr. King and Mr. Prout when he mistook 'em for poachers. I—I might ha' known when they led me on so that they 'eld the inner line of communications. It's—it's a plain do, sir, if you ask *me*; an' they're gloatin' over it in the dormitory.'

The Head saw—saw even to the uttermost farthing—and his mouth twitched a little under his moustache.

'Send them to me at once, Sergeant. This case needn't wait over.'

'Good evening,' said he when the three appeared under escort. 'I want your undivided attention for a few minutes. You've known me for five years, and I've known you for—twenty-five. I think we understand one another perfectly. I am now going to pay you a tremendous compliment. (The brown one, please, Sergeant. Thanks. You needn't wait.) I'm going to execute you without rhyme, Beetle, or reason. I know you went to Colonel Dabney's covers because you were invited. I'm not even going to send the Sergeant with a note to ask if your statement is true; because I am convinced that, on this occasion, you have adhered strictly to the truth. I know, too, that you were not drinking. (You can take off that virtuous expression, M'Turk, or I shall begin to fear you don't understand me.) There is not a flaw in any of your characters. And that is why I am going to perpetrate a howling injustice. Your reputations have been injured, haven't they? You have been disgraced before the House, haven't you? You have a peculiarly keen regard for the honour of your House, haven't you? Well, *now* I am going to lick you.'

Six apiece was their portion upon that word.

'And this, I think'—the Head replaced the cane, and flung the written charge into the wastepaper basket—'covers the situation. When you find a variation from the normal—this will be useful to you in later life—always meet him in an abnormal way. And that reminds me. There are a pile of paper-backs on that shelf. You can borrow them if you put them back. I don't think they'll take any harm from being read in the open. They smell of tobacco rather. You will go to prep. this evening as usual. Good-night,' said that amazing man.

'Good-night, and thank you, sir.'

'I swear I'll pray for the Head to-night,' said Beetle. 'Those last two cuts were just flicks on my collar. There's a *Monte Cristo** in that lower shelf. I saw it. Bags I, next time we go to Aves!'

'Dearr man!' said M'Turk. 'No gating. No impots. No beastly questions. All settled. Hullo! what's King goin' in to him for— King and Prout?'

Whatever the nature of that interview, it did not improve either King's or Prout's ruffled plumes, for, when they came out of the Head's house, six eyes noted that the one was red and blue with emotion as to his nose, and that the other was sweating profusely. That sight compensated them amply for the Imperial Jaw with which they were favoured by the two. It seems—and who so astonished as they?—that they had held back material facts; that they were guilty both of *suppressio veri and suggestio falsi** (well-known gods against whom they often offended); further, that they were malignant in their dispositions, untrustworthy in their characters, pernicious and revolutionary in their influences, abandoned to the devils of wilfulness, pride, and a most intolerable conceit. Ninthly, and lastly, they were to have a care and to be very careful.

They were careful, as only boys can be when there is a hurt to be inflicted. They waited through one suffocating week till Prout and King were their royal selves again; waited till there was a House-match—their own House, too—in which Prout was taking part; waited, further, till he had buckled on his pads in the pavilion and stood ready to go forth. King was scoring at the window, and the three sat on a bench without.

Said Stalky to Beetle: 'I say, Beetle, *quis custodiet ipsos custodes?*'

'Don't ask me,' said Beetle. 'I'll have nothin' private with you. Ye can be as private as ye please the other end of the bench; and I wish ye a very good afternoon.'

M'Turk yawned.

'Well, ye should ha' come up to the Lodge like Christians instead o' chasin' your—a-hem—boys through the length an' breadth of my covers. *I* think these House-matches are all rot. Let's go over to Colonel Dabney's an' see if he's collared any more poachers.'

That afternoon there was joy in Aves.

Slaves of the Lamp

PART I

THE music-room on the top floor of Number Five was filled with the 'Aladdin'* company at rehearsal. Dickson Quartus, commonly known as Dick Four, was Aladdin, stage-manager, ballet-master, half the orchestra, and largely librettist, for the 'book' had been rewritten and filled with local allusions. The pantomime was to be given next week, in the down-stairs study occupied by Aladdin, Abanazar, and the Emperor of China. The Slave of the Lamp, with the Princess Badroulbadour and the Widow Twankey, owned Number Five study across the same landing, so that the company could be easily assembled. The floor shook to the stamp-and-go of the ballet, while Aladdin, in pink cotton tights, a blue and tinsel jacket, and a plumed hat, banged alternately on the piano and his banjo. He was the moving spirit of the game, as befitted a senior who had passed his Army Preliminary and hoped to enter Sandhurst next spring.

Aladdin came to his own at last, Abanazar lay poisoned on the floor, the Widow Twankey danced her dance, and the company decided it would 'come all right on the night.'

'What about the last song, though?' said the Emperor, a tallish, fair-headed boy with a ghost of a moustache, at which he pulled manfully. 'We need a rousing old tune.'

' "John Peel"? "Drink, Puppy, Drink"?' suggested Abanazar, smoothing his baggy lilac pyjamas. 'Pussy' Abanazar never looked more than one-half awake, but he owned a soft, slow smile which well suited the part of the Wicked Uncle.

'Stale,' said Aladdin. 'Might as well have "Grandfather's Clock." What's that thing you were humming at prep. last night, Stalky?'

Stalky, The Slave of the Lamp, in black tights and doublet, a black silk half-mask on his forehead, whistled lazily where he lay on the top of the piano. It was a catchy music-hall tune.

Dick Four cocked his head critically, and squinted down a large red nose.

'Once more, and I can pick it up,' he said, strumming. 'Sing the words.'

'Arrah, Patsy, mind the baby! Arrah, Patsy, mind the child!
Wrap him up in an overcoat, he's surely goin' wild!
Arrah, Patsy, mind the baby; just ye mind the child awhile!
He'll kick an' bite an' cry all night! Arrah, Patsy, mind the child!'*

'Rippin'! Oh, rippin'!' said Dick Four. 'Only we shan't have any piano on the night. We must work it with the banjos—play an' dance at the same time. You try, Tertius.'

The Emperor pushed aside his pea-green sleeves of state, and followed Dick Four on a heavy nickel-plated banjo.

'Yes, but I'm dead all this time. Bung in the middle of the stage, too,' said Abanazar.

'Oh, that's Beetle's biznai,' said Dick Four. 'Vamp it up, Beetle. Don't keep us waiting all night. You've got to get Pussy out of the light somehow, and bring us all in dancing at the end.'

'All right. You two play it again,' said Beetle, who, in a gray skirt and a wig of chestnut sausage-curls, set slantwise above a pair of spectacles mended with an old boot-lace, represented the Widow Twankey. He waved one leg in time to the hammered refrain, and the banjos grew louder.

'Um! Ah! Er—"Aladdin now has won his wife," ' he sang, and Dick Four repeated it.

' "Your Emperor is appeased." ' Tertius flung out his chest as he delivered his line.

'Now jump up, Pussy! Say, "I think I'd better come to life!" Then we all take hands and come forward: "We hope you've all been pleased." *Twiggez-vous?*'

'*Nous twiggons*. Good enough. What's the chorus for the final ballet? It's four kicks and a turn,' said Dick Four.

'Oh! Er!

> John Short* will ring the curtain down,
>   And ring the prompter's bell;
> We hope you know before you go,
>   That we all wish you well.'

'Rippin'! Rippin'! Now for the Widow's scene with the Princess. Hurry up, Turkey'

M'Turk, in a violet silk skirt and a coquettish blue turban, slouched forward as one thoroughly ashamed of himself. The Slave of the Lamp climbed down from the piano, and dispassionately kicked him. 'Play up, Turkey,' he said; 'this is serious.' But there fell on the door the knock of authority. It happened to be King, in gown and mortar-board, enjoying a Saturday evening prowl before dinner.

'Locked doors! Locked doors!' he snapped with a scowl. 'What's the meaning of this; and what, may I ask, is the intention of this—this epicene attire?'

'Pantomime, sir. The Head gave us leave,' said Abanazar, as the only member of the Sixth concerned. Dick Four stood firm in the confidence born of well-fitting tights, but the Beetle strove to efface himself behind the piano. A gray princess-skirt* borrowed from a day-boy's mother and a spotted cotton-bodice unsystematically padded with imposition-paper* make one ridiculous. And in other regards Beetle had a bad conscience.

'As usual!' sneered King. 'Futile foolery just when your careers, such as they may be, are hanging in the balance. I see! Ah, I see! The old gang of criminals—allied forces of disorder—Corkran'—the Slave of the Lamp smiled politely—'M'Turk'—the Irishman smiled—'and, of course, the unspeakable Beetle, our friend Gigadibs.' Abanazar, the Emperor, and Aladdin had more or less of characters, and King passed them over. 'Come forth, my inky buffoon, from behind yonder instrument of music! You supply, I presume, the doggerel for this entertainment. 'Esteem yourself to be, as it were, a poet?'

'He's found one of' em,' thought Beetle, noting the flush on King's cheek-bone.

'I have just had the pleasure of reading an effusion of yours to my address, I believe—an effusion intended to rhyme. So—so you despise me, Master Gigadibs,* do you? I am quite aware—you need not explain—that it was ostensibly *not* intended for my edification. I read it with laughter—yes, with laughter. These paper pellets of inky boys—still a boy we are, Master Gigadibs—do not disturb my equanimity.'

''Wonder which it was,' thought Beetle. He had launched many lampoons on an appreciative public ever since he discovered that it was possible to convey reproof in rhyme.

In sign of his unruffled calm, King proceeded to tear Beetle, whom he called Gigadibs, slowly asunder. From his untied shoe-strings to his mended spectacles (the life of a poet at a big school is hard) he held him up to the derision of his associates—with the usual result. His wild flowers of speech—King had an unpleasant tongue—restored him to good humour at the last. He drew a lurid picture of Beetle's latter end as a scurrilous pamphleteer dying in an attic, scattered a few compliments over M'Turk and Corkran, and, reminding Beetle that he must come up for judgment when called upon, went to Common-room, where he triumphed anew over his victims.

'And the worst of it,' he explained in a loud voice over his soup, 'is that I waste such gems of sarcasm on their thick heads. It's miles above them, I'm certain.'

'We-ell,' said the school chaplain slowly, 'I don't know what Corkran's appreciation of your style may be, but young M'Turk reads Ruskin for his amusement.'

'Nonsense! He does it to show off. I mistrust the dark Celt.'

'He does nothing of the kind. I went into their study the other night, unofficially, and M'Turk was gluing up the back of four odd numbers of *Fors Clavigera*.'*

'I don't know anything about their private lives,' said a mathematical master hotly, 'but I've learned by bitter experience that Number Five study are best left alone. They are utterly soulless young devils.' He blushed as the others laughed.

But in the music-room there was wrath and bad language. Only Stalky, Slave of the Lamp, lay on the piano unmoved.

'That little swine Manders minor must have shown him your stuff. He's always suckin' up to King. Go and kill him,' he drawled. 'Which one was it, Beetle?'

'Dunno,' said Beetle, struggling out of the skirt. 'There was one about his hunting for popularity with the small boys, and the other one was one about him in hell, tellin' the Devil he was a Balliol man. I swear both of 'em rhymed all right. By gum! P'raps Manders minor showed him both! *I'll* correct his cæsuras for him.'*

He disappeared down two flights of stairs, flushed a small pink and white boy in a form-room next door to King's study, which, again, was immediately below his own, and chased him up the corridor into a form-room sacred to the revels of the Lower Third. Thence he came back, greatly disordered, to find M'Turk, Stalky, and the others of the company in his study enjoying an unlimited 'brew'—coffee, cocoa, buns, new bread hot and steaming, sardine, sausage, ham-and-tongue paste, pilchards, two jams, and at least as many pounds of Devonshire cream.

'My Hat!' said he, throwing himself upon the banquet. 'Who stumped up for this, Stalky?' It was within a month of term-end, and blank starvation had reigned in the studies for weeks.

'You,' said Stalky serenely.

'Confound you! You haven't been popping my Sunday bags, then?'

'Keep your hair on. It's only your watch.'

'Watch! I lost it—weeks ago. Out on the Burrows, when we tried to shoot the old ram—the day our pistol burst.'

'It dropped out of your pocket (you're so beastly careless, Beetle), and M'Turk and I kept it for you. I've been wearing it for a week, and you never noticed. 'Took it into Bideford after dinner to-day. 'Got thirteen and sevenpence. Here's the ticket.'

'Well, that's pretty average cool,' said Abanazar behind a slab of cream and jam, as Beetle, reassured upon the safety of his Sunday trousers showed not even surprise, much less resentment. Indeed, it was M'Turk who grew angry, saying:

'You gave him the ticket, Stalky? You pawned it? You unmitigated beast! Why, last month you and Beetle sold mine! 'Never got a sniff of any ticket.'

'Ah, that was because you locked your trunk and we wasted half the afternoon hammering it open. We might have pawned it if you'd behaved like a Christian, Turkey.'

'My Aunt!' said Abanazar, 'you chaps are communists.* Vote of thanks to Beetle, though.'

'That's beastly unfair,' said Stalky, 'when I took all the trouble to pawn it. Beetle never knew he had a watch. Oh, I say, Rabbits-Eggs gave me a lift into Bideford this afternoon.'

Rabbits-Eggs was the local carrier—an outcrop of the early Devonian formation. It was Stalky who had invented his unlovely name.* 'He was pretty average drunk, or he wouldn't have done it. Rabbits-Eggs is a little shy of me, somehow. But I swore it was *pax* between us, and gave him a bob. He stopped at two pubs on the way in, so he'll be howling drunk to-night. Oh, don't begin reading, Beetle; there's a council of war on. What the deuce is the matter with your collar?'

"Chivied Manders minor into the Lower Third box-room. 'Had all his beastly little friends on top of me,' said Beetle, from behind a jar of pilchards and a book.

'You ass! Any fool could have told you where Manders would bunk to,' said M'Turk.

'I didn't think,' said Beetle meekly, scooping out pilchards with a spoon.

"Course you didn't. You never do.' M'Turk adjusted Beetle's collar with a savage tug. 'Don't drop oil all over my "Fors," or I'll scrag you!'

'Shut up, you—you Irish Biddy! 'Tisn't your beastly "Fors." It's one of mine.'

The book was a fat, brown-backed volume of the later Sixties,* which King had once thrown at Beetle's head that Beetle might see whence the name Gigadibs came. Beetle had quietly annexed the book, and had seen—several things. The quarter-comprehended verses lived and ate with him, as the be-dropped pages showed. He removed himself from all that world, drifting at large with wondrous Men and Women, till M'Turk hammered the pilchard spoon on his head and he snarled.

'Beetle! You're oppressed and insulted and bullied by King. Don't you feel it?'

'Let me alone! I can write some more poetry about him if I am, I suppose.'

'Mad! Quite mad!' said Stalky to the visitors, as one exibiting strange beasts. 'Beetle reads an ass called Brownin', and M'Turk reads an ass called Ruskin; and——'

'Ruskin isn't an ass,' said M'Turk. 'He's almost as good as the Opium-Eater.* He says we're "children of noble races trained by surrounding art."* That means me, and the way I decorated the study when you two badgers would have stuck up brackets and Christmas cards. Child of a noble race, trained by surrounding art, stop reading, or I'll shove a pilchard down your neck!'

'It's two to one,' said Stalky warningly, and Beetle closed the book, in obedience to the law under which he and his companions had lived for six checkered years.

The visitors looked on delighted. Number Five study had a reputation for more variegated insanity than the rest of the school put together; and, so far as its code allowed friendship with outsiders, it was polite and open-hearted to its neighbours.

'What rot do you want now?' said Beetle.

'King! War!' said M'Turk, jerking his head toward the wall, where hung a small wooden West-African war-drum, a gift to M'Turk from a naval uncle.

'Then we shall be turned out of the study again,' said Beetle, who loved his flesh-pots. 'Mason turned us out for—just warbling on it.' Mason was that mathematical master who had testified in Common-room.

'Warbling?—Oh, Lord!' said Abanazar. 'We couldn't hear ourselves speak in our study when you played the infernal thing. What's the good of getting turned out of your study, anyhow?'

'We lived in the form-rooms for a week, too,' said Beetle tragically. 'And it was beastly cold.'

'Ye-es; but Mason's rooms were filled with rats every day we were out. It took him a week to draw the inference,' said M'Turk. 'He loathes rats. 'Minute he let us go back the rats stopped. Mason's a little shy of us now, but there was no evidence.'

'Jolly well there wasn't,' said Stalky, 'when I got out on the roof and dropped the beastly things down his chimney. But, look here—'question is, are our characters good enough just now to stand a study row?'

'Never mind mine,' said Beetle. 'King swears I haven't any.'

'I'm not thinking of *you*,' Stalky returned scornfully. 'You aren't going up for the Army, you old bat. I don't want to be expelled—and the Head's getting rather shy of us, too.'

'Rot!' said M'Turk. 'The Head never expels except for beastliness* or stealing. But I forgot; you and Stalky *are* thieves—regular burglars.'

The visitors gasped, but Stalky interpreted the parable with large grins.

'Well, you know, that little beast Manders minor saw Beetle and me hammerin' M'Turk's trunk open in the dormitory when we took his watch last month. Of course Manders sneaked to Mason, and Mason solemnly took it up as a case of theft, to get even with us about the rats.'

'That just put Mason into our giddy hands,' said M'Turk blandly. 'We were nice to him, 'cause he was a new master and wanted to win the confidence of the boys. 'Pity he draws inferences, though. Stalky went to his study and pretended to blub, and told Mason he'd lead a new life if Mason would let him off this time, but Mason wouldn't. 'Said it was his duty to report him to the Head.'

'Vindictive swine!' said Beetle. 'It was all those rats! Then *I* blubbed, too, and Stalky confessed that he'd been a thief in regular practice for six years, ever since he came to the school; and that I'd taught him—*à la* Fagin.* Mason turned white with joy. He thought he had us on toast.'

'Gorgeous! Oh, fids!' said Dick Four. 'We never heard of this.'

''Course not. Mason kept it jolly quiet. He wrote down all our statements on impot-paper. There wasn't anything he wouldn't believe,' said Stalky.

'And handed it all up to the Head, *with* an extempore prayer. It took about forty pages,' said Beetle. 'I helped him a lot.'

'And then, you crazy idiots?' said Abanazar.

'Oh, we were sent for; and Stalky asked to have the "depositions" read out, and the Head knocked him spinning into a waste-paper basket. Then he gave us eight cuts apiece—welters—for—for—takin' unheard-of liberties with a new master. I saw his shoulders shaking when we went out. Do you know,' said Beetle pensively, 'that Mason can't look

at us now in second lesson without blushing? We three stare
at him sometimes till he regularly trickles. He's an awfully
sensitive beast.'

'He read *Eric; or, Little by Little*,' said M'Turk; 'so we gave
him *St. Winifred's; or, The World of School*.* They spent all
their spare time stealing at St. Winifred's, when they weren't
praying or getting drunk at pubs. Well, that was only a week
ago, and the Head's a little bit shy of us. He called it
constructive deviltry. Stalky invented it all.'

"Not the least good having a row with a master unless you
can make an ass of him,' said Stalky, extended at ease on the
hearth-rug. 'If Mason didn't know Number Five—well, he's
learn't, that's all. Now, my dearly beloved 'earers'—Stalky
curled his legs under him and addressed the company—'we've
got that strong, perseverin' man* King on our hands. He went
miles out of his way to provoke a conflict.' (Here Stalky
snapped down the black silk domino and assumed the air of
a judge.) 'He has oppressed Beetle, M'Turk, and me, *privatim
et seriatim*,* one by one, as he could catch us. But now he
has insulted Number Five up in the music-room, and in
the presence of these—these ossifers of the Ninety-third,
wot look like hairdressers.* Binjimin, we must make him cry
"*Capivi!*" '*

Stalky's reading did not include Browning or Ruskin.

'And, besides,' said M'Turk, 'he's a Philistine, a basket-
hanger.* He wears a tartan tie. Ruskin says that any man who
wears a tartan tie will, without doubt, be damned ever-
lastingly.'

'Bravo, M'Turk,' cried Tertius; 'I thought he was only a
beast.'

'He's that, too, of course, but he's worse. He has a china
basket with blue ribbons and a pink kitten on it, hung up in
his window to grow musk in. You know when I got all that
old oak carvin' out of Bideford Church, when they were
restoring it (Ruskin says that any man who'll restore a church
is an unmitigated sweep), and stuck it up here with glue?
Well, King came in and wanted to know whether we'd done
it with a fret-saw! Yah! He is the King of basket-hangers!'

Down went M'Turk's inky thumb* over an imaginary arena

full of bleeding Kings. '*Placetne*,* child of a generous race!' he cried to Beetle.

'Well,' began Beetle doubtfully, 'he comes from Balliol, but I'm going to give the beast a chance. You see I can always make him hop with some more poetry. He can't report me to the Head, because it makes him ridiculous. (Stalky's quite right.) But he shall have his chance.'

Beetle opened the book on the table, ran his finger down a page, and began at random:

> 'Or who in Moscow toward the Czar
> With the demurest of footfalls,
> Over the Kremlin's pavement white
> With serpentine and syenite,
> Steps with five other generals——'*

'That's no good. Try another,' said Stalky.

'Hold on a shake; I know what's coming.' M'Turk was reading over Beetle's shoulder—

> 'That simultaneously take snuff,
> For each to have pretext enough,
> And kerchiefwise unfold his sash,
> Which—softness' self—is yet the stuff

(Gummy! What a sentence!)

> To hold fast where a steel chain snaps
> And leave the grand white neck no gash.

(Full stop.)'

''Don't understand a word of it,' said Stalky.

'More fool you! Construe,' said M'Turk. 'Those six bargees* scragged the Czar and left no evidence. *Actum est* * with King.'

'He gave me that book, too,' said Beetle, licking his lips:

> 'There's a great text in Galatians,
> Once you trip on it entails
> Twenty-nine distinct damnations,
> One sure if another fails.' *

Then irrelevantly:

'Setebos! Setebos! and Setebos!
Thinketh he liveth in the cold of the moon.' *

'He's just come in from dinner,' said Dick Four, looking through the window. 'Manders minor is with him.'

"Safest place for Manders minor just now,' said Beetle.

'Then you chaps had better clear out,' said Stalky politely to the visitors. "Tisn't fair to mix you up in a study row. Besides, we can't afford to have evidence.'

'Are you going to begin at once?' said Aladdin.

'Immediately, if not sooner,' said Stalky, and turned out the gas. 'Strong, perserverin' man*—King. Make him cry "*Capivi*."* G'way, Binjimin.'

The company retreated to their neat and spacious study with expectant souls.

'When Stalky blows out his nostrils like a horse,' said Aladdin to the Emperor of China, 'he's on the war-path. 'Wonder what King will get.'

'Beans,'* said the Emperor. 'Number Five generally pays in full.'

"Wonder if I ought to take any notice of it officially,' said Abanazar, who had just remembered that he was a prefect.

'It's none of your business, Pussy. Besides, if you did, we'd have them hostile to us; and we shouldn't be able to do any work,' said Aladdin. 'They've begun already.'

Now that West-African war-drum had been made to signal across estuaries and deltas. Number Five was forbidden to wake the engine within earshot of the school. But a deep devastating drone filled the passages as M'Turk and Beetle scientifically rubbed its top. Anon it changed to the blare of trumpets—of savage pursuing trumpets. Then, as M'Turk slapped one side, smooth with the blood of ancient sacrifice, the roar broke into short coughing howls such as the wounded gorilla throws in his native forest. These were followed by the wrath of King—three steps at a time, up the staircase, with a dry whirr of the gown. Aladdin and company, listening, squeaked with excitement as the door crashed open. King stumbled into the darkness, and cursed those performers by the gods of Balliol and quiet repose.

'Turned out for a week,' said Aladdin, holding the study

door on the crack. 'Key to be brought down to his study in five minutes. "Brutes! Barbarians! Savages! Children!" He's rather agitated. "Arrah, Patsy, mind the baby!" ' he sang in a whisper as he clung to the door-knob, dancing a noiseless war-dance.

King went downstairs again, and Beetle and M'Turk lit the gas to confer with Stalky. But Stalky had vanished.

"Looks like no end of a mess,' said Beetle, collecting his books and mathematical instrument case. 'A week in the form-rooms isn't any advantage to us.'

'Yes, but don't you see that Stalky isn't here, you owl?' said M'Turk. 'Take down the key, and look sorrowful. King 'll only jaw you for half an hour. I'm going to read in the lower form-room.'

'But it's always me,' mourned Beetle.

'Wait till we see,' said M'Turk hopefully. 'I don't know any more than you do what Stalky means, but it's something. Go down and draw King's fire. You're used to it.'

No sooner had the key turned in the door than the lid of the coal-box, which was also the window-seat, lifted cautiously. It had been a tight fit, even for the lithe Stalky, his head between his knees, and his stomach under his right ear. From a drawer in the table he took a well-worn catapult, a handful of buckshot, and a duplicate key of the study; noiselessly he raised the window and kneeled by it, his face turned to the road, the wind-sloped trees, the dark levels of the Burrows, and the white line of breakers falling nine-deep along the Pebble Ridge. Far down the steep-banked Devonshire lane he heard the husky hoot of the carrier's horn. There was a ghost of melody in it, as it might have been the wind in a gin-bottle essaying to sing 'It's a way we have in the Army.'*

Stalky smiled a tight-lipped smile, and at extreme range opened fire: the old horse half wheeled in the shafts.

'Where be gwaine tu?' hiccoughed Rabbits-Eggs. Another buckshot tore through the rotten canvas tilt with a vicious zipp.

'*Habet!*'* murmured Stalky, as Rabbits-Eggs swore into the patient night, protesting that he saw the 'dommed Colleger' who was assaulting him.

*　*　*　*　*

'And so,' King was saying in a high head voice to Beetle, whom he had kept to play with before Manders minor, well knowing that it hurts a Fifth-form boy to be held up to a fag's derision,—'and so, Master Beetle, in spite of all our verses, of which we are so proud, when we presume to come into direct conflict with even so humble a representative of authority as myself, for instance, we are turned out of our studies, are we not?'

'Yes, sir,' said Beetle, with a sheepish grin on his lips and murder in his heart. Hope had nearly left him, but he clung to a well-established faith that never was Stalky so dangerous as when he was invisible.

'You are not required to criticise, thank you. Turned out of our studies, are we, just as if we were no better than little Manders minor. Only inky schoolboys we are, and must be treated as such.'

Beetle pricked up his ears, for Rabbits-Eggs was swearing savagely on the road, and some of the language entered at the upper sash. King believed in ventilation. He strode to the window, gowned and majestic, very visible in the gas-light.

'I zee 'un! I zee 'un!' roared Rabbits-Eggs, now that he had found a visible foe—another shot from the darkness above. 'Yiss, yeou, yeou long-nosed, fower-eyed, gingy-whiskered beggar! Yeu'm tu old for such goin's on. Aie! Poultice yeour nose, I tall 'ee! Poultice yeour long nose!'

Beetle's heart leapt up within him. Somewhere, somehow, he knew, Stalky moved behind these manifestations. There was hope and the prospect of revenge. He would embody the suggestion about the nose in deathless verse. King threw up the window, and sternly rebuked Rabbits-Eggs. But the carrier was beyond fear or fawning. He had descended from the cart, and was stooping by the roadside.

It all fell swiftly as a dream. Manders minor raised his hand to his head with a cry, as a jagged flint cannoned on to some rich tree-calf bindings in the bookshelf. Another quoited along the writing-table. Beetle made zealous feint to stop it, and in that endeavour overturned a student's lamp, which dripped, _viâ_

King's papers and some choice books, greasily on to a Persian rug. There was much broken glass on the window-seat; the china basket—M'Turk's aversion—cracked to flinders, had dropped her musk plant and its earth over the red rep cushions; Manders minor was bleeding profusely from a cut on the cheek-bone; and King, using strange words, every one of which Beetle treasured, ran forth to find the school Sergeant, that Rabbits-Eggs might be instantly cast into jail.

'Poor chap!' said Beetle, with a false, feigned sympathy. 'Let it bleed a little. That'll prevent apoplexy,' and he held the blind head skilfully over the table, and the papers on the table, as he guided the howling Manders to the door.

Then did Beetle, alone with the wreckage, return good for evil. How, in that office, a complete set of 'Gibbon'* was scarred all along the back as by a flint; how so much black and copying ink chanced to mingle with Manders's gore on the table-cloth; why the big gum-bottle, unstoppered, had rolled semicircularly across the floor; and in what manner the white china door-knob grew to be painted with yet more of Manders's young blood, were matters which Beetle did not explain when the rabid King returned to find him standing politely over the reeking hearth-rug.

'You never told me to go, sir,' he said, with the air of Casabianca,* and King consigned him to the outer darkness.

But it was to a boot-cupboard under the staircase on the ground floor that he hastened, to loose the mirth that was destroying him. He had not drawn breath for a first whoop of triumph when two hands choked him dumb.

'Go to the dormitory and get me my things. Bring 'em to Number Five lavatory.* I'm still in tights,' hissed Stalky, sitting on his head. 'Don't run. Walk.'

But Beetle staggered into the form-room next door, and delegated his duty to the yet unenlightened M'Turk, with an hysterical *précis* of the campaign thus far. So it was M'Turk, of the wooden visage, who brought the clothes from the dormitory while Beetle panted on a form. Then the three buried themselves in Number Five lavatory, turned on all the taps, filled the place with steam, and dropped weeping into the baths, where they pieced out the war.

'*Moi! Je! Ich! Ego!*' gasped Stalky. 'I waited till I couldn't hear myself think, while you played the drum! Hid in the coal-locker—and tweaked Rabbits-Eggs—and Rabbits-Eggs rocked King. Wasn't it beautiful? Did you hear the glass?'

'Why, he—he—he,' shrieked M'Turk, one trembling finger pointed at Beetle.

'Why, I—I—I was through it all,' Beetle howled; 'in his study, being jawed.'

'Oh, my soul!' said Stalky with a yell, disappearing under water.

'The—the glass was nothing. Manders minor's head's cut open. La-la-lamp upset all over the rug. Blood on the books and papers. The gum! The gum! The gum! The ink! The ink! The ink! Oh, Lord!'

Then Stalky leaped out, all pink as he was, and shook Beetle into some sort of coherence; but his tale prostrated them afresh.

'I bunked for the boot-cupboard the second I heard King go downstairs. Beetle tumbled in on top of me. The spare key's hid behind the loose board. There isn't a shadow of evidence,' said Stalky. They were all chanting together.

'And he turned us out himself—himself—him*self!*' This from M'Turk. 'He can't begin to suspect us. Oh, Stalky, it's the loveliest thing we've ever done.'

'Gum! Gum! Dollops of gum!' shouted Beetle, his spectacles gleaming through a sea of lather. 'Ink and blood all mixed. I held the little beast's head all over the Latin proses for Monday. Golly, how the oil stunk! And Rabbits-Eggs told King to poultice his nose! Did you hit Rabbits-Eggs, Stalky?'

'Did I jolly well not? Tweaked him all over. Did you hear him curse? Oh, I shall be sick in a minute if I don't stop.'

But dressing was a slow process, because M'Turk was obliged to dance when he heard that the musk basket was broken, and, moreover, Beetle retailed all King's language with emendations and purple insets.

'Shockin'!'* said Stalky, collapsing in a helpless welter of half-hitched trousers. 'So dam' bad, too, for innocent boys like us! 'Wonder what they'd say at "St. Winifred's, *or* The World of School." By gum! That reminds me we owe the Lower

Third one for assaultin' Beetle when he chivied Manders minor. Come on! It's an alibi Samivel;* and besides, if we let 'em off they'll be worse next time.'

The Lower Third had set a guard upon their form-room for the space of a full hour, which to a boy is a lifetime. Now they were busy with their Saturday evening businesses—cooking sparrows over the gas with rusty nibs; brewing unholy drinks in gallipots;* skinning moles with pocket-knives: attending to paper trays full of silk-worms, or discussing the iniquities of their elders with a freedom, fluency, and point that would have amazed their parents. The blow fell without warning. Stalky upset a crowded form of small boys among their own cooking utensils; M'Turk raided the untidy lockers as a terrier digs at a rabbit-hole; while Beetle poured ink upon such heads as he could not appeal to with a Smith's Classical Dictionary. Three brisk minutes accounted for many silk-worms, pet larvæ, French exercises, school caps, half-prepared bones and skulls, and a dozen pots of home-made sloe jam. It was a great wreckage, and the form-room looked as though three conflicting tempests had smitten it.

'Phew!' said Stalky, drawing breath outside the door (amid groans of 'Oh, you beastly ca-ads! You think yourselves awful funny,' and so forth). '*That's* all right. Never let the sun go down upon your wrath. Rummy little devils, fags. 'Got no notion o' combinin'.'

'Six of 'em sat on my head when I went in after Manders minor,' said Beetle. 'I warned 'em what they'd get, though.'

'Everybody paid in full—beautiful feelin',' said M'Turk absently, as they strolled along the corridor. ''Don't think we'd better say much about King, though, do you, Stalky?'

'Not much. Our line is injured innocence, of course—same as when old Foxibus reported us on suspicion of smoking in the Bunkers. If I hadn't thought of buyin' the pepper and spillin' it all over our clothes, he'd have smelt us. King was gha-astly facetious about that. 'Called us bird-stuffers in form for a week.'

'Ah, King hates the Natural History Society because little Hartopp is president. 'Mustn't do anything in the Coll. without glorifyin' King,' said M'Turk. 'But he must be a putrid ass, you know, to suppose at our time o' life we'd go out and stuff birds like fags.'

'Poor old King!' said Beetle. 'He's awf'ly unpopular in Common-room, and they'll chaff his head off about Rabbits-Eggs. Golly! How lovely! How beautiful! How holy! But you should have seen his face when the first rock came in! *And* the earth from the basket!'

So they were all stricken helpless for five minutes.

They repaired at last to Abanazar's study, and were received reverently.

'What's the matter?' said Stalky, quick to realise new atmospheres.

'You know jolly well,' said Abanazar. 'You'll be expelled if you get caught. King is a gibbering maniac.'

'Who? Which? What? Expelled for how? We only played the war-drum. We've got turned out for that already.'

'Do you chaps mean to say you didn't make Rabbits-Eggs drunk and bribe him to rock King's rooms?'

'Bribe him? No, that I'll swear we didn't,' said Stalky, with a relieved heart, for he loved not to tell lies. 'What a low mind you've got, Pussy! We've been down having a bath. Did Rabbits-Eggs rock King? Strong, perseverin' man King? Shockin'!'

'Awf'ly. King's frothing at the mouth. There's bell for prayers. Come on.'

'Wait a sec,' said Stalky, continuing the conversation in a loud and cheerful voice, as they descended the stairs. 'What did Rabbits-Eggs rock King for?'

'I know,' said Beetle, as they passed King's open door. 'I was in his study.'

'Hush, you ass!' hissed the Emperor of China.

'Oh, he's gone down to prayers,' said Beetle, watching the shadow of the House-master on the wall. 'Rabbits-Eggs was only a bit drunk, swearin' at his horse, and King jawed him through the window, and then, of course, he rocked King.'

'Do you mean to say,' said Stalky, 'that King began it?'

King was behind them, and every well-weighed word went up the staircase like an arrow. 'I can only swear,' said Beetle, 'that King cursed like a bargee. Simply disgustin'. I'm goin' to write to my father about it.'

'Better report it to Mason,' suggested Stalky. 'He knows our tender consciences. Hold on a shake. I've got to tie my bootlace.'

The other study hurried forward. They did not wish to be dragged into stage asides of this nature. So it was left to M'Turk to sum up the situation beneath the guns of the enemy.

'You see,' said the Irishman, hanging on the banister, 'he begins by bullying little chaps; then he bullies the big chaps; then he bullies some one who isn't connected with the Coll., and then he catches it. Serves him jolly well right. . . . I beg your pardon, sir. I didn't see you were coming down the staircase.'

The black gown tore past like a thunder-storm, and in its wake, three abreast, arms linked, the Aladdin Company rolled up the big corridor to prayers, singing with most innocent intention:

'Arrah, Patsy, mind the baby! Arrah, Patsy, mind the child!
Wrap him up in an overcoat, he's surely goin' wild!
Arrah, Patsy, mind the baby; just ye mind the child awhile!
He'll kick an' bite an' cry all night! Arrah, Patsy, mind the child!'

An Unsavoury Interlude

IT was a maiden aunt of Stalky who sent him both books, with the inscription, 'To dearest Artie, on his sixteenth birthday'; it was M'Turk who ordered their hypothecation;* and it was Beetle, returned from Bideford, who flung them on the window-sill of Number Five study with news that Bastable would advance but ninepence on the two; *Eric; or, Little by Little*, being almost as great a drug as *St. Winifred's*. 'An' I don't think much of your aunt. We're nearly out of cartridges, too—Artie, dear.'

Whereupon Stalky rose up to grapple with him, but M'Turk sat on Stalky's head, calling him a 'pure-minded boy' till peace was declared. As they were grievously in arrears with a Latin prose, as it was a blazing July afternoon, and as they ought to have been at a House cricket-match, they began to renew their acquaintance, intimate and unholy, with the volumes.

'Here we are!' said M'Turk. ' "Corporal punishment produced on Eric the worst effects. He burned *not* with remorse or regret"—make a note o' that, Beetle—"but with shame and violent indignation. He glared"—oh, naughty Eric! Let's get to where he goes in for drink.'

'Hold on half a shake. Here's another sample. "The Sixth," he says, "is the palladium of all public schools." But this lot'—Stalky rapped the gilded book—'can't prevent fellows drinkin' and stealin', an' lettin' fags out of window at night, an'—an' doin' what they please. Golly, what we've missed—not goin' to St. Winifred's! . . .'

'I'm sorry to see any boys of my House taking so little interest in their matches.'

Mr. Prout could move very silently if he pleased, though that is no merit in a boy's eyes. He had flung open the study-door without knocking—another sin—and looked at them suspiciously. 'Very sorry, indeed, I am to see you frowsting in your studies.'

'We've been out ever since dinner, sir,' said M'Turk wearily. One House-match is just like another, and their 'ploy' of that week happened to be rabbit-shooting with saloon-pistols.*

'I can't see a ball when it's coming, sir,' said Beetle. 'I've had my gig-lamps* smashed at the Nets till I got excused. I wasn't any good even as a fag, then, sir.'

'Tuck is probably your form. Tuck and brewing. Why can't you three take any interest in the honour of your House?'

They had heard that phrase till they were wearied. The 'honour of the House' was Prout's weak point, and they knew well how to flick him on the raw.

'If you order us to go down, sir, of course we'll go,' said Stalky, with maddening politeness. But Prout knew better than that. He had tried the experiment once at a big match, when the three, self-isolated, stood to attention for half an hour in full view of all the visitors, to whom fags, subsidised for that end, pointed them out as victims of Prout's tyranny. And Prout was a sensitive man.

In the infinitely petty confederacies of the Common-room, King and Macrea, fellow House-masters, had borne it in upon him that by games, and games alone, was salvation wrought. Boys neglected were boys lost. They must be disciplined. Left to himself, Prout would have made a sympathetic House-master; but he was never so left, and, with the devilish insight of youth, the boys knew to whom they were indebted for his zeal.

'Must we go down, sir?' said M'Turk.

'I don't want to order you to do what a right-thinking boy should do gladly. I'm sorry.' And he lurched out with some hazy impression that he had sown good seed on poor ground.

'Now what does he suppose is the use of that?' said Beetle.

'Oh, he's cracked. King jaws him in Common-room about not keepin' us up to the mark, and Macrea burbles about "dithcipline," an' old Heffy sits between 'em sweatin' big drops. I heard Oke [the Common-room butler] talking to Richards [Prout's House-servant] about it down in the basement the other day when I went down to bag some bread,' said Stalky.

'What did Oke say?' demanded M'Turk, throwing *Eric* into a corner.

' "Oh," he said, "they make more nise nor a nest full o' jackdaws, an' half of it like we'd no ears to our heads that waited on 'em. They talks over old Prout—what he've done an' left undone about his boys. An' how their boys be fine boys, an' his'n be dom bad." Well, Oke talked like that, you know, and Richards got awf'ly wrathy. He has a down on King for something or other. 'Wonder why?'

'Why, King talks about Prout in form-room—makes allusions, an' all that—only half the chaps are such asses they can't see what he's drivin' at. And d'you remember what he said about the "Casual House" last Tuesday? He meant us. They say he says perfectly beastly things to his own House, making fun of Prout's,' said Beetle.

'Well, we didn't come here to mix up in their rows,' M'Turk said wrathfully. 'Who'll bathe after call-over? King's takin' it in the cricket-field. Come on.' Turkey seized his straw* and led the way.

They reached the sun-blistered pavilion over against the gray Pebble Ridge just before roll-call, and, asking no questions, gathered from King's voice and manner that his House was on the road to victory.

'Ah, ha!' said he, turning to show the light of his countenance. 'Here we have the ornaments of the Casual House at last. You consider cricket beneath you, I believe'— the flannelled crowd sniggered—'and from what I have seen this afternoon, I fancy many others of your House hold the same view. And may I ask what you purpose to do with your noble selves till tea-time?'

'Going down to bathe, sir,' said Stalky.

'And whence this sudden zeal for cleanliness? There is nothing about you that particularly suggests it. Indeed, so far as I remember—I may be at fault—but a short time ago——'

'Five years, sir,' said Beetle hotly.

King scowled. 'One of you was that thing called a water-funk. Yes, a water-funk. So now you wish to wash? It is well. Cleanliness never injured a boy or—a House. We will proceed to business,' and he addressed himself to the call-over board.

'What the deuce did you say anything to him for, Beetle?' said M'Turk angrily, as they strolled towards the big, open sea-baths.

''Twasn't fair—remindin' one of bein' a water-funk. My first term, too. Heaps of chaps are—when they can't swim.'

'Yes, you ass; but he saw he'd fetched you. You ought never to answer King.'

'But it wasn't fair, Stalky.'

'My Hat! You've been here six years, and you expect fairness. Well, you *are* a dithering idiot.'

A knot of King's boys, also bound for the baths, hailed them, beseeching them to wash—for the honour of their House.

'That's what comes of King's jawin' and messin'. Those young animals wouldn't have thought of it unless he'd put it into their heads. Now they'll be funny about it for weeks,' said Stalky. 'Don't take any notice.'

The boys came nearer, shouting an opprobrious word. At last they moved to windward, ostentatiously holding their noses.

'That's pretty,' said Beetle. 'They'll be sayin' our House stinks next.'

When they returned from the baths, damp-headed, languid, at peace with the world, Beetle's forecast came only too true. They were met in the corridor by a fag—a common, Lower-Second fag—who at arm's length handed them a carefully wrapped piece of soap 'with the compliments of King's House.'

'Hold on,' said Stalky, checking immediate attack. 'Who put you up to this, Nixon? Rattray and White? [Those were two leaders in King's House.] Thank you. There's no answer.'

'Oh, it's too sickening to have this kind o' rot shoved on to a chap. What's the sense of it? What's the fun of it?' said M'Turk.

'It will go on to the end of the term, though.' Beetle wagged his head sorrowfully. He had worn many jests threadbare on his own account.

In a few days it became an established legend of the school

that Prout's House did not wash and were therefore noisome. Mr. King was pleased to smile succulently in form when one of his boys drew aside from Beetle with certain gestures.

'There seems to be some disability attaching to you, my Beetle, or else why should Burton major withdraw, so to speak, the hem of his garments? I confess I am still in the dark. Will some one be good enough to enlighten me?'

Naturally, he was enlightened by half the Form.

'Extraordinary! Most extraordinary! However, each House has its traditions, with which I would not for the world interfere. *We* have a prejudice in favour of washing. Go on, Beetle—from '*Jugurtha tamen*'*—and, if you can, avoid the more flagrant forms of guessing.'

Prout's House was furious because Macrea's and Hartopp's Houses joined King's to insult them. They called a House-meeting after dinner—an excited and angry meeting of all save the prefects, whose dignity, though they sympathised, did not allow them to attend. They read ungrammatical resolutions, and made speeches beginning, 'Gentlemen, we have met on this occasion,' and ending with, 'It's a beastly shame,' precisely as Houses have done since time and schools began.

Number Five study attended, with its usual air of bland patronage. At last M'Turk, of the lanthorn jaws, delivered himself:

'You jabber and jaw and burble, and that's about all you can do. What's the good of it? King's House 'll only gloat because they've drawn you, and King 'll gloat, too. Besides, that resolution of Orrin's is chock-full of bad grammar, and King 'll gloat over *that*.'

'I thought you an' Beetle would put it right, an'—an' we'd post it in the corridor,' said the composer meekly.

'*Pas si je le connai.** I'm not goin' to meddle with the biznai,' said Beetle. 'It's a gloat for King's House. Turkey's quite right.'

'Well, won't Stalky, then?'

But Stalky puffed out his cheeks and squinted down his nose in the style of Panurge,* and all he said was, 'Oh, you abject burblers!'

'You're three beastly scabs!' was the instant retort of the democracy, and they went out amid execrations.

'This is piffling,' said M'Turk. 'Let's get our sallies, and go and shoot bunnies.'

Three saloon-pistols, with a supply of bulleted breech-caps, were stored in Stalky's trunk, and this trunk was in their dormitory, and their dormitory was a three-bed attic one, opening out of a ten-bed establishment, which, in turn, communicated with the great range of dormitories that ran practically from one end of the College to the other. Marcrea's House lay next to Prout's, King's next to Marcrea's, and Hartopp's beyond that again. Carefully locked doors divided House from House, but each House, in its internal arrangements—the College had originally been a terrace of twelve large houses*—was a replica of the next; one straight roof covering all.

They found Stalky's bed drawn out from the wall to the left of the dormer window, and the latter end of Richards protruding from a two-foot-square cupboard in the wall.

'What's all this? I've never noticed it before. What are you tryin' to do, Fatty?'

'Fillin' basins, Muster Corkran.' Richards's voice was hollow and muffled. 'They've been savin' me trouble. Yiss.'

''Looks like it,' said M'Turk. 'Hi! You'll stick if you don't take care.'

Richards backed puffing.

'I can't rache un. Yiss, 'tess a turncock, Muster M'Turk. They've took an' runned all the watter-pipes a storey higher in the houses—runned 'em all along under the 'ang of the heaves, like. Runned 'em in last holidays. I can't rache the turncock.'

'Let me try,' said Stalky, diving into the aperture.

'Slip 'ee to the left, then, Muster Corkran. Slip 'ee to the left, an' feel in the dark.'

To the left Stalky wriggled, and saw a long line of lead-pipe disappearing up a triangular tunnel, whose roof was the rafters and boarding of the College roof, whose floor was sharp-edged joists, and whose side was the rough studding of the lath and plaster wall under the dormer.

''Rummy show. How far does it go?'

'Right along, Muster Corkran—right along from end to end. Her runs under the 'ang of the heaves. Have 'ee rached the

stopcock yet? Mr. King got un put in to save us carryin'
watter from downstairs to fill the basins. No place for a lusty
man like old Richards. I'm tu thickabout to go ferritin'.
Thank 'ee, Muster Corkran.'

The water squirted through the tap just inside the cupboard,
and, having filled the basins, the grateful Richards waddled
away.

The boys sat round-eyed on their beds considering the
possibilities of this trove. Two floors below them they could
hear the hum of the angry House; for nothing is so still as a
dormitory in mid-afternoon of a midsummer term.

'It has been papered over till now.' M'Turk examined the
little door. 'If we'd only known before!'

'I vote we go down and explore. No one will come up this
time o' day. We needn't keep *cave*.'*

They crawled in, Stalky leading, drew the door behind
them, and on all fours embarked on a dark and dirty road full
of plaster, odd shavings, and all the raffle that builders leave
in the waste-room of a house. The passage was perhaps three
feet wide, and, except for the straggling light round the edges
of the cupboards (there was one to each dormer), almost
pitchy dark.

'Here's Macrea's House,' said Stalky, his eye at the crack of
the third cupboard. 'I can see Barnes's name on his trunk.
Don't make such a row, Beetle! We can get right to the end
of the Coll. Come on! . . . We're in King's House now—I can
see a bit of Rattray's trunk. How these beastly boards hurt
one's knees!' They heard his nails scraping on plaster.

'That's the ceiling below. Look out! If we smashed that the
plaster 'ud fall down in the lower dormitory,' said Beetle.

'Let's,' whispered M'Turk.

'An' be collared first thing? Not much. Why, I can shove my
hand ever so far up between these boards.'

Stalky thrust an arm to the elbow between the joists.

'No good stayin' here. I vote we go back and talk it over.
It's a crummy place. 'Must say I'm grateful to King for his
waterworks.'

They crawled out, brushed one another clean, slid the
saloon-pistols down a trouser-leg, and hurried forth to a deep

and solitary Devonshire lane in whose flanks a boy might sometimes slay a young rabbit. They threw themselves down under the rank elder bushes, and began to think aloud.

'You know,' said Stalky at last, sighting at a distant sparrow, 'we could hide our sallies in there like anything.'

'Huh!' Beetle snorted, choked, and gurgled. He had been silent since they left the dormitory.

'Did you ever read a book called *The History of a House* or something? I got it out of the library the other day. A Frenchwoman wrote it—Violet somebody.* But it's translated, you know; and it's very interestin'. Tells you how a house is built.'

'Well, if you're in a sweat to find that out, you can go down to the new cottages they're building for the coastguard.'

'My Hat! I will.' He felt in his pockets. 'Give me tuppence, some one.'

'Rot! Stay here, and don't mess about in the sun.'

'Gi' me tuppence.'

'I say, Beetle, you aren't stuffy about anything, are you?' said M'Turk, handing over the coppers. His tone was serious, for though Stalky often, and M'Turk occasionally, manœuvred on his own account, Beetle had never been known to do so in all the history of the confederacy.

'No, I'm not. I'm thinking.'

'Well, we'll come, too,' said Stalky, with a general's suspicion of his aides.

''Don't want you.'

'Oh, leave him alone. He's been taken worse with a poem,' said M'Turk. 'He'll go burbling down to the Pebble Ridge and spit it all up in the study when he comes back.'

'Then why did he want the tuppence, Turkey? He's gettin' too beastly independent. Hi! There's a bunny. No, it ain't. It's a cat, by Jove! You plug first.'

Twenty minutes later a boy with a straw hat at the back of his head, and his hands in his pockets, was staring at workmen as they moved about a half-finished cottage. He produced some ferocious tobacco, and was passed from the forecourt into the interior, where he asked many questions.

'Well, let's have your beastly epic,' said Turkey, as they

burst into the study, to find Beetle deep in Viollet-le-Duc and some drawings. 'We've had no end of a lark.'

'Epic? What epic? I've been down to the coastguard.'

'No epic? Then we will slay you, O Beadle,'* said Stalky, moving to the attack. 'You've got something up your sleeve. *I* know, when you talk in that tone!'

'Your Uncle Beetle'—with an attempt to imitate Stalky's war-voice—'is a Great Man.'

'Oh no; he jolly well isn't anything of the kind. You deceive yourself, Beetle. Scrag him, Turkey!'

'A Great Man,' Beetle gurgled from the floor. '*You* are futile—look out for my tie!—futile burblers. I am the Great Man. I gloat. Ouch! Hear me!'

'Beetle, de-ah'—Stalky dropped unreservedly on Beetle's chest—'we love you, an' you're a poet. If I ever said you were a doggaroo,* I apologise; but you know as well as we do that you can't do anything by yourself without mucking it.'

'I've got a notion.'

'And you'll spoil the whole show if you don't tell your Uncle Stalky. Cough it up, ducky, and we'll see what we can do. Notion, you fat impostor—I knew you had a notion when you went away! Turkey said it was a poem.'

'I've found out how houses are built. Le' me get up. The floor-joists of one room are the ceiling-joists of the room below.'

'Don't be so filthy technical.'

'Well, the man told me. The floor is laid on top of those joists—those boards on edge that we crawled over—but the floor stops at a partition. Well, if you get behind a partition, same as you did in the attic, don't you see that you can shove anything you please under the floor between the floor-boards and the lath and plaster of the ceiling below? Look here. I've drawn it.'

He produced a rude sketch, sufficient to enlighten the allies. There is no part of the modern school curriculum that deals with architecture, and none of them had yet reflected whether floors and ceilings were hollow or solid. Outside his own immediate interests the boy is as ignorant as the savage he so admires; but he has also the savage's resource.

'I see,' said Stalky. 'I shoved my hand there. An' then?'

'An' then ... They've been calling us stinkers, you know. We might shove somethin' under—sulphur, or something that stunk pretty bad—an' stink 'em out. I know it can be done somehow.' Beetle's eyes turned to Stalky handling the diagrams.

'Stinks?' said Stalky interrogatively. Then his face grew luminous with delight. 'By gum! I've got it. Horrid Stinks! Turkey!' He leaped at the Irishman. 'This afternoon—just after Beetle went away! *She's* the very thing!'

'Come to my arms, my beamish boy,' carolled M'Turk, and they fell into each other's arms dancing. 'Oh, frabjous day! Calloo, callay!* She will! She will!'

'Hold on,' said Beetle. 'I don't understand.'

'Dearr man! It shall, though. Oh, Artie, my pure-souled youth, let us tell our darling Reggie about Pestiferous Stinkadores.'

'Not until after call-over. Come on!'

'I say,' said Orrin stiffly, as they fell into their places along the walls of the gymnasium. 'The House are goin' to hold another meeting.'

'Hold away, then.' Stalky's mind was elsewhere.

'It's about you three this time.'

'All right, give 'em my love. .... *Here, sir,*' and he tore down the corridor.

Gambolling like kids at play, with bounds and side-starts, with caperings and curvettings, they led the almost bursting Beetle to the rabbit-lane, and from under a pile of stones drew forth the new-slain corpse of a cat. Then did Beetle see the inner meaning of what had gone before, and lifted up his voice in thanksgiving for that the world held warriors so wise as Stalky and M'Turk.

'Well-nourished old lady, ain't she?' said Stalky. 'How long d'you suppose it'll take her to get a bit whiff in a confined space?'

'Bit whiff! What a coarse brute you are!' said M'Turk. 'Can't a poor pussy-cat get under King's dormitory floor to die without your pursuin' her with your foul innuendoes?'

'What did she die under the floor for?' said Beetle, looking to the future.

'Oh, they won't worry about *that* when they find her,' said Stalky.

'A cat may look at a king.' M'Turk rolled down the bank at his own jest. 'Pussy, you don't know how useful you're goin' to be to three pure-souled, high-minded boys.'

'They'll have to take up the floor for her, same as they did in Number Nine when the rat croaked. Big medicine—heap big medicine!* Phew! Oh, Lord, I wish I could stop laughin',' said Beetle.

'Stinks! Hi, stinks! Clammy ones!' M'Turk gasped as he regained his place. 'And'—the exquisite humour of it brought them sliding down together in a tangle—'it's all for the honour of the House, too!'

'An' they're holdin' another meetin'—on us,' Stalky panted, his knees in the ditch and his face in the long grass. 'Well, let's get the bullet out of her and hurry up. The sooner she's bedded out the better.'

Between them they did some grisly work with a penknife; between them (ask not who buttoned her to his bosom) they took up the corpse and hastened back, Stalky arranging their plan of action at the full trot.

The afternoon sun, lying in broad patches on the bed-rugs, saw three boys and an umbrella disappear into a dormitory wall. In five minutes they returned, brushed themselves all over, washed their hands, combed their hair, and descended.

'Are you sure you shoved her far enough under?' said M'Turk suddenly.

'Hang it, man, I shoved her the full length of my arm and Beetle's brolly. That must be about six feet. She's bung in the middle of King's big upper ten-bedder. Eligible central situation, *I* call it. She'll stink out his chaps, and Hartopp's and Macrea's, when she really begins to fume. I swear your Uncle Stalky is a great man. Do you realise what a great man he is, Beetle?'

'Well, I had the notion first, hadn't I, only——'

'You couldn't do it without your Uncle Stalky, could you?'

'They've been calling us stinkers for a week now,' said M'Turk. 'Oh, won't they catch it!'

'Stinker! Yah! Stink-ah!' rang down the corridor.

'And she's there,' said Stalky, a hand on either boy's shoulder. 'She—is—there, gettin' ready to surprise 'em. Presently she'll begin to whisper to 'em in their dreams. Then she'll whiff. Golly, how she'll whiff! Oblige me by thinkin' of it for two minutes.'

They went to their study in more or less of silence. There they began to laugh—laugh as only boys can. They laughed with their foreheads on the tables, or on the floor; laughed at length, curled over the backs of chairs or clinging to a book-shelf; laughed themselves limp.

And in the middle of it Orrin entered on behalf of the House.

'Don't mind us, Orrin; sit down. You don't know how we respect and admire you. There's something about your pure, high, young forehead, full of the dreams of innocent boy-hood,* that's no end fetchin'. It is, indeed.'

'The House sent me to give you this.' He laid a folded sheet of paper on the table and retired with an awful front.

'It's the resolution! Oh, read it, some one. I'm too silly-sick with laughin' to see,' said Beetle.

Stalky jerked it open with a precautionary sniff.

'Phew! Phew! Listen. "*The House notices with pain and contempt the attitude of indiference*"—how many f's in indifference, Beetle?'

'Two for choice.'

'Only one here—"*adopted by the occupants of Number Five Study in relation to the insults offered to Mr. Prout's House at the recent meeting in Number Twelve form-room, and the House hereby pass a vote of censure on the said study.*" That's all.'

'And she bled all down my shirt, too!' said Beetle.

'An' I'm catty all over,' said M'Turk, 'though I washed twice.'

'An' I nearly broke Beetle's brolly plantin' her where she would blossom!'

The situation was beyond speech, but not laughter. There was some attempt that night to demonstrate against the three in their dormitory; so they came forth.

'You see,' Beetle began suavely as he loosened his braces, 'the trouble with you is that you're a set of unthinkin' asses.

You've no more brains than spidgers.* We've told you that heaps of times, haven't we?'

'We'll give all three of you a dormitory lickin'. You always jaw at us as if you were prefects,' cried one.

'Oh no, you won't,' said Stalky, 'because you know that if you did you'd get the worst of it sooner or later. *We* aren't in any hurry. *We* can afford to wait for our little revenges. You've made howlin' asses of yourselves, and just as soon as King gets hold of your precious resolution tomorrow you'll find that out. If you aren't sick an' sorry by to-morrow night, I'll—I'll eat my hat.'

But or ever the dinner-bell rang the next day Prout's were sadly aware of their error. King received stray members of that House with an exaggerated attitude of fear. Did they purpose to cause him to be dismissed from the College by unanimous resolution? What were their views concerning the government of the school, that he might hasten to give effect to them? He would not offend them for worlds; but he feared—he sadly feared—that his own House, who did not pass resolutions (but washed), might somewhat deride.

King was a happy man, and his House, basking in the favour of his smile, made that afternoon a long penance to the misled Prout's. And Prout himself, with a dull and lowering visage, tried to think out the rights and wrongs of it all, only plunging deeper into bewilderment. Why should his House be called 'stinkers'? Truly, it was a small thing, but he had been trained to believe that straws show which way the wind blows, and that there is no smoke without fire. He approached King in Common-room with a sense of injustice, but King was pleased to be full of airy persiflage that tide, and brilliantly danced dialectical rings round Prout.

'Now,' said Stalky at bedtime, making pilgrimage through the dormitories before the prefects came up, '*now* what have you got to say for yourselves? Foster, Carton, Finch, Longbridge, Marlin, Brett! I heard you chaps catchin' it from King—he made made hay of you—an' all you could do was to wriggle an' grin an' say, "Yes, sir," an' "No, sir," an' "Oh, sir," an' "Please, sir"! You an' your resolution! Urh!'

'Oh, shut up, Stalky.'

'Not a bit of it. You're a gaudy lot* of resolutionists, you are! You've made a sweet mess of it. Perhaps you'll have the decency to leave us alone next time.'

Here the House grew angry, and in many voices pointed out how this blunder would never have come to pass if Number Five study had helped them from the first.

'But you chaps are so beastly conceited, an'—an' you swaggered into the meetin' as if we were a lot of idiots,' growled Orrin of the resolution.

'That's precisely what you *are!* That's what we've been tryin' to hammer into your thick heads all this time,' said Stalky. 'Never mind, we'll forgive you. Cheer up. You can't help bein' asses, you know,' and, the enemy's flank deftly turned, Stalky hopped into bed.

That night was the first of sorrow among the jubilant King's. By some accident of under-floor draughts the cat did not vex the dormitory beneath which she lay, but the next one to the right; stealing on the air rather as a pale-blue sensation than as any poignant offence. But the mere adumbration of an odour is enough for the sensitive nose and clean tongue of youth. Decency demands that we draw several carbolised sheets over what the dormitory said to Mr. King and what Mr. King replied. He was genuinely proud of his House and fastidious in all that concerned their well-being. He came; he sniffed; he said things. Next morning a boy in that dormitory confided to his bosom friend, a fag of Macrea's, that there was trouble in their midst which King would fain keep secret.

But Macrea's boy had also a bosom friend in Prout's, a shock-headed fag of malignant disposition, who, when he had wormed out the secret, told—told it in a high-pitched treble that rang along the corridor like a bat's squeak.

'An'—an' they've been calling us "stinkers" all this week. Why, Harland minor says they simply can't sleep in his dormitory for the stink. Come on!'

'With one shout and with one cry'* Prout's juniors hurled themselves into the war, and through the interval between first and second lesson some fifty twelve-year-olds were embroiled on the gravel outside King's windows to a tune whose *leit-motif* was the word 'stinker.'

'Hark to the minute-gun* at sea!' said Stalky. They were in their study collecting books for second lesson—Latin, with King. 'I thought his azure brow was a bit cloudy at prayers.

> She is comin', sister Mary,
> She is—'

'If they make such a row now, what will they do when she really begins to look up an' take notice?'

'Well, no vulgar repartee, Beetle. All we want is to keep out of this row like gentlemen.'

' "'Tis but a little faded flower."* Where's my Horace? Look here, I don't understand what she means by stinkin' out Rattray's dormitory first. We holed in under White's, didn't we?' asked M'Turk, with a wrinkled brow.

'Skittish little thing. She's rompin' about all over the place, I suppose.'

'My Aunt! King 'll be a cheerful customer at second lesson. I haven't prepared my Horace one little bit, either,' said Beetle. 'Come on!'

They were outside the form-room door now. It was within five minutes of the bell, and King might arrive at any moment.

Turkey elbowed into a cohort of scuffling fags, cut out Thornton tertius (he that had been Harland's bosom friend), and bade him tell his tale.

It was a simple one, interrupted by tears. Many of King's House had already battered him for libel.

'Oh, it's nothing,' M'Turk cried. 'He says that King's House stinks. That's all.'

'Stale!' Stalky shouted. 'We knew that years ago, only we didn't choose to run about shoutin' "Stinker!" We've got some manners, if they haven't. Catch a fag, Turkey, and make sure of it.'

Turkey's long arm closed on a hurried and anxious ornament of the Lower Second.

'Oh, M'Turk, please let me go. I don't stink—I swear I don't!'

'Guilty conscience!' cried Beetle. 'Who said you did?'

'What d'you make of it?' Stalky punted the small boy into Beetle's arms.

'Snf! Snf! He does, though. I think it's leprosy—or thrush. P'raps it's both. Take it away.'

'Indeed, Master Beetle'—King generally came to the House-door for a minute or two as the bell rang—'we are vastly indebted to you for your diagnosis, which seems to reflect almost as much credit on the natural unwholesomeness of your mind as it does upon your pitiful ignorance of the diseases of which you discourse so glibly. We will, however, test your knowledge in other directions.'

That was a merry lesson, but, in his haste to scarify Beetle, King clean neglected to give him an imposition, and since at the same time he supplied him with many priceless adjectives for later use, Beetle was well content, and applied himself most seriously throughout third lesson (algebra with little Hartopp) to composing a poem entitled 'The Lazar-house.'

After dinner King took his House to bathe in the sea off the Pebble Ridge. It was an old promise; but he wished he could have evaded it, for all Prout's lined up by the Fives Court and cheered with intention. In his absence not less than half the school invaded the infected dormitory to draw their own conclusions. The cat had gained in the last twelve hours, but a battlefield of the fifth day could not have been so flamboyant as the spies reported.

'My word, she *is* doin' herself proud,' said Stalky. 'Did you ever smell anything like it? Ah, an' she isn't under White's dormitory at all yet.'

'But she will be. Give her time,' said Beetle. 'She'll twine like a giddy honeysuckle. What howlin' Lazarites* they are! No House is justified in making itself a stench in the nostrils of decent—'

'High-minded, pure-souled boys. *Do* you burn with remorse and regret?' said M'Turk, as they hastened to meet the House coming up from the sea. King had deserted it, so speech was unfettered. Round its front played a crowd of skirmishers—all Houses mixed—flying, re-forming, shrieking insults. On its tortured flanks marched the Hoplites,* seniors hurling jests one after another—simple and primitive jests of the Stone Age. To these the three added themselves, dispassionately, with an air of aloofness, almost sadly.

'And they look all right, too,' said Stalky. 'It can't be Rattray, can it? Rattray?'

No answer.

'Rattray, dear? He seems stuffy about something or other. Look here, old man, we don't bear any malice about your sending that soap to us last week, do we? Be cheerful, Rat. You can live this down all right. I dare say it's only a few fags. Your House *is* so beastly slack, though.'

'You aren't going back to the House, are you?' said M'Turk. The victims desired nothing better. 'You've simply no conception of the reek up there. Of course, frowzin' as you do, you wouldn't notice it; but, after this nice wash and the clean, fresh air, even you'd be upset. 'Much better camp on the Burrows. We'll get you some straw. Shall we?' The House hurried in to the tune of 'John Brown's body,' sung by loving school-mates, and barricaded themselves in their form-room. Straightway Stalky chalked a large cross, with 'Lord, have mercy upon us,' on the door,* and left King to find it.

The wind shifted that night and wafted a carrion-reek into Macrea's dormitories; so that boys in nightgowns pounded on the locked door between the Houses, entreating King's to wash. Number Five study went to second lesson with not more than half a pound of camphor apiece in their clothing; and King, too wary to ask for explanations, gibbered awhile and hurled them forth. So Beetle finished yet another poem at peace in the study.

'They're usin' carbolic now. Malpas told me,' said Stalky. 'King thinks it's the drains.'

'She'll need a lot o' carbolic,' said M'Turk. 'No harm tryin', I suppose. It keeps King out of mischief.'

'I swear I thought he was goin' to kill me when I sniffed just now. He didn't mind Burton major sniffin' at me the other day, though. He never stopped Alexander howlin' "Stinker!" into our form-room before—before we doctored 'em. He just grinned,' said Stalky. 'What was he frothing over you for, Beetle?'

'Aha! That was my subtle jape. I had him on toast. You know he always jaws about the learned Lipsius.'*

' "Who at the age of four"—*that* chap?' said M'Turk.

'Yes. Whenever he hears I've written a poem. Well, just as I was sittin' down, I whispered. "How is our learned Lipsius?" to Burton major. Old Butt grinned like an owl. He didn't know what I was drivin' at; but King jolly well did. That was really why he hove us out. Ain't you grateful? Now shut up. I'm goin' to write the "Ballad of the Learned Lipsius." '

'Keep clear of anything coarse, then,' said Stalky. 'I shouldn't like to be coarse on this happy occasion.'

'Not for wo-orlds. What rhymes to "stenches," some one?'

In Common-room at lunch King discoursed acridly to Prout of boys with prurient minds, who perverted their few and baleful talents to sap discipline and corrupt their equals, to deal in foul imagery and destroy reverence.

'But you didn't seem to consider this when your House called us—ah—stinkers. If you hadn't assured me that you never interfere with another man's House, I should almost believe that it was a few casual remarks of yours that started all this nonsense.'

Prout had endured much, for King always took his temper to meals.

'You spoke to Beetle yourself, didn't you? Something about not bathing, and being a water-funk?' the school chaplain put in. 'I was scoring in the pavilion that day.'

'I may have—jestingly. I really don't pretend to remember every remark I let fall among small boys; and full well I know the Beetle has no feelings to be hurt.'

'Maybe; but he, or they—it comes to the same thing—have the fiend's own knack of discovering a man's weak place. I confess I rather go out of my way to conciliate Number Five study. It may be soft, but so far, I believe, I am the only man here whom they haven't maddened by their—well—attentions.'

'That is all beside the point. I flatter myself I can deal with them alone as occasion arises. But if they feel themselves morally supported by those who should wield absolute and open-handed justice, then I say that my lot is indeed a hard one. Of all things I detest, I admit that anything verging on disloyalty among ourselves is the first.'

The Common-room looked at one another out of the corners of their eyes, and Prout blushed.

'I deny it absolutely,' he said. 'Er—in fact, I own that I personally object to all three of them. It is not fair, therefore, to——'

'How long do you propose to allow it?' said King.

'But surely,' said Marcrea, deserting his usual ally, 'the blame, if there be any, rests with you, King. You can't hold them responsible for the—you prefer the good old Anglo-Saxon, I believe—stink in your House. My boys are complaining of it now.'

'What can you expect? You know what boys are. Naturally they take advantage of what to them is a heaven-sent opportunity,' said little Hartopp. 'What *is* the trouble in your dormitories, King?'

Mr. King explained that as he had made it the one rule of his life never to interfere with another man's House, so he expected not to be too patently interfered with. They might be interested to learn—here the chaplain heaved a weary sigh—that he had taken all steps that, in his poor judgment, would meet the needs of the case. Nay, further, he had himself expended, with no thought of reimbursement, sums, the amount of which he would not specify, on disinfectants. This he had done because he knew by bitter—by most bitter—experience that the management of the College was slack, dilatory, and inefficient. He might even add almost as slack as the administration of certain Houses which now thought fit to sit in judgment on his actions. With a short summary of his scholastic career, and a *précis* of his qualifications, including his degrees, he withdrew, slamming the door.

'Heigho!' said the chaplain. 'Ours is a dwarfing life—a belittling life, my brethren. God help all schoolmasters! They need it.'

'I don't like the boys, I own'—Prout dug viciously with his fork into the table-cloth—'and I don't pretend to be a strong man, as you know. But I confess I can't see any reason why I should take steps against Stalky and the others because King happens to be annoyed by—by——'

'Falling into the pit he has digged,'* said little Hartopp.

'Certainly not, Prout. No one accuses you of setting one House against another through sheer idleness.'

'A belittling life—a belittling life.' The chaplain rose. 'I go to correct French exercises. By dinner King will have scored off some unlucky child of thirteen; he will repeat to us every word of his brilliant repartees, and all will be well.'

'But about those three. Are they so prurient-minded?'

'Nonsense,' said little Hartopp. 'If you thought for a minute, Prout, you would see that the "precocious flow of fetid imagery" that King complains of is borrowed wholesale from King. *He* "nursed the pinion that impelled the steel."* Naturally he does not approve. Come into the smoking-room for a minute. It isn't fair to listen to boys; but they should be now rubbing it into King's House outside. Little things please little minds.'

The dingy den off the Common-room was never used for anything except gowns. Its windows were ground glass; one could not see out of it, but one could hear almost every word on the gravel outside. A light and wary footstep came up from Number Five.

'Rattray!' in a subdued voice—Rattray's study fronted that way. 'D'you know if Mr. King's anywhere about? I've got a—' M'Turk discreetly left the end of his sentence open.

'No. He's gone out,' said Rattray unguardedly.

'Ah! The learned Lipsius is airing himself, is he? His Royal Highness has gone to fumigate.' M'Turk climbed on the railings, where he held forth like the never-wearied rook.

'Now in all the Coll. there was no stink like the stink of King's House, for it stank vehemently and none knew what to make of it. Save King. And he washed the fags *privatim et seriatim*.* In the fishpools of Heshbon* washed he them, with an apron about his loins.'

'Shut up, you mad Irishman!' There was the sound of a golf-ball spurting up the gravel.

'It's no good getting wrathy, Rattray. We've come to jape with you. Come on, Beetle. They're all at home. You can wind 'em.'

'Where's the Pomposo Stinkadore? 'Tisn't safe for a pure-souled, high-minded boy to be seen round his House these days. Gone out, has he? Never mind, I'll do the best I can, Rattray. I'm *in loco parentis* just now.'

('One for you, Prout,' whispered Macrea, for this was Mr. Prout's pet phrase.)

'I have a few words to impart to you, my young friend. We will discourse together awhile.'

Here the listening Prout sputtered: Beetle, in a strained voice, had chosen a favourite gambit of King's.

'I repeat, Master Rattray, we will confer, and the matter of our discourse shall not be stinks, for that is a loathsome and obscene word. We will, with your good leave—granted, I trust, Master Rattray, granted, I trust—study this—this scabrous upheaval of latent demoralisation. What impresses me most is not so much the blatant indecency with which you swagger abroad under your load of putrescence' (you must imagine this discourse punctuated with golf-balls, but old Rattray was ever a bad shot) 'as the cynical immorality with which you revel in your abhorrent aromas. Far be it from me to interfere with another's House——'

('Good Lord!' said Prout, 'but this *is* King.'

'Line for line, letter for letter. Listen,' said little Hartopp.)

'But to say that you stink, as certain lewd fellows of the baser sort* aver, is to say nothing—less than nothing. In the absence of your beloved House-master, for whom no one has a higher regard than myself, I will, if you will allow me, explain the grossness—the unparalleled enormity—the appalling fetor of the stenches (I believe in the good old Anglo-Saxon word), stenches, sir, with which you have seen fit to infect your House. . . . Oh, bother! I've forgotten the rest, but it was very beautiful. Aren't you grateful to us for labourin' with you this way, Rattray? Lots of chaps 'ud never have taken the trouble, but we're grateful, Rattray.'

'Yes, we're horrid grateful,' grunted M'Turk. 'We don't forget that soap. We're polite. Why ain't you polite, Rat?'

'Hallo!' Stalky cantered up, his cap over one eye. 'Exhortin' the Whiffers, eh? I'm afraid they're too far gone to repent. Rattray! White! Perowne! Malpas! No answer. This is distressin'. This is truly distressin'. Bring out your dead,* you glandered* lepers!'

'You think yourself funny, don't you?' said Rattray, stung from his dignity by this last. 'It's only a rat or something under the floor. We're going to have it up to-morrow.'

'Don't try to shuffle it off on a poor dumb animal, and dead, too. I loathe prevarication. 'Pon my soul, Rattray——'

'Hold on. The Hartoffles never said "'Pon my soul" in all his life,' said Beetle critically.

('Ah!' said Prout to little Hartopp.)

'Upon my word, sir, upon my word, sir, I expected better things of you, Rattray. Why can you not own up to your misdeeds like a man? Have *I* ever shown any lack of confidence in *you*?'

('It's not brutality,' murmured little Hartopp, as though answering a question no one had asked. 'It's boy; only boy.')

'And this was the House.' Stalky changed from a pecking, fluttering voice to tragic earnestness. 'This was the—the— open cesspit that dared to call us "stinkers." And now—and now, it tries to shelter itself behind a dead rat. You annoy me, Rattray. You disgust me! You irritate me unspeakably! Thank Heaven, I am a man of equable temper——'

('This is to your address, Macrea,' said Prout.

'I fear so, I fear so.')

'Or I should scarcely be able to contain myself before your mocking visage.'

'*Cave!*'* in an undertone. Beetle had spied King sailing down the corridor.

'And what may you be doing here, my little friends?' the House-master began. 'I had a fleeting notion—correct me if I am wrong (the listeners with one accord choked)—that if I found you outside my House I should visit you with dire pains and penalties.'

'We were just goin' for a walk, sir,' said Beetle.

'And you stopped to speak to Rattray *en route*?'

'Yes, sir. We've been throwing golf-balls,' said Rattray, coming out of the study.

('Old Rat is more of a diplomat than I thought. So far he is strictly within the truth,' said little Hartopp. 'Observe the ethics of it, Prout.')

'Oh, you were sporting with them, were you? I must say I

do not envy you your choice of associates. I fancy they might have been engaged in some of the prurient discourse with which they have been so disgustingly free of late. I should strongly advise you to direct your steps most carefully in the future. Pick up those golf-balls.' He passed on.

*   *   *   *   *

Next day Richards, who had been a carpenter in the Navy, and to whom odd jobs were confided, was ordered to take up a dormitory floor; for Mr. King held that something must have died there.

'We need not neglect all our work for a trumpery incident of this nature; though I am quite aware that little things please little minds. Yes, I have decreed the boards to be taken up after lunch under Richards' auspices. I have no doubt it will be vastly interesting to a certain type of so-called intellect; but any boy of my House or another's found on the dormitory stairs will *ipso facto** render himself liable to three hundred lines.'

The boys did not collect on the stairs, but most of them waited outside King's. Richards had been bound to cry the news from the attic window, and, if possible, to exhibit the corpse.

"'Tis a cat, a dead cat!' Richards' face showed purple at the window. He had been in the chamber of death and on his knees for some time.

'Cat be blowed!' cried M'Turk. 'It's a dead fag left over from last term. Three cheers for King's dead fag!'

They cheered lustily.

'Show it, show it! Let's have a squint at it!' yelled the juniors. 'Give her to the Bug-hunters. [This was the Natural History Society.] The cat looked at the King—and died of it! Hoosh! Yai! Yaow! Maiow! Ftzz!' were some of the cries that followed.

Again Richards appeared.

'She've been'—he checked himself suddenly—'dead a long taime.'

The school roared.

'Well, come on out for a walk,' said Stalky in a well-chosen pause. 'It's all very disgustin', and I do hope that the Lazar-house won't do it again.'

'Do what?' a King's boy cried furiously.

'Kill a poor innocent cat every time you want to get off washing. It's awfully hard to distinguish between you as it is. I prefer the cat, I must say. She isn't quite so whiff. What are you goin' to do, Beetle?'

'*Je vais gloater. Je vais gloater tout le* blessed afternoon. *Jamais j'ai gloaté comme je gloaterai aujourd'hui. Nous bunkerons aux* bunkers.'

And it seemed good to them so to do.

* * * * *

Down in the basement, where the gas flickers and the boots stand in racks, Richards, amid his blacking-brushes, held forth to Oke of the Common-room, Gumbly of the dining-halls, and fair Lena of the laundry.

'Yiss. Her were in a shockin' staate an' condition. Her nigh made me sick, I tal 'ee. But I rowted un out, and I rowted un out, an' I made all shipshape, though her smelt like to bilges.'

'Her died mousin', I rackon, poor thing,' said Lena.

'Then her moused different to any made cat o' God's world, Lena. I up with the top-board, an' she were lying on her back, an' I turned un ovver with the brume-handle, an' 'twas her back was all covered with the plaster from 'twixt the lathin'. Yiss, I tal 'ee. An' under her head there lay, like, so's to say, a little pillow o' plaster druv up in front of her by raison of her slidin' along on her back. No cat niver went mousin' on her back, Lena. Some one had shoved her along right underneath, so far as they could shove un. Cats don't make theyselves pillows for to die on. Shoved along, she were, when she was settin' for to be cold, laike.'

'Oh, yeou'm too clever to live, Fatty. Yeou go get wed an' taught some sense,' said Lena, the affianced of Gumbly.

''Larned a little 'fore iver some maidens was born. Sarved in the Queen's Navy, I have, where yeou'm taught to use your eyes. Yeou go 'tend your own business, Lena.'

'Do 'ee mean what you'm been tellin' us?' said Oke.

'Ask me no questions, I'll give 'ee no lies. Bullet-hole clane

thru from side to side, an' tu heart-ribs broke like withies. I
seed un when I turned un ovver. They'm clever, oh, they'm
clever, but they'm not too clever for old Richards! 'Twas on
the born tip o' my tongue to tell, tu, but . . . he said us niver
washed, he did. Let his-dom boys call us "stinkers," he did.
Sarved un dom well raight, I say!'

Richards spat on a fresh boot and fell to his work,
chuckling.

The Impressionists

THEY had dropped into the chaplain's study for a Saturday night smoke—all four House-masters—and the three briars and the one cigar reeking in amity proved the Rev. John Gillett's good generalship. Since the discovery of the cat, King had been too ready to see affront where none was meant, and the Reverend John, buffer-state and general confidant, had worked for a week to bring about a good understanding. He was fat, clean-shaven, except for a big moustache, of an imperturbable good temper, and, those who loved him least said, a guileful Jesuit. He smiled benignantly upon his handiwork—four sorely-tried men talking without very much malice.

'Now remember,' he said, when the conversation turned that way, 'I impute nothing. But every time that any one has taken direct steps against Number Five study, the issue has been more or less humiliating to the taker.'

'I can't admit that. I pulverise the egregious Beetle daily for his soul's good; and the others with him,' said King.

'Well, take your own case, King, and go back a couple of years. Do you remember when Prout and you were on their track—for hutting and trespass, wasn't it? Have you forgotten Colonel Dabney?'

The others laughed. King did not care to be reminded of his career as a poacher.

'That was one instance. Again, when you had rooms below them—I always said that that was entering the lion's den—you turned them out.'

'For making disgusting noises. Surely, Gillett, you don't excuse——'

'All I say is that you turned them out. That same evening your study was wrecked.'

'By Rabbits-Eggs—most beastly drunk—from the road,' said King. 'What has that——?'

The Reverend John went on.

'Lastly, they conceive that aspersions are cast upon their personal cleanliness—a most delicate matter with all boys. Very good. Observe how, in each case, the punishment fits the crime. A week after your House calls them "stinkers," King, your House is, not to put too fine a point on it, stunk out by a dead cat who chooses to die in the one spot where she can annoy you most. Again the long arm of coincidence! *Summa.** You accuse them of trespass. Through some absurd chain of circumstances—they may or may not be at the other end of it—you and Prout are made to appear as trespassers. You evict them. For a time your study is made untenable. I have drawn the parallel in the last case. Well?'

'She was under the centre of White's dormitory,' said King. 'There are double floor-boards there to deaden noise. No boy, even in my own House, could possibly have pried up the boards without leaving some trace—and Rabbits-Eggs was phenomenally drunk that other night.'

'They are singularly favoured by fortune. That is all I ever said. Personally, I like them immensely, and I believe I have a little of their confidence. I confess I like being called "Padre." They are at peace with me; consequently I am not treated to bogus confessions of theft.'

'You mean Mason's case?' said Prout heavily. 'That always struck me as peculiarly scandalous. I thought the Head should have taken up the matter more thoroughly. Mason may be misguided, but at least he is thoroughly sincere and means well.'

'I confess I cannot agree with you, Prout,' said the Reverend John. 'He jumped at some silly tale of theft on their part; accepted another boy's evidence without, so far as I can see, any inquiry; and—frankly, I think he deserved all he got.'

'They deliberately outraged Mason's best feelings,' said Prout. 'A word to me on their part would have saved the whole thing. But they preferred to lure him on; to play on his ignorance of their characters——'

'That may be,' said King, 'but I don't like Mason. I dislike him for the very reason that Prout advances to his credit. He means well.'

'Our criminal tradition is not theft—among ourselves, at least,' said little Hartopp.

'For the head of a House that raided seven head of cattle from the innocent pot-wallopers* of Northam, isn't that rather a sweeping statement?' said Macrea.

'Precisely so,' said Hartopp, unabashed. 'That, with gate-lifting, and a little poaching and hawk-hunting on the cliffs, is our salvation.

'It does us far more harm as a school—' Prout began.

'Than any hushed-up scandal could? Quite so. Our reputation among the farmers is most unsavoury. But I would much sooner deal with any amount of ingenious crime of that nature than—some other offences.'

'They may be all right, but they are unboylike, abnormal, and, in my opinion, unsound,' Prout insisted. 'The moral effect of their performances must pave the way for greater harm. It makes me doubtful how to deal with them. I might separate them.'

'You might, of course; but they have gone up the school together for six years. I shouldn't care to do it,' said Macrea.

'They use the editorial "we,"' said King irrelevantly. 'It annoys me. "Where's your prose, Corkran?" "Well, sir, we haven't quite done it yet. We'll bring it in a minute," and so on. And the same with the others.'

'There's great virtue in that "we,"' said little Hartopp. 'You know I take them for trig. M'Turk may have some conception of the meaning of it; but Beetle is as the brutes that perish about sines and cosines. He copies serenely from Stalky, who positively rejoices in mathematics.'

'Why don't you stop it?' said Prout.

'It rights itself at the exams. Then Beetle shows up blank sheets, and trusts to his "English" to save him from a fall. I fancy he spends most of his time with me in writing verse.'

'I wish to Heaven he would transfer a little of his energy in that direction to Elegiacs.' King jerked himself upright. 'He is, with the single exception of Stalky, the very vilest manufacturer of "barbarous hexameters"* that I have dealt with.'

'The work is combined in that study,' said the chaplain. 'Stalky does the mathematics, M'Turk the Latin, and Beetle attends to their English and French. At least, when he was in the sick-house last month—'

'Malingering,' Prout interjected.

'Quite possibly. I found a very distinct falling off in their "Roman d'un Jeune Homme Pauvre"* translations.'

'I think it is profoundly immoral,' said Prout. 'I've always been opposed to the study system.'

'It would be hard to find any study where the boys don't help each other; but in Number Five the thing has probably been reduced to a system,' said little Hartopp. 'They have a system in most things.'

'They confess as much,' said the Reverend John. 'I've seen M'Turk being hounded up the stairs to elegise the "Elegy in a Churchyard,"* while Beetle and Stalky went to punt-about.'*

'It amounts to systematic cribbing,' said Prout, his voice growing deeper and deeper.

'No such thing,' little Hartopp returned. 'You can't teach a cow the violin.'

'In intention it is cribbing.'

'But we spoke under the seal of the confessional, didn't we?' said the Reverend John.

'You say you've heard them arranging their work in this way, Gillett,' Prout persisted.

'Good Heavens! Don't make me Queen's evidence, my dear fellow. Hartopp is equally incriminated. If they ever found out that I had sneaked, our relations would suffer—and I value them.'

'I think your attitude in this matter is weak,' said Prout, looking round for support. 'It would be really better to break up the study—for a while—wouldn't it?'

'Oh, break it up by all means,' said Macrea. 'We shall see then if Gillett's theory holds water.'

'Be wise, Prout. Leave them alone or calamity will overtake you; and what is much more important, they will be annoyed with me. I am too fat, alas! to be worried by bad boys. Where are you going?'

'Nonsense! They would not dare—but I am going to think this out,' said Prout. 'It needs thought. In intention they cribbed, and I must think out my duty.'

'He's perfectly capable of putting the boys on their honour.

It's *I* that am a fool!' The Reverend John looked round remorsefully. 'Never again will I forget that a master is not a man. Mark my words,' said the Reverend John. 'There will be trouble.'

* * * * *

But by the yellow Tiber
Was tumult and affright.*

Out of the blue sky (they were still rejoicing over the cat war) Mr. Prout had dropped into Number Five, read them a lecture on the enormity of cribbing, and bidden them return to the form-rooms on Monday. They had raged, solo and chorus, all through the peaceful Sabbath, for their sin was more or less the daily practice of all the studies.

'What's the good of cursing?' said Stalky at last. 'We're all in the same boat. We've got to go back and consort with the House. A locker in the form-room, and a seat at prep. in Number Twelve.' He looked regretfully round the cosy study which M'Turk, their leader in matters of Art, had decorated with a dado, a stencil, and cretonne hangings.

'Yes! Heffy lurchin' into the form-rooms like a frowzy old retriever, to see if we aren't up to something. You know he never leaves his House alone, these days,' said M'Turk. 'Oh, it will be giddy!'

' "Why aren't you down watchin' cricket? I like a robust, healthy boy. You mustn't frowst in a form-room. Why don't you take an interest in your House?" Yah!' quoted Beetle.

'Yes, why don't we! Let's! We'll take an interest in the House. We'll take no end of interest in the House. He hasn't had us in the form-rooms for a year. We've learned a lot since then. Oh, we'll make it a be-autiful House before we've done! 'Member that chap in *Eric* or *St. Winifred's*—Belial somebody?* I'm goin' to be Belial,' said Stalky, with an ensnaring grin.

'Right O!' said Beetle, 'and I'll be Mammon. I'll lend money at usury—that's what they do at all schools accordin' to the B. O. P.* 'Penny a week on a shillin'. That'll startle Heffy's weak intellect. You can be Lucifer, Turkey.'

'What have I got to do?' M'Turk also smiled.

'Head conspiracies—and cabals—and boycotts. Go in for that "stealthy intrigue" that Heffy is always talkin' about. Come on!'

The House received them on their fall with the mixture of jest and sympathy always extended to boys turned out of their study. The known aloofness of the three made them more interesting.

'Quite like old times, ain't it?' Stalky selected a locker and flung in his books. 'We've come to sport with you, my young friends, for a while, because our beloved House-master has hove us out of our diggin's.'

''Serve you jolly well right,' said Orrin, 'you cribbers!'

'This will never do,' said Stalky. 'We can't maintain our giddy prestige, Orrin, de-ah, if you make these remarks.'

They wrapped themselves lovingly about the boy, thrust him to the opened window, and drew down the sash to the nape of his neck. With an equal swiftness they tied his thumbs together behind his back with a piece of twine, and then, because he kicked furiously, removed his shoes.

There Mr. Prout happened to find him a few minutes later, guillotined and helpless, surrounded by a convulsed crowd who would not assist.

Stalky, in an upper form-room, had gathered himself allies against vengeance. Orrin presently tore up at the head of a boarding-party, and the form-room grew one fog of dust through which boys wrestled, stamped, shouted, and yelled. A desk was carried away in the tumult, a knot of warriors reeled into and split a door-panel, a window was broken, and a gas-jet fell. Under cover of the confusion the three escaped to the corridor, whence they called in and sent up passers-by to the fray.

'Rescue, King's! King's! King's! Number Twelve form-room! Rescue, Prout's—Prout's! Rescue, Macrea's! Rescue, Hartopp's!'

The juniors hurried out like bees aswarm, asking no questions, clattered up the staircase, and added themselves to the embroilment.

'Not bad for the first evening's work,' said Stalky, rearranging his collar. 'I fancy Prout 'll be somewhat annoyed.

We'd better establish an *alibi*.' So they sat on Mr. King's railings till prep.

'You see,' quoth Stalky, as they strolled up to prep. with the ignoble herd, 'if you get the Houses well mixed up an' scufflin', it's even bettin' that some ass will start a real row. Hullo, Orrin, you look rather metagrobolised.'*

'It was all your fault, you beast! You started it. We've got two hundred lines apiece, and Heffy's lookin' for you. Just see what that swine Malpass did to my eye!'

'I like your saying *we* started it. Who called us cribbers? Can't your infant mind connect cause and effect yet? Some day you'll find out that it don't pay to jest with Number Five.'

'Where's that shillin' you owe me?' said Beetle suddenly.

Stalky could not see Prout behind him, but returned the lead without a quaver.

'I only owed you ninepence, you old usurer.'

'You've forgotten the interest,' said M'Turk. 'A halfpenny a week per bob is Beetle's charge. You must be beastly rich, Beetle.'

'Well, Beetle lent me sixpence.' Stalky came to a full stop and made as to work it out on his fingers. 'Sixpence on the nineteenth, didn't he?'

'Yes; but you've forgotten you paid no interest on the other bob—the one I lent you before.'

'But you took my watch as security.' The game was developing itself almost automatically.

'Never mind. Pay me my interest, or I'll charge you interest on interest. Remember I've got your note-of-hand!' shouted Beetle.

'You're a cold-blooded Jew,' Stalky groaned.

'Hush!' said M'Turk very loudly indeed; then started as Prout came upon them.

'I didn't see you in that disgraceful affair in the form-room just now,' said he.

'What, sir? We're just come up from Mr. King's,' said Stalky. 'Please, sir, what am I to do about prep.? They've broken the desk you told me to sit at, and the form's just swimming with ink.'

'Find another seat—find another seat. D'you expect me to

dry-nurse you? I wish to know whether you are in the habit of advancing money to your associates, Beetle?'

'No, sir; not as a general rule, sir.'

'It is a most reprehensible habit. I thought that my House, at least, would be free from it. Even with my opinion of you, I hardly thought it was one of your vices.'

'There's no harm in lending money, sir, is there?'

'I am not going to bandy words with you on your notions of morality. How much have you lent Corkran?'

'I—I don't quite know,' said Beetle. It is difficult to improvise a going concern on the spur of the minute.

'You seemed certain enough just now.'

'I think it's two and fourpence,' said M'Turk, with a glance of cold scorn at Beetle.

In the hopelessly involved finances of the study there was just that sum to which both M'Turk and Beetle laid claim, as their share in the pledging of Stalky's second-best Sunday trousers. But Stalky had maintained for two terms that the money was his commission for effecting the pawn; and had, of course, spent it on a study 'brew.'

'Understand this, then. You are not to continue your operations as a money-lender. Two and fourpence, you said, Corkran?'

Stalky had said nothing, and continued so to do.

'Your influence for evil is quite strong enough without buying a hold over your companions.' He felt in his pockets, and (oh, joy!) produced a florin and fourpence. 'Bring me what you call Corkran's note-of-hand, and be thankful that I do not carry the matter any further. The money is stopped from your pocket-money, Corkran. The receipt to my study, at once.'

Little they cared! Two and fourpence in a lump is worth six weekly sixpences any hungry day of the week.

'But what the dooce *is* a note-of-hand?' said Beetle. 'I only read about it in a book.'

'Now you've jolly well got to make one,' said Stalky.

'Yes—but our ink don't turn black till next day. 'S'pose he'll spot that?'

'Not him. He's too worried,' said M'Turk. 'Sign your name

on a bit of impot-paper, Stalky, and write, "I O U two and fourpence." Aren't you grateful to me for getting that out of Prout? Stalky 'd never have paid. . . . Why, you ass!'

Mechanically Beetle had handed over the money to Stalky as treasurer of the study. The custom of years is not lightly broken.

In return for the document, Prout explained to Beetle the enormity of money-lending, which, like everything except compulsory cricket, corrupted Houses and destroyed good feeling among boys, made youth cold and calculating, and opened the door to all evil. Finally, did Beetle know of any other cases? If so, it was his duty as proof of repentance to let his House-master know. No names need be mentioned.

Beetle did not know—at least, he was not quite sure, sir. How could he give evidence against his friends? The House might, of course—here he feigned an anguished delicacy—be full of it. He was not in a position to say. He had not met with any open competition in his trade; but if Mr. Prout considered it was a matter that affected the honour of the House (Mr. Prout did consider it precisely that), perhaps the House-prefects would be better . . .

He spun it out till half-way through prep.

'And,' said the amateur Shylock, returning to the form-room and dropping at Stalky's side, 'if he don't think the House is putrid with it, I'm severial Dutchmen—that's all. . . . I've been to Mr. Prout's study, sir.' This to the prep.-master. 'He said I could sit where I liked, sir. . . . Oh, he is just tricklin' with emotion . . . . Yes, sir, I'm only askin' Corkran to let me have a dip in his ink.'

After prayers, on the road to the dormitories, Harrison and Craye, senior House-prefects, zealous in their office, waylaid them with great anger.

'What have you been doing to Heffy this time, Beetle? He's been jawing us all the evening.'

'What has His Serene Transparency been vexin' you for?' said M'Turk.

'About Beetle lendin' money to Stalky,' began Harrison; 'and then Beetle went and told him that there was any amount of money-lendin' in the House.'

'No, you don't,' said Beetle, sitting on a boot-basket. 'That's just what I didn't tell him. I spoke the giddy truth. He asked me if there was much of it in the House; and I said I didn't know.'

'He thinks you're a set of filthy Shylocks,'* said M'Turk. 'It's just as well for you he don't think you're burglars. You know he never gets a notion out of his conscientious old head.'

'Well-meanin' man. Did it all for the best.' Stalky curled gracefully round the stair-rail. 'Head in a drain-pipe. Full confession in the left boot.* Bad for the honour of the House—very.'

'Shut up,' said Harrison. 'You chaps always behave as if you were jawin' us when we come to jaw you.'

'You're a lot too cheeky,' said Craye.

'I don't quite see where the cheek comes in, except on your part, in interferin' with a private matter between me an' Beetle after it has been settled by Prout.' Stalky winked cheerfully at the others.

'That's the worst of clever little swots,' said M'Turk, addressing the gas. 'They get made prefects before they have any tact, and then they annoy chaps who could really help 'em to look after the honour of the House.'

'We won't trouble you to do that!' said Craye hotly.

'Then what are you badgerin' us for?' said Beetle. 'On your own showing, you've been so beastly slack, looking after the House, that Prout believes it's a nest of money-lenders. I've told him that I've lent money to Stalky, and no one else. I don't know whether he believes me, but that finishes my case. The rest is *your* business.'

'Now we find out'—Stalky's voice rose—'that there is apparently an organised conspiracy throughout the House. For aught we know, the fags may be lendin' and borrowin' far beyond their means. *We* aren't responsible for it. We're only the rank and file.'

'Are you surprised we don't wish to associate with the House?' said M'Turk, with dignity. 'We've kept ourselves to ourselves in our study till we were turned out, and now we find ourselves let in for—for this sort of thing. It's simply disgraceful.'

'Then you hector and bullyrag us on the stairs,' said Stalky, 'about matters that are your business entirely. You know we aren't prefects.'

'You threatened us with a prefects' lickin' just now,' said Beetle, boldly inventing as he saw the bewilderment in the faces of the enemy.

'And if you expect you'll gain anything from us by your way of approachin' us, you're jolly well mistaken. That's all. Good-night.'

They clattered upstairs, injured virtue on every inch of their backs.

'But—but what the dickens have *we* done?' said Harrison, amazedly, to Craye.

'I don't know. Only—it always happens that way when one has anything to do with them. They're so beastly plausible.'

And Mr. Prout called the good boys into his study anew, and succeeded in sinking both his and their innocent minds ten fathoms deeper in blindfolded bedazement. He spoke of steps and measures, of tone and loyalty in the House and to the House, and urged them to take up the matter tactfully.

So they demanded of Beetle whether he had any connection with any other establishment. Beetle promptly went to his House-master, and wished to know by what right Harrison and Craye had reopened a matter already settled between him and his House-master. In injured innocence no boy excelled Beetle.

Then it occurred to Prout that he might have been unfair to the culprit, who had not striven to deny or palliate his offence. He sent for Harrison and Craye, reprehending them very gently for the tone they had adopted to a repentant sinner, and when they returned to their study, they used the language of despair. They then made headlong inquisition through the House, driving the fags to the edge of hysterics, and unearthing, with tremendous pomp and parade, the natural and inevitable system of small loans that prevails among small boys.

'You see, Harrison, Thornton minor lent me a penny last Saturday, because I was fined for breaking the window; and I spent it at Keyte's.* I didn't know there was any harm in it. And Wray major borrowed twopence from me when my uncle sent me a post-office order—I cashed it at Keyte's—for five bob; but he'll pay me back before the holidays. We didn't know there was anything wrong in it.'

They waded through hours of this kind of thing, but found no usury, or anything approaching to Beetle's gorgeous scale of interest. The seniors—for the school had no tradition of deference to prefects outside compulsory games—told them succinctly to go about their business. They would not give evidence on any terms. Harrison was one idiot, and Craye was another; but the greatest of all, they said, was their House-master.

When a House is thoroughly upset, however good its conscience, it breaks into knots and coteries—small gatherings in the twilight, box-room committees, and groups in the corridor. And when from group to group, with an immense affectation of secrecy, three wicked boys steal, crying 'Cave'* when there is no need of caution, and whispering 'Don't tell!' on the heels of trumpery confidences that instant invented, a very fine air of plot and intrigue can be woven round such a House.

At the end of a few days, it dawned on Prout that he moved in an atmosphere of perpetual ambush. Mysteries hedged him on all sides, warnings ran before his heavy feet, and countersigns were muttered behind his attentive back. M'Turk and Stalky invented many absurd and idle phrases—catch-words that swept through the house as fire through stubble. It was a rare jest, and the only practical outcome of the Usury Commission, that one boy should say to a friend, with awful gravity, 'Do you think there's much of it going on in the house?' The other would reply, 'Well, one can't be too careful, you know.' The effect on a House-master of humane conscience and good intent may be imagined. Again, a man who has sincerely devoted himself to gaining the esteem of his charges does not like to hear himself described, even at a distance, as 'Popularity Prout' by a dark and scowling Celt with a fluent tongue. A rumour that stories—unusual stories—are told in the form-rooms, between the lights, by a boy who does not command his confidence, agitates such a man; and even elaborate and tender politeness—for the courtesy that wise grown men offer to a bewildered child was the courtesy which Stalky wrapped round Prout—restores not his peace of mind.

'The tone of the House seems changed—changed for the worse,' said Prout to Harrison and Craye. 'Have you noticed it? I don't for an instant impute——'

He never imputed anything; but, on the other hand, he never did anything else, and, with the best intentions in the world, he had reduced the House-prefects to a state as nearly bordering on nervous irritation as healthy boys can know. Worst of all, they began at times to wonder whether Stalky & Co. had not some truth in their often repeated assertions that Prout was 'a gloomy ass.'

'As you know, I am not the kind of man who puts himself out for every little thing he hears. *I* believe in letting the House work out their own salvation—with a light guiding hand on the reins, of course. But there is a perceptible lack of reverence—a lower tone in matters that touch the honour of the House, a sort of hardness.'

> "Oh, Prout he is a nobleman, a nobleman, a nobleman!
>   Our Heffy is a nobleman—
>   He does an awful lot,
>   Because his popularity—
>   Oh, pop-u-pop-u-larity—
>   His giddy popularity
>   Would suffer did he not!"

The study door stood ajar; and the song, borne by twenty clear voices, came faint from a form-room. The fags rather liked the tune; the words were Beetle's.

'That's a thing no sensible man objects to,' said Prout, with a lop-sided smile; 'but, you know, straws show which way the wind blows. Can you trace it to any direct influence? I am speaking to you now as heads of the House.'

'There isn't the least doubt of it,' said Harrison angrily. 'I know what you mean, sir. It all began when Number Five study came to the form-rooms. There's no use blinkin' it, Craye. You know that, too.'

'They make things rather difficult for us, sometimes,' said

Craye. 'It's more their manner than anything else, that Harrison means.'

'Do they hamper you in the discharge of your duties, then?'

'Well, no, sir. They only look on and grin—and turn up their noses generally.'

'Ah,' said Prout sympathetically.

'I think, sir,' said Craye, plunging into the business boldly, 'it would be a great deal better if they were sent back to their study—better for the House. They are rather old to be knocking about the form-rooms.'

'They are younger than Orrin, or Flint, and a dozen others that I can think of.'

'Yes, sir; but that's different, somehow. They're rather influential. They have a knack of upsettin' things in a quiet way that one can't take hold of. At least, if one does——'

'And you think they would be better in their own study again?'

Emphatically Harrison and Craye were of that opinion. As Harrison said to Craye, afterwards, 'They've weakened our authority. They're too big to lick; they've made an exhibition of us over this usury business, and we're a laughing-stock to the rest of the school. I'm going up ['for Sandhurst' understood] next term. They've managed to knock me out of half my work already, with their—their lunacy. If they go back to their study we may have a little peace.'

'Hullo, Harrison.' M'Turk ambled round the corner, with a roving eye on all possible horizons. 'Bearin' up, old man? That's right. Live it down! Live it down!'

'What d'you mean?'

'You look a little pensive,' said M'Turk. 'Exhaustin' job superintendin' the honour of the House, ain't it? By the way, how are you off for mares'-nests?'

'Look here,' said Harrison, hoping for instant reward. 'We've recommended Prout to let you go back to your study.'

'The dooce you have! And who under the sun are *you*, to interfere between us and our House-master? Upon my Sam, you two try us very hard—you do, indeed. Of course we don't know how far you abuse your position to prejudice us with Mr. Prout; but when you deliberately stop me to tell me you've been makin' arrangements behind our back—in secret—with Prout—I—I don't know really what we ought to do.'

'That's beastly unfair!' cried Craye.

'It is.' M'Turk had adopted a ghastly solemnity that sat well on his long, lean face. 'Hang it all! A prefect's one thing and an usher's another; but you seem to combine 'em. You recommend this—you recommend that! *You* say how and when we go back to our study!'

'But—but—we thought you'd like it, Turkey. We did, indeed. You know you'll be ever so much more comfortable there.' Harrison's voice was almost tearful.

M'Turk turned away as if to hide his emotions.

'They're broke!' He hunted up Stalky and Beetle in a box-room. 'They're sick! They've been beggin' Heffy to let us go back to Number Five. Poor devils! Poor little devils!'

'It's the olive branch,' was Stalky's comment. 'It's the giddy white flag, by gum! Come to think of it, we *have* metagrobolised 'em.'

Just after tea that day, Mr. Prout sent for them to say that if they chose to ruin their future by neglecting their work, it was entirely their own affair. He wished them, however, to understand that their presence in the form-rooms could not be tolerated one hour longer. He personally did not care to think of the time he must spend in eliminating the traces of their evil influences. How far Beetle had pandered to the baser side of youthful imagination he would ascertain later; and Beetle might be sure that if Mr. Prout came across any soul-corrupting consequences—

'Consequences of what, sir?' said Beetle, genuinely bewildered this time; and M'Turk quietly kicked him on the ankle for being 'fetched' by Prout.

Beetle, the House-master continued, knew very well what was intended. Evil and brief had been their careers under his eye; and as one standing *in loco parentis* to their yet uncontaminated associates, he was bound to take his precautions. The return of the study key closed the sermon.

'But what was the baser-side-of-imagination business?'* said Beetle on the stairs.

'I never knew such an ass as you are for justifyin' yourself,' said M'Turk. 'I hope I jolly well skinned your ankle. Why do you let yourself be drawn by everybody?'

'Draws be blowed! I must have tickled him up in some way I didn't know about. If I'd had a notion of that before, of course I could have rubbed it in better. It's too late now. What a pity! "Baser side." What was he drivin' at?'

'Never mind,' said Stalky. 'I knew we could make it a happy little House. I said so, remember—but I swear I didn't think we'd do it so soon.'

* * * * *

'No,' said Prout most firmly in Common-room. 'I maintain that Gillett is wrong. True, I let them return to their study.'

'With your known views on cribbing, too?' purred little Hartopp. 'What an immoral compromise!'

'One moment,' said the Reverend John. 'I—we—all of us have exercised an absolutely heart-breaking discretion for the last ten days. Now we want to know. Confess—have you known a happy minute since——'

'As regards my House, I have not,' said Prout. 'But you are entirely wrong in your estimate of those boys. In justice to the others—in self-defence——'

'Ha! I said it would come to that,' murmured the Reverend John.

'——I was forced to send them back. Their moral influence was unspeakable—simply unspeakable.'

And bit by bit he told his tale, beginning with Beetle's usury, and ending with the House-prefects' appeal.

'Beetle in the *rôle* of Shylock is new to me,' said King, with twitching lips. 'I heard rumours of it——'

'Before!' said Prout.

'No, after you had dealt with them; but I was careful not to inquire. I never interfere with——'

'I myself,' said Hartopp, 'would cheerfully give him five shillings if he could work out one simple sum in compound interest without three gross errors.'

'Why—why—why!' Mason, the mathematical master,

stuttered, a fierce joy on his face. 'You've been had—precisely the same as me!'

'And so you held an inquiry?' Little Hartopp's voice drowned Mason's ere Prout caught the import of the sentence.

'The boy himself hinted at the existence of a good deal of it in the House,' said Prout.

'He is past master in that line,' said the chaplain. 'But, as regards the honour of the House——'

'They lowered it in a week. I have striven to build it up for years. My own House-prefects—and boys do not willingly complain of each other—besought me to get rid of them. You say you have their confidence, Gillett: they may tell you another tale. As far as I am concerned, they may go to the devil in their own way. I'm sick and tired of them,' said Prout bitterly.

But it was the Reverend John, with a smiling countenance, who went to the devil just after Number Five had cleared away a very pleasant little brew (it cost them two and fourpence) and was settling down to prep.

'Come in, Padre, come in,' said Stalky, thrusting forward the best chair. 'We've only met you official-like these last ten days.'

'You were under sentence,' said the Reverend John. 'I do not consort with malefactors.'

'Ah, but we're restored again,' said M'Turk. 'Mr. Prout has relented.'

'Without a stain on our characters,' said Beetle. 'It was a painful episode, Padre, most painful.'

'Now, consider for a while, and perpend, *mes enfants*. It is about your characters that I've called to-night. In the language of the schools, what the dooce *have* you been up to in Mr. Prout's House? It isn't anything to laugh over. He says that you so lowered the tone of the House he had to pack you back to your studies. Is that true?'

'Every word of it, Padre.'

'Don't be flippant, Turkey. Listen to me. I've told you very often that no boys in the school have a greater influence for good or evil than you have. You know I don't talk about ethics and moral codes, because I don't believe that the young of the human animal realises what they mean for some years to come. All the same, I don't want to think you've been perverting the juniors. Don't interrupt, Beetle. Listen to me! Mr. Prout has a notion that you have been corrupting our associates somehow or other.'

'Mr. Prout has so many notions, Padre,' said Beetle wearily. 'Which one is this?'

'Well, he tells me that he heard you telling a story in the twilight in the form-room, in a whisper. And Orrin said, just as he opened the door, "Shut up, Beetle; it's too beastly." Now then?'

'You remember Mrs. Oliphant's *Beleaguered City** that you lent me last term?' said Beetle.

The Padre nodded.

'I got the notion out of that. Only, instead of a city, I made it the Coll. in a fog—besieged by ghosts of dead boys, who hauled chaps out of their beds in the dormitory. All the names are quite real. You tell it in a whisper, you know—with the names. Orrin didn't like it one little bit. None of 'em have ever let me finish it. It gets just awful at the end.'

'But why in the world didn't you explain to Mr. Prout, instead of leaving him under the impression——'

'Padre Sahib,' said M'Turk, 'it isn't the least good explainin' to Mr. Prout. If he hasn't one impression, he's bound to have another.'

'He'd do it with the best o' motives. He's *in loco parentis*,' purred Stalky.

'You young demons!' the Reverend John replied. 'And am I to understand that the—the usury business was another of your House-master's impressions?'

'Well—we helped a little in that,' said Stalky. 'I did owe Beetle two and fourpence—at least, Beetle says I did, but I never intended to pay him. Then we started a bit of an argument on the stairs, and—and Mr. Prout dropped into it accidental. That was how it was, Padre. He paid me cash down like a giddy Dook (stopped it out of my pocket-money just the same), and Beetle gave him my note-of-hand all correct. I don't know what happened after that.'

'I was too truthful,' said Beetle. 'I always am. You see, he was under an impression, Padre, and I suppose I ought to have corrected that impression; but of course I couldn't be quite certain that his House wasn't given over to money-lendin', could I? I thought the House-prefects might know more about it than I did. They ought to. They're giddy palladiums of public schools.'*

'They did, too—by the time they'd finished,' said M'Turk. 'As nice a pair of conscientious, well-meanin', upright, pure-souled boys as you'd ever want to meet, Padre. They turned the House upside down—Harrison and Craye—with the best motives in the world.'

'They said so.'

> They said it very loud and clear,
> They went and shouted in our ear,'*

said Stalky.

'My own private impression is that all three of you will infallibly be hanged,' said the Reverend John.

'Why, we didn't do anything,' replied M'Turk. 'It was all Mr. Prout. Did you ever read a book about Japanese wrestlers? My uncle—he's in the Navy—gave me a beauty once.'

'Don't try to change the subject, Turkey.'

'I'm not, sir, I'm givin' an illustration—same as a sermon. These wrestler-chaps have got some sort of trick that lets the other chap do all the work. Then they give a little wriggle, and he upsets himself. It's called shibbuwichee or tokonoma,* or somethin'. Mr. Prout's a shibbuwicher. It isn't our fault.'

'Did you suppose we went round corruptin' the minds of the fags?' said Beetle. 'They haven't any, to begin with; and if they had, they're corrupted long ago. I've been a fag, Padre.'

'Well, I fancied I knew the normal range of your iniquities; but if you take so much trouble to pile up circumstantial evidence against yourselves, you can't blame any one if——'

'We don't blame any one, Padre. We haven't said a word against Mr. Prout, have we?' Stalky looked at the others. 'We love him. He hasn't a notion how we love him.'

'H'm! You dissemble your love very well. Have you ever thought who got you turned out of your study, in the first place?'

'It was Mr. Prout turned us out,' said Stalky, with significance.

'Well, I was that man. I didn't mean it; but some words of mine, I'm afraid, gave Mr. Prout the impression——'

Number Five laughed aloud.

'You see it's just the same thing with you, Padre,' said M'Turk. 'He *is* quick to get an impression, ain't he? But you mustn't think we don't love him, 'cause we do. There isn't an ounce of vice about him.'

A double knock fell on the door.

'The Head to see Number Five study in his study at once,' said the voice of Foxy, the school Sergeant.

'Whew!' said the Reverend John. 'It seems to me that there is a great deal of trouble coming for some people.'

'My word! Mr. Prout's gone and told the Head,' said Stalky. 'He's a moral double-ender. Not fair, luggin' the Head into a House-row.'

'I should recommend a copy-book on a—h'm—safe and certain part,' said the Reverend John disinterestedly.

'Huh! He licks across the shoulders, an' it would slam like a beastly barn-door,' said Beetle. 'Good-night, Padre. We're in for it.'

Once more they stood in the presence of the Head—Belial, Mammon, and Lucifer. But they had to deal with a man more subtle than them all. Mr. Prout had talked to him, heavily and sadly, for half an hour; and the Head had seen all that was hidden from the House-master.

'You've been bothering Mr. Prout,' he said pensively. 'House-masters aren't here to be bothered by boys more than is necessary. I don't like being bothered by these things. You are bothering *me*. That is a very serious offence. You see it?'

'Yes, sir.'

'Well, now, I purpose to bother you, on personal and private grounds, because you have broken into my time. You are much too big to lick, so I suppose I shall have to mark my displeasure in some other way. Say, a thousand lines apiece, a week's gating, and a few things of that kind. Much too big to lick, aren't you?'

'Oh no, sir,' said Stalky cheerfully; for a week's gating in the summer term is serious.

'Ve-ry good. Then we will do what we can. I wish you wouldn't bother me.'

It was a fair, sustained, equable stroke, with a little draw to it, but what they felt most was his unfairness in stopping to talk between executions. Thus:

'Among the—lower classes this would lay me open to a charge of—assault. You should be more grateful for your—privileges than you are. There is a limit—one finds it by experience, Beetle—beyond which it is never safe to pursue private vendettas, because—don't move—sooner or later one comes—into collision with the—higher authority, who has studied the animal. *Et ego*—M'Turk, please—*in Arcadia vixi.** There's a certain flagrant injustice about this that ought to appeal to—your temperament. And that's all! You will tell your House-master that you have been formally caned by me.'

'My word!' said M'Turk, wriggling his shoulder-blades all down the corridor. 'That was business! The Prooshian* Bates has an infernal straight eye.'

'Wasn't it wily of me to ask for the lickin',' said Stalky, 'instead of those impots?'

'Rot! We were in for it from the first. *I* knew the cock of his old eye,' said Beetle. 'I was within an inch of blubbing.'

'Well, I didn't exactly smile,' Stalky confessed.

'Let's go down to the lavatory and have a look at the damage. One of us can hold the glass and t'others can squint.'

They proceeded on these lines for some ten minutes. The wales were very red and very level. There was not a penny to choose between any of them for thoroughness, efficiency, and a certain clarity of outline that stamps the work of the artist.

'What are you doing down there?' Mr. Prout was at the head of the lavatory stairs, attracted by the noise of splashing.

'We've only been caned by the Head, sir, and we're washing off the blood. The Head said we were to tell you. We were coming to report ourselves in a minute, sir. (*Sotto voce.*) That's a score for Heffy!'

'Well, he deserves to score something, poor devil,' said M'Turk, putting on his shirt. 'We've sweated a stone and a half off him since we began.'

'But look here, why aren't we wrathy with the Head? He said it was a flagrant injustice. So it is!' said Beetle.

'Dearr man,' said M'Turk, and vouchsafed no further answer.

It was Stalky who laughed till he had to hold on by the edge of a basin.

'You *are* a funny ass! What's the for?' said Beetle.

'I'm—I'm thinking of the flagrant injustice of it!'

The Moral Reformers

THERE was no disguising the defeat. The victory was to Prout, but they grudged it not. If he had broken the rules of the game by calling in the Head, they had had a good run for their money.

The Reverend John sought the earliest opportunity of talking things over. Members of a bachelor Common-room, in a school where masters' studies are designedly dotted among studies and form-rooms, can, if they choose, see a great deal of their charges. Number Five had spent some cautious years in testing the Reverend John. He was emphatically a gentleman. He knocked at a study door before entering; he comported himself as a visitor and not a strayed lictor;* he never prosed, and he never carried over into official life the confidences of idle hours. Prout was ever an unmitigated nuisance; King came solely as the avenger of blood; even little Hartopp, talking natural history, seldom forgot his office; but the Reverend John was a guest desired and beloved by Number Five.

Behold him, then, in their only arm-chair, a bent briar between his teeth, chin down in three folds on his clerical collar, and blowing like an amiable whale, while Number Five discoursed of life as it appeared to them, and specially of that last interview with the Head—in the matter of usury.

'One licking once a week would do you an immense amount of good,' he said, twinkling and shaking all over; 'and, as you say, you were entirely in the right.'

'Ra-ather, Padre! We could have proved it if he'd let us talk,' said Stalky; 'but he didn't. The Head's a downy bird.'

'He understands you perfectly. Ho! ho! Well, you worked hard enough for it.'

'But he's awfully fair. He doesn't lick a chap in the morning an' preach at him in the afternoon,' said Beetle.

'He can't; he ain't in Orders, thank goodness,'* said M'Turk. Number Five held the very strongest views on clerical head-masters, and were ever ready to meet their pastor in argument.

'Almost all other schools have clerical Heads,' said the Reverend John gently.

'It isn't fair on the chaps,' Stalky replied. 'Makes 'em sulky. Of course it's different with you, sir. You belong to the school—same as we do. I mean ordinary clergymen.'

'Well, I am a most ordinary clergyman; and Mr. Hartopp's in Orders too.'

'Ye—es, but he took 'em after he came to the Coll. We saw him go up for his exam. That's all right,' said Beetle. 'But just think if the Head went and got ordained!'

'What would happen, Beetle?'

'Oh, the Coll. 'ud go to pieces in a year, sir. There's no doubt o' that.'

'How d'you know?' The Reverend John was smiling.

'We've been here nearly six years now. There are precious few things about the Coll. we don't know,' Stalky replied. 'Why, even you came the term after I did, sir. I remember your asking our names in form your first lesson. Mr. King, Mr. Prout, and the Head, of course, are the only masters senior to us—in that way.'

'Yes, we've changed a good deal—in Common-room.'

'Huh!' said Beetle, with a grunt. 'They came here, an' they went away to get married. Jolly good riddance, too!'

'Doesn't our Beetle hold with matrimony?'

'No, Padre; don't make fun of me. I've met chaps in the holidays who've got married House-masters. It's perfectly awful! They have babies and teething and measles and all that sort of thing right bung *in* the school; and the masters' wives give tea-parties—tea-parties, Padre!—and ask the chaps to breakfast.'

'That don't matter so much,' said Stalky. 'But the House-masters let their Houses alone, and they leave everything to the prefects. Why, in one school, a chap told me, there were big baize doors and a passage about a mile long between the House and the master's house. They could do just what they pleased.'

'Satan rebuking sin with a vengence.'

'Oh, larks are right enough; but you know what we mean, Padre. After a bit it gets worse an' worse. Then there's a big bust-up and a row that gets into the papers, and a lot of chaps are expelled, you know.'

'Always the wrong uns; don't forget that. Have a cup of cocoa, Padre?' said M'Turk, with the kettle.

'No thanks; I'm smoking. Always the wrong uns? Pro-ceed, my Stalky.'

'And then'—Stalky warmed to the work—'everybody says, "Who'd ha' thought it? Shockin' boys! Wicked little kids!" It all comes of havin' married House-masters, I think.'

'A Daniel come to judgment!'*

'But it does,' M'Turk interrupted. 'I've met chaps in the holidays, an' they've told me the same thing. It looks awfully pretty for one's people to see—a nice separate house with a nice lady in charge an' all that. But it isn't. It takes the House-masters off their work, and it gives the prefects a heap too much power, an'—an'—it rots up everything. You see it isn't as if we were just an ordinary school. We take crammers' rejections as well as good little boys like Stalky. We've got to do that to make our name, of course, and we get 'em into Sandhurst somehow or other, don't we?'

'True, O Turk. Like a book thou talkest, Turkey.'

'And so we want rather different masters, don't you think so, to other places? We aren't like the rest of the schools.'

'It leads to all sorts of bullyin', too, a chap told me,' said Beetle.

'Well, you do need most of a single man's time, I must say.' The Reverend John considered his hosts critically. 'But do you never feel that the world—the Common-room—is too much with you sometimes?'*

'Not exactly—in summer, anyhow.' Stalky's eye roved contentedly to the window. 'Our bounds are pretty big, too, and they leave us to ourselves a good deal.'

'For example, here am I sitting in your study, very much in your way, eh?'

'Indeed you aren't, Padre. Sit down. Don't go, sir. You know we're glad whenever you come.'

There was no doubting the sincerity of the voices. The

Reverend John flushed a little with pleasure and refilled his briar.

'And we generally know where the Common-room are,' said Beetle triumphantly. 'Didn't you come through our lower dormitories last night after ten, sir?'

'I went to smoke a pipe with your Housemaster. No, I didn't give him any impressions. I took a short cut through your dormitories.'

'I sniffed a whiff of 'baccy this mornin'. Yours is stronger than Mr. Prout's. *I* knew,' said Beetle, wagging his head.

'Good heavens!' said the Reverend John absently. It was some years before Beetle perceived that this was rather a tribute to innocence than observation. The long, light, blindless dormitories, devoid of inner doors, were crossed at all hours of the night by masters visiting one another; for bachelors sit up later than married folk. Beetle had never dreamed that there might be a purpose in this steady policing.

'Talking about bullying,' the Reverend John resumed, 'you all caught it pretty hot when you were fags, didn't you?'

'Well, we must have been rather awful little beasts,' said Beetle, looking serenely over the gulf between eleven and sixteen. 'My Hat, what bullies they were then—Fairburn, "Gobby" Maunsell, and all that gang!'

'"Member when "Gobby" called us the Three Blind Mice, and we had to get up on the lockers and sing while he buzzed inkpots at us?' said Stalky. 'They were bullies if you like!'

'But there isn't any of it now,' said M'Turk soothingly.

'That's where you make a mistake. We're all inclined to say that everything is all right as long as we ourselves aren't hurt. I sometimes wonder if it is extinct—bullying.'

'Fags bully each other horrid; but the upper forms are supposed to be swottin' for exams. They've got something else to think about,' said Beetle.

'Why? What do you think?' Stalky was watching the chaplain's face.

'I have my doubts.' Then, explosively, 'On my word, for three moderately intelligent boys you aren't very observant. I suppose you were too busy making things warm for your

House-master to see what lay under your noses when you were in the form-rooms last week?'

'What, sir? I—I swear we didn't see anything,' said Beetle.

'Then I'd advise you to look. When a little chap is whimpering in a corner and wears his clothes like rags, and never does any work, and is notoriously the dirtiest little "corridor-caution" in the Coll., something's wrong somewhere.'

'That's Clewer,' said M'Turk under his breath.

'Yes, Clewer. He comes to me for his French. It's his first term, and he's almost as complete a wreck as you were, Beetle. He's not naturally clever, but he has been hammered till he's nearly an idiot.'

'Oh no. They sham silly to get off more lickings,' said Beetle. '*I* know that.'

'I've never actually seen him knocked about,' said the Reverend John.

'The genuine article don't do that in public,' said Beetle. 'Fairburn never touched me when any one was looking on.'

'You needn't swagger about it, Beetle,' said M'Turk. 'We all caught it in our time.'

'But I got it worse than any one,' said Beetle. 'If you want an authority on bullyin', Padre, come to me. Corkscrews—brush-drill— keys— head-knucklin'—arm-twistin'— rockin'—Ag Ags—and all the rest of it.'

'Yes. I do want you as an authority, or rather I want your authority to stop it—all of you.'

'What about Abana and Pharpar,* Padre—Harrison and Craye? They are Mr. Prout's pets,' said M'Turk a little bitterly. 'We aren't even sub-prefects.'

'I've considered that, but, on the other hand, since most bullying is mere thoughtlessness——'

'Not one little bit of it, Padre,' said M'Turk. 'Bullies like bullyin'. They mean it. They think it up in lesson and practise it in the quarters.'

'Never mind. If the thing goes up to the prefects it may make another House-row. You've had one already. Don't laugh. Listen to me. I ask you—my own Tenth Legion*—to take the thing up quietly. I want little Clewer made fairly clean and decent——'

'Blowed if *I* wash him!' whispered Stalky.

'Decent and self-respecting. As for the other boy, whoever he is, you can use your influence'—a purely secular light flickered in the chaplain's eye—'in any way you please to—to dissuade him. That's all. I'll leave it to you. Good-night, *mes enfants.*'

* * * * *

'Well, what are we goin' to do?' Number Five stared at each other.

'Young Clewer would give his eyes for a place to be quiet in. *I* know that,' said Beetle. 'If we made him a study-fag, eh?'

'No!' said M'Turk firmly. 'He's a dirty little brute, and he'd mess up everything. Besides, we ain't goin' to have any beastly Erickin'. D'you want to walk about with your arm round his neck?'*

'He'd clean out the jam-pots, anyhow; an' the burnt-porridge saucepan—it's filthy now.'

'Not good enough,' said Stalky, bringing up both heels with a crash on the table. 'If we find the merry jester who's been bullyin' him an' make him happy, that'll be all right. Why didn't we spot him when we were in the form-rooms, though?'

'Maybe a lot of fags have made a dead set at Clewer. They do that sometimes.'

'Then we'll have to kick the whole of the lower school in our House—on spec. Come on,' said M'Turk.

'Keep your hair on! We mustn't make a fuss about the biznai. Whoever it is, he's kept quiet or we'd have seen him,' said Stalky. 'We'll walk round and sniff about till we're sure.'

They drew the House form-rooms, accounting for every junior and senior against whom they had suspicions—investigated, at Beetle's suggestion, the lavatories and box-rooms, but without result. Everybody seemed to be present save Clewer.

'Rum!' said Stalky, pausing outside a study door. 'Golly!'

A thin piping mixed with tears came muffled through the panels.

'As beautiful Kitty one morning was tripping—'*

'Louder, you young devil, or I'll buzz a book at you!'

       'With a pitcher of milk——'

Oh, Campbell, please don't!

           To the fair of——'

A book crashed on something soft, and squeals arose.

'Well, I never thought it was a study-chap, anyhow. That accounts for our not spotting him,' said Beetle. 'Sefton and Campbell are rather hefty chaps to tackle. Besides, one can't go into their study like a form-room.'

'What swine!' M'Turk listened. 'Where's the fun of it? I suppose Clewer's faggin' for them.'

'They aren't prefects. That's one good job,' said Stalky, with his war-grin. 'Sefton and Campbell! Um! Campbell and Sefton! Ah! One of 'em's a crammer's pup.'

The two were precocious hairy youths between seventeen and eighteen, sent to the school in despair by parents who hoped that six months' steady cram might, perhaps, jockey them into Sandhurst. Nominally they were in Mr. Prout's House; actually they were under the Head's eye; and since he was very careful never to promote strange new boys to prefectship, they considered they had a grievance against the school. Sefton had spent three months with a London crammer, and the tale of his adventures there lost nothing in the telling. Campbell, who had a fine taste in clothes and a fluent vocabulary, followed his lead in looking down loftily on the rest of the world. This was only their second term, and the school, used to what it profanely called 'crammers' pups,' had treated them with rather galling reserve. But their whiskers—Sefton owned a real razor—and their moustaches were beyond question impressive.

'Shall we go in an' dissuade 'em?' M'Turk asked. 'I've never had much to do with 'em, but I'll bet my hat Campbell's a funk.'

'No—o! That's *oratio directa*,' said Stalky, shaking his head. 'I like *oratio obliqua*.* 'Sides, where'd our moral influence be then? Think o' that!'

'Rot! What are you goin' to do?' Beetle turned into Lower Number Nine form-room, next door to the study.

'Me?' The lights of war flickered over Stalky's face. 'Oh, I want to jape with 'em. Shut up a bit!'

He drove his hands into his pockets and stared out of window at the sea, whistling between his teeth. Then a foot tapped the floor; one shoulder lifted; he wheeled, and began the short quick double-shuffle—the war-dance of Stalky in meditation. Thrice he crossed the empty form-room, with compressed lips and expanded nostrils, swaying to the quick-step. Then he halted before the dumb Beetle and softly knuckled his head, Beetle bowing to the strokes. M'Turk nursed one knee and rocked to and fro. They could hear Clewer howling as though his heart would break.

'Beetle is the sacrifice,' Stalky said at last. 'I'm sorry for you, Beetle. 'Member Galton's *Art of Travel** [one of the forms had been studying that pleasant work] an' the kid whose bleatin' excited the tiger?'

'Oh, curse!' said Beetle uneasily. It was not his first season as a sacrifice. 'Can't you get on without me?'

"Fraid not, Beetle, dear. You've got to be bullied by Turkey an' me. The more you howl, o' course, the better it'll be. Turkey, go an' covet a stump and a box-rope for somewhere. We'll tie him up for a kill—*à la* Galton. 'Member when "Molly" Fairburn made us cock-fight with our shoes off, an' tied up our knees?'

'But that hurt like sin.'

"Course it did. What a clever chap you are, Beetle! Turkey 'll knock you all over the place. 'Member we've had a big row all round, an' I've trapped you into doin' this. Lend us your wipe.'*

Beetle was trussed for cock-fighting; but, in addition to the transverse stump between elbow and knee, his knees were bound with a box-rope. In this posture, at a push from Stalky he rolled over sideways, covering himself with dust.

'Ruffle his hair, Turkey. Now you get down, too. "The bleatin' of the kid excites the tiger." You two are in such a sweatin' wax with me that you only curse. 'Member that. I'll tickle you up with a stump. You'll have to blub, Beetle.'

'Right O! I'll work up to it in half a shake.' said Beetle.

'Now begin—and remember the bleatin' o' the kid.'

'Shut up, you brutes! Let me up! You've nearly cut my knees off. Oh, you *are* beastly cads! Do shut up. 'Tisn't a joke!' Beetle's protest was, in tone, a work of art.

'Give it to him, Turkey! Kick him! Roll him over! Kill him! Don't funk, Beetle, you brute. Kick him again, Turkey.'

'He's not blubbin' really. Roll up, Beetle, or I'll kick you into the fender,' roared M'Turk.

They made a hideous noise among them, and the bait allured their quarry.

'Hullo. What's the giddy jest?' Sefton and Campbell entered to find Beetle on his side, his head against the fender, weeping copiously, while M'Turk prodded him in the back with his toes.

'It's only Beetle,' Stalky explained. 'He's shammin' hurt. I can't get Turkey to go for him properly.'

Sefton promptly kicked both boys, and his face lighted. 'All right, I'll attend to 'em. Get up an' cock-fight, you two. Give me the stump. I'll tickle 'em. Here's a giddy jest! Come on, Campbell. Let's cook 'em.'

Then M'Turk turned on Stalky and called him very evil names.

'You said you were goin' to cock-fight too, Stalky. Come on!'

'More ass you for believin' me, then!' shrieked Stalky.

'Have you chaps had a row?' said Campbell.

'Row?' said Stalky. 'Huh! I'm only educatin' them. D'you know anythin' about cock-fighting, Seffy?'

'Do I know? Why, at Maclagan's, where I was crammin' in town, we used to cock-fight in his drawing-room, and little Maclagan daren't say anything. But we were just the same as men there, of course. Do I know? I'll show you.'

'Can't I get up?' moaned Beetle, as Stalky sat on his shoulder.

'Don't jaw, you fat piffler. You're going to fight Seffy.'

'He'll slay me!'

'Oh, lug 'em into our study,' said Campbell. 'It's nice an' quiet in there. I'll cock-fight Turkey. This is an improvement on young Clewer.'

'Right O! I move it's shoes-off for them an' shoes-on for us,'

said Sefton joyously, and the two were flung down on the
study floor. Stalky rolled them behind an arm-chair.

'Now I'll tie you two up an' direct the bull-fight. Golly,
what wrists you have, Seffy. They're too thick for a wipe; got
a box-rope?' said he.

'Lots in the corner,' Sefton replied. 'Hurry up! Stop
blubbin', you brute, Beetle. We're goin' to have a giddy
campaign. Losers have to sing for the winners—sing odes in
honour of the conqueror. You call yourself a beastly poet,
don't you, Beetle? I'll poet you.' He wriggled into position by
Campbell's side.

Swiftly and scientifically the stumps were thrust through
the natural crooks, and the wrists tied with well stretched box-
ropes to an accompaniment of insults from M'Turk, bound,
betrayed, and voluble behind the chair.

Stalky set away Campbell and Sefton, and strode over to his
allies, locking the door on the way.

'And that's all right,' said he in a changed voice.

'What the devil——?' Sefton began. Beetle's false tears had
ceased; M'Turk, smiling, was on his feet. Together they
bound the knees and ankles of the enemy even more straitly.

Stalky took the arm-chair and contemplated the scene with
his blandest smile. The man trussed for cock-fighting is,
perhaps, the most helpless thing in the world.

' "The bleatin' of the kid excited the tiger." Oh, you
frabjous asses!' He lay back and laughed till he could no more.
The victims took in the situation but slowly.

'We'll give you the finest lickin' you ever had in your young
lives when we get up!' thundered Sefton from the floor.
'You'll laugh the other side of your mouth before you've done.
What the deuce d'you mean by this?'

'You'll see in two shakes,' said M'Turk. 'Don't swear like
that. What we want to know is, why you two hulkin' swine
have been bullyin' Clewer?'

'It's none of your business.'

'What did you bully Clewer for?' The question was repeated
with maddening iteration by each in turn. They knew their work.

'Because we jolly well chose,' was the answer at last. 'Let's
get up.' Even then they could not realise the game.

'Well, now we're goin' to bully you because we jolly well choose. We're goin' to be just as fair to you as you were to Clewer. He couldn't do anything against you. You can't do anything to us. Odd, ain't it?'

'Can't we? You wait an' see.'

'Ah,' said Beetle reflectively, 'that shows you've never been properly jested with. A public lickin' ain't in it with a gentle jape. Bet a bob you'll weep an' promise anything.'

'Look here, young Beetle, we'll half kill you when we get up. I'll promise you that, at any rate.'

'You're going to be half killed first, though. Did you give Clewer Head-knuckles?'

'Did you give Clewer Head-knuckles?' M'Turk echoed. At the twentieth repetition—no boy can stand the torture of one unvarying query, which is the essence of bullying—came confession.

'We did, confound you!'

'Then you'll be knuckled'; and knuckled they were, according to ancient experience. Head-knuckling is no trifle; 'Molly' Fairburn of the old days could not have done better.

'Did you give Clewer Brush-drill?'

This time the question was answered sooner, and Brush-drill was dealt out for the space of five minutes by Stalky's watch. They could not even writhe in their bonds. No brush is employed in Brush-drill.

'Did you give Clewer the Key?'

'No; we didn't. I swear we didn't!' from Campbell, rolling in agony.

'Then we'll give it to you, so you can see what it would be like if you had.'

The torture of the Key—which has no key at all—hurts excessively. They endured several minutes of it, and their language necessitated the gag.

'Did you give Clewer Corkscrews?'

'Yes. Oh, curse your silly souls! Let us alone, you cads.'

They were corkscrewed, and the torture of the Corkscrew—this has nothing to do with corkscrews—is keener than the torture of the Key.

The method and silence of the attacks was breaking their

nerves. Between each new torture came the pitiless, dazing rain of questions, and when they did not answer to the point, Isabella-coloured* handkerchiefs were thrust into their mouths.

'Now are those all the things you did to Clewer? Take out the gag, Turkey, and let 'em answer.'

'Yes, I swear that was all. Oh, you're killing us, Stalky!' cried Campbell.

'Pre-cisely what Clewer said to you. I heard him. Now we're goin' to show you what real bullyin' is. What I don't like about you, Sefton, is, you come to the Coll. with your stick-up collars an' patent-leather boots, an' you think you can teach us something about bullying. *Do* you think you can teach us anything about bullying? Take out the gag and let him answer.'

'No!'—ferociously.

'He says no. Rock him to sleep. Campbell can watch.'

It needs three boys and two boxing-gloves to rock a boy to sleep. Again the operation has nothing to do with its name. Sefton was 'rocked' till his eyes set in his head and he gasped and crowed for breath, sick and dizzy.

'My Aunt!' said Campbell, appalled, from his corner, and turned white.

'Put him away,' said Stalky. 'Bring on Campbell. Now this *is* bullyin'. Oh, I forgot! I say, Campbell, what did you bully Clewer for? Take out his gag and let him answer.'

'I—I don't know. Oh, let me off! I swear I'll make it *pax*. Don't "rock" me!'

' "The bleatin' of the kid excites the tiger." He says he don't know. Set him up, Beetle. Give me the glove an' put in the gag.'

In silence Campbell was 'rocked' sixty-four times.

'I believe I'm goin' to die!' he gasped.

'He says he is goin' to die. Put him away. Now, Sefton! Oh, I forgot! Sefton, what did you bully Clewer for?'

The answer is unprintable; but it brought not the faintest flush to Stalky's downy cheek.

'Make him an Ag Ag, Turkey!'

And an Ag Ag was he made, forthwith. The hard-bought

experience of nearly eighteen years was at his disposal, but he did not seem to appreciate it.

'He says we are sweeps. Put him away! Now, Campbell! Oh, I forgot! I say, Campbell, what did you bully Clewer for?'

Then came the tears—scalding tears; appeals for mercy and abject promises of peace. Let them cease the tortures and Campbell would never lift hand against them. The questions began again—to an accompaniment of keen persuasions.

'You seem hurt, Campbell. Are you hurt?'

'Yes. Awfully!'

'He says he is hurt. Are you broke?'

'Yes, yes! I swear I am. Oh, stop!'

'He says he is broke. Are you humble?'

'Yes!'

'He says he is humble. Are you devilish humble?'

'Yes!'

'He says he is devilish humble. Will you bully Clewer any more?'

'No. No—ooh!'

'He says he won't bully Clewer. Or any one else?'

'No. I swear I won't!'

'Or any one else. What about the lickin' you and Sefton were goin' to give us?'

'I won't! I won't! I swear I won't!'

'He says he won't lick us. Do you esteem yourself to know anything about bullyin'?'

'No, I don't!'

'He says he doesn't know anything about bullyin'. Haven't we taught you a lot?'

'Yes—yes!'

'He says we've taught him a lot. Aren't you grateful?'

'Yes!'

'He says he is grateful. Put him away. Oh, I forgot! I say, Campbell, what did you bully Clewer for?'

He wept anew; his nerves being raw. 'Because I was a bully. I suppose that's what you want me to say?'

'He says he is a bully. Right he is. Put him in the corner. No more japes for Campbell. Now, Sefton!'

'You devils! You young devils!' This and much more as Sefton was punted across the carpet by skilful knees.

' "The bleatin' of the kid excites the tiger." We're goin' to make you beautiful. Where does he keep his shaving-things? [Campbell told.] Beetle, get some water. Turkey, make the lather. We're goin' to shave you, Seffy, so you'd better lie jolly still, or you'll get cut. I've never shaved any one before.'

'Don't! Oh, don't! Please don't!

'Gettin' polite, eh? I'm only goin' to take off one ducky little whisker——'

'I'll—I'll make it *pax*, if you don't. I swear I'll let you off your lickin' when I get up!'

'And half that moustache we're so proud of. He says he'll let us off our lickin'. Isn't he kind?'

M'Turk laughed into the nickel-plated shaving-cup, and settled Sefton's head between Stalky's vice-like knees.

'Hold on a shake,' said Beetle, 'you can't shave long hairs. You've got to cut all that moustache short first, an' then scrope him.'

'Well, I'm not goin' to hunt about for scissors. Won't a match do? Chuck us the match-box. He is a hog, you know; we might as well singe him. Lie still!'

He lit a vesta, but checked his hand. 'I only want to take off half, though.'

'That's all right.' Beetle waved the brush. 'I'll lather up to the middle—see? and you can burn off the rest.'

The thin-haired first moustache of youth fluffed off in flame to the lather-line in the centre of the lip, and Stalky rubbed away the burnt stumpage with his thumb. It was not a very gentle shave, but it abundantly accomplished its purpose.

'Now the whisker on the other side. Turn him over!' Between match and razor this, too, was removed. 'Give him his shaving-glass. Take the gag out. I want to hear what he'll say.'

But there were no words. Sefton gazed at the lop-sided wreck in horror and despair. Two fat tears rolled down his cheek.

'Oh, I forgot! I say, Sefton, what did you bully Clewer for?'

'Leave me alone! Oh, you infernal bullies, leave me alone! Haven't I had enough!'

'He says we must leave him alone,' said M'Turk.

'He says we are bullies, an' we haven't even begun yet,' said Beetle. 'You're ungrateful, Seffy. Golly! You do look an atrocity and a half!'

'He says he has had enough,' said Stalky. 'He errs!'

'Well, to work, to work!' chanted M'Turk, waving a stump. 'Come on, my giddy Narcissus. Don't fall in love with your own reflection!'*

'Oh, let him off,' said Campbell from his corner; 'he's blubbing, too.'

Sefton cried like a twelve-year-old with pain, shame, wounded vanity, and utter helplessness.

'You'll make it *pax*, Sefton, won't you? You can't stand up to those young devils——'

'Don't be rude, Campbell, de-ah,' said M'Turk, 'or you'll catch it again!'

'You *are* devils, you know,' said Campbell.

'What? for a little bullyin'—same as you've been givin' Clewer! How long have you been jestin' with him?' said Stalky. 'All this term?'

'We didn't always knock him about, though!'

'You did when you could catch him,' said Beetle, cross-legged on the floor, dropping a stump from time to time across Sefton's instep. 'Don't I know it!'

'I—perhaps we did.'

'And you went out of your way to catch him? Don't I know it! Because he was an awful little beast, eh? Don't I know it! Now, you see *you*'re awful beasts, and you're gettin' what he got—for bein' a beast. Just because we choose.'

'We never really bullied him—like you've done us.'

'Yah!' said Beetle. 'They never really bully—"Molly" Fairburn didn't. Only knock 'em about a little bit. That's what they say. Only kick their souls out of 'em, and they go and blub in the box-rooms. Shove their heads into the ulsters an' blub. Write home three times a day—yes, you brute, I've done that—askin' to be taken away. You've never been bullied properly, Campbell. I'm sorry you made *pax*.'

'I'm not!' said Campbell, who was a humorist in a way. 'Look out, you're slaying Sefton!'

In his excitement Beetle had used the stump unreflectingly, and Sefton was now shouting for mercy.

'An' you!' he cried, wheeling where he sat. 'You've never been bullied, either. Where were you before you came here?'

'I—I had a tutor.'

'Yah! You would. You never blubbed in your life. But you're blubbin' now, by gum. Aren't you blubbin'?'

'Can't you see, you blind beast?' Sefton fell over sideways, tear-tracks furrowing the dried lather. Crack came the cricket-stump on the curved latter-end of him.

'Blind, am I,' said Beetle, 'and a beast? Shut up, Stalky. I'm goin' to jape a bit with our friend, à la "Molly" Fairburn. *I* think I can see. Can't I see, Sefton?'

'The point is well taken,' said M'Turk, watching the stump at work. 'You'd better say that he sees, Seffy.'

'You do—you can! I swear you do!' yelled Sefton, for strong arguments were coercing him.

'Aren't my eyes lovely?' The stump rose and fell steadily throughout this catechism.

'Yes.'

'A gentle hazel, aren't they?'

'Yes—oh yes!'

'What a liar you are! They're sky-blue. Ain't they sky-blue?'

'Yes—oh yes!'

'You don't know your mind from one minute to another. You must learn—you must learn.'

'What a bait you're in!' said Stalky. 'Keep your hair on, Beetle.'

'I've had it done to me,' said Beetle. 'Now—about my being a beast.'

'*Pax*—oh, *pax!** cried Sefton; 'make it *pax*. I'll give up! Let me off! I'm broke! I can't stand it!'

'Ugh! Just when we were gettin' our hand in!' grunted M'Turk. 'They didn't let Clewer off, I'll swear.'

'Confess—apologise—quick!' said Stalky.

From the floor Sefton made unconditional surrender, more abjectly even than Campbell. He would never touch any one again. He would go softly all the days of his life.

'We've got to take it, I suppose?' said Stalky. 'All right,

Sefton. You're broke? Very good. Shut up, Beetle! But before we let you up, you an' Campbell will kindly oblige us with "Kitty of Coleraine"—à la Clewer.'

'That's not fair,' said Campbell; 'we've surrendered.'

''Course you have. Now you're goin' to do what we tell you—same as Clewer would. If you hadn't surrendered you'd ha' been really bullied. Havin' surrendered—do you follow, Seffy?—you sing odes in honour of the conquerors. Hurry up!'

They dropped into chairs luxuriously. Campbell and Sefton looked at each other, and, neither taking comfort from that view, struck up 'Kitty of Coleraine.'

'Vile bad,' said Stalky, as the miserable wailing ended. 'If you hadn't surrendered it would have been our painful duty to buzz books at you for singin' out o' tune. Now then.'

He freed them from their bonds, but for several minutes they could not rise. Campbell was first on his feet, smiling uneasily. Sefton staggered to the table, buried his head in his arms, and shook with sobs. There was no shadow of fight in either—only amazement, distress, and shame.

'Ca—can't he shave clean before tea, please?' said Campbell. 'It's ten minutes to bell.'

Stalky shook his head. He meant to escort the half-shaved one to that meal.

M'Turk yawned in his chair and Beetle mopped his face. They were all dripping with excitement and exertion.

'If I knew anything about it, I swear I'd give you a moral lecture,' said Stalky severely.

'Don't jaw; they've surrendered,' said M'Turk.

'This moral suasion biznai takes it out of a chap.'

'Don't you see how gentle we've been? We might have called Clewer in to look at you,' said Stalky. 'The bleatin' of the tiger excites the kid. But we didn't. We've only got to tell a few chaps in Coll. about this and you'd be hooted all over the shop. Your life wouldn't be worth havin'. But we aren't goin' to do that, either. We're strictly moral suasers, Campbell; so, unless you or Seffy split about this, no one will.'

'I swear you're a brick,' said Campbell. 'I suppose I was rather a brute to Clewer,'

'It looked like it,' said Stalky. 'But I don't think Seffy need come into hall with cock-eye whiskers. Horrid bad for the fags if they saw him. He can shave. Ain't you grateful, Sefton?'

The head did not lift. Sefton was deeply asleep.

'That's rummy,' said M'Turk, as a snore mixed with a sob. "Cheek, *I* think; or else he's shammin'.'

'No, 'tisn't,' said Beetle. 'When "Molly" Fairburn had attended to me for an hour or so I used to go bung off to sleep on a form sometimes. Poor devil! But he called me a beastly poet, though.'

'Well, come on.' Stalky lowered his voice. 'Good-bye, Campbell. 'Member, if you don't talk, nobody will.'

There should have been a war-dance, but that all three were so utterly tired that they almost went to sleep above the tea-cups in their study, and slept till prep.

*   *   *   *   *

'A most extraordinary letter. Are *all* parents incurably mad? What do you make of it?' said the Head, handing a closely-written eight pages to the Reverend John.

' "The only son of his mother, and she a widow."* That is the least reasonable sort.' The chaplain read with pursed lips.

'If half those charges are true he should be in the sick-house; whereas he is disgustingly well. Certainly he has shaved. I noticed that.'

'Under compulsion, as his mother points out. How delicious! How salutary!'

'You haven't to answer her. It isn't often I don't know what has happened in Coll.; but this is beyond me.'

'If you asked me I should say seek not to propitiate. When one is forced to take crammers' pups——'

'He was perfectly well at extra-tuition—with me—this morning,' said the Head absently. 'Unusually well-behaved, too.'

'——they either educate the school, or the school, as in this case, educates them. I prefer our own methods,' the chaplain concluded.

'You think it was that?' A lift of the Head's eyebrow.

'I'm sure of it! And nothing excuses his trying to give the
Coll. a bad name.'

'That's the line I mean to take with him,' the Head
answered.

The Augurs* winked.

*   *   *   *   *

A few days later the Reverend John called on Number Five.
'Why haven't we seen you before, Padre?' said they.

'I've been watching times and seasons and events and
men—and boys,' he replied. 'I am pleased with my Tenth
Legion. I make them my compliments. Clewer was throwing
ink-balls in form this morning, instead of doing his work. He
is now doing fifty lines for—unheard-of audacity.'

'You can't blame us, sir,' said Beetle. 'You told us to remove
the—er—pressure. That's the worst of a fag.'

'I've known boys five years his senior throw ink-balls,
Beetle. To such an one have I given two hundred lines—not
so long ago. And now I come to think of it, were those lines
ever shown up?'

'Were they, Turkey?' said Beetle unblushingly.

'Don't you think Clewer looks a little cleaner, Padre?'
Stalky interrupted.

'We're no end of moral reformers,' said M'Turk.

'It was all Stalky, but it was a lark,' said Beetle.

'I have noticed the moral reform in several quarters. Didn't
I tell you you had more influence than any boys in the Coll.
if you cared to use it?'

'It's a trifle exhaustin' to use frequent—our kind of moral
suasion. Besides, you see, it only makes Clewer cheeky.'

'I wasn't thinking of Clewer; I was thinking of—the other
people, Stalky.'

'Oh, we didn't bother much about the other people,' said
M'Turk. 'Did we?'

'But I did—from the beginning.'

'Then you knew, sir?'

A downward puff of smoke.

'Boys educate each other, they say, more than we can or

dare. If I had used one half of the moral suasion you may or may not have employed——'

'With the best motives in the world. Don't forget our pious motives, Padre,' said M'Turk.

'I suppose I should be now languishing in Bideford jail, shouldn't I? Well, to quote the Head, in a little business which we have agreed to forget, that strikes me as flagrant injustice. ... What are you laughing at, you young sinners? Isn't it true? I will not stay to be shouted at. What I looked into this den of iniquity for was to find out if any one cared to come down for a bathe off the Ridge. But I see you won't.'

'Won't we, though! Half a shake, Padre Sahib, till we get our towels, and *nous sommes avec vous!*'

TO THE COMPANIONS

HORACE, Ode 17, Bk. V.

HOW comes it that, at even-tide,
　　When level beams should show most truth,
Man, failing, takes unfailing pride
　　In memories of his frolic youth?

Venus and Liber* fill their hour;
　　The games engage, the law-courts prove;
Till hardened life breeds love of power
　　Or Avarice, Age's final love.

Yet at the end, these comfort not—
　　Nor any triumph Fate decrees—
Compared with glorious, unforgot-
　　ten innocent enormities

Of frontless days before the beard,
　　When, instant on the casual jest,
The God Himself of Mirth appeared
　　And snatched us to His heaving breast.

And we—not caring who He was
　　But certain He would come again—
Accepted all He brought to pass
　　As Gods accept the lives of men . . .

Then He withdrew from sight and speech,
　　Nor left a shrine. How comes it now
While Charon's* keel grates on the beach,
　　He calls so clear: 'Rememberest thou?'

The United Idolaters

HIS name was Brownell and his reign was brief. He came from the Central Anglican Scholastic Agency, a soured, clever, reddish man picked up by the Head at the very last moment of the summer holidays in default of Macrea (of Macrea's House) who wired from Switzerland that he had smashed a knee mountaineering, and would not be available that term.

Looking back at the affair, one sees that the Head should have warned Mr. Brownell of the College's outstanding peculiarity, instead of leaving him to discover it for himself the first day of the term, when he went for a walk to the beach, and saw 'Potiphar' Mullins, Head of Games, smoking without conceal on the sands. 'Pot,' having the whole of the Autumn Football challenges, acceptances, and Fifteen reconstructions to work out, did not as first comprehend Mr. Brownell's shrill cry of: 'You're smoking! You're smoking, sir!' but he removed his pipe, and answered, placably enough: 'The Army Class is allowed to smoke, sir.'

Mr. Brownell replied: 'Preposterous!'

Pot, seeing that this new person was uninformed, suggested that he should refer to the Head.

'You may be sure I shall—sure I shall, sir! Then we shall see!'

Mr. Brownell and his umbrella scudded off, and Pot returned to his match-plannings. Anon, he observed, much as the Almighty might observe black-beetles, two small figures coming over the Pebble Ridge a few hundred yards to his right. They were a Major and his Minor,* the latter a new boy and, as such, entitled to his brother's countenance for exactly three days—after which he would fend for himself. Pot waited till they were well out on the great stretch of mother-o'-pearl sands; then caused his ground-ash to describe a magnificent whirl of command in the air.

'Come on,' said the Major. 'Run!'

'What for?' said the Minor, who had noticed nothing.

''Cause we're wanted. Leg it!'

'Oh, I can do *that*,' the Minor replied and, at the end of the sprint, fetched up a couple of yards ahead of his brother, and much less winded.

''Your Minor?' said Pot, looking over them, seawards.

'Yes, Mullins,' the Major replied.

'All right. Cut along!' They cut on the word.

'Hi! Fludd Major! Come back!'

Back fled the elder.

'Your wind's bad. Too fat. You grunt like a pig. 'Mustn't do it! Understand? Go away!'

'What was all that for?' the Minor asked on the Major's return.

'To see if we could run, you fool!'

'Well, I ran faster than you, anyhow,' was the scandalous retort.

'Look here, Har—Minor,* if you go on talking like this, you'll get yourself kicked all round Coll. An' you mustn't stand like you did when a prefect's talkin' to you.'

The Minor's eyes opened with awe. 'I thought it was only one of the masters,' said he.

'Masters! It was Mullins—Head o' Games. You *are* a putrid young ass!'

By what seemed pure chance, Mr. Brownell ran into the school chaplain, the Reverend John Gillett, beating up against the soft, September rain that no native ever troubled to wear a coat for.

'I was trying to catch you after lunch,' the latter began. 'I wanted to show you our objects of local interest.'

'Thank you! I've seen all *I* want,' Mr. Brownell answered. 'Gillett, *is* there anything about me which suggests the Congenital Dupe?'

'It's early to say, yet,' the chaplain answered. 'Who've you been meeting?'

'A youth called Mullins, I believe.' And, indeed, there was Potiphar, ground-ash, pipe, and all, quarter-decking* serenely below the Pebble Ridge.

'Oh! I see. Old Pot—our Head of Games.'

'He was smoking. He's smoking *now*! Before those two little boys, too!' Mr. Brownell panted. 'He had the audacity to tell me that——'

'Yes,' the Reverend John cut in. 'The Army Class is allowed to smoke—not in their studies, of course, but within limits, out of doors. You see we have to compete against the crammers' establishments, where smoking's usual.'

This was true! Of the only school in England was this the cold truth, and for the reason given, in that unprogressive age!

'Good Heavens!' said Mr. Brownell to the gulls and the gray sea. 'And I was never warned!'

'The Head *is* a little forgetful. *I* ought to have—— But it's all right,' the chaplain added soothingly. 'Pot won't—er—give you away.'

Mr. Brownell, who knew what smoking led to, testified out of his twelve years' experience of what he called the Animal Boy. He left little unexplored or unexplained.

'There may be something in what you say,' the Reverend John assented. 'But as a matter of fact, their actual smoking doesn't amount to much. They talk a great deal about their brands of tobacco. Practically, it makes them rather keen on putting down smoking among the juniors—as an encroachment on their privilege, you see. They lick 'em twice as hard for it as *we'd* dare to.'

'Lick?' Mr. Brownell cried. 'One expels! One expels! *I* know the end of these practices.' He told his companion, in detail, with anecdotes and inferences, a great deal more about the Animal Boy.

'Ah!' said the Reverend John to himself. 'You'll leave at the end of the term; but you'll have a deuce of a time first.' Aloud: 'We-ell, I suppose no one can be sure of any school's tendency at any given moment, but, personally, I should incline to believe that we're reasonably free from the—er—monastic microbes of—er—older institutions.'

'But a school's a school. You can't get out of *that*! It's preposterous! You must admit *that*,' Mr. Brownell insisted.

They were within hail of Pot by now, and the Reverend John asked him how Affairs of State stood.

'All right, thank you, sir. How are you, sir?'

'Loungin' round and sufferin',* my son. What about the dates for the Exeter and Tiverton matches?'

'As late in the term as we can get 'em, don't you think, sir?'

'Quite! Specially Blundell's.* They're our dearest foe,' he explained to the frozen Mr. Brownell. 'Aren't we rather light in the scrum just now, Mullins?'

"Fraid so, sir: but Packman's playin' forward this term.'

'*At* last!' cried the Reverend John. (Packman was Pot's second-in-command, who considered himself a heaven-born half-back, but Pot had been working on him diplomatically.) 'He'll be a pillar, at any rate. Lend me one of your fuzees, please. I've only got matches.'

Mr. Brownell was unused to this sort of talk. 'A bad beginning to a bad business,' he muttered as they returned to College.

Pot finished out his meditations; from time to time rubbing up the gloss on his new seven-and-sixpenny silver-mounted, rather hot, myall-wood* pipe, with its very thin crust in the bowl.

As the Studies brought back brackets and pictures for their walls, so did they bring odds and ends of speech—theatre, opera, and music-hall gags—from the great holiday world; some of which stuck for a term, and others were discarded. Number Five was unpacking, when Dick Four (King's House) of the red nose and dramatic instincts, who with Pussy and Tertius inhabited the study below, loafed up and asked them 'how their symptoms seemed to segashuate.'* They said nothing at the time, for they knew Dick had a giddy naval uncle who took him to the Pavilion and the Cri,* and all would be explained later. But, before they met again, Beetle came across two fags at war in a box-room, one of whom cried to the other: 'Turn me loose, or I'll knock the natal stuffin' out of you.'* Beetle demanded why he, being offal, presumed to use this strange speech. The fag said it came out of a new book about rabbits and foxes and turtles and niggers, which was in his locker. (*Uncle Remus* was a popular holiday gift-book in Shotover's* year: when Cetewayo* lived in Melbury Road, Arabi Pasha* in Egypt, and Spofforth* on the Oval.) Beetle had it out and read for some time, standing by the window, ere he carried it off to Number Five and began at once to give a wonderful story of a Tar Baby. Stalky tore it from him because he sputtered incoherently; M'Turk, for the same cause, wrenching it from Stalky. There was no prep. that night. The book was amazing, and full of quotations that one could hurl like javelins. When they came down to prayers, Stalky, to show he was abreast of the latest movement, pounded on the door of Dick Four's study shouting a couplet that pleased him:

> 'Ti-yi! Tungalee!
> I eat um pea! I pick um pea!'*

Upon which Dick Four, hornpiping and squinting, and not at all unlike a bull-frog, came out and answered from the bottom of his belly, whence he could produce incredible noises:

> 'Ingle-go-jang, my joy, my joy!
> Ingle-go-jang, my joy!
> I'm right at home, my joy, my joy!——'*

The chants' seemed to answer the ends of their being created for the moment. They all sang them the whole way up the corridor, and, after prayers, bore the burdens dispersedly to their several dormitories where they found many who knew the book of the words, but who, boylike, had waited for a lead ere giving tongue. In a short time the College was as severely infected with *Uncle Remus* as it had been with *Pinafore* and *Patience*.* King realised it specially because he was running Macrea's House in addition to his own and, Dick Four said, was telling his new charges what he thought of his 'esteemed colleague's' methods of House-control.

The Reverend John was talking to the Head in the latter's study, perhaps a fortnight later.

'If you'd only wired *me*,' he said. 'I could have dug up something that might have tided us over. This man's dangerous.'

'*Mea culpa!*'* the Head replied. 'I had so much on hand. Our Governing Council alone—— But what do *We** make of him?'

'Trust Youth! *We* call him "Mister."'

' "Mister Brownell"?'

'Just "Mister." It took *Us* three days to plumb his soul.'

'And he doesn't approve of Our institutions? You say he is On the Track—eh? He suspects the worst?'*

The school chaplain nodded.

'We-ell. *I* should say that that was the one tendency we had *not* developed. Setting aside we haven't even a curtain in a dormitory, let alone a lock to any form-room door—there has to be tradition in these things.'

'So I believe. So, indeed, one knows. And—'tisn't as if I ever preached on personal purity either.'

The Head laughed. 'No, or you'd join Brownell at term-end. By the way, what's this new line of Patristic discourse you're giving us in church? I found myself listening to some of it last Sunday.'

'Oh! My Early Christianity sermons? I bought a dozen ready made in Town just before I came down. Some one who knows his Gibbon must have done 'em. Aren't they good?' The Reverend John, who was no hand at written work, beamed self-approvingly. There was a knock and Pot entered.

The weather had defeated him, at last. All footer-grounds, he reported, were unplayable, and must be rested. His idea, to keep things going, was Big and Little Side Paper-chases thrice a week. For the juniors, a shortish course on the Burrows, which he intended to oversee personally the first few times, while Packman lunged Big Side across the inland and upland ploughs, for proper sweats. There was some question of bounds that he asked authority to vary; and, would the Head please say which afternoons would interfere least with the Army Class, Extra Tuition.

As to bounds, the Head left those, as usual, entirely to Pot. The Reverend John volunteered to shift one of his extra-tu. classes from four to five P.M. till after prayers—nine to ten. The whole question was settled in five minutes.

'*We* hate paper-chases, don't we, Pot?' the Headmaster asked as the Head of Games rose.

'Yes, sir, but it keeps 'em in training. Good night, sir.'

'To go back——' drawled the Head when the door was well

shut. 'No-o. I do *not* think so! . . . Ye-es! He'll leave at the end of the term . . . A-aah! How does it go? "Don't 'spute wid de squinch-owl. Jam de shovel in de fier."* Have you come across that extraordinary book, by the way?'

'Oh, yes. *We*'ve got it badly too. It has some sort of elemental appeal, I suppose.'

Here Mr. King came in with a neat little scheme for the reorganisation of certain details in Macrea's House, where he had detected reprehensible laxities. The Head sighed. The Reverend John only heard the beginnings of it. Then he slid out softly. He remembered he had not written to Macrea for quite a long time.

The first Big Side Paper-chase, in blinding wet, was as vile as even the groaning and bemired Beetle had prophesied. But Dick Four had managed to run his own line when it skirted Bideford, and turned up at the Lavatories half an hour late cherishing a movable tumour beneath his sweater.

'Ingle-go-jang!' he chanted, and slipped out a warm but coy land-tortoise.

'My Sacred Hat!' cried Stalky. 'Brer Terrapin! Where you catchee? What you makee-do *aveck*?'

This was Stalky's notion of how they talked in *Uncle Remus*; and he spake no other tongue for weeks.

'I don't know yet; but I had to get him. 'Man with a barrow full of 'em in Bridge Street. 'Gave me my choice for a bob. Leave him alone, you owl! He won't swim where you've been washing your filthy self! "*I*'m right at home, my joy, my joy."' Dick's nose shone like Bardolph's* as he bubbled in the bath.

Just before tea-time, he, Pussy, and Tertius broke in upon Number Five, processionally, singing:

> 'Ingle-go-jang, my joy, my joy!
> Ingle-go-jang, my joy!
> I'm right at home, my joy, my joy!
> Ingle-go-jang, my joy!'

Brer Terrapin, painted *or* and *sable**—King's House-colours—swung by a neatly contrived belly-band from the end of a broken jumping-pole. They thought rather well of taking him in to tea. They called at one or two studies on the way, and were warmly welcomed; but when they reached the still shut doors of the dining-hall (Richards, ex-Petty Officer, R.N.,* was always unpunctual—but they needn't have called him 'Stinking Jim'*) the whole school shouted approval. After the meal, Brer Terrapin was borne the round of the form-rooms from Number One to Number Twelve, in an unbroken roar of homage.

'To-morrow,' Dick Four announced, 'we'll sacrifice to him. Fags in blazin' paper-baskets!' and with thundering 'Ingle-go-jangs' the Idol retired to its shrine.

It had been a satisfactory performance. Little Hartopp, surprised labelling 'rocks' in Number Twelve, which held the Natural History Museum, had laughed consumedly; and the Reverend John, just before prep. complimented Dick that he had not a single dissenter to his following. In this respect that affair was an advance on Byzantium and Alexandria which, of course, were torn by rival sects led by militant Bishops or zealous heathen. *Vide*, (Beetle,) *Hypatia*,* and (if Dick Four ever listened, instead of privily swotting up his Euclid, in Church) the Reverend John's own sermons. Mr. King, who had heard the noise but had not appeared, made no comment till dinner, when he told the Common-room ceiling that he entertained the lowest opinion of Uncle Remus's buffoonery, but opined that it might interest certain types of intellect. Little Hartopp, School Librarian, who had, by special request, laid in an extra copy of the book, differed acridly. He had, he said, heard or overheard every salient line of *Uncle Remus* quoted, appositely too, by boys whom he would not have credited with intellectual interests. Mr. King repeated that he was wearied by the senseless and childish repetitions of immature minds. He recalled the *Patience* epidemic. Mr. Prout did not care for *Uncle Remus*—the dialect put him off— but he thought the Houses were getting a bit out of hand. There was nothing one could lay hold of, of course—'As yet,' Mr. Brownell interjected darkly. 'But this larking about in form-rooms,' he added, 'had potentialities which, if *he* knew anything of the Animal Boy, would develop—or had developed.'

'I shouldn't wonder,' said the Reverend John. 'This is the first time to my knowledge that Stalky has ever played second-fiddle to any one. Brer Terrapin was entirely Dick Four's notion. By the way, he was painted *your* House-colours, King.'

'Was he?' said King artlessly. 'I have always held that our Dickson Quartus had the rudiments of imagination. We will look into it—look into it.'

'In our loathsome calling, more things are done by judicious letting alone than by any other,' the Reverend John grunted.

'I can't subscribe to that,' said Mr. Prout. '*You* haven't a House,' and for once Mr. King backed Prout.

'Thank Heaven I haven't! Or I should be like you two. Leave 'em alone! Leave 'em alone! Haven't you ever seen puppies fighting over a slipper for hours?'

'Yes, but Gillett admits that Dickson Quartus was the only begetter* of this manifestation. I wasn't aware that the—er—Testacean had been tricked out in *my* colours,' said King.

And at that very hour, Number Five study—'prep.' thrown to the winds—were toiling inspiredly at a Tar Baby* made up of Beetle's sweater, and half-a-dozen lavatory-towels; a condemned cretonne curtain and, ditto, baize table-cloth for 'natal stuffin''; an ancient, but air-tight puntabout-ball for the head; all three play-box ropes for bindings; and most of Richards' weekly blacking-allowance for Prout's House's boots, to give tone to the whole.

'Gummy!' said Beetle when their curtain-pole had been taken down and Tar Baby hitched to the end of it by a loop in its voluptuous back. 'It looks pretty average indecent, somehow.'

'You can use it this way, too,' Turkey demonstrated, handling the curtain-pole like a flail. 'Now, shove it in the fireplace to dry an' we'll wash up.'

'But—but,' said Stalky, fascinated by the unspeakable front and behind of the black and bulging horror. 'How *come* he lookee so hellish?'

'Dead easy! If you do anything with your whole heart, Ruskin says, you always pull off something dam'-fine. Brer Terrapin's only a natural animal; but Tar Baby's Art,' M'Turk explained.

'I see! "If you're anxious for to shine in the high aesthetic line."* Well, Tar Baby's the filthiest thing *I*'ve ever seen in my life,' Stalky concluded. 'King'll be rabid.'

The United Idolaters set forth, side by side, at five o'clock next afternoon; Brer Terrapln, wlde awake, and swimming hard into nothing; Tar Baby lurching from side to side with a lascivious abandon that made Foxy, the school Sergeant, taking defaulters' drill in the corridor, squawk like an outraged hen. And when they ceremoniously saluted each other, like aristocratic heads on revolutionary pikes, it beat the previous day's performance out of sight and mind. The very fags, offered up, till the bottoms of the paper-baskets carried away, as heave-offerings* before them, fell over each other for the honour; and House by House, when the news spread, dropped its doings, and followed the Mysteries—not without song . . .

Some say it was a fag of Prout's who appealed for rescue from Brer Terrapin to Tar Baby; others, that the introits to the respective creeds ('Ingle-go-jang'—'Ti-yi-Tungalee!') carried in themselves the seeds of dissent. At any rate, the cleavage developed as swiftly as in a new religion, and by tea-time when they were fairly hoarse, the rolling world was rent to the death between Ingles *versus* Tungles, and Brer Terrapin had swept out Number Eleven form-room to the War-cry: 'Here I come a-bulgin' and a-bilin'.'* Prep. stopped further developments, but they agreed that, as a recreation for wet autumn evenings, the jape was unequalled, and called for its repetition on Saturday.

That was a brilliant evening, too. Both sides went into prayers practically re-dressing themselves. There was a smell of singed fag down the lines and a watery eye or so; but nothing to which the most fastidious could have objected. The Reverend John hinted something about roof-lifting noises.

'Oh, *no*, Padre Sahib. We were only billin' an' cooin' a bit,' Stalky explained. 'We haven't really begun. There's goin' to be a tug-o'-war next Saturday with Miss Meadows'* bed-cord——'

' "Which in dem days would ha' hilt a mule," ' the Reverend John quoted. 'Well, I've got to be impartial. I wish you both good luck.'

The week, with its three paper-chases, passed uneventfully, but for a certain amount of raiding and reprisals on new lines that might have warned them they were playing with fire. The juniors had learned to use the sacred war-chants as signals of distress; oppressed Ingles squealing for aid against oppressing Tungles, and *vice versa*; so that one never knew when a peaceful form-room would flare up in song and slaughter. But not a soul dreamed, for a moment, that that Saturday's jape would develop into—what it did! They were rigidly punctilious about the ritual; exquisitely careful as to the weights on Miss Meadows' bed-cord, kindly lent by Richards, who said he knew nothing about mules, but guaranteed it would hold a barge's crew; and if Dick Four chose to caparison himself as Archimandrite of Joppa, black as burned cork could make him, why, Stalky, in a nightgown kilted up beneath his sweater, was equally the Pope Symmachus,* just converted from heathendom but given to alarming relapses.

It began after tea—say 6.50 P.M. It got into its stride by 7.30 when Turkey, with pillows bound round the ends of forms, invented the Royal Battering-Ram Corps. It grew and—it grew till a quarter to nine when the prefects, most of whom had fought on one side or the other, thought it time to stop and went in with ground-ashes and the bare hand for ten minutes. . . .

Honours for the action were not awarded by the Head till Monday morning when he dealt out one dozen lickings to selected seniors, eight 'millies' (one thousand), fourteen 'usuals' (five hundred lines), minor impositions past count, and a stoppage of pocket-money on a scale and for a length of time unprecedented in modern history.

He said the College was within an ace of being burned to the ground when the gas-jet in Number Eleven form-room— where they tried to burn Tar Baby, fallen for the moment into the hands of the enemy—was wrenched off, and the lit gas spouted all over the ceiling till some one plugged the pipe with dormitory soap. He said that nothing save his consideration for their future careers kept him from expelling the wanton ruffians who had noosed all the decks in Number Twelve and swept them up in one crackling mound, barring a couple that had pitched-poled through the window. This, again, had been no man's design but the inspiration of necessity when Tar Baby's bodyguard, surrounded but defiant, was only rescued at the last minute by Turkey's immortal flank-attack with the battering-rams that carried away the door of Number Nine. He said that the same remarks applied to the fireplace and mantelpiece in Number Seven which everybody had seen fall out of the wall of their own motion after Brer Terrapin had hitched Miss Meadows' bed-cord to the bars of the grate.

He said much more, too; but as King pointed out in Common-room that evening, his canings were inept, he had *not* confiscated the Idols and, above all, had not castigated, as King would have castigated, the disgusting childishness of all concerned.

'Well,' said little Hartopp, 'I saw the prefects choking them off as we came into prayers. You've reason to reckon that in the scale of suffering.'

'And more than half the damage was done under *your* banner, King,' the Reverend John added.

'That doesn't affect my judgment; though, as a matter of fact, I believe Brer Terrapin triumphed over Tar Baby all along the line. Didn't he, Prout?'

'It didn't seem to me a fitting time to ask. The Tar Babies were handicapped of course, by not being able to—ah—tackle a live animal.'

'I confess,' Mr. Brownell volunteered, 'it was the studious perversity of certain aspects of the orgy which impressed *me*. And yet, what can one exp——'

'How do you mean?' King demanded. 'Dickson Quartus may be eccentric, but——'

'I was alluding to the vile and calculated indecency of that black doll.'

Mr. Brownell had passed Tar Baby going down to battle, all round and ripe, before Turkey had began to use it as Bishop Odo's* holy-water sprinkler.

'It is possible you didn't——'

'*I* never noticed anything,' said Prout. 'If there had been, I should have been the first——'

Here little Hartopp sniggered, which did not cool the air.

'Peradventure,' King began with due intake of the breath. 'Peradventure even *I* might have taken cognizance of the matter both for my own House's sake and for my colleague's . . . No! Folly I concede. Utter childishness and complete absence of discipline in *all* quarters, as the natural corollary to dabbling in so-called transatlantic humour, I frankly admit. But that there was anything esoterically obscene in the outbreak I absolutely deny.'

'They've been fighting for weeks over those things,' said Mr. Prout. ''Silly, of course, but I don't see how it can be dangerous.'

'Quite true. Any House-master of experience knows *that*, Brownell,' the Reverend John put in reprovingly.

'Given a normal basis of tradition and conduct—certainly,' Mr. Brownell answered. 'But with such amazing traditions as exist here, no man with any experience of the Animal Boy can draw your deceptive inferences. That's all *I* mean.'

Once again, and not for the first time, but with greater heat he testified what smoking led to—what, indeed, he was morally certain existed in full blast under their noses . . .

Gloves were off in three minutes. Pessimists, no more than poets, love each other and, even when they work together, it is one thing to pessimise congenially with an ancient and tried associate who is also a butt, and another to be pessimised over by an inexperienced junior, even though the latter's college career may have included more exhibitions—nay, even pot-huntings*—than one's own. The Reverend John did his best to pour water on the flames. Little Hartopp, perceiving that it was pure oil, threw in canfuls of his own, from the wings. In the end, words passed which would have made the Common-room uninhabitable for the future, but that Macrea had written (the Reverend John had seen the letter) saying that his knee was fairly re-knit and he was prepared to take on again at half-term. This happened to be the only date since the Creation beyond which Mr. Brownell's self-respect would not permit him to stay one hour. It solved the situation, amid puffings and blowings and bitter epigrams, and a most distinguished stateliness of bearing all round, till Mr. Brownell's departure.

'My dear fellow!' said the Reverend John to Macrea, on the first night of the latter's return. 'I *do* hope there was nothing in my letters to you—you asked me to keep you posted—that gave you any idea King wasn't doing his best with your House according to his lights?'

'Not in the least,' said Macrea. 'I've the greatest respect for King, but after all, one's House is one's House. One can't stand it being tinkered with by well-meaning outsiders.'

To Mr. Brownell on Bideford station-platform, the Reverend John's last words were:

'Well, well. You mustn't judge us too harshly. I dare say there's a great deal in what you say. Oh, Yes! King's conduct was inexcusable, absolutely inexcusable! About the smoking? Lamentable, but we must all bow down, more or less, in the House of Rimmon.* *We* have to compete with the Crammers' Shops.'

To the Head, in the silence of his study, next day: 'He didn't seem to me the kind of animal who'd keep to advantage in our atmosphere. Luckily he lost his temper (King and he are own brothers) and he couldn't withdraw his resignation.'

'Excellent. After all, it's only a few pounds to make up. I'll slip it in under our recent—er—barrack damages. And what do *We* think of it all, Gillett?'

'*We* do not think at all—any of us,' said the Reverend John. 'Youth is its own prophylactic, thank Heaven.'

And the Head, not usually devout,* echoed, 'Thank Heaven!'

'It was worth it,' Dick Four pronounced on review of the profit-and-loss account with Number Five in his study.

'Heap-plenty-*bong-assez*,' Stalky assented.

'But why didn't King ra'ar up an' cuss Tar Baby?' Beetle asked.

'You preter-pluperfect,* fat-ended fool!' Stalky began—

'Keep your hair on! We *all* know the Idolaters wasn't our Uncle Stalky's idea. But why didn't King—'

'Because Dick took care to paint Brer Terrapin King's House-colours. You can always conciliate King by soothin' his putrid *esprit-de-maisong*.* Ain't that true, Dick?'

Dick Four, with the smile of modest worth unmasked, said it was so.

'An' now,' Turkey yawned. 'King an' Macrea'll jaw for the rest of the term how he ran his House when Macrea was tryin' to marry fat widows in Switzerland. Mountaineerin'! 'Bet Macrea never went near a mountain.'

"One good job, though. I go back to Macrea for Maths. He *does* know something,' said Stalky.

'Why? Didn't "Mister" know anythin'?' Beetle asked.

"Bout as much as *you*,' was Stalky's reply.

'*I* don't go about pretending to. What was he like?'

' "Mister"? Oh, rather like King—King and water.'

Only water was not precisely the fluid that Stalky thought fit to mention.

THE CENTAURS

U P came the young Centaur-colts from the plains
    they were fathered in—
  Curious, awkward, afraid.
Burrs in their hocks and their tails, they were
    gathered in
  Mobs and run up to the yard to be made.

Starting and shying at straws, with sidlings and
    plungings,
  Buckings and whirlings and bolts;
Greener than grass, but full-ripe for their bridlings
    and lungings,
  Up to the yards and to Chiron* they bustled the
    colts . . .

First the light web and the cavesson; then the
    linked keys
  To jingle and turn on the tongue. Then, with
    cocked ears,
The hour of watching and envy, while comrades
    at ease
  Passaged and backed, making naught of these
    terrible gears

Next, over-pride and its price at the low-seeming
    fence,
  Too oft and too easily taken—the world-beheld
    fall!
And none in the yard except Chiron to doubt the
    immense,
  Irretrievable shame of it all! . . .

Last, the trained squadron, full-charge—the
    sound of a going
  Through dust and spun clods, and strong kicks,
    pelted home as they went,

And repaid at top-speed; till the order to halt
   without slowing
Brought every colt on his haunches—and
   Chiron content!

Regulus

Regulus, a Roman general, defeated the Carthaginians 256 B.C., but was next year defeated and taken prisoner by the Carthaginians, who sent him to Rome with an embassy to ask for peace or an exchange of prisoners. Regulus strongly advised the Roman Senate to make no terms with the enemy. He then returned to Carthage and was put to death.

THE Fifth Form had been dragged several times in its collective life, from one end of the school Horace to the other. Those were the years when Army examiners gave thousands of marks for Latin, and it was Mr. King's hated business to defeat them.

Hear him, then, on a raw November morning at second lesson.

'Aha!' he began, rubbing his hands. '*Cras ingens iterabimus aequor.** Our portion to-day is the Fifth Ode of the Third Book, I believe—concerning one Regulus, a gentleman. And how often have we been through it?'

'Twice, sir,' said Malpass, head of the Form.

Mr. King shuddered. 'Yes, twice, quite literally,' he said. 'To-day, with an eye to your Army *viva-voce* examinations— ugh!—I shall exact somewhat freer and more florid renditions. With feeling and comprehension if that be possible. I except'—here his eye swept the back benches—'our friend and companion Beetle, from whom, now as always, I demand an absolutely literal translation.' The form laughed subserviently.

'Spare his blushes! Beetle charms us first.'

Beetle stood up, confident in the possession of a guaranteed construe, left behind by M'Turk, who had that day gone into the sick-house with a cold. Yet he was too wary a hand to show confidence.

'*Credidimus*, we—believe—we have believed,' he opened in hesitating slow time, '*tonantem Jovem*, thundering Jove—

regnare, to reign—*caelo*, in heaven. *Augustus*, Augustus—
habebitur, will be held or considered—*praesens divus*, a present
God—*adjectis Britannis*, the Britons being added—*imperio*, to
the Empire—*gravibusque Persis*, with the heavy—er, stern
Persians.'

'What?'

'The grave or stern Persians.' Beetle pulled up with the 'Thank-
God-I-have-done-my-duty'* air of Nelson in the cockpit.

'I am quite aware,' said King, 'that the first stanza is about
the extent of your knowledge, but continue, sweet one,
continue. *Gravibus*, by the way, is usually translated as
"troublesome." '

Beetle drew a long and tortured breath. The second stanza
(which carried over to the third) of that Ode is what is
technically called a 'stinker.' But M'Turk had done him
handsomely.

'*Milesne Crassi*, had—has the soldier of Crassus—*vixit*,
lived—*turpis maritus*, a disgraceful husband——'

'You slurred the quantity of the word after *turpis*,' said
King. 'Let's hear it.'

Beetle guessed again, and for a wonder hit the correct
quantity. 'Er—a disgraceful husband—*conjuge barbara*, with a
barbarous spouse.'

'Why do you select *that* disgustful equivalent out of all the
dictionary?' King snapped. 'Isn't "wife" good enough for
you?'

'Yes, sir. But what do I do about this bracket, sir? Shall I
take it now?'

'Confine yourself at present to the soldier of Crassus.'

'Yes, sir. *Et*, and—*consenuit*, has he grown old—*in armis*, in
the—er—arms—*hostium socerorum*, of his father-in-law's
enemies.'

'Who? How? Which?'

'Arms of his enemies' fathers-in-law, sir.'

'Tha-anks. By the way, what meaning might you attach to
in armis?'

'Oh, weapons—weapons of war, sir.' There was a virginal
note in Beetle's voice as though he had been falsely accused
of uttering indecencies. 'Shall I take the bracket now, sir?'

'Since it seems to be troubling you.'

'*Pro Curia*, O for the Senate House—*inversique mores*, and manners upset—upside down.'

'Ve-ry like your translation. Meantime, the soldier of Crassus?'

'*Sub rege Medo*, under a Median King—*Marsus et Apulus*, he being a Marsian and an Apulian.'

'Who? The Median King?'

'No, sir. The soldier of Crassus. *Oblittus* agrees with *milesne Crassi*, sir,' volunteered too hasty Beetle.

'Does it? It doesn't with *me*.'

'*Oh-blight-us*,'* Beetle corrected hastily, 'forgetful—*anciliorum*, of the shields, or trophies—*et nominis*, and the—his name—*et togae*, and the toga—*eternaeque Vestae*, and eternal Vesta—*incolumi Jove*, Jove being safe—*ot urbe Roma*, and the Roman city.' With an air of hardly restrained zeal—'Shall I go on, sir?'

Mr. King winced. 'No, thank you. You have indeed given us a translation! May I ask if it conveys any meaning whatever to your so-called mind?'

'Oh, I think so, sir.' This with gentle toleration for Horace and all his works.

'We envy you. Sit down.'

Beetle sat down relieved, well knowing that a reef of uncharted genitives stretched ahead of him, on which in spite of M'Turk's sailing-directions he would infallibly have been wrecked.

Rattray, who took up the task, steered neatly through them and came unscathed to port.

'Here we require drama,' said King. 'Regulus himself is speaking now. Who shall represent the provident-minded Regulus? Winton, will you kindly oblige?'

Winton of King's House, a long, heavy, tow-headed Second Fifteen forward, overdue for his First Fifteen colours, and in aspect like an earnest, elderly horse, rose up, and announced, among other things, that he had seen 'signs affixed to Punic deluges.'* Half the Form shouted for joy, and the other half for joy that there was something to shout about.

Mr. King opened and shut his eyes with great swiftness. '*Signa adfixa delubris*,' he gasped. 'So *delubris* is "deluges" is it? Winton, in all our dealings, have I ever suspected you of a jest?'

'No, sir,' said the rigid and angular Winton, while the Form rocked about him.

'And yet you assert *delubris* means "deluges." Whether I am a fit subject for such a jape is, of course, a matter of opinion, but. . . . Winton, you are normally conscientious. May we assume you looked out *delubris*?'

'No, sir.' Winton was privileged to speak that truth dangerous to all who stand before Kings.

'Made a shot at it then?'

Every line of Winton's body showed he had done nothing of the sort. Indeed, the very idea that 'Pater' Winton (and a boy is not called 'Pater' by companions for his frivolity) would make a shot at anything was beyond belief. But he replied, 'Yes,' and all the while worked with his right heel as though he were heeling a ball at punt-about.

Though none dared to boast of being a favourite with King, the taciturn, three-cornered Winton stood high in his Housemaster's opinion. It seemed to save him neither rebuke nor punishment, but the two were in some fashion sympathetic.

'Hm!' said King drily. 'I was going to say—*Flagitio additis damnum*,* but I think—I think I see the process. Beetle, the translation of *delubris*, please.'

Beetle raised his head from his shaking arm long enough to answer: 'Ruins, sir.'

There was an impressive pause while King checked off crimes on his fingers. Then to Beetle the much-enduring man addressed winged words:

'Guessing,' said he. 'Guessing, Beetle, as usual, from the look of *delubris* that it bore some relation to *diluvium* or deluge, you imparted the result of your half-baked lucubrations to Winton who seems to have been lost enough to have accepted it. Observing next, your companion's fall, from the presumed security of your undistinguished position in the rear-guard, you took another pot-shot. The turbid chaos of your mind threw up some memory of the word "dilapidations" which you have pitifully attempted to disguise under the synonym of "ruins." '

As this was precisely what Beetle had done he looked hurt
but forgiving. 'We will attend to this later,' said King. 'Go on,
Winton, and retrieve yourself.'

Delubris happened to be the one word which Winton had
not looked out and had asked Beetle for, when they were
settling into their places. He forged ahead with no further
trouble. Only when he rendered *scilicet* as 'forsooth,' King
erupted.

'Regulus,' he said, 'was not a leader-writer for the penny
press, nor, for that matter, was Horace. Regulus says: "The
soldier ransomed by gold will come keener for the fight—will
he by—by gum!" *That's* the meaning of *scilicet*. It indicates
contempt—bitter contempt. "Forsooth," forsooth! You'll be
taking about "speckled beauties" and "eventually transpire"
next. Howell, what do you make of that doubled "Vidi ego—
ego vidi"? It wasn't put in to fill up the metre, you know.'

'Isn't it intensive, sir?' said Howell, afflicted by a genuine
interest in what he read. 'Regulus was a bit in earnest about
Rome making no terms with Carthage—and he wanted to let
the Romans understand it, didn't he, sir?'

'Less than your usual grace, but the fact. Regulus *was* in
earnest. He was also engaged at the same time in cutting his
own throat with every word he uttered. He knew Carthage
which (your examiners won't ask you this so you needn't take
notes) was a sort of God-forsaken nigger Manchester. Regulus
was not thinking about his own life. He was telling Rome the
truth. He was playing for his side. Those lines from the
eighteenth to the fortieth ought to be written in blood. Yet
there are things in human garments which will tell you that
Horace was a flaneur—a man about town. Avoid such beings.
Horace knew a very great deal. *He* knew! *Erit ille fortis*—"will
he be brave who once to faithless foes has knelt?" And again
(stop pawing with your hooves, Thornton!) *hic unde vitam
sumeret inscius*. That means roughly—but I perceive I am
ahead of my translators. Begin at *hic unde*, Vernon, and let us
see if you have the spirit of Regulus.'

Now no one expected fireworks from gentle Paddy Vernon,
sub-prefect of Hartopp's House, but, as must often be the case
with growing boys, his mind was in abeyance for the time

being, and he said, all in a rush, on behalf of Regulus: '*O magna Carthago probrosis altior Italiae ruinis*, O Carthage, thou wilt stand forth higher than the ruins of Italy.'

Even Beetle, most lenient of critics, was interested at this point, though he did not join the half-groan of reprobation from the wiser heads of the Form.

'*Please* don't mind me,' said King, and Vernon very kindly did not. He ploughed on thus: 'He (Regulus) is related to have removed from himself the kiss of the shameful wife and of his small children as less by the head, and, being stern, to have placed his virile visage on the ground.'

Since King loved 'virile' about as much as he did 'spouse' or 'forsooth' the Form looked up hopefully. But Jove thundered not.

'Until,' Vernon continued, 'he should have confirmed the sliding fathers as being the author of counsel never given under an alias.'

He stopped, conscious of stillness round him like the dread calm of the typhoon's centre. King's opening voice was sweeter than honey.

'I am painfully aware by bitter experience that I cannot give you any idea of the passion, the power, the—the essential guts of the lines which you have so foully outraged in our presence. But——' the note changed, 'so far as in me lies, I will strive to bring home to you, Vernon, the fact that there exist in Latin a few pitiful rules of grammar, of syntax, nay, even of declension, which were not created for your incult sport—your Bœotian* diversion. You will, therefore, Vernon, write out and bring to me to-morrow a word-for-word English-Latin translation of the Ode, together with a full list of all adjectives—an adjective is not a verb, Vernon, as the Lower Third will tell you—all adjectives, their number, case, and gender. Even now I haven't begun to deal with you faithfully.'

'I—I'm very sorry, sir,' Vernon stammered.

'You mistake the symptoms, Vernon. You are possibly discomfited by the imposition, but sorrow postulates some sort of mind, intellect, *nous*. Your rendering of *probrosis** alone stamps you as lower than the beasts of the field. Will some one take the taste out of our mouths? And—talking of tastes——' He coughed. There was a distinct flavour of chlorine gas in the air. Up went an eyebrow, though King knew perfectly well what it meant.

'Mr. Hartopp's sti—science class next door,' said Malpass.

'Oh yes. I had forgotten. Our newly established Modern Side, of course. Perowne, open the windows; and Winton, go on once more from *interque maerentes*.'

'And hastened away,' said Winton, 'surrounded by his mourning friends, into—into illustrious banishment. But I got that out of Conington,* sir,' he added in one conscientious breath.

'I am aware. The master generally knows his ass's crib, though I acquit *you* of any intention that way. Can you suggest anything for *egregius exul*? Only "egregious exile"? I fear "egregious" is a good word ruined. No! You can't in this case improve on Conington. Now then for *atqui sciebat quae sibi barbarus tortor pararet*. The whole force of it lies in the *atqui*.'

'Although he knew,' Winton suggested.

'Stronger than that, I think.'

'He who knew well,' Malpass interpolated.

'Ye-es. "Well though he knew." I don't like Conington's "well-witting." It's Wardour Street.'*

'Well though he knew what the savage torturer was—was getting ready for him,' said Winton.

'Ye-es. Had in store for him.'

'Yet he brushed aside his kinsmen and the people delaying his return.'

'Ye-es; but then how do you render *obstantes*?'

'If it's a free translation mightn't *obstantes* and *morantem* come to about the same thing, sir?'

'Nothing comes to "about the same thing" with Horace, Winton. As I have said, Horace was not a journalist. No, I take it that his kinsmen bodily withstood his departure, whereas the crowd—*populumque*—the democracy stood about futilely pitying him and getting in the way. Now for that noblest of endings—*quam si clientum*,' and King ran off into the quotation:

> 'As though some tedious business o'er
>   Of clients' court, his journey lay
> Towards Venafrum's grassy floor
>   Or Sparta-built Tarentum's bay.*

All right, Winton. Beetle, when you've quite finished dodging the fresh air yonder, give me the meaning of *tendens*—and turn down your collar.'

'Me, sir? *Tendens*, sir? Oh! Stretching away in the direction of, sir.'

'Idiot! Regulus was not a feature of the landscape. He was a man, self-doomed to death by torture. *Atqui sciebat*—knowing it—having achieved it for his country's sake—can't you hear that *atqui* cut like a knife?—he moved off with some dignity. That is why Horace out of the whole golden Latin tongue chose the one word *tendens*—which is utterly untranslatable.'

The gross injustice of being asked to translate it, converted Beetle into a young Christian martyr, till King buried his nose in his handkerchief again.

'I think they've broken another gas-bottle next door, sir,' said Howell. 'They're always doing it.' The Form coughed as more chlorine came in.

'Well, I suppose we must be patient with the Modern Side,' said King. 'But it is almost insupportable for this Side. Vernon, what are you grinning at?'

Vernon's mind had returned to him glowing and inspired. He chuckled as he underlined his Horace.

'It appears to amuse you,' said King. 'Let us participate. What is it?'

'The last two lines of the Tenth Ode, in this book, sir,' was Vernon's amazing reply.

'What? Oh, I see. *Non hoc semper erit liminis aut aquae caelestis patiens latus.*[1] King's mouth twitched to hide a grin. 'Was that done with intention?'

'I—I thought it fitted, sir.'

'It does. It's distinctly happy. What put it into your thick head, Paddy?'

[1] 'This side will not always be patient of rain and waiting on the threshold.'

'I don't know, sir, except we did the Ode last term.'

'And you remembered? The same head that minted *probrosis* as a verb! Vernon, you are an enigma. No! This Side will *not* always be patient of unheavenly gases and waters. I will make representations to our so-called Moderns. Meantime (who shall say I am not just?) I remit you your accrued pains and penalties in regard to *probrosim, probrosis, probrosit* and other enormities. I oughtn't to do it, but this Side is occasionally human. By no means bad, Paddy.'

'Thank you, sir,' said Vernon, wondering how inspiration had visited him.

Then King, with a few brisk remarks about Science, headed them back to Regulus, of whom and of Horace and Rome and evil-minded commercial Carthage and of the democracy eternally futile, he explained, in all ages and climes, he spoke for ten minutes; passing thence to the next Ode—*Delicta majorum*—where he fetched up, full-voiced, upon—'*Dis te minorem quod geris imperas*' (Thou rulest because thou bearest thyself as lower than the Gods)—making it a text for a discourse on manners, morals, and respect for authority as distinct from bottled gases, which lasted till the bell rang. Then Beetle, concertinaing his books, observed to Winton, 'When King's really on tap he's an interestin' dog. Hartopp's chlorine uncorked him.'

'Yes; but why did you tell me *delubris* was "deluges," you silly ass?' said Winton.

'Well, that uncorked him too. Look out, you hoof-handed old owl!' Winton had cleared for action as the Form poured out like puppies at play and was scragging Beetle. Stalky from behind collared Winton low. The three fell in confusion.

'*Dis te minorem quod geris imperas,*' quoth Stalky, ruffling Winton's lint-white locks. "Mustn't jape with Number Five study. Don't be too virtuous. Don't brood over it. 'Twon't count against you in your future caree-ah. Cheer up, Pater.'

'Pull him off my—er—essential guts, will you?' said Beetle from beneath. 'He's squashin' 'em.'

They dispersed to their studies.

* * * * *

No one, the owner least of all, can explain what is in a growing boy's mind. It might have been the blind ferment of

adolescence; Stalky's random remarks about virtue might have
stirred him; like his betters he might have sought popularity
by way of clowning; or, as the Head asserted years later, the
only known jest of his serious life might have worked on him,
as a sober-sided man's one love colours and dislocates all his
after days. But, at the next lesson, mechanical drawing with
Mr. Lidgett who as drawing-master had very limited powers
of punishment, Winton fell suddenly from grace and let loose
a live mouse in the form-room. The whole Form, shrieking
and leaping high, threw at it all the plaster cones, pyramids,
and fruit in high relief—not to mention ink-pots—that they
could lay hands on. Mr. Lidgett reported at once to the Head;
Winton owned up to his crime, which, venial in the Upper
Third, pardonable at a price in the Lower Fourth, was, of
course, rank ruffianism on the part of a Fifth Form boy; and
so, by graduated stages, he arrived at the Head's study just
before lunch, penitent, perturbed, annoyed with himself
and—as the Head said to King in the corridor after the meal—
more human than he had known him in seven years.

'You see,' the Head drawled on, 'Winton's only fault is a
certain costive and unaccommodating virtue. So this comes
very happily.'

'I've never noticed any sign of it,' said King. Winton was
in King's House, and though King as pro-consul might, and
did, infernally oppress his own Province, once a black and
yellow cap was in trouble at the hands of the Imperial
authority King fought for him to the very last steps of
Caesar's throne.

'Well, you yourself admitted just now that a mouse was
beneath the occasion,' the Head answered.

'It was.' Mr. King did not love Mr. Lidgett. 'It should have
been a rat. But—but—I hate to plead it—it's the lad's first
offence.'

'Could you have damned him more completely, King?'

'Hm. What is the penalty?' said King, in retreat, but
keeping up a rear-guard action.

'Only my usual few lines of Virgil to be shown up by tea-
time.'

The head's eyes turned slightly to that end of the corridor

where Mullins, Captain of the Games ('Pot,' 'old Pot,' or 'Potiphar' Mullins), was pinning up the usual Wednesday notice—'Big, Middle, and Little Side Football—A to K, L to Z, 3 to 4.45 P.M.

You cannot write out the Head's usual few (which means five hundred) Latin lines and play football for one hour and three-quarters between the hours of 1.30 and 5 P.M. Winton had evidently no intention of trying to do so, for he hung about the corridor with a set face and an uneasy foot. Yet it was law in the school, compared with which that of the Medes and Persians* was no more than a non-committal resolution, that any boy, outside the First Fifteen, who missed his football for any reason whatever, and had not a written excuse, duly signed by competent authority, to explain his absence, would receive not less than three strokes with a ground-ash from the Captain of the Games, generally a youth between seventeen and eighteen years, rarely under eleven stone ('Pot' was nearer thirteen), and always in hard condition.

King knew without inquiry that the Head had given Winton no such excuse.

'But he is practically a member of the First Fifteen. He has played for it all this term,' said King. 'I believe his Cap should have arrived last week.'

'His Cap has not been given him. Officially, therefore, he is naught. I rely on old Pot.'

'But Mullins is Winton's study-mate,' King persisted.

Pot Mullins and Pater Winton were cousins and rather close friends.

'That will make no difference to Mullins—or Winton, if I know 'em,' said the Head.

'But—but,' King played his last card desperately, 'I was going to recommend Winton for extra sub-prefect in my House, now Carton has gone.'

'Certainly,' said the Head. 'Why not? He will be excellent by tea-time, I hope.'

At that moment they saw Mr. Lidgett, tripping down the corridor, waylaid by Winton.

'It's about that mouse-business at mechanical drawing,' Winton opened, swinging across his path.

'Yes, yes, highly disgraceful,' Mr. Lidgett panted.

'I know it was,' said Winton. 'It—it was a cad's trick because——'

'Because you knew I couldn't give you more than fifty lines,' said Mr. Lidgett.

'Well, anyhow I've come to apologise for it.'

'Certainly,' said Mr. Lidgett, and added, for he was a kindly man, 'I think that shows quite right feeling. I'll tell the Head at once I'm satisfied.'

'No—no!' The boy's still unmended voice jumped from the growl to the squeak. 'I didn't mean *that*! I—I did it on principle. Please don't—er—do anything of that kind.'

Mr. Lidgett looked him up and down and, being an artist, understood.

'Thank you, Winton,' he said. 'This shall be between ourselves.'

'You heard?' said King, indecent pride in his voice.

'Of course. You thought he was going to get Lidgett to beg him off the impot.'

King denied this with so much warmth that the Head laughed and King went away in a huff.

'By the way,' said the Head, 'I've told Winton to do his lines in your form-room—not in his study.'

'Thanks,' said King over his shoulder, for the Head's orders had saved Winton and Mullins, who was doing extra Army work in the study, from an embarrassing afternoon together.

An hour later, King wandered into his still form-room as though by accident. Winton was hard at work.

'Aha!' said King, rubbing his hands. 'This does not look like games, Winton. Don't let me arrest your facile pen. Whence this sudden love for Virgil?'

'Impot from the Head, sir, for that mouse-business this morning.'

'Rumours thereof have reached us. That was a lapse on your part into Lower Thirdery which I don't quite understand.'

The 'tump-tump' of the puntabouts before the sides settled to games came through the open window. Winton, like his House-master, loved fresh air. Then they heard Paddy Vernon, sub-prefect on duty, calling the roll in the field and marking defaulters. Winton wrote steadily. King curled himself up on a desk, hands round knees. One would have said that the man was gloating over the boy's misfortune, but the boy understood.

'*Dis te minorem quod geris imperas*,' King quoted presently. 'It is necessary to bear oneself as lower than the local gods— even than drawing-masters who are precluded from effective retaliation. I *do* wish you'd tried that mouse-game with me, Pater.'

Winton grinned; then sobered. 'It was a cad's trick, sir, to play on Mr. Lidgett.' He peered forward at the page he was copying.

'Well, "the sin *I* impute to each frustrate ghost"*——' King stopped himself. 'Why do you goggle like an owl? Hand me the Mantuan* and I'll dictate. No matter. Any rich Virgilian measures will serve. I may peradventure recall a few.' He began:

> 'Tu regere imperio populos Romane memento;
> Hae tibi erunt artes pacisque imponere morem,
> Parcere subjectis et debellare superbos.*

There you have it all, Winton. Write that out twice and yet once again.'

For the next forty minutes, with never a glance at the book, King paid out the glorious hexameters (and King could read Latin as though it were alive), Winton hauling them in and coiling them away behind him as trimmers in a telegraph-ship's hold coil away deep-sea cable. King broke from the Aeneid to the Georgics and back again, pausing now and then to translate some specially loved line or to dwell on the treble-shot texture of the ancient fabric. He did not allude to the coming interview with Mullins except at the last, when he said, 'I think at this juncture, Pater, I need not ask you for the precise significance of *atqui sciebat quae sibi barbarus tortor*.'

The ungrateful Winton flushed angrily, and King loafed out to take five o'clock call-over, after which he invited little Hartopp to tea and a talk on chlorine gas. Hartopp accepted the challenge like a bantam, and the two went up to King's

study about the same time as Winton returned to the form-
room beneath it to finish his lines.

Then half a dozen of the Second Fifteen who should have
been washing strolled in to condole with 'Pater' Winton,
whose misfortune and its consequences were common talk.
No one was more sincere than the long, red-headed, knotty-
knuckled 'Paddy' Vernon, but, being a careless animal, he
joggled Winton's desk.

'Curse you for a silly ass!' said Winton. 'Don't do that.'

No one is expected to be polite while under punishment, so
Vernon, sinking his sub-prefectship, replied peacefully
enough:

'Well, don't be wrathy, Pater.'

'I'm not,' said Winton. 'Get out! This ain't your House
form-room.'

"Form-room don't belong to you. Why don't you go to your
own study?' Vernon replied.

'Because Mullins is there waitin' for the victim,' said Stalky
delicately, and they all laughed. 'You ought to have shaken
that mouse out of your trouser-leg, Pater. That's the way I did
in my youth. Pater's revertin' to his second childhood. Never
mind, Pater, we all respect you and your future caree-ah.'

Winton, still writhing, growled. Vernon leaning on the desk
somehow shook it again. Then he laughed.

'What are you grinning at?' Winton asked.

'I was only thinkin' of you being sent up to take a lickin'
from Pot. I swear I don't think it's fair. You've never shirked
a game in your life, and you're as good as in the First Fifteen
already. Your Cap ought to have been delivered last week,
oughtn't it?'

It was law in the school that no man could by any means
enjoy the privileges and immunities of the First Fifteen till the
black velvet cap with the gold tassel, made by dilatory Exeter
outfitters, had been actually set on his head. Ages ago, a large-
built and unruly Second Fifteen had attempted to change this
law, but the prefects of that age were still larger, and the lively
experiment had never been repeated.

'Will you,' said Winton very slowly, 'kindly mind your own
damned business, you cursed, clumsy, fat-headed fool?'

The form-room was as silent as the empty field in the darkness outside. Vernon shifted his feet uneasily.

'Well, *I* shouldn't like to take a lickin' from Pot,' he said.

'Wouldn't you?' Winton asked, as he paged the sheets of lines with hands that shook.

'No, I shouldn't,' said Vernon, his freckles growing more distinct on the bridge of his white nose.

'Well, I'm going to take it'—Winton moved clear of the desk as he spoke. 'But *you*'re going to take a lickin' from me first.' Before any one realised it, he had flung himself neighing against Vernon. No decencies were observed on either side, and the rest looked on amazed. The two met confusedly, Vernon trying to do what he could with his longer reach; Winton, insensible to blows, only concerned to drive his enemy into a corner and batter him to pulp. This he managed over against the fireplace, where Vernon dropped half-stunned. 'Now I'm going to give you your lickin',' said Winton. 'Lie there till I get a ground-ash and I'll cut you to pieces. If you move, I'll chuck you out of the window.' He wound his hands into the boy's collar and waistband, and had actually heaved him half off the ground before the others with one accord dropped on his head, shoulders, and legs. He fought them crazily in an awful hissing silence. Stalky's sensitive nose was rubbed along the floor; Beetle received a jolt in the wind that sent him whistling and crowing against the wall; Perowne's forehead was cut, and Malpass came out with an eye that explained itself like a dying rainbow through a whole week.

'Mad! Quite mad!' said Stalky, and for the third time wriggled back to Winton's throat. The door opened and King came in, Hartopp's little figure just behind him. The mound on the floor panted and heaved but did not rise, for Winton still squirmed vengefully. 'Only a little play, sir,' said Perowne. ''Only hit my head against a form.' This was quite true.

'Oh,' said King. '*Dimovit obstantes propinquos.* You, I presume, are the *populus* delaying Winton's return to—Mullins, eh?'

'No, sir,' said Stalky behind his claret-coloured handkerchief. 'We're the *maerentes amicos.*'

'Not bad! You see, some of it sticks after all,' King chuckled to Hartopp, and the two masters left without further inquiries.

The boys sat still on the now passive Winton.

'Well,' said Stalky at last, 'of all the putrid he-asses, Pater, you are *the*——'

'I'm sorry. I'm awfully sorry,' Winton began, and they let him rise. He held out his hand to the bruised and bewildered Vernon. 'Sorry, Paddy. I—I must have lost my temper. I—I don't know what's the matter with me.'

"Fat lot of good that'll do my face at tea,' Vernon grunted. 'Why couldn't you say there was something wrong with you instead of lamming out like a lunatic? Is my lip puffy?'

'Just a trifle. Look at my beak! Well, we got all these pretty marks at footer—owin' to the zeal with which we played the game,' said Stalky, dusting himself. 'But d'you think you're fit to be let loose again, Pater?' 'Sure you don't want to kill another sub-prefect? I wish *I* was Pot. I'd cut your sprightly young soul out.'

'I s'pose I ought to go to Pot now,' said Winton.

'And let all the other asses see you lookin' like this! Not much. We'll all come up to Number Five study and wash off in hot water. Beetle, you aren't damaged. Go along and light the gas-stove.'

'There's a tin of cocoa in my study somewhere,' Perowne shouted after him. 'Rootle round till you find it, and take it up.'

Separately, by different roads, Vernon's jersey pulled half over his head, the boys repaired to Number Five study. Little Hartopp and King, I am sorry to say, leaned over the banisters of King's landing and watched.

'Ve-ry human,' said little Hartopp. 'Your virtuous Winton, having got himself into trouble, takes it out of my poor old Paddy. I wonder what precise lie Paddy will tell about his face.'

'But surely you aren't going to embarrass him by asking?' said King.

'*Your* boy won,' said Hartopp.

'To go back to what we were discussing,' said King quickly,

'do you pretend that your modern system of inculcating unrelated facts about chlorine, for instance, all of which may be proved fallacies by the time the boys grow up, can have any real bearing on education—even the low type of it that examiners expect?'

'I maintain nothing. But is it any worse than your Chinese reiteration of uncomprehended syllables in a dead tongue?'

'Dead, forsooth!' King fairly danced. 'The only living tongue on earth! Chinese! On my word, Hartopp!'

'And at the end of seven years—how often have I said it?' Hartopp went on,—'seven years of two hundred and twenty days of six hours each, your victims go away with nothing, absolutely nothing, except, perhaps, if they've been very attentive, a dozen—no, I'll grant you twenty—one score of totally unrelated Latin tags which any child of twelve could have absorbed in two terms.'

'But—but can't you realise that if our system brings later— at any rate—at a pinch—a simple understanding—grammar and Latinity apart—a mere glimpse of the significance (foul word!) of, we'll say, one Ode of Horace, one twenty lines of Virgil, we've got what we poor devils of ushers are striving after?'

'And what might that be?' said Hartopp.

'Balance, proportion, perspective—life. Your scientific man is the unrelated animal—the beast without background. Haven't you ever realised *that* in your atmosphere of stinks?'

'Meantime you make them lose life for the sake of living, eh?'

'Blind again, Hartopp! I told you about Paddy's quotation this morning. (But he made *probrosis* a verb, he did!) You yourself heard young Corkran's reference to *maerentes amicos*. It sticks—a little of it sticks among the barbarians.'

'Absolutely and essentially Chinese,' said little Hartopp, who, alone of the Common-room, refused to be outfaced by King. 'But I don't yet understand how Paddy came to be licked by Winton. Paddy's supposed to be something of a boxer.'

'Beware of vinegar made from honey,' King replied. 'Pater, like some other people, is patient and long-suffering, but he has his limits. The Head is oppressing him damnably, too. As I pointed out, the boy has practically been in the First Fifteen since term began.'

'But, my dear fellow, I've known you give a boy an impot and refuse him leave off games, again and again.'

'Ah, but that was when there was real need to get at some oaf who couldn't be sensitised in any other way. Now, in our esteemed Head's action I see nothing but——'

The conversation from this point does not concern us.

Meantime Winton, very penitent and especially polite towards Vernon, was being cheered with cocoa in Number Five study. They had some difficulty in stemming the flood of his apologies. He himself pointed out to Vernon that he had attacked a sub-prefect for no reason whatever, and, therefore, deserved official punishment.

'I can't think what was the matter with me to-day,' he mourned. 'Ever since that blasted mouse business——'

'Well, then, don't think,' said Stalky. 'Or do you want Paddy to make a row about it before all the school?'

Here Vernon was understood to say that he would see Winton and all the school somewhere else.

'And if you imagine Perowne and Malpass and me are goin' to give evidence at a prefects' meeting just to soothe your beastly conscience, you jolly well err,' said Beetle. 'I know what you did.'

'What?' croaked Pater, out of the valley of his humiliation.

'You went Berserk. I've read all about it in *Hypatia*.'*

'What's "going Berserk"?' Winton asked.

'Never you mind,' was the reply. 'Now, don't you feel awfully weak and seedy?'

'I *am* rather tired,' said Winton, sighing.

'That's what you ought to be. You've gone Berserk and pretty soon you'll go to sleep. But you'll probably be liable to fits of it all your life,' Beetle concluded. ''Shouldn't wonder if you murdered some one some day.'

'Shut up—you and your Berserks!' said Stalky. 'Go to Mullins now and get it over, Pater.'

'I call it filthy unjust of the Head,' said Vernon. 'Anyhow, you've given me my lickin', old man. I hope Pot'll give you yours.'

'I'm awful sorry—awfully sorry,' was Winton's last word.

It was the custom in that consulship to deal with games' defaulters between five o'clock call-over and tea. Mullins, who was old enough to pity, did not believe in letting boys wait through the night till the chill of the next morning for their punishments. He was finishing off the last of the small fry and their excuses when Winton arrived.

'But, please, Mullins'—this was Babcock tertius, a dear little twelve-year-old mother's darling—'I had an awful hack on the knee. I've been to the Matron about it and she gave me some iodine. I've been rubbing it in all day. I thought that would be an excuse off.'

'Let's have a look at it,' said the impassive Mullins. 'That's a shin-bruise—about a week old. Touch your toes. I'll give you the iodine.'

Babcock yelled loudly as he had many times before. The face of Jevons, aged eleven, a new boy that dark wet term, low in the House, low in the Lower School, and lowest of all in his homesick little mind, turned white at the horror of the sight. They could hear his working lips part stickily as Babcock wailed his way out of hearing.

'Hullo, Jevons! What brings you here?' said Mullins.

'Pl-ease, sir, I went for a walk with Babcock tertius.'

'Did you? Then I bet you went to the tuck-shop—and you paid, didn't you?'

A nod. Jevons was too terrified to speak.

'Of course, and I bet Babcock told you that old Pot 'ud let you off because it was the first time.'

Another nod with a ghost of a smile in it.

'All right.' Mullins picked Jevons up before he could guess what was coming, laid him on the table with one hand, with the other gave him three emphatic spanks, then held him high in air.

'Now you tell Babcock tertius that he's got you a licking from me, and see you jolly well pay it back to him. And when you're prefect of games don't you let any one shirk his footer without a written excuse. Where d'you play in your game?'

'Forward, sir.'

'You can do better than that. I've seen you run like a young buck-rabbit. Ask Dickson from me to try you as three-quarter next game, will you? Cut along.'

Jevons left, warm for the first time that day. enormously set up in his own esteem, and very hot against the deceitful Babcock.

Mullins turned to Winton. 'Your name's on the list, Pater.' Winton nodded.

'I know it. The Head landed me with an impot for that mouse-business at mechanical drawing. No excuse.'

'He meant it then?' Mullins jerked his head delicately towards the ground-ash on the table. 'I heard something about it.'

Winton nodded. 'A rotten thing to do,' he said. "Can't think what I was doing ever to do it. It counts against a fellow so; and there's some more too——'

'All right, Pater. Just stand clear of our photo-bracket, will you?'

The little formality over, there was a pause. Winton swung round, yawned in Pot's astonished face and staggered towards the window-seat.

'What's the matter with you, Dick? Ill?'

'No. Perfectly all right, thanks. Only—only a little sleepy.' Winton stretched himself out, and then and there fell deeply and placidly asleep.

'It isn't a faint,' said the experienced Mullins, 'or his pulse wouldn't act. 'Tisn't a fit or he'd snort and twitch. It can't be sunstroke, this term, and he hasn't been over-training for anything.' He opened Winton's collar, packed a cushion under his head, threw a rug over him and sat down to listen to the regular breathing. Before long Stalky arrived, on pretence of borrowing a book. He looked at the window-seat.

"Noticed anything wrong with Winton lately?' said Mullins.

"Notice anything wrong with my beak?' Stalky replied. 'Pater went Berserk after call-over, and fell on a lot of us for jesting with him about his impot. You ought to see Malpass's eye.'

'You mean that Pater fought?' said Mullins.

'Like a devil. Then he nearly went to sleep in our study just now. I expect he'll be all right when he wakes up. Rummy business! Conscientious old bargee. You ought to have heard his apologies.'

'But Pater can't fight one little bit,' Mullins repeated.

"'Twasn't fighting. He just tried to murder every one.' Stalky described the affair, and when he left Mullins went off to take counsel with the Head, who, out of a cloud of blue smoke, told him that all would yet be well.

'Winton,' said he, 'is a little stiff in his moral joints. He'll get over that. If he asks you whether to-day's doings will count against him in his——'

'But you know it's important to him, sir. His people aren't—very well off,' said Mullins.

'That's why I'm taking all this trouble. You must reassure him, Pot. I have overcrowded him with new experiences. Oh, by the way, has his Cap come?'

'It came at dinner, sir.' Mullins laughed.

Sure enough, when he waked at tea-time, Winton proposed to take Mullins all through every one of his day's lapses from grace, and 'Do you think it will count against me?' said he.

'Don't you fuss so much about yourself and your silly career,' said Mullins. 'You're all right. And oh—here's your First Cap at last. Shove it up on the bracket and come on to tea.'

They met King on their way, stepping statelily and rubbing his hands. 'I have applied,' said he, 'for the services of an additional sub-prefect in Carton's unlamented absence. Your name, Winton, seems to have found favour with the powers that be, and—and all things considered—I am disposed to give my support to the nomination. You are therefore a quasi-lictor.'*

'Then it didn't count against me,' Winton gasped as soon as they were out of hearing.

A Captain of Games can jest with a sub-prefect publicly.

'You utter ass!' said Mullins, and caught him by the back of his stiff neck and ran him down to the hall where the sub-prefects, who sit below the salt, made him welcome with the economical bloater-paste of mid-term.

King and little Hartopp were sparring in the Reverend John
Gillett's study at 10 P.M.—classical *versus* modern as usual.

'Character—proportion—background,' snarled King. 'That
is the essence of the Humanities.'

'Analects of Confucius,'* little Hartopp answered.

'Time,' said the Reverend John behind the soda-water. 'You
men oppress me. Hartopp, what did you say to Paddy in your
dormitories to-night? Even *you* couldn't have overlooked his face.'

'But I did,' said Hartopp calmly. 'I wasn't even humorous
about it, as some clerics might have been. I went straight
through and said naught.'

'Poor Paddy! Now, for my part,' said King, 'and you know
I am not lavish in my praises, I consider Winton a first-class
type; absolutely first-class.'

'Ha-ardly,' said the Reverend John. 'First-class of the
second class, I admit. The very best type of second class
but'—he shook his head—'it should have been a rat. Pater'll
never be anything more than a Colonel of Engineers.'

'What do you base that verdict on?' said King stiffly.

'He came to me after prayers—with all his conscience.'

'Poor old Pater. Was it the mouse?' said little Hartopp.

'That, and what he called his uncontrollable temper, and his
responsibilities as sub-prefect.'

'And you?'

'If we had had what is vulgarly called a pi-jaw he'd have had
hysterics. So I recommended a dose of Epsom salts. He'll take
it, too—conscientiously. Don't eat me, King. Perhaps he'll be
a K.C.B.'*

Ten o'clock struck and the Army Class boys in the further
studies coming to their houses after an hour's extra work
passed along the gravel path below. Some one was chanting,
to the tune of 'White sand and grey sand,'* *Dis te minorem
quod geris imperas*. He stopped outside Mullins' study. They
heard Mullins' window slide up and then Stalky's voice:

'Ah! Good-evening, Mullins, my *barbarus tortor*. We're the
waits. We have come to inquire after the local Berserk. Is he
doin' as well as can be expected in his new caree-ah?'

'Better than you will, in a sec, Stalky,' Mullins grunted.

"Glad of that. We thought he'd like to know that Paddy has been carried to the sick-house in ravin' delirium. They think it's concussion of the brain.'

'Why, he was all right at prayers,' Winton began earnestly, and they heard a laugh in the background as Mullins slammed down the window.

"Night, Regulus,' Stalky sang out, and the light footsteps went on.

'You see. It sticks. A little of it sticks among the barbarians,' said King.

'Amen,' said the Reverend John. 'Go to bed.'

A TRANSLATION*

HORACE, Ode 3, Bk. V.

There are whose study is of smells,
    And to attentive schools rehearse
How something mixed with something else
    Makes something worse.

Some cultivate in broths impure
    The clients of our body—these,
Increasing without Venus, cure,
    Or cause, disease.

Others the heated wheel extol,
    And all its offspring, whose concern
Is how to make it farthest roll
    And fastest turn.

Me, much incurious if the hour
    Present, or to be paid for, brings
Me to Brundusium by the power
    Of wheels or wings;

Me, in whose breast no flame hath burned
    Life-long, save that by Pindar lit,
Such lore leaves cold: I am not turned
    Aside to it.

More than when, sunk in thought profound
    Of what the unaltering Gods require,
My steward (friend *but* slave) brings round
    Logs for my fire.

A Little Prep.

THE Easter term was but a month old when Stettson major, a day-boy, contracted diphtheria, and the Head was very angry. He decreed a new and narrower set of bounds—the infection had been traced to an out-lying farmhouse—urged the prefects to lick all trespassers severely, and promised extra attentions from his own hand. There were no words bad enough for Stettson major, quarantined at his mother's house, who had lowered the school-average of health. This he said in the gymnasium after prayers. Then he wrote some two hundred letters to as many anxious parents and guardians, and bade the school carry on. The trouble did not spread, but, one night, a dog-cart drove to the Head's door, and in the morning the Head had gone, leaving all things in charge of Mr. King, senior House-master. The Head often ran up to town, where the school devoutly believed he bribed officials for early proofs of the Army Examination papers; but this absence was unusually prolonged.

'Downy old bird!' said Stalky to the allies, one wet afternoon, in the study. 'He must have gone on a bend an' been locked up, under a false name.'

'What for?' Beetle entered joyously into the libel.

'Forty shillin's or a month for hackin' the chucker-out of the Pavvy* on the shins. Bates always has a spree when he goes to town. 'Wish he was back, though. I'm about sick o' King's "whips an' scorpions"* an' lectures on public-school spirit—yah!—and scholarship!'

' "Crass an' materialised brutality of the middle-classes—readin' solely for marks. Not a scholar in the whole school," '

M'Turk quoted, pensively boring holes in the mantelpiece with a hot poker.

'That's rather a sickly way of spending an afternoon. 'Stinks, too. Let's come out an' smoke. Here's a treat.' Stalky held up a long Indian cheroot. "Bagged it from my pater last holidays. I'm a bit shy of it, though; it's heftier than a pipe. We'll smoke it palaver-fashion. Hand it round, eh? Let's lie up behind the old harrow on the Monkey-farm Road.'

'Out of bounds. Bounds beastly strict these days, too. Besides, we shall cat.'* Beetle sniffed the cheroot critically. 'It's a regular Pomposo Stinkadore.'*

'You can; I shan't. What d'you say, Turkey?'

'Oh, may's well, I s'pose.'

'Chuck on your cap, then. It's two to one, Beetle. Hout you come!'

They saw a group of boys by the notice-board in the corridor; little Foxy, the school Sergeant, among them.

'More bounds, I expect,' said Stalky. 'Hullo, Foxibus, who are you in mournin' for?' There was a broad band of crape round Foxy's arm.

'He was in my old Regiment,' said Foxy, jerking his head towards the notices, where a newspaper cutting was thumb-tacked between call-over lists.

'By gum!' quoth Stalky, uncovering as he read. 'It's old Duncan—Fat-Sow Duncan—killed on duty at something or other Kotal. "*Rallyin' his men with conspicuous gallantry.*" He would, of course. "*The body was recovered.*" That's all right. They cut 'em up sometimes, don't they, Foxy?'

'Horrid,' said the Sergeant briefly.

'Poor old Fat-Sow! I was a fag when he left. How many does that make to us, Foxy?'

'Mr. Duncan, he is the ninth. He came here when he was no bigger than little Grey tertius. My old Regiment, too. Yiss, nine to us, Mr. Corkran, up to date.'

The boys went out into the wet, walking swiftly.

"Wonder how it feels—to be shot and all that,' said Stalky, as they splashed down a lane. 'Where did it happen, Beetle?'

'Oh, out in India somewhere. We're always rowin' there. But look here, Stalky, what is the good o' sittin' under a hedge an' cattin'? It's be-eastly cold. It's be-eastly wet, and we'll be collared as sure as a gun.'

'Shut up! Did you ever know your Uncle Stalky get you into a mess yet?' Like many other leaders, Stalky did not dwell on past defeats.

They pushed through a dripping hedge, landed among water-logged clods, and sat down on a rust-coated harrow. The cheroot burned with sputterings of saltpetre. They smoked it gingerly, each passing to the other between closed forefinger and thumb.

'Good job we hadn't one apiece, ain't it?' said Stalky, shivering through set teeth. To prove his words he immediately laid all before them, and they followed his example. . . .

'I told you,' moaned Beetle, sweating clammy drops. 'Oh, Stalky, you *are* a fool!'

'*Je cat, tu cat, il cat. Nous cattons!*' M'Turk handed up his contribution and lay hopelessly on the cold iron.

'Something's wrong with the beastly thing. I say, Beetle, have you been droppin' ink on it?'

But Beetle was in no case to answer. Limp and empty, they sprawled across the harrow, the rust marking their ulsters in red squares and the abandoned cheroot-end reeking under their very cold noses. Then—they had heard nothing—the Head himself stood before them—the Head who should have been in town bribing examiners—the Head fantastically attired in old tweeds and a deer-stalker!

'Ah,' he said, fingering his moustache. 'Very good. I might have guessed who it was. You will go back to the College and give my compliments to Mr. King and ask him to give you an extra-special licking. You will then do me five hundred lines. I shall be back to-morrow. Five hundred lines by five o'clock to-morrow. You are also gated for a week. This is not exactly the time for breaking bounds. *Extra*-special, please.'

He disappeared over the hedge as lightly as he had come. There was a murmur of women's voices in the deep lane.

'Oh, you Prooshian brute!'* said M'Turk as the voices died away. 'Stalky, it's all your silly fault.'

'Kill him! Kill him!' gasped Beetle.

'I ca-an't. I'm going to cat again . . . I don't mind that, but King 'll gloat over us horrid. Extra-special, ooh!'

Stalky made no answer—not even a soft one. They went to College and received that for which they had been sent. King enjoyed himself most thoroughly, for by virtue of their seniority the boys were exempt from his hand, save under special order. Luckily, he was no expert in the gentle art.

' "Strange, how desire doth outrun performance," '* said Beetle irreverently, quoting from some Shakespeare play that they were cramming that term. They regained their study and settled down to the imposition.

'You're quite right, Beetle.' Stalky spoke in silky and propitiating tones. 'Now if the Head had sent us up to a prefect, we'd have got something to remember!'

'Look here,' M'Turk began with cold venom, 'we aren't going to row you about this business, because it's too bad for a row; but we want you to understand you're jolly well excommunicated, Stalky. You're a plain ass.'

'How was I to know that the Head 'ud collar us? What was he doin' in those ghastly clothes, too?'

'Don't try to raise a side-issue,' Beetle grunted severely.

'Well, it was all Stettson major's fault. If he hadn't gone an' got diphtheria 'twouldn't have happened. But don't you think it rather rummy—the Head droppin' on us that way?'

'Shut up! You're dead!' said Beetle. 'We've chopped your spurs off your beastly heels. We've cocked your shield upside down, and—and I don't think you ought to be allowed to brew for a month.'

'Oh, stop jawin' at me. I want——'

'Stop? Why—why, we're gated for a week.' M'Turk almost howled as the agony of the situation overcame him. 'A lickin' from King, five hundred lines, *and* a gating. D'you expect us to kiss you, Stalky, you beast?'

'Drop rottin' for a minute. I want to find out about the Head bein' where he was.'

'Well, you have. You found him quite well and fit. Found him making love to Stettson major's mother. That was her in the lane—I heard her. And *so* we were ordered a licking before a day-boy's mother. Bony old widow, too,' said M'Turk. 'Anything else you'd like to find out?'

'I don't care. I swear I'll get even with him some day,' Stalky growled.

''Looks like it,' said M'Turk. 'Extra-special, week's gatin' and five hundred . . . and now you're goin' to row about it! 'Help scrag him, Beetle!' Stalky had thrown his Virgil at them.

The Head returned next day without explanation, to find the lines waiting for him and the school a little relaxed under Mr. King's viceroyalty. Mr. King had been talking at and round and over the boys' heads, in a lofty and promiscuous style, of public-school spirit and the traditions of ancient seats; for he always improved an occasion. Beyond waking in two hundred and fifty young hearts a lively hatred of all other foundations, he accomplished little—so little, indeed, that when, two days after the Head's return, he chanced to come across Stalky & Co., gated but ever resourceful, playing marbles in the corridor, he said that he was not surprised—not in the least surprised. This was what he had expected from persons of their *morale*.

'But there isn't any rule against marbles, sir. Very interestin' game,' said Beetle, his knees white with chalk and dust. Then he received two hundred lines for insolence, besides an order to go to the nearest prefect for judgment and slaughter.

This is what happened behind the closed doors of Flint's study, and Flint was then Head of the Games:—

'Oh, I say, Flint. King has sent me to you for playin' marbles in the corridor an' shoutin' "alley tor" an' "knuckle down."'

'What does he suppose I have to do with that?' was the answer.

'Dunno. Well?' Beetle grinned wickedly. 'What am I to tell him? He's rather wrathy about it.'

'If the Head chooses to put a notice in the corridor forbiddin' marbles, I can do something; but I can't move on a House-master's report. He knows that as well as I do.'

The sense of this oracle Beetle conveyed, all unsweetened, to King, who hastened to interview Flint.

Now Flint had been seven and a half years at the College, counting six months with a London crammer, from whose roof he had returned, homesick, to the Head for the final Army polish. There were four or five other seniors who had gone through much the same mill, not to mention boys, rejected by other establishments on account of a certain overwhelmingness, whom the Head had wrought into very fair shape. It was not a Sixth to be handled without gloves, as King found.

'Am I to understand it is you intention to allow Board-school games* under your study windows, Flint? If so, I can only say——' He said much, and Flint listened politely.

'Well, sir, if the Head sees fit to call a prefects' meeting we are bound to take the matter up. But the tradition of the school is that the prefects can't move in any matter affecting the whole school without the Head's direct order.'

Much more was then delivered; both sides a little losing their temper.

After tea, at an informal gathering of prefects in his study, Flint related the adventure.

'He's been playin' for this for a week, and now he's got it. You know as well as I do that if he hadn't been gassing at us the way he has, that young devil Beetle wouldn't have dreamed of marbles.'

'We know that,' said Perowne, 'but that isn't the question. On Flint's showin' King has called the prefects names enough to justify a first-class row. Crammers' rejections, ill-regulated hobble-de-hoys, wasn't it? Now it's impossible for prefects——'

'Rot,' said Flint. 'King's the best classical cram we've got; and 'tisn't fair to bother the Head with a row. He's up to his eyes with extra-tu. and Army work as it is. Besides, as I told King, we aren't a public school. We're a limited liability company payin' four per cent. My father's a shareholder, too.'*

'What's that got to do with it?' said Venner, a red-headed boy of nineteen.

'Well, seems to me that we should be interferin' with ourselves. We've got to get into the Army or—get out, haven't we? King's hired by the Council to teach us. All the rest's flumdiddle. Can't you see?'

It might have been because he felt the air was a little thunderous that the Head took his after-dinner cheroot to Flint's study; but he so often began an evening in a prefect's room that nobody suspected when he drifted in politely, after the knocks that etiquette demanded.

'Prefects' meeting?' A cock of one wise eye-brow.

'Not exactly, sir; we're just talking things over. Won't you take the easy chair?'

'Thanks. Luxurious infants, you are.' He dropped into Flint's big half-couch and puffed for a while in silence. 'Well, since you're all here, I may confess that I'm the mute with the bow-string.'*

The young faces grew serious. The phrase meant that certain of their number would be withdrawn from all further games for extra-tuition. It might also mean future success at Sandhurst; but it was present ruin for the First Fifteen.

'Yes, I've come for my pound of flesh.* I ought to have had you out before the Exeter match; but it's our sacred duty to beat Exeter.'

'Isn't the Old Boys' match sacred, too, sir?' said Perowne. The Old Boys' match was the event of the Easter term.

'We'll hope they aren't in training. Now for the list. First I want Flint. It's the Euclid that does it. You must work deductions with me. Perowne, extra mechanical drawing. Dawson goes to Mr. King for extra Latin, and Venner to me for German. Have I damaged the First Fifteen much?' He smiled sweetly.

'Ruined it, I'm afraid, sir,' said Flint. 'Can't you let us off till the end of the term?'

'Impossible. It will be a tight squeeze for Sandhurst this year.'

'And all to be cut up by those vile Afghans, too,' said Dawson. ''Wouldn't think there'd be so much competition, would you?'

'Oh, that reminds me. Crandall is coming down with the Old

Boys—I've asked twenty of them, but we shan't get more than
a weak team. I don't know whether he'll be much use, though.
He was rather knocked about, recovering poor old Duncan's
body.'

'Crandall major—the Gunner?' Perowne asked.

'No, the minor—"Toffee" Crandall—in a Native Infantry
regiment. He was almost before your time, Perowne.'

'The papers didn't say anything about him. We read about
Fat-Sow, of course. What's Crandall done, sir?'

'I've brought over an Indian paper that his mother sent me.
It was rather a—hefty, I think you say—piece of work. Shall
I read it?'

The Head knew how to read. When he had finished the
quarter-column of small type everybody thanked him politely.

'Good for the old Coll.!' said Perowne. 'Pity he wasn't in
time to save Fat-Sow, though. That's nine to us, isn't it, in the
last three years?'

'Yes . . . And I took old Duncan off all games for extra-tu.
five years ago this term,' said the Head. 'By the way, who do
you hand over the Games to, Flint?'

'Haven't thought yet. Who'd you recommend, sir?'

'No, thank you. I've heard it casually hinted behind my
back that the Prooshian Bates is a downy bird, but he isn't
going to make himself responsible for a new Head of the
Games. Settle it among yourselves. Good-night.'

'And that's the man,' said Flint, when the door shut, 'that
you want to bother with a dame's school row.'

'I was only pullin' your fat leg,' Perowne returned hastily.
'You're so easy to draw, Flint.'

'Well, never mind that. The Head's knocked the First
Fifteen to bits, and we've got to pick up the pieces, or the Old
Boys will have a walk-over. Let's promote all the Second
Fifteen and make Big Side play up. There's heaps of talent
somewhere that we can polish up between now and the
match.'

The case was represented so urgently to the school that even
Stalky and M'Turk, who affected to despise football, played
one Big-Side game seriously. They were forthwith promoted
ere their ardour had time to cool, and the dignity of their Caps

demanded that they should keep some show of virtue. The match-team was worked at least four days out of seven, and the school saw hope ahead.

With the last week of the term the Old Boys began to arrive, and their welcome was nicely proportioned to their worth. Gentlemen cadets from Sandhurst and Woolwich, who had only left a year ago, but who carried enormous side, were greeted with a cheerful 'Hullo! What's the Shop* like?' from those who had shared their studies. Militia subalterns had more consideration, but it was understood they were not precisely of the true metal. Recreants who, failing for the Army, had gone into business or banks were received for old sake's sake, but in no way made too much of. But when the real subalterns, officers and gentlemen full-blown—who had been to the ends of the earth and back again and so carried no side—came on the scene strolling about with the Head, the school divided right and left in admiring silence. And when one laid hands on Flint, even upon the Head of the Games, crying, 'Good Heavens! What do you mean by growing in this way? You were a beastly little fag when I left,' visible halos encircled Flint. They would walk to and fro in the corridor with the little red school Sergeant, telling news of old regiments; they would burst into form-rooms sniffing the well-remembered smells of ink and whitewash; they would find nephews and cousins in the lower forms and present them with enormous wealth; or they would invade the gymnasium and make Foxy show off the new stock on the bars.

Chiefly, though, they talked with the Head, who was father-confessor and agent-general to them all; for what they shouted in their unthinking youth, they proved in their thoughtless manhood—to wit, that the Prooshian Bates was 'a downy bird.' Young blood who had stumbled into an entanglement with a pastry-cook's daughter at Plymouth; experience who had come into a small legacy but mistrusted lawyers; ambition halting at cross-roads, anxious to take the one that would lead him farthest; extravagance pursued by the money-lender; arrogance in the thick of a regimental row—each carried his trouble to the Head; and Chiron* showed him, in language quite unfit for little boys, a quiet and safe way round, out, or under. So they overflowed his house, smoked his cigars, and drank his health as they had drunk it all the earth over when two or three of the old school had forgathered.

'Don't stop smoking for a minute,' said the Head. 'The more you're out of training the better for us. I've demoralised the First Fifteen with extra-tu.'

'Ah, but we're a scratch lot. Have you told 'em we shall need a substitute even if Crandall can play?' said a Lieutenant of Engineers with the D.S.O.* to his credit.

'He wrote me he'd play, so he can't have been much hurt. He's coming down to-morrow morning.'

'Crandall minor that was, and brought off poor Duncan's body?' The Head nodded. 'Where are you going to put him? We've turned you out of house and home already, Head Sahib.' This was a Squadron-Commander of Bengal Lancers, home on leave.

'I'm afraid he'll have to go up to his old dormitory. You know Old Boys can claim that privilege. Yes, I think leetle Crandall minor must bed down there once more.'

'Bates Sahib'—a Gunner flung a heavy arm round the Head's neck—'You've got something up your sleeve. Confess! I know that twinkle.'

'Can't you see, you cuckoo?' a Submarine Miner interrupted. 'Crandall goes up to the dormitory as an object-lesson, for moral effect and so forth. Isn't that true, Head Sahib?'

'It is. You know too much, Purvis. I licked you for that in '79.'

'You did, sir, and it's my private belief you chalked the cane.'

'N-no. But I've a very straight eye. Perhaps that misled you.'

That opened the flood-gates of fresh memories, and they all told tales out of school.

When Crandall minor that was—Lieutenant R. Crandall of an ordinary Indian regiment—arrived from Exeter on the morning of the match, he was cheered along the whole front of the College, for the prefects had repeated the sense of that which the Head had read them in Flint's study. When Prout's

House understood that he would claim his Old Boy's right to a bed for one night, Beetle ran into King's House next door and executed a public 'gloat' up and down the enemy's big form-room; departing in a haze of ink-pots.

'What d'you take any notice of those rotters for?' said Stalky, playing substitute for the Old Boys, magnificent in black jersey, white knickers, and black stockings. 'I talked to *him* up in the dormitory when he was changin'. 'Pulled his sweater down for him. He's cut about all over the arms— horrid purply ones. He's goin' to tell us about it to-night. I asked him to when I was lacin' his boots.'

'Well, you *have* got cheek,' said Beetle enviously.

"Slipped out before I thought. But he wasn't a bit angry. He's no end of a chap. I swear I'm goin' to play up like beans. Tell Turkey!'

The technique of that match belongs to a bygone age. Scrimmages were tight and enduring; hacking was direct and to the purpose; and round the scrimmage stood the school, crying, 'Put down your heads and shove!' Toward the end everybody lost all sense of decency, and mothers of day-boys too close to the touch-line heard language not included in the bills. No one was actually carried off the field, but both sides felt happier when time was called, and Beetle helped Stalky and M'Turk into their overcoats. The two had met in the many-legged heart of things, and as Stalky said, had 'done each other proud.' As they swaggered woodenly behind the teams—substitutes do not rank as equals of hairy men—they passed a pony-carriage near the wall, and a husky voice cried, 'Well played. Oh, played indeed!' It was Stettson major, white-cheeked and hollow-eyed, who had fought his way to the ground under escort of an impatient coachman.

'Hullo, Stettson,' said Stalky, checking. 'Is it safe to come near you yet?'

'Oh yes. I'm all right. They wouldn't let me out before, but I had to come to the match. Your mouth looks pretty plummy.'

'Turkey trod on it accidental-done-a-purpose. Well, I'm glad you're better, because we owe you something. You and your membranes got us into a sweet mess, young man.'

'I heard of that,' said the boy, giggling. 'The Head told me.'

'Dooce he did! When?'

'Oh, come on up to Coll. My shin 'll stiffen if we stay jawin' here.'

'Shut up, Turkey. I want to find out about this. Well?'

'He was stayin' at our house all the time I was ill.'

'What for? Neglectin' the Coll. that way? 'Thought he was in town.'

'I was off my head, you know, and they said I kept on callin' for him.'

'Cheek! You're only a day-boy.'

'He came just the same, and he about saved my life. I was all bunged up one night—just goin' to croak, the doctor said—and they stuck a tube or somethin' in my throat, and the Head sucked out the stuff.'

'Ugh! 'Shot if *I* would!'

'He ought to have got diphtheria himself, the doctor said. So he stayed on at our house instead of going back. I'd ha' croaked in another twenty minutes, the doctor says.'

Here the coachman, being under orders, whipped up and nearly ran over the three.

'My Hat!' said Beetle. 'That's pretty average heroic.'

'Pretty average!' M'Turk's knee in the small of his back cannoned him into Stalky, who punted him back. 'You ought to be hung!'

'And the Head ought to get the V.C.,' said Stalky. 'Why, he might have been dead *and* buried by now. But he wasn't. But he didn't. Ho! ho! He just nipped through the hedge like a lusty old blackbird. Extra-special, five hundred lines, an' gated for a week—all sereno!'

'I've read o' somethin' like that in a book,' said Beetle. 'Gummy, what a chap! Just think of it!'

'I'm thinking,' said M'Turk; and he delivered a wild Irish yell that made the team turn round.

'Shut your fat mouth,' said Stalky, dancing with impatience. 'Leave it to your Uncle Stalky, and he'll have the Head on toast. If you say a word, Beetle, till I give you leave, I swear I'll slay you. *Habeo capitem crinibus minimis.* I've got him by the short hairs! Now look as if nothing had happened.'

There was no need of guile. The school was too busy cheering
the drawn match. It hung round the lavatories regardless of
muddy boots while the team washed. It cheered Crandall minor
whenever it caught sight of him, and it cheered more wildly
than ever after prayers, because the Old Boys in evening dress,
openly twirling their moustaches, attended, and instead of with
the masters, ranged themselves along the wall immediately
before the prefects; and the Head called them over, too—majors,
minors, and tertiuses, after their old names.

'Yes, it's all very fine,' he said to his guests after dinner, 'but
the boys are getting a little out of hand. There will be trouble
and sorrow later, I'm afraid. You'd better turn in early,
Crandall. The dormitory will be sitting up for you. I don't
know to what dizzy heights you may climb in your profession,
but I do know you'll never get such absolute adoration as
you're getting now.'

'Confound the adoration. I want to finish my cigar, sir.'

'It's all pure gold. Go where glory waits, Crandall—minor.'

The setting of that apotheosis was a ten-bed attic dormitory,
communicating through doorless openings with three others.
The gas flickered over the raw pine wash-stands. There was
an incessant whistling of draughts, and outside the naked
windows the sea beat on the Pebble Ridge.

'Same old bed—same old mattress, I believe,' said Crandall,
yawning. 'Same old everything. Oh, but I'm lame! I'd no
notion you chaps could play like this.' He caressed a battered
shin. 'You've given us all something to remember you by.'

It needed a few minutes to put them at their ease; and, in
some way they could not understand, they were more easy
when Crandall turned round and said his prayers—a ceremony
he had neglected for some years.

'Oh, I am sorry. I've forgotten to put out the gas.'

'Please don't bother,' said the prefect of the dormitory.
'Worthington does that.'

A nightgowned twelve-year-old, who had been waiting to
show off, leaped from his bed to the bracket and back again,
by way of a washstand.

'How d'you manage when he's asleep?' said Crandall,
chuckling.

'Shove a cold cleek* down his neck.'

'It was a wet sponge when I was junior in the dormitory. . . . Hullo! What's happening?'

The darkness had filled with whispers, the sound of trailing rugs, bare feet on bare boards, protests, giggles, and threats such as:

'Be quiet, you ass! . . . *Squattez-vous* on the floor, then! . . . I swear you aren't going to sit on *my* bed! . . . Mind the tooth-glass,' and so forth.

'Sta—Corkran said,' the prefect began, his tone showing his sense of Stalky's insolence, 'that perhaps you'd tell us about that business with Duncan's body.'

'Yes—yes—yes,' ran the keen whispers. 'Tell us.'

'There's nothing to tell. What on earth are you chaps hoppin' about in the cold for?'

'Never mind us,' said the voices. 'Tell about Fat-Sow.'

So Crandall turned on his pillow and spoke to the generation he could not see.

'Well, about three months ago he was commanding a treasure-guard—a cart full of rupees to pay troops with—five thousand rupees in silver. He was comin' to a place called Fort Pearson, near Kalabagh.'*

'I was born there,' squeaked a small fag. 'It was called after my uncle.'

'Shut up—you and your uncle! Never mind *him*, Crandall.'

'Well, ne'er mind. The Afridis* found out that this treasure was on the move, and they ambushed the whole show a couple of miles before he got to the fort, and cut up the escort. Duncan was wounded, and the escort hooked it. There weren't more than twenty Sepoys* all told, and there were any amount of Afridis. As things turned out, I was in charge at Fort Pearson. 'Fact was, I'd heard the firing and was just going to see about it, when Duncan's men came up. So we all turned back together. They told me something about an officer, but I couldn't get the hang of things till I saw a chap under the wheels of the cart out in the open, propped up on one arm, blazing away with a revolver. You see, the escort had abandoned the cart, and the Afridis—they're an awfully suspicious gang—thought the retreat was a trap—sort of draw, you know—and the cart was the bait. So they had left poor old Duncan alone. 'Minute they spotted how few *we* were, it was a race across the flat who should reach old Duncan first. We ran, and they ran, and we won, and after a little hackin' about they pulled off. I never knew it was one of us till I was right on top of him. There are heaps of Duncans in the service, and of course the name didn't remind me. He wasn't changed at all hardly. He'd been shot through the lungs, poor old man, and he was pretty thirsty. I gave him a drink and sat down beside him, and—funny thing, too—he said, "Hullo, Toffee!" and I said, "Hullo, Fat-Sow! Hope you aren't hurt," or something of the kind. But he died in a minute or two—never lifted his head off my knees. . . . I say, you chaps out there will get your death of cold. Better go to bed.'

'All right. In a minute. But your cuts—your cuts. How did you get wounded?'

'That was when we were taking the body back to the Fort. They came on again, and there was a bit of a scrimmage.'

'Did you kill any one?'

'Yes. Shouldn't wonder. Good-night.'

'Good-night. Thank you, Crandall. Thanks awf'ly, Crandall. Good-night.'

The unseen crowds withdrew. His own dormitory rustled into bed and lay silent for a while.

'I say, Crandall'—Stalky's voice was tuned to a wholly foreign reverence.

'Well, what?'

'Suppose a chap found another chap croaking with diphtheria—all bunged up with it—and they stuck a tube in his throat and the chap sucked the stuff out, what would you say?'

'Um,' said Crandall reflectively. 'I've only heard of one case, and that was a doctor. He did it for a woman.'

'Oh, this wasn't a woman. It was only a boy.'

'Makes it all the finer, then. It's about the bravest thing a man can do. Why?'

'Oh, I heard of a chap doin' it. That's all.'

'Then he's a brave man.'

'Would *you* funk it?'

'Ra-ather. Anybody would. Fancy dying of diphtheria in cold blood.'

'Well—ah! Er! Look here!' That sentence ended in a grunt, for Stalky had leaped out of bed and with M'Turk was sitting on the head of Beetle, who would have sprung the mine there and then.

Next day, which was the last of the term and given up to a few wholly unimportant examinations, began with wrath and war. Mr. King had discovered that nearly all his House— it lay, as you know, next door but one to Prout's in the long range of buildings—had unlocked the doors between the dormitories and had gone in to listen to a story told by Crandall. He went to the Head, clamorous, injured, appealing; for he never approved of allowing so-called young men of the world to contaminate the morals of boyhood. 'Very good,' said the Head. He would attend to it.

'Well, I'm awf'ly sorry,' said Crandall guiltily. 'I don't think I told 'em anything they oughtn't to hear. Don't let them get into trouble on my account.'

'Tck!' the Head answered, with the ghost of a wink. 'It isn't the boys that make trouble; it's the masters. However, Prout and King don't approve of dormitory gatherings on this scale, and one must back up the House-masters. Moreover, it's hopeless to punish two Houses only, so late in the term. We must be fair and include everybody. Let's see. They have a holiday task for the Easters, which, of course, none of them will ever look at. We will give the whole school, except prefects and study-boys, regular prep. to-night; and the Common-room will have to supply a master to take it. We must be fair to all.'

'Prep. on the last night of the term. Whew!' said Crandall, thinking of his own wild youth. 'I fancy there will be larks.'

The school, frolicking among packed trunks, whooping down the corridor, and 'gloating' in form-rooms, received the news with amazement and rage. No school in the world did prep. on the last night of the term. This thing was monstrous, tyrannical, subversive of law, religion, and morality. They would go into the form-rooms, and they would take their degraded holiday task with them, but—here they smiled and speculated what manner of man the Common-room would send up against them. The lot fell on Mason, credulous and enthusiastic, who loved youth. No other master was anxious to take that prep., for the school lacked the steadying influence of tradition; and men accustomed to the ordered routine of ancient foundations found it occasionally insubordinate. The four long form-rooms, in which all below the rank of study-boys worked, received him with thunders of applause. Ere he had coughed twice they favoured him with a metrical summary of the marriage-laws of Great Britain, as recorded by the High Priest of the Israelites and commented on by the leader of the host. The lower forms reminded him that it was the last day, and that therefore he must 'take it all in play.' When he dashed off to rebuke them, the Lower Fourth and Upper Third began with one accord to be sick, loudly and realistically. Mr. Mason tried, of all vain things under heaven, to argue with them, and a bold soul at a back desk bade him 'take fifty lines for not 'olding up 'is 'and before speaking.' As one who prided himself upon the precision of his English this cut Mason to the quick, and while he was trying to discover the offender, the Upper and Lower Second, three form-rooms away, turned out the gas and threw ink-pots. It was a pleasant and stimulating prep. The study-boys and prefects heard the echoes of it far off, and the Common-room at dessert smiled.

Stalky waited, watch in hand, till half-past eight.

'If it goes on much longer the Head will come up,' said he. 'We'll tell the studies first, and then the form-rooms. Look sharp!'

He allowed no time for Beetle to be dramatic or M'Turk to drawl. They poured into study after study, told their tale, and went again so soon as they saw they were understood, waiting for no comment; while the noise of that unholy prep. grew and deepened. By the door of Flint's study they met Mason flying towards the corridor.

'He's gone to fetch the Head. Hurry up! Come on!'

They broke into Number Twelve form-room abreast and panting.

'The Head! The Head! The Head!' That call stilled the

tumult for a minute, and Stalky leaping to a desk shouted, 'He went and sucked the diphtheria stuff out of Stettson major's throat when we thought he was in town. Stop rotting, you asses! Stettson major would have croaked if the Head hadn't done it. The Head might have died himself. Crandall says it's the bravest thing any livin' man can do, and'—his voice cracked—'the Head don't know we know!'

M'Turk and Beetle, jumping from desk to desk, drove the news home among the junior forms. There was a pause, and then, Mason behind him, the Head entered. It was in the established order of things that no boy should speak or move under his eye. He expected the hush of awe. He was received with cheers—steady, ceaseless cheering. Being a wise man he went away, and the forms were silent and a little frightened.

'It's all right,' said Stalky. 'He can't do much. 'Tisn't as if you'd pulled the desks up like we did when old Carleton took prep. once. Keep it up! Hear 'em cheering in the studies!' He rocketed out with a yell, to find Flint and the prefects lifting the roof off the corridor.

When the Head of a limited liability company, paying four per cent., is cheered on his saintly way to prayers, not only by four form-rooms of boys waiting punishment, but by his trusted prefects, he can either ask for an explanation or go his road with dignity, while the senior House-master glares like an excited cat and points out to a white and trembling mathematical master that certain methods—not his, thank God—usually produce certain results. Out of delicacy the Old Boys did not attend that call-over; and it was to the school drawn up in the gymnasium that the Head spoke icily.

'It is not often that I do not understand you; but I confess I do not to-night. Some of you, after your idiotic performances at prep., seem to think me a fit person to cheer. I am going to show you that I am not.'

Crash—crash—crash—came the triple cheer that disproved it, and the Head glowered under the gas.

'That is enough. You will gain nothing. The little boys (the Lower School did not like that form of address) will do me three hundred lines apiece in the holidays. I shall take no further notice of them. The Upper School will do me one thousand lines apiece in the holidays, to be shown up the evening of the day they come back. And further—'

'Gummy, what a glutton!' Stalky whispered.

'For your behaviour towards Mr. Mason I intend to lick the whole of the Upper School to-morrow when I give you your journey-money. This will include the three study-boys I found dancing on the form-room desks when I came up. Prefects will stay after call-over.'

The school filed out in silence, but gathered in groups by the gymnasium door waiting what might befall.

'And now, Flint,' said the Head, 'will you be good enough to give me some explanation of your conduct?'

'Well, sir,' said Flint desperately, 'if you save a chap's life at the risk of your own when he's dyin' of diphtheria, and the Coll. finds it out, wha-what can you expect, sir?'

'Um, I see. Then that noise was not meant for—ah, cheek. I can connive at immorality, but I cannot stand impudence. However, it does not excuse their insolence to Mr. Mason. I'll forgo the lines this once, remember; but the lickings hold good.'

When this news was made public, the school, lost in wonder and admiration, gasped at the Head as he went to his house. Here was a man to be reverenced. On the rare occasions when he caned he did it very scientifically, and the execution of a hundred boys would be epic—immense.

'It's all right, Head Sahib. *We* know,' said Crandall, as the Head slipped off his gown with a grunt in his smoking-room. 'I found out just now from our substitute. He was gettin' my opinion of your performance last night in the dormitory. I didn't know then that it was you he was talkin' about. Crafty young animal. Freckled chap with eyes—Corkran, I think his name is.'

'Oh, I know him, thank you,' said the Head; and reflectively, 'Ye-es, I should have included them even if I hadn't seen 'em.'

'If the old Coll. weren't a little above themselves already, we'd chair you down the corridor,' said the Engineer. 'Oh, Bates, how could you? You might have caught it yourself, and where would we have been then?'

'I always knew you were worth twenty of us any day. Now I'm sure of it,' said the Squadron-Commander, looking round for contradictions.

'He isn't fit to manage a school, though. Promise you'll never do it again, Bates Sahib. We—we can't go away comfy in our minds if you take these risks,' said the Gunner.

'Bates Sahib, you aren't ever goin' to cane the whole Upper School, are you?' said Crandall.

'I can connive at immorality, as I said, but I can't stand impudence. Mason's lot is quite hard enough even when I back him. Besides, the men at the golf-club heard them singing "Aaron and Moses."* I shall have complaints about that from the parents of day-boys. Decency must be preserved.'

'We're coming to help, ' said all the guests.

*   *   *   *   *

The Upper School were caned one after the other, their overcoats over their arms, the brakes waiting in the road below to take them to the station, their journey-money on the table. The Head began with Stalky, M'Turk, and Beetle. He dealt faithfully by them.

'And here's your journey-money. Good-bye, and pleasant holidays.'

'Good-bye. Thank you, sir. Good-bye.'

They shook hands.

'Desire don't outrun performance*—much—this mornin'. We got the cream of it,' said Stalky. 'Now wait till a few chaps come out, and we'll really cheer him.'

'Don't want on our account, please,' said Crandall, speaking for the Old Boys. 'We're going to begin now.'

It was very well so long as the cheering was confined to the corridor, but when it spread to the gymnasium, when the boys awaiting their turn cheered, the Head gave it up in despair, and the remnant flung themselves upon him to shake hands.

Then they seriously devoted themselves to cheering till the brakes were hustled off the premises in dumb show.

'Didn't I say I'd get even with him!' said Stalky on the box-seat, as they swung into the narrow Northam street. 'Now all together—takin' time from your Uncle Stalky:

> It's a way we have in the Army,
> It's a way we have in the Navy,
> It's a way we have in the Public Schools,
> Which nobody can deny!'*

The Flag of their Country

IT was winter and bitter cold of mornings. Consequently Stalky and Beetle—M'Turk being of the offensive type that makes ornate toilet under all circumstances—drowsed till the last moment before turning out to call-over in the gas-lit gymnasium. It followed that they were often late; and since every unpunctuality earned them a black mark, and since three black marks a week meant defaulters' drill, equally it followed that they spent hours under the Sergeant's hand. Foxy drilled the defaulters with all the pomp of his old parade-ground.

'Don't think it's any pleasure to me' (his introduction never varied). 'I'd much sooner be smoking a quiet pipe in my own quarters—but I see we 'ave the Old Brigade on our 'ands this afternoon. If I only 'ad you regular, Muster Corkran,' said he, dressing the line.

'You've had me for nearly six weeks, you old glutton. Number off from the right!'

'Not *quite* so previous, please. I'm taking this drill. Left, half—turn! Slow—march.' Twenty-five sluggards, all old offenders, filed into the gymnasium. 'Quietly provide yourselves with the requisite dumb-bells; returnin' quietly to your place. Number off from the right, in *a* low voice. Odd numbers one pace to the front. Even numbers stand fast. Now, leanin' forward from the 'ips, takin' your time from me.'

The dumb-bells rose and fell, clashed and were returned as one. The boys were experts at the weary game.

'Ve-ry good. I shall be sorry when any of you resume your 'abits of punctuality. Quietly return dumb-bells. We will now try some simple drill.'

'Ugh! I know that simple drill.'

'It would be 'ighly to your discredit if you did not, Muster Corkran. *At* the same time, it is not so easy as it looks.'

'Bet you a bob, I can drill as well as you, Foxy.'

'We'll see later. Now try to imagine you ain't defaulters at

all, but an 'arf company on parade, me bein' your commandin'
officer. There's no call to laugh. If you're lucky, most of you
will 'ave to take drills 'arf your life. Do me a little credit.
You've been at it long enough, goodness knows.'

They were formed into fours, marched, wheeled, and
countermarched, the spell of ordered motion strong on them.
As Foxy said, they had been at it a long time.

The gymnasium door opened, revealing M'Turk in charge
of an old gentleman.

The Sergeant, leading a wheel, did not see. 'Not so bad,' he
murmured. 'Not 'arf so bad. The pivot-man of the wheel *honly*
marks time, Muster Swayne. Now, Muster Corkran, you say
you know the drill? Oblige me by takin' over the command
and, reversin' my words step by step, relegate them to their
previous formation.'

'What's this? What's this?' cried the visitor authoritatively.

'A—a little drill, sir,' stammered Foxy, saying nothing of
first causes.

'Excellent—excellent. I only wish there were more of it,' he
chirruped. 'Don't let me interrupt. You were just going to
hand over to some one, weren't you?' He sat down, breathing
frostily in the chill air.

'I shall muck it. I know I shall,' whispered Stalky uneasily; and his discomfort was not lightened by a murmur
from the rear rank that the old gentleman was General
Collinson, a member of the College Board of Council.

'Eh—what?' said Foxy.

'Collinson, K.C.B.*—He commanded the Pompadours—
my father's old regiment,' hissed Swayne major.

'Take your time,' said the visitor. '*I* know how it feels. Your
first drill—eh?'

'Yes, sir.' He drew an unhappy breath. ''Tention. Dress!'
The echo of his own voice restored his confidence.

The wheel was faced about, flung back, broken into fours,
and restored to line without a falter. The official hour of
punishment was long past, but no one thought of that. They
were backing up Stalky—Stalky in deadly fear lest his voice
should crack.

'He does you credit, Sergeant,' was the visitor's comment.

'A good drill—and good material to drill. Now, it's an extraordinary thing: I've been lunching with your Headmaster and he never told me you had a cadet-corps in the College.'

'We 'aven't, sir. This is only a little drill,' said the Sergeant.

'But aren't they keen on it?' said M'Turk, speaking for the first time, with a twinkle in his deep-set eyes.

'Why aren't *you* in it, though, Willy?'

'Oh, I'm not punctual enough,' said M'Turk. 'The Sergeant only takes the pick of us.'

'Dismiss! Break off!' cried Foxy, fearing an explosion in the ranks. 'I—I ought to have told you, sir, that——'

'But you should have a cadet-corps.' The General pursued his own line of thought. 'You *shall* have a cadet-corps, too, if my recommendation in Council is any use. I don't know when I've been so pleased. Boys animated by a spirit like yours should set an example to the whole school.'

'They do,' said M'Turk.

'Bless my soul! Can it be so late? I've kept my fly* waiting half an hour. Well, I must run away. Nothing like seeing things for oneself. Which end of the building does one get out at? Will you show me, Willy? Who was that boy who took the drill?'

'Corkran, I think his name is.'

'You ought to know him. That's the kind of boy you should cultivate. Evidently an unusual sort. A wonderful sight. Five-and-twenty boys, who, I dare say, would much sooner be playing cricket—' (it was the depth of winter; but grown people, especially those who have lived long in foreign parts, make these little errors, and M'Turk did not correct him)— 'drilling for the sheer love of it. A shame to waste so much good stuff; but I think I can carry my point.'

'An' who's your friend with the white whiskers?' demanded Stalky, on M'Turk's return to the study.

'General Collinson. He comes over to shoot with my father sometimes. Rather a decent old bargee, too. He said I ought to cultivate your acquaintance, Stalky.'

'Did he tip you?'

M'Turk exhibited a blessed whole sovereign.

'Ah,' said Stalky, annexing it, for he was treasurer. 'We'll have a hefty brew. You'd pretty average cool cheek, Turkey, to jaw about our keenness an' punctuality.'

'Didn't the old boy know we were defaulters?' said Beetle.

'Not him. He came down to lunch with the Head. I found him pokin' about the place on his own hook afterwards, an' I thought I'd show him the giddy drill. When I found he was so pleased, I wasn't goin' to damp his giddy ardour. He mightn't ha' given me the quid if I had.'

'Wasn't old Foxy pleased? Did you see him get pink behind the ears?' said Beetle. 'It was an awful score for him. Didn't we back him up beautifully? Let's go down to Keyte's and get some cocoa and sassingers.'*

They overtook Foxy, speeding down to retail the adventure to Keyte, who in his time had been Troop Sergeant-Major in a cavalry regiment, and now, a war-worn veteran, was local postmaster and confectioner.

'You owe us something,' said Stalky, with meaning.

'I'm 'ighly grateful, Muster Corkran. I've 'ad to run against you pretty hard in the way o' business, now and then, but I will say that outside o' business—bounds an' smokin', an' such like—I don't wish to have a more trustworthy young gentleman to 'elp me out of a hole. The way you 'andled the drill was beautiful, though I say it. Now, if you come regular henceforward——'

'But he'll have to be late three times a week,' said Beetle. 'You can't expect a chap to do that—just to please you, Foxy.'

'Ah, that's true. Still, if you could manage it—and you, Muster Beetle—it would give you a big start when the cadet-corps is formed. I expect the General will recommend it.'

They raided Keyte's very much at their own sweet will, for the old man, who knew them well, was deep in talk with Foxy.

'I make what we've taken seven and six,' Stalky called at last over the counter; 'but you'd better count for yourself.'

'No—no. I'd take your word any day, Muster Corkran.—In the Pompadours, was he, Sergeant? We lay with them once—at Umballa, I think it was.'

'I don't know whether this ham-and-tongue tin is eighteen pence or one an' four.'

'Say one an' fourpence, Muster Corkran. . . . Of course, Sergeant, if it was any use to give my time, I'd be pleased to do it, but I'm too old. I'd like to see a drill again.'

'Oh, come on, Stalky,' cried M'Turk. 'He isn't listenin' to you. Chuck over the money.'

'I want the quid changed, you ass. Keyte! Private Keyte! Corporal Keyte! Terroop-Sergeant-Major Keyte, will you give me change for a quid?'

'Yes—yes, of course. Seven an' six.' He stared abstractedly, pushed the silver over, and melted away into the darkness of the back room.

'Now those two 'll jaw about the Mutiny till tea-time,' said Beetle.

'Old Keyte was at Sobraon,'* said Stalky. 'Hear him talk about that sometimes! Beats Foxy hollow.'

*   *   *   *   *

The Head's face, inscrutable as ever, was bent over a pile of letters.

'What do you think?' he said at last to the Reverend John Gillett.

'It's a good idea. There's no denying that—an estimable idea.'

'We concede that much. Well?'

'I have my doubts about it—that's all. The more I know of boys the less do I profess myself capable of following their moods; but I own I shall be very much surprised if the scheme takes. It—it isn't the temper of the school. We prepare for the Army.'

'My business—in this matter—is to carry out the wishes of the Council. They demand a volunteer cadet-corps. A volunteer cadet-corps will be furnished. I have suggested, however, that we need not embark upon the expense of uniforms till we are drilled. General Collinson is sending us fifty lethal weapons—cut-down Sniders, he calls them—all carefully plugged.'

'Yes, that is necessary in a school that uses loaded saloon-pistols to the extent we do.' The Reverend John smiled.

'Therefore there will be no outlay except the Sergeant's time.'

'But if he fails you will be blamed.'

'Oh, assuredly. I shall post a notice in the corridor this afternoon, and——'

'I shall watch the result.'

*   *   *   *   *

'Kindly keep your 'ands off the new arm-rack.'

Foxy wrestled with a turbulent crowd in the gymnasium. 'Nor it won't do even a condemned Snider any good to be continual snappin' the lock, Mr. Swayne.—Yiss, the uniforms will come later, when we're more proficient; at present we will confine ourselves to drill. I am 'ere for the purpose of takin' the names o' those willin' to join.—Put down that Snider, Muster Hogan!'

'What are you goin' to do, Beetle?' said a voice.

'I've had all the drill *I* want, thank you.'

'What! After all you've learned? Come on. Don't be a scab! They'll make you corporal in a week,' cried Stalky.

'I'm not goin' up for the Army.' Beetle touched his spectacles.

'Hold on a shake, Foxy,' said Hogan. 'Where are you goin' to drill us?'

'Here—in the gym—till you are fit an' capable to be taken out on the road.' The Sergeant threw a chest.

'For all the Northam cads* to look at? Not good enough, Foxibus.'

'Well, we won't make a point of it. You learn your drill first, an' later we'll see.'

'Hullo,' said Ansell of Macrea's, shouldering through the mob. 'What's all this about a giddy cadet-corps?'

'It will save you a lot o' time at Sandhurst,' the Sergeant replied promptly. 'You'll be dismissed your drills early if you go up with a good groundin' before'and.'

'Hm! 'Don't mind learnin' my drill, but I'm not goin' to ass about the country with a toy Snider. Perowne, what are you goin' to do? Hogan's joinin'.'

''Don't know whether I've the time,' said Perowne. 'I've got no end of extra-tu. as it is.'

'Well, call this extra-tu.,' said Ansell. ''Twon't take us long to mug up the drill.'

'Oh, that's right enough, but what about marchin' in public?' said Hogan, not foreseeing that three years later he should die in the Burmese sunlight outside Minhla Fort.*

'Afraid the uniform won't suit your creamy complexion?' M'Turk asked with a villainous sneer.

'Shut up, Turkey. You aren't goin' up for the Army.'

'No, but I'm goin' to send a substitute. Hi! Morrell an' Wake! You two fags by the arm-rack, you've got to volunteer.'

Blushing deeply—they had been too shy to apply before—the youngsters sidled towards the Sergeant.

'But I don't want the little chaps—not at first,' said the Sergeant disgustedly. 'I want—I'd like some of the Old Brigade—the defaulters—to stiffen 'em a bit.'

'Don't be ungrateful, Sergeant. They're nearly as big as you get 'em in the Army now.' M'Turk read the papers of those years and could be trusted for general information, which he used as he used his 'tweaker.' Yet he did not know that Wake minor would be a bimbashi* of the Egyptian Army ere his thirtieth year.

Hogan, Swayne, Stalky, Perowne, and Ansell were deep in consultation by the vaulting-horse, Stalky as usual laying down the law. The Sergeant watched them uneasily, knowing that many waited on their lead.

'Foxy don't like my recruits,' said M'Turk, in a pained tone, to Beetle. 'You get him some.'

Nothing loath, Beetle pinioned two more fags—each no taller than a carbine.

'Here you are, Foxy. Here's food for powder. Strike for your hearths an' homes, you young brutes—an' be jolly quick about it.'

'Still he isn't happy,' said M'Turk.

'For the way we have with our Army
Is the way we have with our Navy.'

Here Beetle joined in. They had found the poem in an old volume of *Punch*, and it seemed to cover the situation:

'An' both of 'em lead to adversity,
Which nobody can deny!'

'You be quiet, young gentlemen. If you can't 'elp—don't 'inder.' Foxy's eye was still on the council by the horse. Carter, White, and Tyrrell, all boys of influence, had joined it. The rest fingered the rifles irresolutely.

'Half a shake,' cried Stalky. 'Can't we turn out those rotters before we get to work?'

'Certainly,' said Foxy. 'Any one wishful to join will stay 'ere. Those who do not so intend will go out, quietly closin' the door be'ind 'em.'

Half a dozen of the earnest-minded rushed at M'Turk and Beetle, and they had just time to escape into the corridor.

'Well, why don't you join?' Beetle asked, resettling his collar.

'Why didn't you?'

'What's the good? We aren't goin' up for the Army. Besides, I know the drill—all except the manual, of course. 'Wonder what they're doin' inside?'

'Makin' a treaty with Foxy. Didn't you hear Stalky say: "That's what we'll do—an' if he don't like it he can lump it"? They'll use Foxy for a cram. Can't you see, you idiot? They're goin' up for Sandhurst or the Shop* in less than a year. They'll learn their drill an' then they'll drop it like a shot. D'you suppose chaps with their amount of extra-tu. are takin' up volunteerin' for fun?'

'Well, I don't know. I thought of doin' a poem about it— rottin' 'em, you know—"The Ballad of the Dogshooters"— eh?'

'I don't think you can, because King 'll be down on the corps like a cartload o' bricks. He hasn't been consulted. He's sniffin' round the notice-board now. Let's lure him.' They strolled up carelessly towards the House-master—a most meek couple.

'How's this?' said King, with a start of feigned surprise. 'Methought you would be learning to fight for your country.'

'I think the company's full, sir,' said M'Turk.

'It's a great pity,' sighed Beetle.

'Forty valiant defenders, have we, then? How noble! What devotion! I presume that it is possible that a desire to evade their normal responsibilities may be at the bottom of this zeal.

Doubtless they will be accorded special privileges, like the Choir and the Natural History Society—one must not say Bug-hunters.'

'Oh, I suppose so, sir,' said M'Turk cheerily. 'The Head hasn't said anything about it yet, but he will, of course.'

'Oh, sure to.'

'It is just possible, my Beetle,' King wheeled on the last speaker, 'that the House-masters—a necessary but somewhat neglected factor in our humble scheme of existence—may have a word to say on the matter. Life, for the young at least, is not all weapons and munitions of war. Education is incidentally one of our aims.'

'What a consistent pig he is,' cooed M'Turk, when they were out of earshot. 'One always knows where to have him. Did you see how he rose to that draw about the Head and special privileges?'

'Confound him, he might have had the decency to have backed the scheme. I could do such a lovely ballad, rottin' it; and now I'll have to be a giddy enthusiast. It don't bar our pulling Stalky's leg in the study, does it?'

'Oh no; but in the Coll. we must be pro-cadet-corps like anything. Can't you make up a giddy epigram, à la Catullus,* about King objectin' to it?' Beetle was at this noble task when Stalky returned all hot from his first drill.

'Hullo, my ramrod-bunger!' began M'Turk. 'Where's your dead dog? Is it Defence or Defiance?'*

'Defiance,' said Stalky, and leaped on him at that word. 'Look here, Turkey, you mustn't rot* the corps. We've arranged it beautifully. Foxy swears he won't take us out into the open till we want to go.'

'*Dis*-gustin' exhibition of immature infants apin' the idiosyncrasies of their elders. Snff!'

'Have you drawn King, Beetle?' Stalky asked in a pause of the scuffle.

'Not exactly; but that's his genial style.'

'Well, listen to your Uncle Stalky—who is a Great Man. Moreover and subsequently, Foxy's goin' to let us drill the corps in turn—*privatim et seriatim*—so that we'll all know how to handle a half company anyhow. *Ergo*, an' *propter hoc,** when we go to the Shop we shall be dismissed drill early; thus, my beloved 'earers, combinin' education with wholesome amusement.'

'I knew you'd make a sort of extra-tu. of it, you cold-blooded brute,' said M'Turk. 'Don't you want to die for your giddy country?'

'Not if I can jolly well avoid it. So you mustn't rot the corps.'

'We'd decided on that, years ago,' said Beetle scornfully. 'King 'll do the rottin'.'

'Then you've got to rot King, my giddy poet. Make up a good catchy Limerick, and let the fags sing it.'

'Look here, you stick to volunteerin', and don't jog the table.'

'He won't have anything to take hold of,' said Stalky, with dark significance.

They did not know what that meant till, a few days later, they proposed to watch the corps at drill. They found the gymnasium door locked and a fag on guard.

'This is sweet cheek,' said M'Turk, stooping.

''Mustn't look through the key-hole,' said the sentry.

'I like that. Why, Wake, you little beast, I made you volunteer.'

'Can't help it. My orders are not to allow any one to look.'

'S'pose we do?' said M'Turk. 'S'pose we jolly well slay you?'

'My orders are, I am to give the name of anybody who interferes with me on my post, to the corps, an' they'd deal with him after drill, accordin' to martial law.'

'What a brute Stalky is!' said Beetle. They never doubted for a moment who had devised that scheme.

'You esteem yourself a giddy centurion, don't you?' said Beetle, listening to the crash and rattle of grounded arms within.

'My orders are, not to talk except to explain my orders—they'll lick me if I do.'

'M'Turk looked at Beetle. The two shook their heads and turned away.

'I swear Stalky *is* a great man,' said Beetle after a long pause.

'One consolation is that this sort of secret-society biznai will drive King wild.'

It troubled many more then King, but the members of the corps were muter than oysters. Foxy, being bound by no vow, carried his woes to Keyte.

'I never come across such nonsense in my life. They've tiled the lodge, inner and outer guard all complete,* and then they get to work, keen as mustard.'

'But what's it all for?' asked the ex-Troop Sergeant-Major.

'To learn their drill. You never saw anything like it. They begin after I've dismissed 'em—practisin' tricks; but out into the open they will not come—not for ever so. The 'ole thing is pre-posterous. If you're a cadet-corps, I say, be a cadet-corps, instead o' hidin' be'ind locked doors.'

'And what do the authorities say about it?'

'That beats me again.' The Sergeant spoke fretfully. 'I go to the 'Ead an' 'e gives me no help. There's times when I think he's makin' fun o' me. I've never been a Volunteer-sergeant, thank God—but I've always had the consideration to pity 'em. I'm glad o' that.'

'I'd like to see 'em,' said Keyte. 'From your statements, Sergeant, I can't get at what they're after.'

'Don't ask me, Major! Ask that freckle-faced young Corkran. He's their generalissimo.'

One does not refuse a warrior of Sobraon, or deny the only pastry-cook within bounds. So Keyte came, by invitation, leaning upon a stick, tremulous with old age, to sit in a corner and watch.

'They shape well. They shape well. They shape uncommon well,' he whispered between evolutions.

'Oh, *this* isn't what they're after. Wait till I dismiss 'em.'

At the 'break-off' the ranks stood fast. Perowne fell out, faced them, and, refreshing his memory by glimpses at a red-bound, metal-clasped book, drilled them for ten minutes. (This is that Perowne who was shot in Equatorial Africa by his own men.)

Ansell followed him, and Hogan followed Ansell. All three were implicitly obeyed.

Then Stalky laid aside his Snider, and, drawing a long

breath, favoured the company with a blast of withering invective.

"Old 'ard, Muster Corkran. That ain't in any drill,' cried Foxy.

'All right, Sergeant. You never know what you may have to say to your men.—For pity's sake, try to stand up without leanin' against each other, your blear-eyed, herrin'-gutted gutter-snipes. It's no pleasure to *me* to comb you out. That ought to have been done before you came here, you—you Militia broom-stealers!'

'The old touch—the old touch. We know it,' said Keyte, wiping his rheumy eyes. 'But where did he pick it up?'

'From his father—or his uncle. Don't ask me! Half of 'em must have been born within earshot o' the barracks.' (Foxy was not far wrong in his guess.) 'I've heard more back-talk since this volunteerin' nonsense began than I've heard in a year in the service.'

'There's a rear-rank man lookin' as though his belly were in the pawn-shop. Yes, you, Private Ansell,' and Stalky tongue-lashed the victim for three minutes, in gross and in detail.

'Hullo!' He returned to his normal tone. 'First blood to me. You flushed, Ansell. You wriggled.'

"Couldn't help flushing,' was the answer. "Don't think I wriggled, though.'

'Well, it's your turn now.' Stalky resumed his place in the ranks.

'Lord, Lord! It's as good as a play,' chuckled the attentive Keyte.

Ansell, too, had been blessed with relatives in the service, and slowly, in a lazy drawl—his style was more reflective than Stalky's—descended the abysmal depths of personality.

'Blood to me!' he shouted triumphantly. 'You couldn't stand it, either.' Stalky was a rich red, and his Snider shook visibly.

'I didn't think I would,' he said, struggling for composure, 'but after a bit I got in no end of a bait. Curious, ain't it?'

'Good for the temper,' said the slow-moving Hogan, as they returned arms to the rack.

'Did you ever?' said Foxy, hopelessly, to Keyte.

'I don't know much about volunteers, but it's the rummiest show I ever saw. I can see what they're gettin' at, though. Lord! how often I've been told off an' dressed down in my day! They shape well—extremely well they shape.'

'If I could get 'em out into the open, there's nothing I couldn't do with 'em, Major. Perhaps when the uniforms come down, they'll change their tune.'

Indeed it was time that the corps made some concession to the curiosity of the school. Thrice had the guard been maltreated and thrice had the corps dealt out martial law to the offender. The school raged. What was the use, they asked, of a cadet-corps which none might see? Mr. King congratulated them on their invisible defenders, and they could not parry his thrusts. Foxy was growing sullen and restive. A few of the corps openly expressed doubts as to the wisdom of their course; and the question of uniforms loomed on the near horizon. If those were issued, they would be forced to wear them.

But as so often happens in this life, the matter was suddenly settled from without.

The Head had duly informed the Council that their recommendation had been acted upon, and that, so far as he could learn, the boys were drilling.

He said nothing of the terms on which they drilled. Naturally, General Collinson was delighted and told his friends. One of his friends rejoiced in a friend, a Member of Parliament—a zealous, an intelligent, and, above all, a patriotic person, anxious to do the most good in the shortest possible time. But we cannot answer, alas! for the friends of our friends. If Collinson's friend had introduced him to the General, the latter would have taken his measure and saved much. But the friend merely spoke of his friend; and since no two people in this world see eye to eye, the picture conveyed to Collinson was inaccurate. Moreover, the man was an M.P., an impeccable Conservative, and the General had the English soldier's lurking respect for any member of the Court of Last Appeal. The man was going down into the West country, to spread light in some benighted constituency. Wouldn't it be a good idea if, armed with the General's recommendation, he, taking the admirable and newly-established cadet-corps for his text, spoke a few words—'Just talked to the boys a little—eh? You know the kind of thing that would be acceptable; and he'd be the very man to do it. The sort of talk that boys understand, you know.'

'They didn't talk to 'em much in my time,' said the General suspiciously.

'Ah! but times change—with the spread of education and so on. The boys of to-day are the men of to-morrow. An impression in youth is likely to be permanent. And in these times, you know, with the country going to the dogs!'

'You're quite right.' The island was then entering on five years of Mr. Gladstone's rule;* and the General did not like what he had seen of it. He would certainly write to the Head, for it was beyond question that the boys of to-day made the men of to-morrow. That, if he might say so, was uncommonly well put.

In reply, the Head stated that he should be delighted to welcome Mr. Raymond Martin, M.P., of whom he had heard so much; to put him up for the night, and to allow him to address the school on any subject that he conceived would interest them. If Mr. Martin had not yet faced an audience of this particular class of British youth, the Head had no doubt that he would find it an interesting experience.

'And I don't think I am very far wrong in that last,' he confided to the Reverend John. 'Do you happen to know anything of one Raymond Martin?'

'I was at College with a man of that name,' the chaplain replied. 'He was without form and void,* so far as I remember, but desperately earnest.'

'He will address the Coll. on "Patriotism" next Saturday.'

'If there is one thing our boys detest more than another it is having their Saturday evenings broken into. Patriotism has no chance beside "brewing."'

'Nor art either. D'you remember our "Evening with Shakespeare"?' The Head's eyes twinkled. 'Or the humorous gentleman with the magic-lantern?'

*   *   *   *   *

'An' who the dooce is this Raymond Martin, M.P.?' demanded

Beetle, when he read the notice of the lecture in the corridor. 'Why do the brutes always turn up on a Saturday?'

'Ouh! Reomeo, Reomeo. Wherefore art thou Reomeo?' said M'Turk over his shoulder, quoting the Shakespeare artiste of last term. 'Well, he won't be as bad as her, I hope. Stalky, are you properly patriotic? Because if you ain't, this chap's goin' to make you.'

''Hope he won't take up the whole of the evening. I suppose we've got to listen to him.'

''Wouldn't miss him for the world,' said M'Turk. 'A lot of chaps thought that Romeo-Romeo woman was a bore. *I* didn't. I liked her! 'Member when she began to hiccough in the middle of it? P'raps he'll hiccough. Who-ever gets into the gym first, bags seats for the other two.'

* * * *

There was no nervousness, but a brisk and cheery affability about Mr. Raymond Martin, M.P., as he drove up, watched by many eyes, to the Head's house.

''Looks a bit of a bargee,'* was M'Turk's comment. ''Shouldn't be surprised if he was a Radical. He rowed the driver about the fare. I heard him.'

'That was his giddy patriotism,' Beetle explained.

After tea they joined the rush for seats, secured a private and invisible corner, and began to criticise. Every gas-jet was lit. On the little dais at the far end stood the Head's official desk, whence Mr. Martin would discourse, and a ring of chairs for the masters.

Entered then Foxy, with official port, and leaned something like a cloth rolled round a stick against the desk. No one in authority was yet present, so the school applauded, crying: 'What's that, Foxy? What are you stealin' the gentleman's brolly for?—We don't birch here. We cane! Take away that bauble!—Number off from the right'—and so forth, till the entry of the Head and the masters ended all demonstrations.

'One good job—the Common-room hate this as much as we do. Watch King wrigglin' to get out of the draught.'

'Where's the Raymondiferous Martin? Punctuality, my beloved 'earers, is the image o' war——'

'Shut up. Here's the giddy Duke. Golly, what a dewlap!'
Mr. Martin, in evening dress, was undeniably throaty—a tall,
generously-designed, pink-and-white man. Still, Beetle need
not have been coarse.

'Look at his back while he's talkin' to the Head. Vile bad
from to turn your back on the audience! He's a Philistine—a
Bopper*—a Jebusite an' a Hivite.'* M'Turk leaned back and
sniffed contemptuously.

In a few colourless words the Head introduced the speaker
and sat down amid applause. When Mr. Martin took the
applause to himself, they naturally applauded more than ever.
It was some time before he could begin. He had no knowledge
of the school—its tradition or heritage. He did not know that
the last census showed that eighty per cent of the boys had
been born abroad—in camp, cantonment, or upon the high
seas; or that seventy-five per cent were sons of officers in one
or other of the services—Willoughbys, Paulets, De Castros,
Maynes, Randalls, after their kind—looking to follow their
fathers' profession. The Head might have told him this, and
much more; but, after an hour-long dinner in his company,
the Head decided to say nothing whatever. Mr. Raymond
Martin seemed to know so much already.

He plunged into his speech with a long-drawn, rasping
'Well, boys,' that, though they were not conscious of it, set
every young nerve ajar. He supposed they knew—hey?—what
he had come down for? It was not often that he had an
opportunity to talk to boys. He supposed that boys were very
much the same kind of persons—some people thought them
rather funny persons—as they had been in his youth.

'This man,' said M'Turk, with conviction, 'is *the* Gadarene
Swine.'*

But they must remember that they would not always be
boys. They would grow up into men, because the boys of to-
day made the men of to-morrow, and upon the men of to-
morrow the fair fame of their glorious native land depended.

'If this goes on, my beloved 'earers, it will be my painful duty
to rot this bargee.' Stalky drew a long breath through his nose.

''Can't do that,' said M'Turk. 'He ain't chargin' anything
for his Romeo.'

And so they ought to think of the duties and responsibilities of the life that was opening before them. Life was not all—he enumerated a few games, and, that nothing might be lacking to the sweep and impact of his fall, added 'marbles.' 'Yes, life was not,' he said, 'all marbles.'

There was one tense gasp—among the juniors almost a shriek—of quivering horror. He was a heathen—an outcast—beyond the extremest pale of toleration—self-damned before all men! Stalky bowed his head in his hands. M'Turk, with a bright and cheerful eye, drank in every word, and Beetle nodded solemn approval.

Some of them, doubtless, expected in a few years to have the honour of a commission from the Queen, and to wear a sword. Now, he himself had had some experience of these duties, as a Major in a volunteer regiment, and he was glad to learn that they had established a volunteer corps in their midst. The establishment of such an establishment conduced to a proper and healthy spirit, which, if fostered, would be of great benefit to the land they loved and were so proud to belong to. Some of those now present expected, he had no doubt—some of them anxiously looked forward to leading their men against the bullets of England's foes; to confronting the stricken field in all the pride of their youthful manhood.

Now the reserve of a boy is tenfold deeper than the reserve of a maid, she being made for one end only by blind Nature, but man for several. With a large and healthy hand, he tore down these veils, and trampled them under the well-intentioned feet of eloquence. In a raucous voice he cried aloud little matters, like the hope of Honour and the dream of Glory, that boys do not discuss even with their most intimate equals; cheerfully assuming that, till he spoke, they had never considered these possibilities. He pointed them to shining goals, with fingers which smudged out all radiance on all horizons. He profaned the most secret places of their souls with outcries and gesticulations. He bade them consider the deeds of their ancestors in such fashion that they were flushed to their tingling ears. Some of them—the rending voice cut a frozen stillness—might have had relatives who perished in defence of their country. [They thought, not a few of them, of an old sword in a passage, or above a breakfast-room table, seen and fingered by stealth since they could walk.] He adjured them to emulate those illustrious examples; and they looked all ways in their extreme discomfort.

Their years forbade them even to shape their thoughts clearly to themselves. They felt savagely that they were being outraged by a fat man who considered marbles a game.

And so he worked towards his peroration—which, by the way, he used later with overwhelming success at a meeting of electors—while they sat, flushed and uneasy, in sour disgust. After many many words, he reached for the cloth-wrapped stick and thrust one hand in his bosom. This—this was the concrete symbol of their land—worthy of all honour and reverence! Let no boy look on this flag who did not purpose to worthily add to its imperishable lustre. He shook it before them—a large calico Union Jack, staring in all three colours, and waited for the thunder of applause that should crown his effort.

They looked in silence. They had certainly seen the thing before—down at the coastguard station, or through a telescope, half-mast high when a brig went ashore on Braunton sands; above the roof of the Golf Club, and in Keyte's window, where a certain kind of striped sweetmeat bore it in paper on each box. But the College never displayed it; it was no part of the scheme of their lives; the Head had never alluded to it; their fathers had not declared it unto them. It was a matter shut up, sacred and apart. What, in the name of everything caddish, was he driving at, who waved that horror before their eyes? Happy thought! Perhaps he was drunk.

The Head saved the situation by rising swiftly to propose a vote of thanks, and at his first motion the school clapped furiously, from a sense of relief.

'And I am sure,' he concluded, the gaslight full on his face, 'that you will all join me in a very hearty vote of thanks to Mr. Raymond Martin for the most enjoyable address he has given us.'

To this day we shall never know the rights of the case. The Head vows that he did no such thing; or that, if he did, it must have been something in his eye; but those who were present are persuaded that he winked, once, openly and solemnly, after the word 'enjoyable.' Mr. Raymond Martin got his applause full tale. As he said, 'Without vanity, I think my few words went to their hearts. I never knew boys could cheer like that.'

He left as the prayer-bell rang, and the boys lined up against the wall. The flag lay still unrolled on the desk, Foxy regarding it with pride, for he had been touched to the quick by Mr. Martin's eloquence. The Head and the Common-room, standing back on the dais, could not see the glaring offence, but a prefect left the line, rolled it up swiftly, and as swiftly tossed it into a glove-and-foil locker.

Then, as though he had touched a spring, broke out the low murmur of content, changing to quick-volleyed hand-clapping.

They discussed the speech in the dormitories. There was not one dissentient voice. Mr. Raymond Martin, beyond question, was born in a gutter, and bred in a Board-school,* where they played marbles. He was further (I give the barest handful from great store) a Flopshus Cad, an Outrageous Stinker, a Jelly-bellied Flag-flapper (this was Stalky's contribution), and several other things which it is not seemly to put down.

The volunteer cadet-corps fell in next Monday, depressedly, with a face of shame. Even then, judicious silence might have turned the corner.

Said Foxy: 'After a fine speech like what you 'eard night before last, you ought to take 'old of your drill with re-newed activity. I don't see how you can avoid comin' out an' marchin' in the open now.'

'Can't we get out of it, then, Foxy?' Stalky's fine old silky tone should have warned him.

'No, not with his giving the flag so generously. He told me before he left this morning that there was no objection to the corps usin' it as their own. It's a handsome flag.'

Stalky returned his rifle to the rack in dead silence, and fell out. His example was followed by Hogan and Ansell.

Perowne hesitated. 'Look here, oughtn't we——?' he began.

'I'll get it out of the locker in a minute,' said the Sergeant, his back turned. 'Then we can——'

'Come on!' shouted Stalky. 'What the devil are you waiting for? Dismiss! Break off.'

'Why—what the—where the——?'

The rattle of Sniders, slammed into the rack, drowned his voice, as boy after boy fell out.

'I—I don't know that I shan't have to report this to the Head,' he stammered.

'Report, then, and be damned to you,' cried Stalky, white to the lips, and ran out.

*   *   *   *   *

'Rummy thing!' said Beetle to M'Turk. 'I was in the study, doin' a simply lovely poem about the Jelly-bellied Flag-flapper, an' Stalky came in, an' I said "Hullo!" an' he cursed me like a bargee, and then he began to blub like anything. Shoved his head on the table and howled. Hadn't we better do something?'

M'Turk was troubled. 'P'raps he's smashed himself up somehow.'

They found him, with very bright eyes, whistling between his teeth.

'Did I take you in, Beetle? I thought I would. Wasn't it a good draw? Didn't you think I was blubbin'? Didn't I do it well? Oh, you fat old ass!' And he began to pull Beetle's ears and cheeks, in the fashion that was called 'milking.'

'I knew you were blubbin',' Beetle replied composedly. 'Why aren't you at drill?'

'Drill! What drill?'

'Don't try to be a clever fool. Drill in the gym.'

"Cause there isn't any. The volunteer cadet-corps is broke up—disbanded—dead—putrid—corrupt—stinkin'. An' if you look at me like that, Beetle, I'll slay you too. . . . Oh yes, an' I'm goin' to be reported to the Head for swearin'.'

THE BIRTHRIGHT

*THE miracle of our land's speech—so known
And long received, none marvel when 'tis shown!*

We have such wealth as Rome at her most pride
Had not or (having) scattered not so wide;
Nor with such arrant prodigality
Beneath her any pagan's foot let lie . . .
Lo! Diamond that cost some half their days
To find and t'other half to bring to blaze:
Rubies of every heat, wherethrough we scan
The fiercer and more fiery heart of man:
Emerald that with the uplifted billow vies,
And Sapphires evening remembered skies:
Pearl perfect, as immortal tears must show,
Bred, in deep waters, of a piercing woe;
And tender Turkis, so with charms y-writ,
Of woven gold, Time dares not bite on it.
Thereafter, in all manners worked and set,
Jade, coral, amber, crystal, ivories, jet,—
Showing no more than various fancies, yet,
Each a Life's token or Love's amulet. . . .
Which things, through timeless arrogance of use,
We neither guard nor garner, but abuse;
So that our scholars—nay, our children—fling
In sport or jest treasure to arm a King;
And the gross crowd, at feast or market, hold
Traffic perforce with dust of gems and gold!

The Propagation of Knowledge

THE Army Class 'English,' which included the Upper Fifth, was trying to keep awake; for 'English' (Literature—Augustan epoch—eighteenth century) came at last lesson, and that, on a blazing July afternoon, meant after every one had been bathing. Even Mr. King found it hard to fight against the snore of the tide along the Pebble Ridge, and spurred himself with strong words.

Since, said he, the pearls of English Literature existed only to be wrenched from their settings and cast before young swine* rooting for marks, it was his loathed business—in anticipation of the Army Preliminary Examination which, as usual, would be held at the term's end, under the auspices of an official Examiner sent down *ad hoc*—to prepare for the Form a General Knowledge test-paper, which he would give them next week. It would cover their studies, up to date, of the Augustans and *King Lear*, which was the selected—and strictly expurgated—Army Exam. play for that year. Now, English Literature, as he might have told them, was *not* divided into water-tight compartments, but flowed like a river. For example, Samuel Johnson, glory of the Augustans and no mean commentator of Shakespeare, was but one in a mighty procession which——

At this point Beetle's nodding brows came down with a grunt on the desk. He had been soaking and sunning himself in the open sea-baths built out on the rocks under the cliffs, from two-fifteen to four-forty.

The Army Class took Johnson off their minds. With any luck, Beetle would last King till the tea-bell. King rubbed his hands and began to carve him. He had gone to sleep to show his contempt (*a*) for Mr. King, who might or might not matter, and (*b*) for the Augustans, who none the less were not to be sneered at by one whose vast and omnivorous reading, for which such extraordinary facilities had been granted (this was because the Head had allowed Beetle the run of his

library), naturally overlooked such *epigonoi** as Johnson,
Swift, Pope, Addison, and the like. Harrison Ainsworth* and
Marryat* doubtless appealed——

Even so, Beetle salt-encrusted all over except his spectacles, and steeped in delicious languors, was sliding back
to sleep again, what 'Taffy' Howell, the leading light of
the Form, who knew his Marryat as well as Stalky did
his Surtees, began in his patent, noiseless whisper: ' "Allow
me to observe—in the most delicate manner in the world—just
to hint——" '

'Under pretext of studying literature, a desultory and
unformed mind would naturally return, like the dog of
Scripture——'*

' "You're a damned trencher-scrapin', napkin-carryin',
shillin'-seekin', up-an'-down-stairs &c." ' Howell breathed.

Beetle choked aloud on the sudden knowledge that King
was the ancient and eternal Chucks—later Count Shucksen—
of *Peter Simple.** He had not realised it before.

'Sorry, sir. I'm afraid I've been asleep, sir,' he sputtered.

The shout of the Army Class diverted the storm. King was
grimly glad that Beetle had condescended to honour truth so
far. Perhaps he would now lend awakened ear to a summary
of the externals of Dr. Johnson, as limned by Macaulay.* And
he read, with intention, the just historian's outline of a
grotesque figure with untied shoe-strings, that twitched and
grunted, gorged its food, bit its finger-nails, and neglected its
ablutions. The Form hailed it as a speaking likeness of Beetle;
nor were they corrected.

Then King implored him to vouchsafe his comrades one
single fact connected with Dr. Johnson which might at any
time have adhered to what, for decency's sake, must, Mr.
King supposed, be called his mind.

Beetle was understood to say that the only thing he could
remember was in French.

'You add, then, the Gallic tongue to your accomplishments?
The information plus the accent? 'Tis well! Admirable
Crichton,* proceed!'

And Beetle proceeded with the text of an old Du Maurier*
drawing in a back-number of *Punch:*

'De tous ces défunts cockolores
Le moral Fénélon,*
Michel Ange et Johnson
(Le Docteur) sont les plus awful bores.'*

To which Howell, wooingly, just above his breath:
' "Oh, *won't* you come up, come up?" '*

Result, as the tea-bell rang, one hundred lines, to be shown up at seven-forty-five that evening. This was meant to blast the pleasant summer interval between tea and prep. Howell, a favourite in 'English' as well as Latin, got off; but the Army Class crashed in to tea with a new Limerick.

The imposition was a matter of book-keeping, so far as Beetle was concerned; for it was his custom of rainy afternoons to fabricate store of lines in anticipation of just these accidents. They covered such English verse as interested him at the moment, and helped to fix the stuff in his memory. After tea, he drew the required amount from his drawer in Number Five study, thrust it into his pocket, went up to the Head's house, and settled himself in the big Outer Library where, ever since the Head had taken him off all mathematics, he did précis-work and French translation. Here he buried himself in a close-printed, thickish volume which had been his chosen browse for some time. A hideous account of a hanging, drawing, and quartering had first attracted him to it; but later he discovered the book (*Curiosities of Literature** was its name) full of the finest confused feeding—such as forgeries and hoaxes, Italian literary societies, religious and scholastic controversies of old when men (even that most dreary John Milton, of *Lycidas*) slanged each other, not without dust and heat,* in scandalous pamphlets; personal peculiarities of the great; and a hundred other fascinating inutilities. This evening he fell on a description of wandering, mad Elizabethan beggars, known as Tom-a-Bedlams, with incidental references to Edgar who plays at being a Tom-a-Bedlam in *Lear*, but whom Beetle did not consider at all funny. Then, at the foot of a left-hand page, leaped out on him a verse—of incommunicable splendour, opening doors into inexplicable worlds—from a song which Tom-a-Bedlams were supposed to sing. It ran:

> With a heart of furious fancies
>   Whereof I am commander,
> With a burning spear and a horse of air,
>   To the wilderness I wander.
> With a knight of ghosts and shadows
>   I summoned am to tourney,
> Ten leagues beyond the wide world's end—
>   Methinks it is no journey

He sat, mouthing and staring before him, till the prep.-bell rang and it was time to take his lines up to King's study and lay them, as hot from the press, in the impot-basket* appointed. He carried his dreams on to Number Five. They knew the symptoms of old.

'Readin' again,' said Stalky, like a wife welcoming her spouse from the pot-house.

'Look here, I've found out something——' Beetle began. 'Listen——'

'No, you don't—till afterwards. It's Turkey's prep.' This meant it was a Horace Ode through which Turkey would take them for a literal translation, and all possible pitfalls. Stalky gave his businesslike attention, but Beetle's eye was glazed and his mind adrift throughout, and he asked for things to be repeated. So, when Turkey closed the Horace, justice began to be executed.

'I'm all right,' he protested, 'I swear I heard a lot of what Turkey said. Shut up! Oh, shut *up*! *Do* shut up, you putrid asses.' Beetle was speaking from the fender, his head between Turkey's knees, and Stalky largely over the rest of him.

'What's the metre of the beastly thing?' M'Turk waved his Horace. 'Look it up, Stalky. Twelfth of the Third.'*

'*Ionicum a minore*,'* Stalky reported, closing his book in turn. 'Don't let him forget it'; and Turkey's Horace marked the metre on Beetle's skull, with special attention to elisions. It hurt.

> 'Miserar' est neq' amori dare ludum neque dulci
>   Mala vino laver aut ex——*

Got it? You liar! You've no ear at all! Chorus, Stalky!'

Both Horaces strove to impart the measure, which was altogether different from its accompaniment. Presently Howell dashed in from his study below.

'Look *out*! If you make this infernal din we'll have some one up the staircase in a sec.'

'We're teachin' Beetle Horace. He was goin' to burble us some muck he'd read,' the tutors explained.

''Twasn't muck! It was about those Tom-a-Bedlams in *Lear*.'

'Oh!' said Stalky. 'Why didn't you say so?'

''Cause you didn't listen. They had drinkin'-horns an' badges, and there's a Johnson note on Shakespeare about the meanin' of Edgar sayin' "My horn's dry." But Johnson's dead-wrong about it. Aubrey* says——'

'Who's Aubrey?' Howell demanded. 'Does King know about him?'

'Dunno. Oh yes, an' Johnson started to learn Dutch when he was seventy.'

'What the deuce for?' Stalky asked.

'For a change after his Dikker,* I suppose,' Howell suggested.

'And I looked up a lot of other English stuff, too. I'm goin' to try it all on King.'

'Showin'-off as usual,' said the acid M'Turk, who, like his race, lived and loved to destroy illusions.

'No. For a draw.* He's an unjust dog! If you read, he says you're showin'-off. If you don't, you're a mark-huntin' Philistine.* What does he want you to do, curse him?'

'Shut up, Beetle!' Stalky pronounced. 'There's more than draws in this. You've cribbed your maths off me ever since you came to Coll. You don't know what a cosine is, even *now*. Turkey does all your Latin.'

'I like that! Who does both your *Picciolas*?'*

'French don't count. It's time you began to work for your giddy livin' an' help us. *You* aren't goin' up for anythin' that matters. Play for your side, as Heffles says, or die the death! You don't want to die the death, again, do you? Now, let's hear about that stinkard Johnson swottin' Dutch. You're sure it was Sammivel, not Binjimin?* You *are* so dam' inaccurate!'

Beetle conducted an attentive class on the curiosities of literature for nearly a quarter of an hour. As Stalky pointed out, he promised to be useful.

The Horace Ode next morning ran well; and King was content. Then, in full feather, he sailed round the firmament at large, and, somehow, apropos to something or other, used the word 'della Cruscan'*—'if any of you have the faintest idea of its origin.' Some one hadn't caught it correctly which gave Beetle just time to whisper 'Bran—an' mills' to Howell, who said, promptly: 'Hasn't it somethin' to do with mills—an' bran, sir?' King cast himself into poses of stricken wonder. 'Oddly enough,' said he, 'it has.'

They were then told a great deal about some silly Italian Academy of Letters which borrowed its office furniture from the equipment of mediæval flour-mills. And: 'How has our Ap-Howell* come by his knowledge?' Howell, being, indeed, Welsh, thought that it might have been something he had read in the holidays. King openly purred over him.

'If that had been *me*,' Beetle observed while they were toying with sardines between lessons, 'he'd ha' dropped on me for showin'-off.'

'See what we're savin' you from,' Stalky answered. 'I'm playin' Johnson, 'member, this afternoon.'

That, too, came cleanly off the bat; and King was gratified by this interest in the Doctor's studies. But Stalky hadn't a ghost of a notion how he had come by the fact.

'Why didn't you say your father told you?' Beetle asked at tea.

'My-y Lord! Have you ever seen the guv'nor?' Stalky collapsed shrieking among the piles of bread and butter. 'Well, look here. Taffy goes in to-morrow about those drinkin' horns an' Tom-a-Bedlams. You cut up to the library after tea, Beetle. You know what King's English papers are like. Look out useful stuff for answers an' we'll divvy* at prep.'

At prep., then, Beetle, loaded with assorted curiosities, made his forecast. He argued that there were bound to be a good many 'what-do-you-know-abouts' those infernal Augustans. Pope was generally a separate item; but the odds were that Swift, Addison, Steele, Johnson, and Goldsmith would be lumped under one head. Dryden was possible, too, though rather outside the Epoch.

'Dryden. Oh! "Glorious John!" 'Know *that* much, anyhow,' Stalky vaunted.

'Then lug in Claude Halcro in the *Pirate,** Beetle advised. 'He's always sayin' "Glorious John." King's a hog on Scott, too.'

'No-o. I don't read Scott. You take this Hell Crow* chap, Taffy.'

'Right. What about Addison, Beetle?' Howell asked.

''Drank like a giddy fish.'

'We all know that,' chorused the gentle children.

'He said, "See how a Christian can die"; an' he hadn't any conversation, 'cause some one or other——'

'Guessin' again, *as* usual,' M'Turk sneered. 'Who?'

''Cynical man called Mandeville*—said he was a silent parson in a tie-wig.'

'Right-ho! I'll take the silent parson with wig and 'purtenances. Taffy can have the dyin' Christian,' Stalky decided.

Howell nodded, and resumed: 'What about Swift, Beetle?'

''Died mad. Two girls.* 'Saw a tree, an' said: "I shall die at the top."* Oh yes, an' his private amusements were "ridiculous an' trivial."*'

Howell shook a wary head. 'Dunno what that might let me in for with King. You can have it, Stalky.'

'I'll take that,' M'Turk yawned. 'King doesn't matter a curse to me, an' he knows it. "Private amusements contemptible."' He breathed all Ireland into the last perverted word.

'Right,' Howell assented. 'Bags I* the dyin' tree, then.'

''Cheery lot, these Augustans,' Stalky sighed. ''Any more of 'em been croakin' lately, Beetle?'

'My Hat!' the far-seeing Howell struck in. 'King always gives us a stinker half-way down. What about Richardson—that "Clarissa" chap, y'know?'

'I've found out lots about him,' said Beetle, promptly. 'He was the "Shakespeare of novelists."'

}

'King won't stand that. He says there's only one Shakespeare. 'Mustn't rot about Shakespeare to King,' Howell objected.

'An' he was "always delighted with his own works," ' Beetle continued.

'Like you,' Stalky pointed out.

'Shut up. Oh yes, an'——' he consulted some hieroglyphics on a scrap of paper—'the—the impassioned Diderot* (dunno who *he* was) broke forth: "O Richardson, thou singular genius!" '

Howell and Stalky rose together, each clamouring that he had bagged that first.

'I *must* have it!' Howell shouted. 'King's never seen me breakin' forth with the impassioned Diderot. He's *got* to! Give me Diderot, you impassioned hound!'

'Don't upset the table. There's tons more. An' his genius was "fertile and prodigal." '

'All right! *I* don't mind bein' "fertile and prodigal" for a change,' Stalky volunteered. 'King's going to enjoy this exam. If he was the Army Prelim. chap we'd score.'

'The Prelim. questions will be pretty much like King's stuff,' Beetle assured them.

'But it's always a score to know what your examiner's keen on,' Howell said, and illustrated it with an anecdote. "Uncle of mine stayin' with my people last holidays——'

'Your Uncle Diderot?' Stalky asked.

'No, you ass! Captain of Engineers. He told me he was up for a Staff exam. to an old Colonel-bird who believed that the English were the Lost Tribes of Israel, or something like that. He'd written tons o' books about it.'

'All Sappers* are mad,' said Stalky. 'That's one of the things the guv'nor *did* tell me.'

'Well, ne'er mind. My uncle played up, o' course. 'Said he'd always believed it, too. And *so* he got nearly top-marks for field-fortification. 'Didn't know a thing about it, either, he said.'

'Good biznai!' said Stalky. 'Well, go on, Beetle. What about Steele?'

'Can't I keep anything for myself?'

'Not *much*!* King'll ask you where you got it from, and you'd show off, an' he'd find out. This ain't your silly English Literature, you ass. It's our marks. Can't you see that?'

Beetle very soon saw it was exactly as Stalky had said.

Some days later a happy, and therefore not too likeable, King was explaining to the Reverend John in his own study how effort, zeal, scholarship, the Humanities, and perhaps a little natural genius for teaching, could inspire even the mark-hunting minds of the young. His text was the result of his General Knowledge paper on the Augustans and *King Lear*.

'Howell,' he said, 'I was not surprised at. He *has* intelligence. But, frankly, I did not expect young Corkran to burgeon. Almost one might believe he occasionally read a book.'

'And M'Turk too?'

'Yes. He had somehow arrived at a rather just estimate of Swift's lighter literary diversions. They *are* contemptible. And in the "Lear" questions—they were all attracted by Edgar's character—Stalky had dug up something about Aubrey on Tom-a-Bedlams from some unknown source. Aubrey, of all people! I'm sure I only alluded to him once or twice.'

'Stalky among the prophets of "English"! And he didn't remember where he'd got it either?'

'No. Boys are amazingly purblind and limited. But if they keep this up at the Army Prelim., it is conceivable the Class may not do itself discredit. I told them so.'

'I congratulate you. Ours is the hardest calling in the world, with the least reward. By the way, who are they likely to send down to examine us?'

'It rests between two, I fancy. Martlett—with me at Balliol—and Hume. *They* wisely chose the Civil Service. Martlett has published a brochure on Minor Elizabethan Verse—journeyman work, of course—enthusiasms, but no grounding. Hume I heard of lately as having infected himself in Germany with some Transatlantic abomination about Shakespeare and Bacon.* He was Sutton.'* (The Head, by the way, was a Sutton man.)

King returned to his examination-papers and read extracts

from them, as mothers repeat the clever sayings of their babes.

'Here's old Taffy Howell, for instance—apropos to Diderot's eulogy of Richardson. "The impassioned Diderot broke forth: 'Richardson, thou singular genius!' " '

It was the Reverend John who stopped himself, just in time, from breaking forth. He recalled that, some days ago, he had heard Stalky on the stairs of Number Five, hurling the boots of many fags at Howell's door and bidding the 'impassioned Diderot' within 'break forth' at his peril.

'Odd,' said he, gravely, when his pipe drew again. 'Where did Diderot say that?'

'I've forgotten for the moment. Taffy told me he'd picked it up in the course of holiday reading.'

'Possibly. One never knows what heifers the young are ploughing with. Oh! How did Beetle do?'

'The necessary dates and his handwriting defeated him, I'm glad to say. I cannot accuse myself of having missed any opportunity to castigate that boy's inordinate and intolerable conceit. But I'm afraid it's hopeless. I think I touched him somewhat, though, when I read Macaulay's stock piece on Johnson. The others saw it at once.'

'Yes, you told me about that at the time,' said the Reverend John, hurriedly.

'And our esteemed Head having taken him off maths for this précis-writing—whatever that means!—has turned him into a most objectionable free-lance. He was without any sense of reverence before, and promiscuous cheap fiction—which is all that his type of reading means—aggravates his worst points. When it came to a trial he was simply nowhere.'

'Ah, well! Ours is a hard calling—specially if one's sensitive. Luckily, I'm too fat.' The Reverend John went out to bathe off the Pebble Ridge, girt with a fair linen towel whose red fringe signalled from half a mile away.

There lurked on summer afternoons, round the fives-court or the gym, certain watchful outcasts who had exhausted their weekly ration of three baths, and who were too well known to Cory the bathman to outface him by swearing that they hadn't. These came in like sycophantic pups at walk, and when the Reverend John climbed the Pebble Ridge, more than a dozen of them were at his heels, with never a towel among them. One could only bathe off the Ridge with a House-master, but by custom, a dozen details above a certain age, no matter whence recruited, made a 'House' for bathing, if any kindly master chose so to regard them. Beetle led the low, growing reminder: 'House! House, sir? We've got a House now, Padre.'

'Let it be law as it is desired,' boomed the Reverend John. On which word they broke forward, hirpling* over the unstable pebbles and stripping as they ran, till, when they touched the sands, they were as naked as God had made them, and as happy as He intended them to be.

It was half-flood—dead-smooth, except for the triple line of combers, a mile from wing to wing, that broke evenly with a sound of ripping canvas, while their sleek rear-guards formed up behind. One swam forth, trying to copy the roll, rise, and dig-out of the Reverend John's side-stroke, and manœuvred to meet them so that they should crash on one's head, when for an instant one glanced down arched perspectives of beryl, before all broke in fizzy, electric diamonds, and the pulse of the main surge slung one towards the beach. From a good comber's crest one was hove up almost to see Lundy* on the horizon. In its long cream-streaked trough, when the top had turned over and gone on, one might be alone in mid-Atlantic. Either way it was divine. Then one capered on the sands till one dried off, retrieved scattered flannels, gave thanks in chorus to the Reverend John, and lazily trailed up to five-o'clock call-over, taken on the lower cricket field.

'Eight this week,' said Beetle, and thanked Heaven aloud.

'Bathing seems to have sapped your mind,' the Reverend John remarked. 'Why did you do so vilely with the Augustans?'

'They *are* vile, Padre. So's *Lear*.'

'The other two did all right, though.'

'I expect they've been swottin',' Beetle grinned.

'I've expected that, too, in my time. But I want to hear about the "impassioned Diderot," please.'

'Oh, that was Howell, Padre. You mean when Diderot broke

forth: "Richardson, thou singular genius"? He'd read it in the holidays somewhere.'

'I *beg* your pardon. Naturally, Taffy would read Diderot in the holidays. Well, I'm sorry I can't lick you for this; but if any one ever finds out anything about it, you've only yourself to thank.'

Beetle went up to Coll. and to the Outer Library, where he had on tap the last of a book called *Elsie Venner*, by a man called Oliver Wendell Holmes—all about a girl who was interestingly allied to rattlesnakes.* He finished what was left of her, and cast about for more from the same hand, which he found on the same shelf, with the trifling difference that the writer's Christian name was now Nathaniel,* and he did not deal in snakes. The authorship of Shakespeare was his theme—not that Shakespeare with whom King oppressed the Army Class, but a lowborn, poaching, ignorant, immoral village lout who could not have written one line of any play ascribed to him. (Beetle wondered what King would say to Nathaniel if ever they met.) The real author was Francis Bacon, of Bacon's Essays, which did not strike Beetle as any improvement. He had 'done' the Essays last term. But evidently Nathaniel's views annoyed people, for the margins of his book—it was second-hand, and the old label of a public library still adhered—flamed with ribald, abusive, and contemptuous comments by various hands. They ranged from 'Rot!' 'Rubbish!' and such like to crisp counter-arguments. And several times some one had written: 'This beats Delia.'* One copious annotator dissented, saying: 'Delia is supreme in this line,' 'Delia beats this hollow,' 'See Delia's Philosophy, page so and so.' Beetle grieved he could not find anything about Delia (he had often heard King's views on lady-writers as a class) beyond a statement by Nathaniel, with pencilled exclamation-points rocketing all round it, that 'Delia Bacon discovered in Francis Bacon a good deal more than Macaulay.' Taking it by and large, with the kind help of the marginal notes, it appeared that Delia and Nathaniel between them had perpetrated every conceivable outrage against the Head-God of King's idolatry: and King was particular about his idols. Without pronouncing on the merits of the controversy, it occurred to Beetle that a well-mixed dose of Nathaniel ought to work on King like a seidlitz powder.* At this point a pencil and a half sheet of impot-paper came into action, and he went down to tea so swelled with Baconian heresies and blasphemies that he could only stutter between mouthfuls. He returned to his labours after the meal, and was visibly worse at prep.

'I say,' he began, 'have you ever heard that Shakespeare never wrote his own beastly plays?'

"Fat lot of good to us!' said Stalky. 'We've got to swot 'em up just the same. Look here! This is for English parsin' to-morrow. It's *your* biznai.' He read swiftly from the school *Lear* (Act II. Sc. 2) thus:

> STEWARD: 'Never any:
> It pleased the King his master, very late,
> To strike at me, upon his misconstruction;
> When he, conjunct, an' flatterin' his displeasure,
> Tripped me behind: bein' down, insulted, railed,
> And put upon him such a deal of man,
> That worthy'd him, got praises of the King
> For him attemptin' who was self-subdued;
> And, in the fleshment of this dread exploit,
> Drew on me here again.

'Now then, my impassioned bard, *construez*! That's Shakespeare.'

"Give it up! He's drunk,' Beetle declared at the end of a blank half minute.

'No, he isn't,' said Turkey. 'He's a steward—on the estate—chattin' to his employers.'

'Well—look here, Turkey. You ask King if Shakespeare ever wrote his own plays, an' he won't give a dam' what the steward said.'

'I've not come here to play with ushers,'* was M'Turk's view of the case.

'I'd do it,' Beetle protested, 'only he'd slay *me*! He don't love me when I ask about things. I can give you the stuff to draw him—tons of it!' He broke forth into a précis, interspersed with praises, of Nathaniel Holmes and his commentators—especially the latter. He also mentioned Delia, with sorrow that he had not read her. He spoke through nearly the whole of prep.; and the upshot of it was that M'Turk relented and promised to approach King next 'English' on the authenticity of Shakespeare's plays.

The time and tone chosen were admirable. While King was warming himself by a preliminary canter round the Form's literary deficiencies, Turkey coughed in a style which suggested a reminder to a slack *employé* that it was time to stop chattering and get to work. As King began to bristle, Turkey inquired: 'I'd be glad to know, sir, if it's true that Shakespeare did not write his own plays at all?'

'Good God!' said King most distinctly. Turkey coughed again piously. 'They all say so in Ireland, sir.'

'Ireland—Ireland—Ireland!' King overran Ireland with one blast of flame that should have been written in letters of brass for instruction to-day. At the end, Turkey coughed once more, and the cough said: 'It is Shakespeare, and not my country, that you are hired to interpret to me.' He put it directly, too: 'An' is it true at all about the alleged plays, sir?'

'It is not,' Mr. King whispered, and began to explain, on lines that might, perhaps, have been too freely expressed for the parents of those young (though it gave their offspring delight), but with a passion, force, and wealth of imagery which would have crowned his discourse at any university. By the time he drew towards his peroration the Form was almost openly applauding. Howell noiselessly drummed the cadence of 'Bonnie Dundee'* on his desk; Paddy Vernon framed a dumb: 'Played! Oh, *well* played, sir!' at intervals; Stalky kept tally of the brighter gems of invective; and Beetle sat aghast but exulting among the spirits he had called up. For though their works had never been mentioned, and though Mr. King said he had merely glanced at the obscene publications, he seemed to know a tremendous amount about Nathaniel and Delia—especially Delia.

'I told you so!' said Beetle, proudly, at the end.

'What? *Him!* I wasn't botherin' myself to listen to him an' his Delia,' M'Turk replied.

Afterwards King fought his battle over again with the Reverend John in the Common-room.

'Had I been that triple ass Hume, I might have risen to the bait. As it is, I flatter myself I left them under no delusions as to Shakespeare's authenticity. Yes, a small drink, please. Virtue has gone out of me indeed.* But *where* did they get it from?'

'The devil! The young devil!' the Reverend John muttered, half aloud.

'I could have excused devilry. It was ignorance. Sheer, crass, insolent provincial ignorance! I tell you, Gillett, if the Romans had dealt faithfully with the Celt, *ab initio*,* this—this would never have happened.'

'Quite so. I should like to have heard your remarks.'

'I've told 'em to tell me what they remember of them, with their own conclusions, in essay form next week.'

Since he had loosed the whirlwind, the fair-minded Beetle offered to do Turkey's essay for him. On Turkey's behalf, then, he dealt with Shakespeare's lack of education, his butchering, poaching, drinking, horse-holding, and errand-running as Nathaniel had described them; lifted from the same source pleasant names, such as 'rustic' and 'sorry poetaster,'* on which last special hopes were built; and expressed surprise that one so ignorant 'could have done what he was attributed to.' His own essay contained no novelties. Indeed, he withheld one or two promising 'subsequently transpireds' for fear of distracting King.

But, when the essays were read, Mr. King confined himself wholly to Turkey's pitiful, puerile, jejune, exploded, unbaked, half-bottomed thesis. He touched, too, on the 'lie in the soul,'* which was, fundamentally, vulgarity—the negation of Reverence and the Decencies. He broke forth into an impassioned defence of 'mere atheism,' which he said was often no more than mental flatulence—transitory and curable by knowledge of life—in no way comparable, for essential enormity, with the debasing pagan abominations to which Turkey had delivered himself. He ended with a shocking story about one Jowett,* who seemed to have held some post of authority where King came from, and who had told an atheistical undergraduate that if he could not believe in a

Personal God by five that afternoon he would be expelled—as, with tears of rage in his eyes, King regretted that he could not expel M'Turk. And Turkey blew his nose in the middle of it.

But the aim of education being to develop individual judgment, King could not well kill him for his honest doubts about Shakespeare. And he himself had several times quoted, in respect to other poets: 'There lives more faith in honest doubt, Believe me, than in half the creeds.'* So he treated Turkey in form like a coiled puff-adder; and there was a tense peace among the Augustans. The only ripple was the day before the Army Examiner came, when Beetle inquired if he 'need take this exam., sir, as I'm not goin' up for anything.' Mr. King said there was great need—for many reasons, none of them flattering to vanity.

As far as the Army Class could judge, the Examiner was not worse than his kind, and the written 'English' paper ran closely on the lines of King's mid-term General Knowledge test. Howell played his 'impassioned Diderot' to the Richardson lead; Stalky his parson in the wig; M'Turk his contemptible Swift; Beetle, Steel's affectionate notes out of the spunging-house* to 'Dearest Prue,' all in due order. There were, however, one or two leading questions about Shakespeare. A boy's hand shot up from a back bench.

'In answering Number Seven—reasons for Shakespeare's dramatic supremacy,' he said, 'are we to take it Shakespeare *did* write the plays he is supposed to have written, sir?'

The Examiner hesitated an instant. 'It is generally assumed that he did.' But there was no reproof in his words. Beetle began to sit down slowly.

Another hand and another voice: 'Have we got to say we believe he did, sir? Even if we do nott?'*

'You are not called upon to state your beliefs. But we can go into that at *viva voce** this afternoon—if it interests you.'

'Thank you, sir.'

'What did you do that for?' Paddy Vernon demanded at dinner.

'It's the Lost Tribes of Israel game, you ass,' said Howell.

'To make sure,' Stalky amplified. 'If he was like King, he'd have shut up Beetle an' Turkey at the start, but he'd have thought King gave us the Bacon notion. Well, he didn't shut 'em up; so they're playin' it again this afternoon. If he stands it then, he'll be sure King gave us the notion. Either way, it's dead-safe for us—*an'* King.'

At the afternoon's *viva voce*, before they sat down to the Augustans, the Examiner wished to hear, 'with no bearing on the examination, of course,' from those two condidates who had asked him about Question Seven. Which were they?

'Take off your gigs,* you owl,' said Stalky between his teeth. Beetle pocketed them and looked into blurred vacancy with a voice coming out of it that asked: 'Who—what gave you that idea about Shakespeare?' From Stalky's kick he knew the question was for him.

'Some people say, sir, there's a good deal of doubt about it nowadays, sir.'

'Ye-es, that's true, but——'

'It's his knowin' so much about legal phrases.' Turkey was in support—a lone gun barking somewhere to his right.

'That is a crux, I admit. Of course, whatever one may think privately, officially Shakespeare *is* Shakespeare. But how have *you* been taught to look at the question?'

'Well, Holmes says it's impossible he could——'

'On the legal phraseology alone, sir,' M'Turk chimed in.

'Ah, but the theory is that Shakespeare's experiences in the society of that day brought him in contact with all the leading intellects.' The Examiner's voice was quite colloquial now.

'But they didn't think much of actors then, sir, did they?' This was Howell cooing like a cushat dove.* 'I mean——'

The Examiner explained the status of the Elizabethan actor in some detail, ending: 'And that makes it the more curious, doesn't it?'

'And this Shakespeare was supposed to be writin' plays and actin' in 'em *all* the time?' M'Turk asked, with sinister meaning.

'Exactly what I—what lots of people have pointed out. Where did he get the time to acquire all his special knowledge?'

'Then it looks as if there was something in it, doesn't it, sir?'

'That,' said the Examiner, squaring his elbows at ease on the desk, 'is a very large question which——'

'Yes, sir!'—in half-a-dozen eagerly attentive keys. . . .

For decency's sake a few Augustan questions were crammed in conscience-strickenly, about the last ten minutes. Howell took them since they involved dates, but the answers, though highly marked, were scarcely heeded. When the clock showed six-thirty the Examiner addressed them as 'Gentlemen'; and said he would have particular pleasure in speaking well of this Army Class, which had evinced such a genuine and unusual interest in English Literature, and which reflected the greatest credit on their instructors. He passed out: the Form upstanding, as custom was.

'He's goin' to congratulate King,' said Howell. 'Don't make a row! "Don't—make—a—noise—Or else you'll wake the Baby!" '* . . .

Mr. King of Balliol, after Mr. Hume of Sutton had complimented him, as was only just, before all his colleagues in Common-room, was kindly taken by the Reverend John to his study, where he exploded on the hearth-rug.

'He—he thought *I* had loosed this—this rancid Baconian rot among them. He complimented me on my breadth of mind—my being abreast of the times! You heard him? That's how they think at Sutton. It's an open stye! A lair of bestial! They have a chapel there, Gillett, and they pray for their souls—their *souls*!'

'His particular weakness apart, Hume was perfectly sincere about what you'd done for the Army Class. He'll report in that sense, too. That's a feather in your cap, and a deserved one. He said their interest in Literature was unusual. That is *all* your work, King.'

'But I bowed down in the House of Rimmon* while he Baconised all over me!—poor devil of an usher that I am! You heard it! I ought to have spat in his eye! Heaven knows I'm as conscious of my own infirmities as my worst enemy can be; but what have I done to deserve this! What *have* I done?'

'That's just what I was wondering,' the Reverend John replied. 'Have you, perchance, done anything?'

'Where? How?'

'In any Army Class, for example.'

'Assuredly not! My Army Class? I couldn't wish for a better—keen, interested enough to read outside their allotted task—intelligent, receptive! They're head and shoulders above last year's. The idea that I, forsooth, should, even by inference, have perverted their minds with this imbecile and unspeakable girls'-school tripe that Hume professes! *You* at least know that I have my standards; and in Literature and in the Classics, I hold *maxima debetur pueris reverentia.*'[1]

'It's singular, not plural, isn't it?' said the Reverend John. 'But you're absolutely right as to the principle! . . . Ours is a deadly calling, King—specially if one happens to be sensitive.'

---

[1] The greatest respect is due to young persons.

The Satisfaction of a Gentleman

LONG before the days of 'Cyrano de Bergerac,'* the Coll. knew that you might discuss his red nose with Dickson Quartus in all amity and safety, so long as it did not turn blue, and he did not gnash his teeth and speak with tongues. If that happened—why, anything might happen; and the worst generally happened after long stretches of lean living. For example, 'Pussy' Abanazar and Tertius, his study-mates, being the junior sub-prefects of that winter term, were in the field, taking Lower School footer—which, of course, took both of their fags*—and Dick coming up from place-kicking found the study fire out, too.

Naturally, he went up to Number Five, immediately overhead, and borrowed from Beetle, *in reposo* on the domestic hearth, a shovelful of burning coals. Coming down with it, he almost ran into Mr. King, his own House-master, at the bottom of the stairs, and from sheer nervous shock tilted out the whole affair at, if not over, his feet. There was some energetic dancing and denouncing, as Beetle noted through the banisters, and when it had ceased Dick had five hundred lines, which did not prevent him from being very happy with Beetle over the spirited action of King's hind-legs among the cinders.

Last lesson that day was English Literature—'Paradise Lost'—and when Harrison major, whose voice is as a lost sheep's, bleated about Satan treading on 'burning marl,'* Beetle sputtered aloud.

King might or might not have guessed the connection. But he said nothing beyond, 'Two hundred Latin lines.' Dick condoled with Beetle after tea; but also developed his own grievance, which was that Beetle had heaped too many coals of fire* on him.

'I like that!' was the retort. 'I kept *on* tellin' you your shovel wouldn't hold 'em, you blue-snouted Mandrill.'* Beetle knew much about the coloration of Mandrills, and would often describe it to Dick.

But this time Dick's nose blue-fired where it stood; he gnashed his teeth, and emitted the war cry of the Royal Line of Ashantee.* (His naval uncle had fought in those parts* and, Dick swore, had taught him all the languages.) What followed, though painful for Beetle who was alone (and Pussy was with Dick), was merely an affair of outposts. The Temple of Janus was opened* ceremonially later. After prayers, Number Five, who were sitting up from nine of ten for 'extra work,' caught a fag of their House about to undress, hustled it into a nightgown over all for tabard, and sent it to Dick's study with a stolen gym boxing-glove, which Turkey called 'the Cartel.'* Dick spared the quavering herald, and pranced up to Number Five, robed in a tablecloth, at the very top of his rarely shown form. As Head of the Gaboon* and the Dahomey Customs,* he talked Fantee,* which includes—with whistlings and quackings—Rabelaisian accounts of the manners of the West Coast, and the etiquette of native courts thereabouts; for his uncle had been an observant officer. It altogether destroyed Number Five. They clung to the table, beseeching Dick to stop and let them get breath; and they topped off the ribald hour with pickled onions and raspberry vinegar for a pledge of naked war.

When they went up to their study next morning, after second lesson, they found, when they could see, everything in it furred with a ghastly, greasy deposit; and a smell fouler than the sight. Dick had shut down their chimney damper, set an old 'gutty' golf ball in a sardine-tin on the new-made fire, jammed their window, plugged up with paper beneath their door, and let nature do the rest. Their pictures left white squares on the walls when they took them down. Turkey felt it most, for Art was his province. Beetle wanted to bore holes in the floor, and pour melted lead through; but, as Stalky pointed out, Pussy and Tertius were sub-prefects, and one could not include their study in the field of unrestricted warfare.

'Dick's flank is covered all right,' he said. 'Beetle ought to have thought of that. Yes, you ass, I *have* thought of snuff; but don't *you* try to think, or you'll hash it. Leave him alone!'

So when the King of Ashantee quacked his triumph at next

call-over, they all looked straitly to their own front, and lifted neither hand nor hoof. Only Pussy, on an exquisite note between apology and authority, reminded Stalky that the day following would be a House-match (Macrea's *v.* King's), which would claim him, Tertius and Dick from three to five. As sub-prefect he could have commanded a truce, but as ally of Dick he had sanctioned the war and had taken part in the execution of Beetle—Death by the Hundred Slices between two forms.

'That's all right,' Stalky answered him. '*We* wouldn't dree-eem of goin' into studies when they're empty.'

'Dick didn't think,' Pussy went on. It was the extreme limit of concession.

'Don't you worry, Kitten. He's goin' to.' After which, Stalky removed from Beetle six penny stamps reserved for correspondence.

''Want 'em all?' said Beetle.

'I didn't. But I will now, you selfish hound. I do all the work an'——'

'*All* right. 'Tisn't *my* fault if I can't write home,' said the robbed one in a relieved voice, and went on plaintively: 'Who's bagged my new socks, curse you?'

'Those Mandrill ones? 'Wouldn't be found dead in 'em. Turkey most likely. He's eesthetic.'

Beetle sighed. They were a church-going pair of a provocative peacock-blue, which, when coquettishly exhibited across an aisle, would make Dick's nose glow through half the sermon.

On Saturday afternoon, with everybody down at the House-match, Stalky brought out the communal frying-pan, and laid in it large slabs of the fattest bacon.

'Old Mother Hunt gave me all that for four-pence. She thinks it's a bit off. Fry it, Beetle.'

The slices rendered as generously as blubber. When the pan was about half full of fat, Stalky fished out three slices and tied each slice to a string from a new penny string-ball. Then he and the others leaned out of their window, and bobbed them against the window of the study below. In that crisp October air, each bob left a white blob of coagulated fat on the pane.

When a slice ceased to register, it was hauled up and reconditioned. At intervals, someone would go down to report on the effect from the ground-level, or to direct the more delicate stipplings. They put on a second coat to make sure, and judged that It would do.

The returning enemy were too full of their game to notice anything till they had washed, and were well at home again. Then, peering from above, Number Five saw Pussy's huge paw put forth, and an experimenting finger drawn through the creamy deposit on the panes.

'Go an' jape with them, Turkey. Get Dick's head well out. Keep that fat just off the bubble, Beetle,' said Stalky.

Turkey presented himself on the area-railings outside the lower study and, as usual, let others make conversation. He had gifts that way. Things had not gone much beyond 'Filthy swine!' when the King of Ashantee, ousting his slower-minded mates, leaned forth, and addressed himself directly to Turkey, with two golf balls, one after the other. Here Stalky took the pan from Beetle, and decanted, say, one pint of pure bacon fat on to Dick's scalp, where it set at once into a frosty wig. The bag of flour, dashed down after it, was sheer waste of the sixth of Beetle's penny stamps. Without a glance at the result, Turkey sauntered back, and pushed the study table against the door.

'All right. To-morrow's Sunday,' said Stalky. 'Good for Dick's topper. But don't you notice him. He's the Lord Anointed.'*

Saturday Prayers were worth attending; but next day's divine service was—just that! Dick's locks had clotted into irregular overlapping scales which, when flattened by a desperate hand, sprang up again unrelatedly. Even his study mates mocked him, but, for Number Five, it was as though he had never been upon earth or in memory. They merely put it about that his was a disease which comes from not brushing the hair, and that presently it would bleed.

That same Sabbath eve—disregarding advice and scorning reinforcements—the Head of the Gaboon tore upstairs alone to call upon them, when, seeing that he appeared to be armed, they fell on him—ankle, waist and neck—without a word. At last he was understood to say something about 'slugs in a saw-pit.'* They let up.

'It's your gloat,' he gasped. 'Let's top off with a duel in the Bunkers. I challenge the lot of you. Death before dishonour! *An*' give me some of that raspberry vinegar.'

''Your sally* any good?' M'Turk asked. He had Number Five's armoury in his own care.

'Hellish stiff. I was bringing it for you to clean a bit. I've got cartridges but no oil.' He picked up from the floor a lock-jawed twenty-two rim-fire Belgian saloon-pistol, which Turkey took over at once.

''Get expelled for duellin',' Beetle observed sourly.

'You abject cur! You're the only one with gig-lamps, too,' Stalky rebuked.

'*You* called me The Mandrill,' said the Head of the Gaboon. 'An' what was that beastliness of yours about my hair bleedin','—thou—thou varlet?' (That was Dick's word of the week, so to say.)

'Oh, *Plica Polonica*,'* said Beetle, and brightly summarised as much as he could recall of Polish Plat out of a Heaven-sent old encyclopedia.

'*Two* shots at Beetle for that,' said Dick icily.

'You shall have 'em!' cried generous Stalky. 'But look here, you can't take us *all* on. What about a quadrilateral duel?' Stalky saw himself excelling Marryat.*

'What for? You each get plugged at three times, same as me. *I* don't mind.'

'What distance?' said Turkey, with his head in his playbox among the oiled rags.

'Dunno, quite. 'Ten paces too much?' Stalky suggested.

'Rot!' Beetle protested. 'You can make a Burrows donkey bray his head off at a hundred yards with dust-shot. I've done it.'

'You unfeelin' brute! Now you can do a little brayin' on your own, an' see how you like it. I vote we make it twelve paces for the duels, and after that we'll pick sides and have a general stalk in the Bunkers.'

'Who's to give the range *then*?' Beetle asked.

'Guess it, you old burbler. Besides, dust-shot don't hardly sting even at point-blank.'

Beetle explained what his spiritual adventures must be ere he lent himself to such speculations. His piety wearied them.

'If you say much more we'll decree you a rabbit—same as Maunsell did young Vivian. *He* made him cock-up at point-blank.' Stalky was referring to an episode of their early and oppressed past.

'Yes, an' Gartside major got hold of it and half cut Maunsell's fat soul out of him in the dormitory. That shows what prefects think of duellin'! An' s'pose King spots us in the Bunkers with his filthy telescope? I've looked through it. I swear you can see the crabs runnin' about on Braunton Sands.' Beetle delivered this all in one passionate breath.

'You're sickenin',' said Turkey. 'Maunsell was bullyin' young Vivian. D'you mean to say *you're* bein' bullied? An', tell me now, has King or Prout or Foxy—has anyone—ever told ye that duellin' is forbidden at Coll.? Don't prevaricate. Have you ever seen it posted in the corridor?'

'Then get Pussy and Tertius for seconds,' Beetle howled.

'I'd not dream of runnin' in on them for a little thing like this,' Turkey concluded, and Dick added:

'Besides, this is a private affair. It's the satisfaction of a gentleman, thou scurvy varlet.'

'Oh, shut up an' listen to your Uncle. The Bunkers to-morrow after call-over. Shots all round—*an'* one extra for Beetle. First blood satisfies Honour. Then we'll pick sides an' have a general stalk till we're out of ammunition.'

'Good business,' said the foe. '*And* a brew for the survivors after tea! My uncle hath remembered me. Selah!* We'd better have it up here and ask Pussy and Tertius. It's safer.'

At that epoch, the young of the English, alone of their kind, understood the exact difference between official and unofficial. Pussy and Tertius said they would be happy to attend the brew and, being men of substance, sent, as it were, milk and honey in advance. They had not been officially informed what the banquet would celebrate, but prying suspicion is beneath true authority.

'Anyhow,' said Pussy to his colleague, 'I've been through Dick's cartridges to make sure. '*All* dust-shot.'

At three, then, next day, after Beetle, the house-keeper, had set out the table for a brew of six, four boys in prudent overcoats ('sallies' pack clumsily beneath short jackets) pushed into the wind for the rushy sand-dunes at the far end of the Pebble Ridge. It is true that certain old men who, though not in the Army, impiously wore red coats, used a fringe of the landscape for a senile diversion known as Golf—Turkey had played it for some weeks and pronounced it 'sickenin' '—but once off the line of their activities—the 'fairway' they called it—a boy might have been in the Sahara.

The Equinox drove the sand into their faces or round their legs, as they dived among the sheep-haunted hollows. The upstanding winter tide roared and trampled along the Pebble Ridge outside till they had to shout to each other, and racing slashes of low sunlight from seaward lit the sands and the bents with fierce coppery glares. In a secluded dell, out of the worst of the wind, Turkey posted Stalky and Dick Four—each edge-on, House-cap pulled down to the eyebrows, left elbow crooked, covering mouth and nose, and pistol ready to level over the crook at the Caution and to fire at the Word. For such had been the tradition of the Giants of the Prime—great names—now even greater Captains who, of course, stood fire daily.

'Squad!' croaked Turkey in Foxy's best manner. 'Fire!' Both pistols popped together. It was a clean miss.

'Didn't you even hear mine?' Stalky called.

The King of Coomassie* shook his head gingerly. It was difficult for him to keep his cap on his matted hair.

'Never mind. I'll get you at the stalk.' Then Stalky in turn placed Turkey and Dick. They fired.

''Heard something that time,' said Dick appreciatively. Turkey had raised his left elbow, knowing that his pistol threw low.

Beetle took the field of honour without parade. His first shot was well to the left.

'Your man is in front of ye,' said M'Turk grimly. 'Reload as ye stand.'

'*Now* you pay for Mandrill!' Dick shouted. But on the 'Fire' Beetle blazed skyward, which, with that uncertain sort of ammunition and by the help of a passing gust, was just enough to sling the charge well forward. The King of Ashantee rubbed his cheek and swore in purest English.

'Blood!' Turkey paced in. ''Tip of Dick's ear bleedin'.'

'Pimple! Pimple!' roared the King. 'I've been scratching it for weeks.'

Turkey dabbed with a handkerchief and held up the evidence.

'Blood! Honour satisfied. 'Let-off for you, Beetle!'

But Beetle was already treading his own conception of a reel to the chant of: '*I*'ve drilled the *Ma*ndrill—the *Ma*ndrill—the *Ma*ndrill!'*

'Bunk!' Stalky warned him. 'Run, you ass!' The King of Ashantee was gnashing his teeth and reloading with intent. 'We'll start the stalk now. I'm on your side, Beetle.'

'Are ye? Then I'm on Dick's,' said M'Turk, wheeling, and fired into the skirts of the flying overcoat.

Beetle was out of that hollow and across several others before he found a ragged bunker—the old 'Cockscomb'— whose crest had been undercut by rabbits. Here he lay down and reloaded, resolved to sell his life dear, but not to go looking for many buyers. He knew what Stalky could be as an ally, and it worried him; but, from broken words that rode the gale, it sounded as though Stalky must have stalked Dick Four, and so committed himself to a definite policy. Beetle's was to reach, as soon as might be, those very old red-coated men whom he had so often scorned. Deeply as they loathed his likes, they would not allow him to be peppered in their fairway. He crawled unfastidiously to the next bunker furthest from the sea, descended its face, and disturbed an old ewe. She bolted up wind, and brought down on him out of a side-ravine Dick Four, wrestling with a jammed pistol and roaring like a gorilla. Just when Beetle—as he ever afterwards explained— was about to blow his silly brains out, Dick scooped up tons of sand, and tossed them into the blast. Beetle ate of it what he could not avoid, rubbed enough of the rest out of his spectacles and eyes to see a little, and ploughed on, the skirts of his unbuttoned overcoat ever being blown forward between the legs. Renewed poppings and yells from the rear indicated either that he had been 'decreed a rabbit' *in absentia*,* or that civil war had broken out. But, like unthinking youth, he did not look back.

He arrived, well on all fours, at the lip of a big crater known in those pure days as The Pit. Directly beneath him stood an ancient in a red coat, scrabbling, like King David,* with a niblick. While Beetle, on both elbows, removed his spectacles to get a little more damp sand off them, the unkind wind hove his coat-tails clean over his head, and plunged him in darkness. Almost at the same instant he felt a pain behind, which urged him to plunge out of it. . . . And thus it was that this innocent boy, with life's golden promise before him, and that withered zealot, trifling blasphemously through his few remaining days, met all of a heap, on much the same selection of *mots justes*—cries of lost souls and defeated generals.

'Blast you! Who *are* you?' the elder began; but Beetle, his spectacles in his hand, disengaged and fled on—he felt at the moment that he could run for ever—to the protection of the fairway. Here, as he cleaned and reshipped his glasses, he realised that his personal grief was now more like the dying memory of an efficient ground-ash than any portent of fatal hæmorrhage. Presently, life, as it tingled through his young system, seemed rather prosperous. At any rate, he had drilled the Mandrill; escaped further active service; the old goat in The Pit had not seen him with his spectacles on, which ought to be a perfect alibi; and a brew of brews awaited him. He returned towards Coll.

A sobbing voice hailed, and Stalky ranged or, rather, tottered alongside. Without turning his head, Beetle asked him what he had done *that* for.

'Because you deserted! You left me to fight a rearguard action alone, you cad!' Then, clinging to Beetle's cold shoulder: 'I didn't mean to. I *swear* I didn't till your coat blew up! Then I couldn't help it. Wasn't it a beauty? Did it sting much? Never mind! Turkey's got it in the ankle—point-blank. He left his silly foot stickin' out of some rushes and Dick thought it was you! Turkey's a bit wrathy.'

Turkey limped up with Dick. They were obviously estranged. Dick was talking about 'lousy Fenians,'* and Turkey's nose was high in air.

'Well?' said Beetle, a thought comforted. Stalky continued:

'Turkey got my cap. I stuck it up to draw his fire. Then he got me on the hand!' A dirty rag round a palm was proof. 'Oh, but before that, I got Dick where I got you, but *much* tighter. Turkey changed sides after Dick plugged him. That was really why I had to plug *you*—to make things fair. 'See, you old burbler?'

'But,' Dick was pleading with Turkey, 'how the devil was I to know you were wearing Beetle's ungodly socks? I couldn't *smell* 'em in this wind, could I? It was your fault for baggin' 'em!'

Beetle chortled. There seemed to be some justice in things after all.

'I hope Turkey plugged you, you murderer,' he rounded on Dick.

'Only once.' Dick rubbed his neck again. He might have lightly brushed a bough of gorse.

'That's nothing.' Beetle looked pointedly at his own salient work on the rim of the ear.

'Yours was an infernal fluke,' said Dick hotly. 'You were in a blue funk all the time,—thou—thou noisome varlet.'

'Thou notch-eared knave,' was the reply.

But the crisis had passed, and Dick beamed; he, too, had a sound taste in epithets.

They were going through pockets for over-looked cartridges (one has to explain so much if any are found), and throwing them into Goosey Pool, when, out of the autumn dusk, a robin-like old man hopped, and almost pecked, at Turkey. The others delicately walked on; Beetle for once leading.

'You were the boy who swore at me just now,' the stranger began.

Turkey took no notice, except that his nose went up a little more.

'I was in a bunker, and you knocked into me. Using filthy language, sir!'

'An' what were ye doin' in the bunker? An' which bunker was it?' Turkey spoke like all the wearied and disbelieving magistracy of the Ireland of those days.

'The Pit,' said the Ancient, being a golfer—which is to say a monomaniac.

Turkey came to life with a jerk.

'Bunkered? In The Pit? With this wind blowin'? Goin' or comin' ye could *nott!*'*

'But I tell you I *did*.' The other seemed to have forgotten his original grievance.

'Ah, then, ye're not worth a curse—an' never will be.'

Turkey rejoined his companions, to whom Beetle was giving a theory of cause and effect. The four linked arms and swept up the old sunken lane to Coll. Honour was satisfied; there remained but their own young appetites. When, just before last lesson, Beetle connected the rubber tube from the gas-bracket to their dear little stove—turning the jet down to that exact degree which will bring milk-cocoa to perfection in one hour and a half—and counted the potted ham-and-tongue jars, the chicken-and-ham sausage, the sardine-tins, the three jams, the condensed milk, the two pounds of Devonshire cream, and the whole pound of real butter, he would not have changed his lot with kings. Nor, as he went to the form-room, did it strike him that a spare, accurately dressed person standing in the Head's porch had anything to do with the old goat he had heard, rather than seen, cursing in The Pit.

Ten minutes before the close of last lesson (their mouths were watering already), Foxy knocked and laid a well-known slip on King's desk.

'The Head to see,' King read, and paused to let suspense soak in. 'Ah! Only our usual three—*plus* Dickson Quartus. This I fear, portends tragedy. All four of you—*at* once—*if* you please!'

They agreed that, for the first time in their knowledge of him, the Head must have been drunk. Nothing else explained his performance.

'The way he *talked* was enough,' said Dick Four. 'All the studies brew, and he knows it. But he went on as if he'd heard of it for the first time.'

'At the top of his voice, too. When Bates is wrathy, he whispers. But he shouted like Rabbits-Eggs.* That proves it,' said Stalky.

'Then, all that putrid rot about "the criminality" of havin'
a tube. *All* the studies have 'em. He said it was theft—of gas!
There you are!' Dick continued.

'An' his rot about 'gorgin'.' He *knows* we can't live on the
muck they give us. He—he said brewin' was "an insult to the
bountiful provision made for us by the authorities." Mad!
Ravin' mad!' This was Beetle's kinder judgment.

Turkey scratched an ankle and spoke—

'Authority! He's never said a word about any authority
except himself since I've been here.'

'Then you think he's tight, too?'

'I do not. If he'd drunk enough to make him talk like that,
he'd have been lyin' on the floor to say it.'

'Anyhow, he licked like hell,' Beetle went on.

'He did *nott*,* either. His arm was never shoulder-high once.'

'But if he wasn't tight, what made him count the cuts aloud?
No one does that, except Justus Prout,' said Stalky.

Dick Four pointed at the untouched table.

'He hasn't confiscated the grub. Better eat it and have Pussy
and Tertius in for cover.'

'Better make sure first,' said Beetle. '*I* don't want the Head
japin' with me again just now. I'll ask Foxy.'

He found him in the gym as usual.

'No orders about it at all,' said the Sergeant, and there was
an unfathomable twinkle in his little red eye.

But Turkey sat on the window-seat asking of nobody:

'For what would he be roarin' like that? The man was out
of his nature, I tell ye.'

*   *   *   *   *

Years—some years—later, Captain 'Pussy' Abanazar, R.E.,*
seconded for duty in the Indian Political, at home on leave,
was invited by the Head to spend a few days of the Easters at
Coll., in a mild, early, Devon spring. Half a dozen of the
Army Class stayed up to read for near exams, and perhaps as
many juniors whose people were abroad. When the last
shouting brake-load had left, and emptiness filled the
universe, the Head turned into a most delightful and
comprehending uncle, so that that forlorn band remembered

those Easters through the rest of their lives. And when Captain Abanazar rolled in, and was to each of them equally a demi-god and an elder brother of the right sort (he tipped like Crœsus*), their caps overflowed.

One soft evening in the Head's private study, with the sea churning up old memories all along the Ridge, Pussy asked:

'Bates Sahib, do you remember lickin' Number Five and Dick Four for brewin' in——' He gave the year and added: 'My first term as a sub, you know.'

The Head smiled and nodded.

'And giving 'em a pi-jaw?'

'Pi-jaws aren't my line. There *was* a jaw, though. Why? What did they think about it?'

'They didn't understand it at all. I believe they thought you were tight.'

'Would I had been! But it was worse. It was cowardice, Pussy—it was bowing down in the House of Rimmon.* And they noticed what I said?'

'I should say they did!'

'No wonder! We had a Board of Directors in those days— retired Colonels—martial men with the habit of command. I'm glad I never had that.'

'Yes, we all deplored your lack of it, Sir.'

'Don't misunderstand me. They were excellent men. I'm sure we were all deeply indebted to them. One of the very best was a Colonel—Coll—Con—wait a minute—Curthwen. But he's in Abraham's bosom* now. (Awkward bedfellow!) He knew about education and the prices of things. *So* useful at Board meetings. I always moved the vote of thanks to him. He was exceptionally nice to me. Advice—the soundest advice. You see, he knew about—er—everything except, yes, golf. He had to come down here to learn that. I only dared go round with him once. I enjoyed it too much. Little runny-nosed Northam caddies told him where to put his horrible feet. Ah! When he came down here, you see, his evenings were quite free, and he could drop in on me at any time, and—er—offer a few suggestions.'

Pussy shuddered all over; and he was not of the smaller makes.

'Yes,' the Head mused. 'It's a shameful story. *That* evening, he dropped in complaining that one of us—you—a boy—had nearly knocked him over in a bunker, and then used filthy language. . . . No. I never found out who the boy was. I could only envy. But the shock and the language—he was, of course, a churchwarden—made him a little—excessive, perhaps. He gave me an hour's sound advice—with a tang to it. Then I walked with him to the old Fives Court to see him off, but he sniffed like a hound opposite Number Five, and said he smelt gas escaping. (You *can't* smell it any other way, can you?) Then he began all over again, Pussy—on economics in the abstract. An eye like a lizard's. That type have the lust of detail. Yes! After one hour, he began again. Then I lied—as overworked children do.'

'By Jove! I remember your warning me about that, when I worked Lower School too hard at footer. It's true of men, too.'

'It is. I lied like a scullion—like the hireling that I was! I told him the gas was already shut off from the studies when not required. I think I told him I kept the key of the meter in my—bath-room. I don't *want* to think what I told him. He was good enough to say he took my word for it, but——'

'Did he? 'Wish I'd been there. Well?'

'He tracked the stink upstairs foot by foot—like Prout on a moral trail. It was I—I—who threw open the study door to show his suspicions were wrong. And there was that glorious brew laid out on the table, and the tube from the gas-jet to the stove! A tiny, little, bright, blue flame, Pussy. It went *wheee-whee*, like a toy balloon deflating. That was *me*! I deflated; he inflated for ten minutes. I am a wicked old man—as you know. I have terrorised infants and perjured myself to mothers, and intrigued with and against my Staff; but I paid for my sins then, Pussy. You'd have loved it.'

'But I'd have dropped him out of the window first,' said Pussy.

'Why? He had the obvious right of it. There *was* the smell. There *was* the waste. (As a matter of fact, it was traced to the basement.) And, I suppose, there *was* a chance of burning down the Coll. Then he was shocked at the brew. He said it showed you didn't appreciate your lawful food. Yes! He sawed at me with his voice Pussy, till I fell. I connived—I confederated with him. I suggested that he should eavesdrop in my private study—yes, here—and listen to what I should say when I sacrificed those innocent children. Thank goodness I have forgotten my discourse, but I know that I addressed them—him, next door, I mean—out of his own Philistine vocabulary. And you say they noticed the falling-off in my style? Aha! *Non omnis moriar!*'* The Head purred.

'They couldn't make any sense of it. And did you count the cuts aloud?'

'Very like. Why should I have stopped at any crime! I was playing up to the Board—to appearances—to expediency—to fear of consequences—to all those little dirty things that I brought you children up to spit upon. Except that I didn't kneel and pray with them—Heavens! he might have exacted *that*!—there was only one redeeming feature. When it came to the execution, that little red cupboard-door stuck.'

'The rope breaking on the gallows,' Pussy amplified. 'It never did with me!'

'And I saw my face in the glass, like an ape's—a frightened, revengeful ape's. (And, so far as I *have* a gospel, it is never to carry things to the sweating-point.) That saved a remnant of my integrity. Saved them something, as well. The licking was a noisy one—for his benefit—but artistically, my dear boy, you understand, a sketch—the merest outline.'

'That squares with the evidence, too. And you didn't confiscate the grub. I know, because I helped eat it.'

'There are limits to my brutality. Besides, he'd gone to gorge at his dreadful Golf Club; and I could have eaten a horse. But it was all abject—paltry—time-serving—unjust. Not that I believe in Justice, but I don't like to think that I ever licked out of personal mortification and revenge.'

'Don't you worry, Bates dear. Those young devils had been out duellin' in the Bunkers the whole afternoon. Every one of 'em was a casualty as he stood to you. What was our allowance for that?'

'Threats of expulsion—followed by twelve of the best. The young scoundrels! But you've taken a load off my mind, Pussy. If I'd known that, I could have paid 'em honourably!'

'Beetle was the chap who attended to your Colonel, too. Stalky plugged him—bending—on the edge of The Pit, and he fell into it, cursing Stalky for all he was worth. The Colonel was bunkered at the bottom. You see?'

'*I* see. Never again will I hear a word against Beetle—unless I say it myself.' The Head spoke with genuine gratitude. 'But how did they hound him into the fray? Was he—er—"decreed a rabbit"?'

'Bates, dear, is there one single dam' thing about us that you don't know?' Pussy spoke after an admiring pause.

'We-ell! It's a shameful confession, but, you see, I loved you all. The rest was only sending you all to bed dead-tired. . . . You want a sheet of impot-paper? You know where it lives. What for?'

'I'm going to restore your prestige an' give Stalky pain. He needs a tonic where he is now, poor devil! . . . Please, Sir, what are common nouns in *io* called?'

What Pussy sent out (as 'code,' at State expense) from the overwhelmed little Post Office ran:

'Capitem vidi. Stop. Constat flagellatio Studii Quinti Ricardique Quarti utsi ob caenam vere propter duellum vestrum inter arenas donata fuisse. Stop. Matutinissime si Capitem decipere vis surgendum. Stop. Amorem expedit. Stop. Felis Catus.'[1]

What Stalky, doing station-master in a freezing internationalised lamp-room, received, after two or three telegraphists of the Nearer and Farther Easts had had their flying shots at it, was:

'Captain vids. Stop. Constance plageltio studdi quinti ricandk que qualte cuts obscene very prabst duel in vestry iter arimas donala puistse. Stop. Matushima so cahutem discipere via sargentson. Stop. Amend expent. Stop. Felix Cotes.'

He had trouble enough on his own fork at the time, so, as Pussy foretold, it proved a tonic. The office of origin and 'studdi quinti' gave him a bearing, but he upset half the railway system of Cathay,* as then working, to arrive at

---

[1] 'Have seen the Head. He says the licking of Number Five Study and Dick Four ostensibly for brewing was really for your duel in the Bunkers. You've got to get up very early to take in the Head. He sends love. The Cat.'

epigraphists with a College education. A Captain of Native
Infantry happened to remember the catchword, 'You must get
up pretty early to take in the Head.' The rest was combined
deductive scholarship. In due time a cable went back, not to
F. Cotes, but to the Head:

'*These from Sinim.* Stop. Knew it all along. Delighted your
character for downiness cleared. Stop. Ours nationally and
personally more than indifferent here. Stop. Best loves for
birthday.*'

Four or five names out of an Army Class followed in school
order.

Not till several years later did Pussy tell Stalky and the
others how they had been deceived; and cruelly rubbed in that
'Knew it all along.' As they were, then, far too senior to go
to war in the ancient formation, they passed the docket over
to Beetle, with instructions to 'report and revenge.'

Which had to be done!

The Last Term

IT was within a few days of the holidays, the term-end examinations, and, more important still, the issue of the College paper which Beetle edited.* He had been cajoled into that office by the blandishments of Stalky and M'Turk and the extreme rigour of study law. Once installed, he discovered, as others have done before him, that his duty was to do the work while his friends criticised. Stalky christened it the *Swillingford Patriot*,* In pious memory of Sponge—and M'Turk compared the output unfavourably with Ruskin and De Quincey. Only the Head took an interest in the publication, and his methods were peculiar. He gave Beetle the run of his brown-bound, tobacco-scented library; prohibiting nothing, recommending nothing. There Beetle found a fat armchair, a silver inkstand, and unlimited pens and paper. There were scores and scores of ancient dramatists; there were Hakluyt,* his voyages; French translations of Muscovite authors called Pushkin and Lermontoff; little tales of a heady and bewildering nature, interspersed with unusual songs—Peacock was that writer's name; there was Borrow's *Lavengro*; an odd theme, purporting to be a translation of something called a 'Rubáiyát,'* which the Head said was a poem not yet come to its own; there were hundreds of volumes of verse—Crashaw; Dryden; Alexander Smith;* L.E.L.;* Lydia Sigourney;* Fletcher and a purple island;* Donne; Marlowe's *Faust*; and—this made M'Turk (to whom Beetle conveyed it) sheer drunk for three days—Ossian;* *The Earthly Paradise*;* *Atalanta in Calydon*;* and Rossetti—to name only a few. Then the Head, drifting in under pretence of playing censor to the paper, would read here a verse and here another of these poets; opening up avenues. And, slow breathing, with half-shut eyes above his cigar, would speak of great men living, and journals, long dead,* founded in their riotous youth; of years when all the planets were little new-lit stars trying to find their places in the uncaring void, and he, the

Head, knew them as young men know one another. So the
regular work went to the dogs, Beetle being full of other
matters and metres, hoarded in secret and only told to M'Turk
of an afternoon, on the sands, walking high and disposedly*
round the wreck of the Armada galleon, shouting and
declaiming against the long-ridged seas.

Thanks in large part to their House-master's experienced
distrust, the three for three consecutive terms had been passed
over for promotion to the rank of prefect—an office that went
by merit, and carried with it the honour of the ground-ash,
and liberty, under restrictions, to use it.

'*But*,' said Stalky, 'come to think of it, we've done more
giddy jesting with the Sixth since we've been passed over than
any one else in the last seven years.'

He touched his neck proudly. It was encircled by the stiffest
of stick-up collars, which custom decreed could be worn only
by the Sixth. And the Sixth saw those collars and said no
word. 'Pussy' Abanazar or Dick Four of a year ago would have
seen them discarded in five minutes or . . . But the Sixth of
that term was made up mostly of young but brilliantly clever
boys, pets of the House-masters, too anxious for their dignity
to care to come to open odds with the resourceful three. So
they crammed their caps at the extreme back of their heads,
instead of a trifle over one eye as the Fifth should, and rejoiced
in patent-leather boots on week-days, and marvellous made-up
ties on Sundays—no man rebuking. M'Turk was going up for
Cooper's Hill,* and Stalky for Sandhurst, in the spring; and
the Head had told them both that, unless they absolutely
collapsed during the holidays, they were safe. As a trainer of
colts, the Head seldom erred in an estimate of form.

He had taken Beetle aside that day and given him much good
advice, not one word of which did Beetle remember when he
dashed up to the study, white with excitement, and poured
out the wondrous tale. It demanded a great belief.

'You begin on a hundred a year?' said M'Turk
unsympathetically. 'Rot!'

'And my passage out! It's all settled. The Head says he's
been breaking me for this for ever so long, and I never knew—
I never knew. One don't begin with writing straight off,

y'know. Begin by filling in telegrams and cutting things out o' papers with scissors.'

'Oh, Scissors! What an ungodly mess you'll make of it,' said Stalky. 'But, anyhow, this will be your last term, too. Seven years, my dearly beloved 'earers—though not prefects.'

'Not half bad years, either,' said M'Turk. 'I shall be sorry to leave the old Coll.; shan't you?'

They looked out over the sea creaming along the Pebble Ridge in the clear winter light. "Wonder where we shall all be this time next year?' said Stalky absently.

'This time five years,' said M'Turk.

'Oh,' said Beetle, 'my leavin's between ourselves. The Head hasn't told any one. I know he hasn't, because Prout grunted at me to-day that if I were more reasonable—yah!—I might be a prefect next term. I suppose he's hard up for his prefects.'

'Let's finish up with a row with the Sixth,' suggested M'Turk.

'Dirty little schoolboys!' said Stalky, who already saw himself a Sandhurst cadet. 'What's the use?'

'Moral effect,' quoth M'Turk. 'Leave an imperishable tradition, and all the rest of it.'

'Better go into Bideford an' pay up our debts,' said Stalky. 'I've got three quid out of my father—*ad hoc*. Don't owe more than thirty bob, either. Cut along, Beetle, and ask the Head for leave. Say you want to correct the *Swillingford Patriot*.'

'Well, I do,' said Beetle. 'It'll be my last issue, and I'd like it to look decent. I'll catch him before he goes to his lunch.'

Ten minutes later they wheeled out in line, by grace released from five o'clock call-over, and all the afternoon lay before them. So also unluckily did King, who never passed without witticisms. But brigades of Kings could not have ruffled Beetle that day.

'Aha! Enjoying the study of light literature, my friends,' said he, rubbing his hands. 'Common mathematics are not for such soaring minds as yours, are they?'

('One hundred a year,' thought Beetle, smiling into vacancy.)

'Our open incompetence takes refuge in the flowery paths of inaccurate fiction. But a day of reckoning approaches, Beetle mine. I myself have prepared a few trifling foolish

questions in Latin prose which can hardly be evaded even by
your practised arts of deception. Ye-es, Latin prose. I think,
if I may say so—but we shall see when the papers are set—
"Ulpian serves *your* need."* "Aha! *Elucescebat*, quoth our
friend." We shall see! We shall see!'

Still no sign from Beetle. He was on a steamer, his passage
paid into the wide and wonderful world—a thousand leagues
beyond Lundy Island.

King dropped him with a snarl.

'He doesn't know. He'll go on correctin' exercises an' jawin'
an' showin' off before the little boys next term—and next.'
Beetle hurried after his companions up the steep path of the
furze-clad hill behind the College.

They were throwing pebbles on the top of the gasometer,
and the grimy gas-man in charge bade them desist. They
watched him oil a turncock sunk in the ground between two
furze-bushes.

'Cokey, what's that for?' said Stalky.

'To turn the gas on to the kitchens', said Cokey. 'If so be
I didn't turn her on, yeou young gen'lemen 'ud be larnin' your
book by candlelight.'

'Um!' said Stalky, and was silent for at least a minute . . .

'Hullo! Where are you chaps going?'

A bend of the lane brought then face to face with Tulke,
senior prefect of King's House—a smallish, white-haired boy,
of the type that must be promoted on account of its intellect,
and ever afterwards appeals to the Head to support its
authority when zeal has outrun discretion.

The three took no sort of notice. They were on lawful pass.
Tulke repeated his question hotly, for he had suffered many
slights from Number Five study, and fancied that he had at
last caught them tripping.

'What the devil is that to you?' Stalky replied, with his
sweetest smile.

'Look here, I'm not goin'—I'm not goin' to be sworn at by
the Fifth!' sputtered Tulke.

'Then cut along and call a prefects' meeting,' said M'Turk,
knowing Tulke's weakness.

The prefect became inarticulate with rage.

'Mustn't yell at the Fifth that way,' said Stalky. 'It's vile bad form.'

'Cough it up, ducky!' M'Turk said calmly.

'I—I want to know what you chaps are doing out of bounds?' This with an important flourish of his ground-ash.

'Ah!' said Stalky. 'Now we're gettin' at it. Why didn't you ask that before?'

'Well, I ask it now. What are you doing?'

'We're admiring you, Tulke,' said Stalky. 'We think you're no end of a fine chap, don't we?'

'We do! We do!' A dog-cart with some girls in it swept round the corner, and Stalky promptly kneeled before Tulke in the attitude of prayer; so Tulke turned a colour.

'I've reason to believe——' he began.

'Oyez! Oyez! Oyez!' shouted Beetle, after the manner of Bideford's town-crier, 'Tulke has reason to believe! Three cheers for Tulke!'

They were given. 'It's all our giddy admiration,' said Stalky. 'You know how we love you, Tulke. We love you so much we think you ought to go home and die. You're too good to live, Tulke.'

'Yes,' said M'Turk. '*Do* oblige us by dyin'. Think how lovely you'd look stuffed!'

Tulke swept up the road with an unpleasant glare in his eye.

'That means a prefects' meeting—sure pop,' said Stalky. 'Honour of the Sixth involved, and all the rest of it. Tulke 'll write notes all this afternoon, and Carson will call us up after tea. They daren't overlook that.'

'Bet you a bob he follows us!' said M'Turk. 'He's King's pet, and it's scalps to both of 'em if we're caught out. We must be virtuous.'

'Then I move we go to Mother Yeo's for a last gorge. We owe her about ten bob, and Mary 'll weep sore when she knows we're leaving,' said Beetle.

'She gave me an awful wipe on the head last time—Mary,' said Stalky.

'She does if you don't duck,' said M'Turk. 'But she generally kisses one back. Let's try Mother Yeo.'

They sought a little bottle-windowed half-dairy, half-restaurant, a dark-browed, two-hundred-year-old house, at the head of a narrow side street. They had patronised it from the days of their fagdom, and were very much friends at home.

'We've come to pay our debts, mother,' said Stalky, sliding his arm round the fifty-six-inch waist of the mistress of the establishment. 'To pay our debts and say good-bye—and—and we're awf'ly hungry.'

'Aie!' said Mother Yeo, 'makkin' love to me! I'm shaamed of 'ee.'

''Rackon us wouldn't du no such thing if Mary was here,' said M'Turk, lapsing into the broad North Devon that the boys used on their campaigns.

'Who'm takin' my name in vain?' The inner door opened, and Mary, fair-haired, blue-eyed, and apple-cheeked, entered with a bowl of cream in her hands. M'Turk kissed her. Beetle followed suit, with exemplary calm. Both boys were promptly cuffed.

'Niver kiss the maid when 'e can kiss the mistress,' said Stalky, shamelessly winking at Mother Yeo, as he investigated a shelf of jams.

''Glad to see one of 'ee dont want his head slapped no more,' said Mary invitingly, in that direction.

'Neu! 'Reckon I can get 'em give me,' said Stalky, his back turned.

'Not by me—yeou little masterpiece!'

''Niver asked 'ee. That's maids to Northam. Yiss—an' Appledore.' An unreproducible sniff, half contempt, half reminiscence, rounded the retort.

'Aie! Yeou won't niver come to no good end. Whutt be 'baout, smellin' the cream?'

''Tees bad,' said Stalky. 'Zmell 'un.'

Incautiously Mary did as she was bid.

'Bidevoor kiss.'

'Niver amiss,' said Stalky, taking it without injury.

'Yeou—yeou—yeou——' Mary began, bubbling with mirth.

'They'm better to Northam—more rich, laike—an' us gets them give back again,' he said, while M'Turk solemnly waltzed Mother Yeo out of breath, and Beetle told Mary the sad news, as they sat down to clotted cream, jam, and hot bread.

'Yiss. Yeou'll niver zee us no more, Mary. We'm goin' to be passons an' missioners.'

'Steady the Buffs?' said M'Turk, looking through the blind. 'Tulke has followed us. He's comin' up the street now.'

'They've niver put us out o' bounds,' said Mother Yeo. 'Bide yeou still, my little dearrs.' She rolled into the inner room to make the score.

'Mary,' said Stalky suddenly, with tragic intensity. 'Do 'ee lov' me, Mary?'

'Iss-fai! 'Talled 'ee zo since yeou was zo high!' the damsel replied.

"Zee 'un comin' up street, then?' Stalky pointed to the unconscious Tulke. 'He've niver been kissed by no sort or manner o' maid in hees borned laife, Mary. Oh, 'tees shaamful!'

'Whutt's to do with me? 'Twill come to 'un in the way o' nature, I rackon.' She nodded her head sagaciously. 'You niver want me to kiss un—sure-*ly*?'

"Give 'ee half-a-crown if 'ee will,' said Stalky, exhibiting the coin.

Half-a-crown was much to Mary Yeo, and a jest was more; but——

'Yeu'm afraid,' said M'Turk, at the psychological moment.

'Aie!' Beetle echoed, knowing her weak point. 'There's not a maid to Northam 'ud think twice. An' yeou such a fine maid, tu!'

M'Turk planted one foot firmly against the inner door lest Mother Yeo should return inopportunely, for Mary's face was set. It was then that Tulke found his way blocked by a tall daughter of Devon—that county of easy kisses, and pleasantest under the sun. He dodged aside politely. She reflected a moment, and laid a vast hand upon his shoulder.

'Where be 'ee gwaine tu, my dearr?' said she.

Over the handkerchief he had crammed into his mouth Stalky could see the boy turn scarlet.

'Gie I a kiss! Don't they larn 'ee manners to College?'

Tulke gasped and wheeled. Solemnly and conscientiously Mary kissed him twice, and the luckless prefect fled.

She stepped into the shop, her eyes full of simple wonder.

"Kissed 'un?' said Stalky, handing over the money.

'Iss, fai! But, oh, my little body, *he*'m no Colleger. 'Zeemed tu-minded to cry, laike.'

'Well, we won't. You couldn't make us cry that way,' said M'Turk. 'Try.'

Whereupon Mary cuffed then all round.

As they went out with tingling ears, said Stalky generally, "Don't think there'll be much of a prefects' meeting.'

'Won't there, just!' said Beetle. 'Look here. If he kissed her—which is our tack—he is a cynically immoral hog, and his conduct is blatant indecency. *Confer orationes Regis furiosissimi** when he collared me readin' "Don Juan." '

"Course he kissed her,' said M'Turk. 'In the middle of the street. With his House-cap on!'

'Time, 3.57 P.M. Make a note o' that. What d'you mean, Beetle?' said Stalky.

'Well! He's a truthful little beast. He may say he was kissed.'

'And then?'

'Why, then!' Beetle capered at the mere thought of it. 'Don't you see? The corollary to the giddy proposition is that the Sixth can't protect 'emselves from outrages an' ravishin's. 'Want nursemaids to look after 'em! We've only got to whisper that to the Coll. Jam for the Sixth! Jam for us! Either way it's jammy!'

'By Gum!' said Stalky. 'Our last term's endin' well. Now you cut along an' finish up your old rag, and Turkey and me will help. We'll go in the back way. No need to bother Randall.'

'Don't play the giddy garden-goat, then?' Beetle knew what help meant, though he was by no means averse to showing his importance before his allies. The little loft behind Randall's printing-office was his own territory, where he saw himself already controlling the *Times*. Here, under the guidance of the inky apprentice, he had learned to find his way more or less circuitously about the case, and considered himself an expert compositor.

The school paper in its locked formes* lay on a stone-topped table, a proof by the side; but not for worlds would Beetle have corrected from the mere proof. With a mallet and a pair of tweezers, he knocked out mysterious wedges of wood that released the forme, picked a letter here and inserted a letter there, reading as he went along and stopping much to chuckle over his own contributions.

'You won't show off like that,' said M'Turk, 'when you've got to do it for your living. Upside down and backwards, isn't it? Let's see if I can read it.'

'Get out!' said Beetle. 'Go and read those formes in the rack there, if you think you know so much.'

'Formes in a rack! What's that? Don't be so beastly professional.'

M'Turk drew off with Stalky to prowl about the office. They left little unturned.

'Come here a shake, Beetle. What's this thing?' said Stalky, in a few minutes. ''Looks familiar.'

Said Beetle, after a glance: 'It's King's Latin prose exam. paper. *In—In Verrem: actio prima.** What a lark!'

'Think o' the pure-souled, high-minded boys who'd give their eyes for a squint at it!' said M'Turk.

'No, Willie dear,' said Stalky; 'that would be wrong and painful to our kind teachers. You wouldn't crib, Willie, would you?'

''Can't read the beastly stuff, anyhow,' was the reply. 'Besides, we're leavin' at the end o' the term, so it makes no difference to us.'

''Member what the Considerate Bloomer did to Spraggon's account of the Puffin'ton Hounds?* We must sugar Mr. King's milk for him,' said Stalky, all lighted from within by a devilish joy. 'Let's see what Beetle can do with those forceps he's so proud of.'

''Don't see how you can make Latin prose much more cock-eye than it is, but we'll try,' said Beetle, transposing an *aliud* and *Asiæ* from two sentences. 'Let's see! We'll put that full-stop a little further on, and begin the sentence with the next capital. Hurrah! Here's three lines that can move up all in a lump.'

' ''One of those scientific rests for which this eminent huntsman is so justly celebrated.''*' Stalky knew the Puffington run by heart.

'Hold on! Here's a *vol—voluntate quidnam* all by itself,' said M'Turk.

'I'll attend to her in a shake. *Quidnam* goes after *Dolabella*.'

'Good old Dolabella,' murmured Stalky. 'Don't break him. Vile prose Cicero wrote, didn't he? He ought to be grateful for——'

'Hullo!' said M'Turk, over another forme. 'What price a giddy ode! *Qui—quis*—oh, it's *Quis multa gracilis,** o' course.'

'Bring it along. We've sugared the milk here,' said Stalky, after a few minutes' zealous toil. 'Never thrash your hounds unnecessarily.'

'*Quis munditiis?* I swear that's not bad,' began Beetle, plying the tweezers. 'Don't that interrogation look pretty? *Heu quoties fidem!* That sounds as if the chap were anxious an' excited. *Cui flavam religas in rosa*—Whose flavour is relegated to a rose. *Mutatosque Deos flebit in antro.*'

'Mute gods weepin' in a cave,' suggested Stalky. ''Pon my Sam, Horace needs as much lookin' after as—Tulke.'

They edited him faithfully till it was too dark to see.

*   *   *   *   *

' "Aha! *Elucescebat,* quoth our friend." Ulpian serves my need, does it? If King can make anything out of *that*, I'm a blue-eyed squatteroo,' said Beetle, as they slid out of the loft window into a back alley of old acquaintance and started on a three-mile trot to the College. But the revision of the classics had detained them over long. They halted, blown and breathless, in the furze at the back of the gasometer, the College lights twinkling below, ten minutes at least late for tea and lock-up.

'It's no good,' puffed M'Turk. 'Bet a bob Foxy is waiting for defaulters under the lamp by the Fives Court. It's a nuisance, too, because the Head gave us long leave, and one doesn't like to break it.'

' "Let me now from the bonded ware'ouse of my knowledge,"*' began Stalky.

'Oh, rot! Don't Jorrock. Can we make a run for it?' snapped M'Turk.

' "Bishops' boots Mr. Radcliffe also condemned, an' spoke

'ighly in favour of tops cleaned with champagne an' abricot jam." Where's that thing Cokey was twiddlin' this afternoon?'

They heard him groping in the wet, and presently beheld a great miracle. The lights of the Coastguard cottages near the sea went out; the brilliantly illuminated windows of the Golf Club disappeared, and were followed by the frontages of the two hotels. Scattered villas dulled, twinkled, and vanished. Last of all, the Coll. lights died also. They were left in the pitchy darkness of a windy winter's night.

' "Blister my kidneys. It *is* a frost. The dahlias are dead!" said Stalky. 'Bunk!'

They squattered through the dripping gorse as the College hummed like an angry hive and the dining-rooms chorussed, 'Gas! gas! gas!' till they came to the edge of the sunk path that divided them from their study. Dropping that ha-ha like bullets, and rebounding like boys, they dashed to the study, in less than two minutes had changed into dry trousers and coat, and, ostentatiously slippered, joined the mob in the dining-hall, which resembled the storm-centre of a South American revolution.

' "Hellish dark and smells of cheese." '* Stalky elbowed his way into the press, howling lustily for gas. 'Cokey must have gone for a walk. Foxy'll have to find him.'

Prout, as the nearest House-master, was trying to restore order, for rude boys were flicking butter-pats across chaos, and M'Turk had turned on the fags' tea-urn, so that many were parboiled and wept with an unfeigned dolor. The Fourth and Upper Third broke into the school song, the '*Vive la Compagnie,*' to the accompaniment of drumming knife-handles; and the junior forms shrilled bat-like shrieks and raided one another's victuals. Two hundred and fifty boys in high condition, seeking for more light, are truly earnest inquirers.

When a most vile smell of gas told them that supplies had been renewed, Stalky, waistcoat unbuttoned, sat gorgedly over what might have been his fourth cup of tea. 'And that's all right,' he said. 'Hullo! 'Ere's Pomponius Ego!'*

It was Carson, the head of the school, a simple, straight-minded soul, and a pillar of the First Fifteen, who crossed over from the prefects' table and in a husky, official voice invited the three to attend in his study in half an hour.

'Prefects' meetin'!' 'Prefects' meetin'!' hissed the tables, and they imitated barbarically the actions and effects of the ground-ash.

'How are we goin' to jest with 'em?' said Stalky, turning half-face to Beetle. 'It's your play this time!'

'Look here,' was the answer, 'all I want you to do is not to laugh. I'm goin' to take charge o' young Tulke's immorality—à la King, and it's goin' to be serious. If you can't help laughin' don't look at me, or I'll go pop.'

'I see. All right,' said Stalky.

M'Turk's lank frame stiffened in every muscle and his eyelids dropped half over his eyes. That last was a war-signal.

The eight or nine seniors, their faces very set and sober, were ranged in chairs round Carson's severely Philistine study. Tulke was not popular among them, and a few who had had experience of Stalky and Company doubted that he might, perhaps, have made an ass of himself. But the dignity of the Sixth was to be upheld. So Carson began hurriedly:

'Look here, you chaps, I've—we've sent for you to tell you you're a good deal too cheeky to the Sixth—have been for some time—and—and we've stood about as much as we're goin' to, and it seems you've been cursin' and swearin' at Tulke on the Bideford road this afternoon, and we're goin' to show you you can't do it. That's all.'

'Well, that's awfully good of you,' said Stalky, 'but we happen to have a few rights of our own, too. You can't, just because you happen to be made prefects, haul up seniors and jaw 'em on spec, like a House-master. We aren't fags, Carson. This kind of thing may do for Davies tertius, but it won't do for us.'

'It's only old Prout's lunacy that we weren't prefects long ago. You know that,' said M'Turk. 'You haven't any tact.'

'Hold on,' said Beetle. 'A prefects' meetin' has to be reported to the Head. I want to know if the Head backs Tulke in this business?'

'Well—well, it isn't exactly a prefects' meeting,' said Carson. 'We only called you in to warn you.'

'But all the prefects are here,' Beetle insisted. 'Where's the difference?'

'My Gum!' said Stalky. 'Do you mean to say you've just called us in for a jaw—after comin' to us before the whole school at tea an' givin' 'em the impression it was a prefects' meeting? 'Pon my Sam, Carson, you'll get into trouble, you will.'

'Hole-an'-corner business—hole-an'-corner business,' said M'Turk, wagging his head. 'Beastly suspicious.'

The Sixth looked at each other uneasily. Tulke had called three prefects' meetings in two terms, till the Head had informed the Sixth that they were expected to maintain discipline without the recurrent menace of his authority. Now, it seemed that they had made a blunder at the outset, but any right-minded boy would have sunk the legality and been properly impressed by the Court. Beetle's protest was distinct 'cheek.'

'Well, you chaps deserve a lickin',' cried one Naughten incautiously. Then was Beetle filled with a noble inspiration.

'For interferin' with Tulke's amours, eh?' Tulke turned a rich sloe colour. 'Oh no, you don't!' Beetle went on. 'You've had your innings. We've been sent up for cursing and swearing at you, and we're goin' to be let off with a warning! *Are* we? Now then, you're going to catch it.'

'I—I—I——' Tulke began. 'Don't let that young devil start jawing.'

'If you've anything to say, you must say it decently,' said Carson.

'Decently? I will. Now look here. When we went into Bideford we met this ornament of the Sixth—is that decent enough?—hanging about on the road with a nasty look in his eye. We didn't know *then* why he was so anxious to stop us, *but* at five minutes to four, when we were in Yeo's shop, we saw Tulke *in* broad daylight, *with* his House-cap on, kissin' an' huggin' a woman *on* the pavement. Is that decent enough for you?'

'I didn't—I wasn't.'

'We saw you?' said Beetle. 'And now—I'll be decent, Carson—you sneak back with her kisses' (not for nothing had

Beetle perused the later poets) 'hot on your lips and call prefects' meetings, which aren't prefects' meetings, to uphold the honour of the Sixth.' A new and heaven-cleft path opened before him that instant. 'And how do we know,' he shouted— 'how do we know how many of the Sixth are mixed up in this abominable affair?'

'Yes, that's what we want to know,' said M'Turk, with simple dignity.

'We meant to come to you about it quietly, Carson, but you *would* have the meeting,' said Stalky sympathetically.

The Sixth were too taken aback to reply. So, carefully modelling his rhetoric on King, Beetle followed up the attack surpassing and surprising himself.

'It—it isn't so much the cynical immorality of the biznai, as the blatant indecency of it, that's so awful. As far as we can see, it's impossible for us to go into Bideford without runnin' up against some prefect's unwholesome amours. There's nothing to snigger over, Naughten. *I* don't pretend to know much about these things—but it seems to me a chap must be pretty far dead in sin' (that was a quotation from the school chaplain) 'when he takes to embracing his paramours' (that was Hakluyt*) 'before all the city' (a reminiscence of Milton). 'He might at least have the decency—you're authorities on decency, I believe—to wait till dark. But he didn't. You didn't! Oh, Tulke. You—you incontinent little animal!'

'Here, shut up a minute. What's all this about, Tulke?' said Carson.

'I—look here. I'm awfully sorry. I never thought Beetle would take this line.'

'Because—you've—no decency—you—thought—I hadn't,' cried Beetle all in one breath.

'Tried to cover it all up with a conspiracy, did you?' said Stalky.

'Direct insult to all three of us,' said M'Turk. 'A most filthy mind you have, Tulke.'

'I'll shove you fellows outside the door if you go on like this,' said Carson angrily.

'That proves it's a conspiracy,' said Stalky, with the air of a virgin martyr.

'I—I was goin' along the street—I swear I was,' cried Tulke, 'and—and I'm awfully sorry about it—a woman came up and kissed me. I swear I didn't kiss her.'

There was a pause, filled by Stalky's long, liquid whistle of contempt, amazement, and derision.

'On my honour,' gulped the persecuted one. 'Oh, do stop him jawing.'

'Very good,' M'Turk interjected. 'We are compelled, of course, to accept your statement.'

'Confound it!' roared Naughten. 'You aren't head-prefect here, M'Turk.'

'Oh, well,' returned the Irishman, 'you know Tulke better than we do. I am only speaking for ourselves. *We* accept Tulke's word. But all I can say is that if I'd been collared in a similarly disgustin' situation, and had offered the same explanation Tulke has, I—I wonder what you'd have said. However, it seems on Tulke's word of honour——'

'And Tulkus—beg pardon—*kiss*, of course—Tulkiss is an honourable man,'* put in Stalky.

'——that the Sixth can't protect 'emselves from bein' kissed when they go for a walk!' cried Beetle, taking up the running with a rush. 'Sweet business, isn't it? Cheerful thing to tell the fags, ain't it? We aren't prefects, of course, but we aren't kissed very much. 'Don't think that sort of thing ever enters our heads; does it, Stalky?'

'Oh no!' said Stalky, turning aside to hide his emotions. M'Turk's face merely expressed lofty contempt and a little weariness.

'Well, you seem to know a lot about it,' interposed a prefect.

''Can't help it—when you chaps shove it under our noses.' Beetle dropped into a drawling parody of King's most biting colloquial style—the gentle rain after the thunderstorm. 'Well, it's all very sufficiently vile and disgraceful, isn't it? I don't know who comes out of it worst: Tulke, who happens to have been caught; or the other fellows who haven't. And we'—here he wheeled fiercely on the other two—'we've got to stand up and be jawed by them because we've disturbed their intrigues.'

'Hang it! I only wanted to give you a word of warning,' said Carson, thereby handing himself bound to the enemy.

'Warn? You?' This with the air of one who finds loathsome gifts in his locker. 'Carson, *would* you be good enough to tell us what conceivable thing there is that you are entitled to warn us about after this exposure? Warn? Oh, it's a little too much! Let's go somewhere where it's clean.'

The door banged behind their outraged innocence.

'Oh, Beetle! Beetle! Beetle! Golden Beetle!' sobbed Stalky, hurling himself on Beetle's panting bosom as soon as they reached the study. 'However did you do it?'

'Dear-r man!' said M'Turk, embracing Beetle's head with both arms, while he swayed it to and fro on the neck, in time to this ancient burden—

> 'Pretty lips—sweeter than—cherry or plum,
> Always look—jolly and—never look glum;
> Seem to say—Come away. Kissy!—come, come!
> Yummy-yum! Yummy-yum! Yummy-yum-yum!'*

'Look out. You'll smash my gig-lamps,'* puffed Beetle, emerging. 'Wasn't it glorious? Didn't I "Eric" 'em splendidly?* Did you spot my cribs from King? Oh, blow!' His countenance clouded. 'There's one adjective I didn't use—obscene. 'Don't know how I forgot that. It's one of King's pet ones, too.'

'Never mind. They'll be sendin' ambassadors round in half a shake to beg us not to tell the school. It's a deuced serious business for them,' said M'Turk. 'Poor Sixth—poor old Sixth!'

'Immoral young rips,' Stalky snorted. 'What an example to pure-souled boys like you and me!'

And the Sixth in Carson's study stood aghast, glowering at Tulke, who was on the edge of tears.

'Well,' said the head-prefect acidly. 'You've made a pretty average ghastly mess of it, Tulke.'

'Why—why didn't you lick that young devil Beetle before he began jawing?' Tulke wailed.

'I knew there'd be a row,' said a prefect of Prout's House. 'But you would insist on the meeting, Tulke.'

'Yes, and a fat lot of good it's done us,' said Naughten. 'They come in here and jaw our heads off when we ought to be

jawin' them. Beetle talks to us as if we were a lot of blackguards
and—and all that. And when they've hung us up to dry, they go
out and slam the door like a House-master. All your fault, Tulke.'

'But I didn't kiss her.'

'You ass! If you'd said you *had* and stuck to it, it would have been
ten times better than what you did,' Naughten retorted. 'Now
they'll tell the whole school—and Beetle 'll make up a lot of beastly
rhymes and nick-names.'

'But, hang it, she kissed me!' Outside his work, Tulke's mind
moved slowly.

'I'm not thinking of you. I'm thinking of us. I'll go up to their
study and see if I can make 'em keep quiet!'

'Tulke's awf'ly cut up about this business,' Naughten began,
ingratiatingly, when he found Beetle.

'Who's kissed him this time?'

'——and I've come to ask you chaps, and especially you, Beetle,
not to let the thing be known all over the school. Of course,
fellows as senior as you are can easily see why.'

'Um!' said Beetle, with the cold reluctance of one who faces an
unpleasant public duty. 'I suppose I must go and talk to the Sixth
again.'

'Not the least need, my dear chap, I assure you,' said Naughten
hastily. 'I'll take any message you care to send.'

But the chance of supplying the missing adjective was too
tempting. So Naughten returned to that still undissolved meeting,
Beetle, white, icy, and aloof, at his heels.

'There seems,' he began, with laboriously crisp articulation,
'there seems to be a certain amount of uneasiness among you as
to the steps we may think fit to take in regard to this last revelation
of the—ah—obscene. If it is any consolation to you to know that
we have decided—for the honour of the school, you understand—
to keep our mouths shut as to these—ah—obscenities, you—ah—
have it.'

He wheeled, his head among the stars, and strode statelily back
to his study, where Stalky and M'Turk lay side by side upon the
table wiping their tearful eyes—too weak to move.

*   *   *   *   *

The Latin prose paper was a success beyond their wildest

dreams. Stalky and M'Turk were, of course, out of all examinations (they did extra-tuition with the Head), but Beetle attended with zeal.

'This, I presume, is a par-ergon* on your part,' said King, as he dealt out the papers. 'One final exhibition ere you are translated to loftier spheres? A last attack on the classics? It seems to confound you already.'

Beetle studied the print with knit brows. 'I can't make head or tail of it,' he murmured. 'What does it mean?'

'No, no!' said King, with scholastic coquetry. 'We depend upon you to give us the meaning. This is an examination, Beetle mine, not a guessing-competition. You will find your associates have no difficulty in——'

Tulke left his place and laid the paper on the desk. King looked, read, and turned a ghastly green.

'Stalky's missing a heap,' thought Beetle. ''Wonder how King'll get out of it?'

'There seems,' King began with a gulp, 'a certain modicum of truth in our Beetle's remark. I am—er—inclined to believe that the worthy Randall must have dropped this in forme—if you know what that means. Beetle, you purport to be an editor. Perhaps you can enlighten the Form as to formes.'

'What, sir? Whose form? I don't see that there's any verb in this sentence at all, an'—an'—the Ode is all different, somehow.'

'I was about to say, before you volunteered your criticism, that an accident must have befallen the paper in type, and that the printer reset it by the light of nature. No—' he held the thing at arm's length—'our Randall is not an authority on Cicero or Horace.'

'Rather mean to shove it off on Randall,' whispered Beetle to his neighbour. 'King must ha' been as screwed as an owl when he wrote it out.'

'But we can amend the error by dictating it.'

'No, sir.' The answer came pat from a dozen throats at once. 'That cuts the time for the exam. Only two hours allowed, sir. 'Tisn't fair. It's a printed-paper exam. How're we goin' to be marked for it? It's all Randall's fault. It isn't *our* fault, anyhow. An exam.'s an exam.,' etc., etc.

Naturally Mr. King considered this was an attempt to undermine his authority, and, instead of beginning dictation at once, delivered a lecture on the spirit in which examinations should be approached. As the storm subsided, Beetle fanned it afresh.

'Eh? What? What was that you were saying to MacLagan?'

'I only said I thought the papers ought to have been looked at before they were given out, sir.'

'Hear, hear!' from a back bench.

Mr. King wished to know whether Beetle took it upon himself personally to conduct the traditions of the school. His zeal for knowledge ate up another fifteen minutes, during which the prefects showed unmistakable signs of boredom.

'Oh, it was a giddy time,' said Beetle, afterwards, in dismantled Number Five. 'He gibbered a bit, and I kept him on the gibber, and then he dictated about a half of Dolabella & Co.'*

'Good old Dolabella! Friend of mine. Yes?' said Stalky tenderly.

'Then we had to ask him how every other word was spelt, of course, and he gibbered a lot more. He cursed me and MacLagan (Mac played up like a trump) and Randall, and the "materialised ignorance of the unscholarly middle classes," "lust for mere marks," and all the rest. It was what you might call a final exhibition—a last attack—a giddy par-ergon.'

'But of course he was blind squiffy when he wrote the paper. I hope you explained *that*?' said Stalky.

'Oh yes. I told Tulke so. I said an immoral prefect an' a drunken House-master were legitimate inferences. Tulke nearly blubbed. He's awfully shy of us since Mary's time.'

Tulke preserved that modesty till the last moment—till the journey-money had been paid, and the boys were filling the brakes that took them to the station. Then the three happily constrained him to wait awhile.

'You see, Tulke, you may be a prefect,' said Stalky, 'but I've left the Coll. Do you see, Tulke, dear?'

'Yes, I see. Don't bear malice, Stalky.'

'Stalky? Curse your impudence, you young cub,' shouted Stalky, magnificent in top-hat, stiff collar, spats, and high-waisted, snuff-coloured ulster. 'I want you to understand that *I*'m Mister Corkran, an' you're a dirty little schoolboy.'

'Besides bein' frabjously* immoral,' said M'Turk. ''Wonder you aren't ashamed to foist your company on pure-minded boys like us!'

'Come on, Tulke,' cried Naughten, from the prefects' brake.

'Yes, we're comin'. Shove up and make room, you Collegers. You've all got to be back next term, with your "Yes, sir," and "Oh, sir," an' "No, sir," an' "Please, sir"; but before we say good-bye we're going to tell you a little story. Go on, Dickie' (this to the driver); 'we're quite ready. Kick that hat-box under the seat, an' don't crowd your Uncle Stalky.'

'As nice a lot of high-minded youngsters as you'd wish to see,' said M'Turk, gazing round with bland patronage. 'A trifle immoral, but then—boys will be boys. It's no good tryin' to look stuffy, Carson. Mister Corkran will now oblige with the story of Tulke an' Mary Yeo!'

Slaves of the Lamp

PART II

THAT very Infant who told the story of the capture of Boh* Na-ghee[1] to Eustace Cleever, novelist, inherited an estateful baronetcy, with vast revenues, resigned the service, and became a landholder, while his mother stood guard over him to see that he married the right girl. But, new to his position, he presented the local volunteers with a full-sized magazine-rifle range, two miles long, across the heart of his estate, and the surrounding families, who lived in savage seclusion among woods full of pheasants, regarded him as an erring maniac. The noise of the firing disturbed their poultry, and Infant was cast out from the society of J.P.'s and decent men till such time as a daughter of the county might lure him back to right thinking. He took his revenge by filling the house with choice selections of old schoolmates home on leave—affable detrimentals,* at whom the bicycle-riding maidens of the surrounding families were allowed to look from afar. I knew when a troopship was in port by the Infant's invitations. Sometimes he would produce old friends of equal seniority; at others, young and blushing giants whom I had left small fags far down in the Lower Second; and to these Infant and the elders expounded the whole duty of Man in the Army.

'I've had to cut the Service,'* and the Infant; 'but that's no reason why my vast stores of experience should be lost to posterity.' He was just thirty, and in that same summer an imperious wire drew me to his baronial castle: 'Got good haul; ex *Tamar*.* Come along.'

It was an unusually good haul, arranged with a single eye to my benefit. There was a baldish, broken-down captain of Native Infantry, shivering with ague behind an indomitable red nose—and they called him Captain Dickson. There was another captain, also of Native Infantry, with a fair moustache; his face was like white glass, and his hands were

[1] "A Conference of the Powers," *Many Inventions*.

fragile, but he answered joyfully to the cry of Tertius. There was an enormously big and well-kept man, who had evidently not campaigned for years, clean-shaved, soft-voiced, and cat-like, but still Abanazar for all that he adorned the Indian Political Service; and there was a lean Irishman,* his face tanned blue-black with the suns of the Telegraph Department. Luckily the baize doors of the bachelors' wing fitted tight, for we dressed promiscuously in the corridor or in each other's rooms, talking, calling, shouting, and anon waltzing by pairs to songs of Dick Four's own devising.

There were sixty years of mixed work to be sifted out between us, and since we had met one another from time to time in the quick scene-shifting of India—a dinner, camp, or a race-meeting here; a dak-bungalow* or railway station up country somewhere else—we had never quite lost touch. Infant sat on the banisters, hungrily and enviously drinking it in. He enjoyed his baronetcy, but his heart yearned for the old days.

It was a cheerful babel of matters personal, provincial, and imperial, pieces of old call-over lists, and new policies, cut short by the roar of a Burmese gong, and we went down not less than a quarter of a mile of stairs to meet Infant's mother, who had known us all in our school-days and greeted us as if those had ended a week ago. But it was fifteen years since, with tears of laughter, she had lent me a gray princess-skirt* for amateur theatricals.

That was a dinner from the Arabian Nights served in an eighty-foot hall full of ancestors and pots of flowering roses, and, this was more impressive, heated by steam. When it was ended and the little mother had gone away—('You boys want to talk, so I shall say good-night now')—we gathered about an apple-wood fire, in a gigantic polished steel grate, under a mantelpiece ten feet high, and the Infant compassed us about with curious liqueurs and that kind of cigarette which serves best to introduce your own pipe.

'Oh, bliss!' grunted Dick Four from a sofa, where he had been packed with a rug over him. 'First time I've been warm since I came home.'

We were all nearly on top of the fire, except Infant, who had been long enough at Home to take exercise when he felt chilled. This is a grisly diversion, but one much affected by the English of the Island.

'If you say a word about cold tubs and brisk walks,' drawled M'Turk, 'I'll kill you, Infant. I've got a liver, too. 'Member when we used to think it a treat to turn out of our beds on a Sunday morning—thermometer fifty-seven degrees if it was summer—and bathe off the Pebble Ridge? Ugh!'

''Thing I don't understand,' said Tertius, 'was the way we chaps used to go down into the lavatories, boil ourselves pink, and then come up with all our pores open into a young snowstorm or a black frost. Yet none of our chaps died, that I can remember.'

'Talkin' of baths,' said M'Turk, with a chuckle, ''member our bath in Number Five, Beetle, the night Rabbits-Eggs rocked King? What wouldn't I give to see old Stalky now! He is the only one of the two Studies not here.'

'Stalky is the great man of his Century,' said Dick Four.

'How d'you know?' I asked.

'How do I know?' said Dick Four scornfully. 'If you've ever been in a tight place with Stalky you wouldn't ask.'

'I haven't seen him since the camp at Pindi in '87,' I said. 'He was goin' strong then—about seven feet high and four feet thick.'

'Adequate chap. Infernally adequate,' said Tertius, pulling his moustache and staring into the fire.

'Got dam' near court-martialled and broke* in Egypt in '84,' the Infant volunteered. 'I went out in the same trooper with him—as raw as he was. Only *I* showed it, and Stalky didn't.'

'What was the trouble?' said M'Turk, reaching forward absently to twitch my dress-tie into position.

'Oh, nothing. His Colonel trusted him to take twenty Tommies out to wash, or groom camels, or something at the back of Suakin, and Stalky got embroiled with Fuzzies five miles in the interior. He conducted a masterly retreat and wiped up eight of 'em. He knew jolly well he'd no right to go out so far, so he took the initiative and pitched in a letter to his Colonel, who was frothing at the mouth, complaining of

the "paucity of support accorded to him in his operations."
Gad, it might have been one fat brigadier slangin' another!
Then he went into the Staff Corps.'

'That—is—entirely—Stalky,' said Abanazar from his
armchair.

'You've come across him too?' I said.

'Oh yes,' he replied in his softest tones. 'I was at the tail of
that—that epic. Don't you chaps know?'

We did not—Infant, M'Turk, and I; and we called for
information very politely.

"'Twasn't anything,' said Tertius. 'We got into a mess up
in the Khye-Kheen Hills* a couple o' years ago, and Stalky
pulled us through. That's all.'

M'Turk gazed at Tertius with all an Irishman's contempt
for the tongue-tied Saxon.

'Heavens!' he said. 'And it's you and your likes govern
Ireland. Tertius, aren't you ashamed?'

'Well, I can't tell a yarn. I can chip in when the other fellow
starts. Ask him.' He pointed to Dick Four, whose nose
gleamed scornfully over the rug.

'I knew you couldn't,' said Dick Four. 'Give me a whisky
and soda. I've been drinking lemon-squash and ammoniated
quinine while you chaps were bathin' in champagne, and my
head's singin' like a top.'

He wiped his ragged moustache above the drink; and, his
teeth chattering in his head, began:

'You know the Khye-Kheen-Malôt expedition when we
scared the souls out of 'em with a field force they daren't fight
against? Well, both tribes—there was a coalition against us—
came in without firing a shot: and a lot of hairy villains, who
had no more power over their men than I had, promised and
vowed all sorts of things. On that very slender evidence, Pussy
dear——

'I was at Simla,' said Abanazar hastily.

'Never mind, you're tarred with the same brush. On the
strength of those tuppeny-ha'penny treaties, your asses of
Politicals reported the country as pacified, and the
Government, being a fool, as usual, began road-makin'—
dependin' on local supply for labour. 'Member that, Pussy?

'Rest of our chaps who'd had no look-in during the campaign didn't think there'd be any more of it, and were anxious to get back to India. But I'd been in two of these little rows before, and I had my suspicions. I engineered myself, *summo ingenio*,* into command of a road-patrol—no shovellin', only marching up and down genteelly with a guard. They'd withdrawn all the troops they could, but I nucleused* about forty Pathans, recruits chiefly, of my regiment, and sat tight at the base-camp while the road-parties went to work, as per Political survey.

"Had some rippin' sing-songs in camp, too,' said Tertius.

'My pup'—thus did Dick Four refer to his subaltern—'was a pious little beast. He didn't like the sing-songs, and so he went down with pneumonia. I rootled round the camp, and found Tertius gassing about as a D.A.Q.M.G.,* which, God knows, he isn't cut out for. There were six or eight of the old Coll. at base-camp (we're always in force for a frontier row), but I'd heard of Tertius as a steady old hack, and I told him he had to shake off his D.A.Q.M.G. breeches and help *me*. Tertius volunteered like a shot, and we settled it with the authorities, and out we went—forty Pathans, Tertius, and me, looking up the road-parties. Macnamara's—'member old Mac, the Sapper, who played the fiddle so damnably at Umballa?*—Mac's party was the last but one. The last was Stalky's. He was at the head of the road with some of his pet Sikhs. Mac said he believed he was all right.'

'Stalky *is* a Sikh,' said Tertius. 'He takes his men to pray at the Durbar Sahib at Amritzar,* regularly as clockwork, when he can.'

'Don't interrupt, Tertius. It was about forty miles beyond Mac's before I found him; and my men pointed out gently, but firmly, that the country was risin'. What kind o' country, Beetle? Well, I'm no word-painter, thank goodness, but *you* might call it a hellish country! When we weren't up to our necks in snow, we were rolling down the khud.* The well-disposed inhabitants, who were to supply labour for the road-making (don't forget that, Pussy dear), sat behind rocks and took pot-shots at us. 'Old, old story!* We all legged it in search of Stalky. I had a feeling that he'd be in good cover, and about dusk we found him and his road-party, as snug as a bug in a rug, in an old Malôt stone fort, with a watch-tower at one corner. It overhung the road they had blasted out of the cliff fifty feet below; and under the road things went down pretty sheer, for five or six hundred feet, into a gorge about half a mile wide and two or three miles long. There were chaps on the other side of the gorge scientifically gettin' our range. So I hammered on the gate and nipped in, and tripped over Stalky in a greasy, bloody old poshteen,* squatting on the ground, eating with his men. I'd only seen him for half a minute about three months before, but I might have met him yesterday. He waved his hand all sereno.

' "Hullo, Aladdin! Hullo, Emperor!" he said. "You're just in time for the performance."

'I saw his Sikhs looked a bit battered. "Where's your command? Where's your subaltern?" I said.

' "Here—all there is of it," said Stalky. "If you want young Everett, he'd dead, and his body's in the watch-tower. They rushed our road-party last week, and got him and seven men. We've been besieged for five days. I suppose they let you through to make sure of you. The whole country's up. 'Strikes me you walked into a first-class trap." He grinned, but neither Tertius nor I could see where the deuce the fun was. We hadn't any grub for our men, and Stalky had only four days' whack* for his. That came of dependin' upon your asinine Politicals, Pussy dear, who told us that the inhabitants were friendly.

'To make us quite comfy, Stalky took us up to the watch-tower to see poor Everett's body, lyin' in a foot o' drifted snow. It looked like a girl of fifteen—not a hair on the little fellow's face. He'd been shot through the temple, but the Malôts had left their mark on him. Stalky unbuttoned the tunic, and showed it to us—a rummy sickle-shaped cut on the chest. 'Member the snow all white on his eyebrows, Tertius? 'Member when Stalky moved the lamp and it looked as if he was alive?'

'Ye-es,' said Tertius, with a shudder. ' "Member the beastly look on Stalky's face, though, with his nostrils all blown out, same as he used to look when he was bullyin' a fag? That was a lovely evening.'

'We held a council of war up there over Everett's body. Stalky said the Malôts and Khye-Kheens were up together; havin' sunk their blood-fueds to settle us. The chaps we'd seen across the gorge were Khye-Kheens. It was about half a mile from them to us as a bullet flies, and they'd made a line of sungars* under the brow of the hill to sleep in and starve us out. The Malôts, he said, were in front of us promiscuous.* There wasn't good cover behind the fort, or they'd have been there, too. Stalky didn't mind the Malôts half as much as he did the Khye-Kheens. He said the Malôts were treacherous curs. What I couldn't understand was, why in the world the two gangs didn't join in and rush us. There must have been at least five hundred of 'em. Stalky said they didn't trust each other very well, because they were ancestral enemies when they were at home; and the only time they'd tried a rush he'd hove a couple of blasting-charges among 'em, and that had sickened 'em a bit.

'It was dark by the time we finished, and Stalky, always sereno, said: "You command now. I don't suppose you mind my taking any action I may consider necessary to reprovision the fort?" I said "Of course not," and then the lamp blew out. So Tertius and I had to climb down the tower steps (we didn't want to stay with Everett) and got back to our men. Stalky had gone off—to count the stores, I supposed. Anyhow, Tertius and I sat up in case of a rush (they were plugging at us pretty generally, you know), relieving each other till the mornin'.

'Mornin' came. No Stalky. Not a sign of him. I took counsel with his senior native officer—a grand, white-whiskered old chap—Rutton Singh, from Jullunder*-way. He only grinned, and said it was all right. Stalky had been out of the fort twice before, somewhere or other, accordin' to him. He said Stalky 'ud come back unchipped, and gave me to understand that Stalky was an invulnerable *Guru* of sorts. All the same, I put the whole command on half rations, and set 'em to pickin' out loop-holes.

'About noon there was no end of a snowstorm, and the enemy stopped firing. We replied gingerly, because we were awfully short of ammunition. 'Don't suppose we fired five shots an hour, but we generally got our man. Well, while I was talking with Rutton Singh I saw Stalky coming down from the watch-tower, rather puffy about the eyes, his poshteen coated with claret-coloured ice.

' "No trustin' these snowstorms," he said. "Nip out quick and snaffle what you can get. There's a certain amount of friction between the Khye-Kheens and the Malôts just now."

'I turned Tertius out with twenty Pathans, and they bucked about in the snow for a bit till they came on to a sort of camp about eight hundred yards away, with only a few men in charge and half-a-dozen sheep by the fire. They finished off the men, and snaffled the sheep and as much grain as they could carry, and came back. No one fired a shot at 'em. There didn't seem to be anybody about, but the snow was falling pretty thick.

' "That's good enough," said Stalky when we got dinner ready and he was chewin' mutton-kababs off a cleanin' rod. "There's no sense riskin' men. They're holding a pow-wow between the Khye-Kheens and the Malôts at the head of the gorge. I don't think these so-called coalitions are much good."

'Do you know what the maniac had done? Tertius and I shook it out of him by instalments. There was an underground granary cellar-room below the watch-tower, and in blasting the road Stalky had blown a hole into one side of it. Being no one else *but* Stalky, he'd kept the hole open for his own ends; and laid poor Everett's body slap over the well of the stairs that led down to it from the watch-tower. He'd had to remove and replace the corpse every time he used the passage. The Sikhs wouldn't go near the place, of course. Well, he'd got out of this hole, and dropped on to the road. Then, in the night *and* a howling snowstorm, he'd dropped over the edge of the khud, made his way down to the bottom of the gorge, forded the nullah* which was half frozen, climbed up on the other side along a track he'd discovered, and come out on the right flank of the Khye-Kheens. He had then—listen to this!— crossed over a ridge that paralleled their rear, walked half a mile behind that, and come out on the left of their line where the gorge gets shallow and where there was a regular track between the Malôt and the Khye-Kheen camps. That was about two in the morning, and, as it turned out, a man spotted him—a Khye-Kheen. So Stalky abolished him quietly, and left him—*with* the Malôt mark on his chest, same as Everett had.

' "I was just as economical as I could be," Stalky said to us, "If he shouted I should have been slain. I'd never had to do that kind of thing but once before, and that was the first time I tried that path. It's perfectly practicable for infantry, you know."

' "What about your first man?" I said.

' "Oh, that was the night after they killed Everett, and I went out lookin' for a line of retreat for my men. A man found me. I abolished him—*privatim*—scragged him. But on thinkin' it over it occurred to me that if I could find the body (I'd hove it down some rocks) I might decorate it with the Malôt mark and leave it to the Khye-Kheens to draw inferences. So I went out again the next night and did. The Khye-Kheens are shocked at the Malôts perpetratin' these two dastardly outrages after they'd sworn to sink all blood-feuds. I lay up behind their sungars early this morning and watched 'em. They all went to confer about it at the head of the gorge. Awf'ly annoyed they are. 'Don't wonder." You know the way Stalky drops out his words, one by one.'

'My God!' said the Infant explosively, as the full depth of the strategy dawned on him.

'Dear r man!' said M'Turk, purring rapturously.

'Stalky stalked,' said Tertius. 'That's all there is to it.'

'No, he didn't,' said Dick Four. 'Don't you remember how he insisted that he had only applied his luck? Don't you remember how Rutton Singh grabbed his boots* and grovelled in the snow, and how our men shouted?'

'None of our Pathans believed that was luck,' said Tertius. 'They swore Stalky ought to have been born a Pathan, and—'member we nearly had a row in the fort when Rutton Singh said Stalky was a Sikh? Gad, how furious the old chap was with my Pathan Jemadar! But Stalky just waggled his finger and they shut up.

'Old Rutton Singh's sword was half out, though, and he swore he'd cremate every Khye-Kheen and Malôt he killed. That made the Jemadar pretty wild, because he didn't mind fighting against his own creed, but he wasn't going to crab a fellow-Mussulman's chances of Paradise. Then Stalky jabbered Pushtu and Punjabi in alternate streaks. Where the deuce did he pick up his Pushtu* from, Beetle?'

'Never mind his language, Dick,' said I. 'Give us the gist of it.'

'I flatter myself I can address the wily Pathan on occasion, but, hang it all, I can't make puns in Pushtu, or top off my arguments with a smutty story, as he did. He played on those two old dogs o' war like a—like a concertina. Stalky said—and the other two backed up his knowledge of Oriental nature— that the Khye-Kheens and the Malôts between 'em would organise a combined attack on us that night, as a proof of good faith. They wouldn't drive it home, though, because neither side would trust the other on account, at Rutton Singh put it, of the little accidents. Stalky's notion was to crawl out at dusk with his Sikhs, manœuvre 'em along this ungodly goat-track that he'd found, to the back of the Khye-Kheen position, and then lob in a few long shots at the Malôts when the attack was well on. "That'll divert their minds and help to agitate 'em," he said. "Then you chaps can come out and sweep up the pieces, and we'll rendezvous at the head of the gorge. After that, I move we get back to Mac's camp and have something to eat." '

'*You* were commandin'?' the Infant suggested.

'I was about three months senior to Stalky, and two months Tertius's senior,' Dick Four replied. '*But* we were all from the same old Coll. I should say ours was the only little affair on record where some one wasn't jealous of some one else.'

'We weren't,' Tertius broke in, 'but there was another row between Gul Sher Khan and Rutton Singh. Our Jemadar said—he was quite right—that no Sikh living could stalk worth a damn; and that Koran Sahib* had better take out the Pathans, who understood that kind of mountain work. Rutton Singh said that Koran Sahib jolly well knew every Pathan was a born deserter, and every Sikh was a gentleman, even if he couldn't crawl on his belly. Stalky struck in with some woman's proverb or other, that had the effect of doublin' both men up with a grin. He said the Sikhs and the Pathans could settle their claims on the Khye-Kheens and Malôts later on, but he was going to take his Sikhs along for this mountain-climbing job, because Sikhs could shoot. They can too. Give 'em a mule-load of ammunition apiece, and they're perfectly happy.'

'And out he gat,' said Dick Four. 'As soon as it was dark, and he'd had a bit of snooze, him and thirty Sikhs went down through the staircase in the tower, every mother's son of 'em salutin' little Everett where It stood propped up against the wall. The last I heard him say was, "Kubbadar! tumbleinga!*"[1] and they tumbleingaed over the black edge of nothing. Close upon 9 P.M. the combined attack developed; Khye-Kheens across the valley, and Malôts in front of us, pluggin' at long range and yellin' to each other to come along and cut our infidel throats. Then they skirmished up to the gate, and began the old game of calling our Pathans renegades, and invitin' 'em to join the holy war. One of our men, a young fellow from Dera Ismail,* jumped on the wall to slang 'em back, and jumped down, blubbing like a child. He'd been hit smack in the middle of the hand. 'Never saw a man yet who could stand a hit in the hand without weepin' bitterly. It tickles up all the nerves. So Tertius took his rifle and smote the others on the head to keep them quiet at the loopholes. The dear children wanted to open the gate and go in at 'em generally, but that didn't suit our book.

'At last, near midnight, I heard the wop, wop, wop, of Stalky's Martinis* across the valley, and some general cursing among the Malôts, whose main body was hid from us by a fold in the hillside. Stalky was brownin'* 'em at a great rate, and very naturally they turned half right and began to blaze at their faithless allies, the Khye-Kheens—regular volley firin'. In less than ten minutes after Stalky opened the diversion they were going it hammer and tongs, both sides and valley. When we could see, the valley was rather a mixed-up affair. The Khye-Kheens had steamed out of their sungars above the gorge to chastise the Malôts, and Stalky—I was watching him through my glasses—had slipped in behind 'em. Very good. The Khye-Kheens had to leg it along the hillside up to where the gorge got shallow and they could cross over to the Malôts,

---

[1] 'Look out; you'll fall!'

who were awfully cheered to see the Khye-Kheens taken in the rear.

'Then it occurred to me to comfort the Khye-Kheens. So I turned out the whole command, and we advanced *à la pas de charge,** doublin' up what, for the sake of argument, we'll call the Malôts' left flank. Even then, if they'd sunk their differences, they could have eaten us alive; but they'd been firin' at each other half the night, and they went on firin'. Queerest thing you ever saw in your born days! As soon as our men doubled up to the Malôts, they'd blaze at the Khye-Kheens more zealously than ever, to show they were on our side, run up the valley a few hundred yards, and halt to fire again. The moment Stalky saw our game he duplicated it his side the gorge; and, by Jove! the Khye-Kheens did just the same thing.'

'Yes, but,' said Tertius, 'you've forgot him playin' "Arrah, Patsy, mind the baby"* on the bugle to hurry us up.'

'Did he?' roared M'Turk. Somehow we all began to sing it, and there was an interruption.

'Rather,' said Tertius, when we were quiet. No one of the Aladdin company could forget that tune. 'Yes, he played "Patsy." Go on, Dick.'

'Finally,' said Dick Four, 'we drove both mobs into each other's arms on a bit of level ground at the head of the valley, and saw the whole crew whirl off, fightin' and stabbin' and swearin' in a blinding snowstorm. They were a heavy, hairy lot, and we didn't follow 'em.

'Stalky had captured one prisoner—an old pensioned Sepoy* of twenty-five years' service, who produced his discharge—an awf'ly sportin' old card. He had been tryin' to make his men rush us early in the day. He was sulky—angry with his own side for their cowardice, and Rutton Singh wanted to bayonet him—Sikhs don't understand fightin' against the Government after you've served it honestly—but Stalky rescued him, and froze on to him tight—with ulterior motives, I believe. When we got back to the fort, we buried young Everett—Stalky wouldn't hear of blowin' up the place—and bunked. We'd only lost ten men, all told.'

'Only ten, out of seventy. How did you lose 'em?' I asked.

'Oh, there was a rush on the fort early in the night, and a few Malôts got over the gate. It was rather a tight thing for a minute or two, but the recruits took it beautifully. Lucky job we hadn't any badly wounded men to carry, because we had forty miles to Macnamara's camp. By Jove, how we legged it! Half way in, old Rutton Singh collapsed, so we slung him across four rifles and Stalky's overcoat; and Stalky, his prisoner, and a couple of Sikhs were his bearers. After that I went to sleep. You can, you know, on the march, when your legs get properly numbed. Mac swears we all marched into his camp snoring, and dropped where we halted. His men lugged us into the tents like gram-bags.* I remember wakin' up and seeing Stalky asleep with his head on old Rutton Singh's chest. *He* slept twenty-four hours. I only slept seventeen, but then I was coming down with dysentery.'

'Coming down with dysentery.'

'Coming down! What rot! He had it on him before we joined Stalky in the fort,' said Tertius.

'Well, *you* needn't talk! You hove your sword at Macnamara and demanded a drumhead court-martial every time you saw him. The only thing that soothed you was putting you under arrest every half-hour. You were off your head for three days.'

''Don't remember a word of it,' said Tertius placidly. 'I remember my orderly giving me milk, though.'

'How did Stalky come out?' M'Turk demanded, puffing hard over his pipe.

'Stalky? Like a serene Brahmini bull.* Poor old Mac was at his Royal Engineer's wits' end to know what to do. You see I was putrid with dysentery, Tertius was ravin', half the men had frost-bite, and Macnamara's orders were to break camp and come in before winter. So Stalky, who hadn't turned a hair, took half his supplies to save him the bother o' luggin' 'em back to the plains, and all the ammunition he could get at, and, *consilio et auxilio* Rutton Singhi, tramped back to his fort with all his Sikhs and his precious prisoner, *and* a lot of dissolute hangers-on that he and the prisoner had seduced into service. He had sixty men of sorts—and his brazen cheek. Mac nearly wept with joy when he went. You see there weren't any explicit orders to Stalky to come in before the passes were blocked: Mac is a great man for orders, and Stalky's a great man for orders—when they suit his book.'

'He told me he was goin' to the Engadine,'* said Tertius. 'Sat on my cot smokin' a cigarette, and makin' me laugh till I cried. Macnamara bundled the whole lot of us down to the plains next day. We were a walkin' hospital.'

'Stalky told me that Macnamara was a simple godsend to him,' said Dick Four. 'I used to see him in Mac's tent listenin' to Mac playin' the fiddle, and, between the pieces, wheedlin' Mac out of picks and shovels and dynamite cartridges hand-over-fist. Well, that was the last we saw of Stalky. A week or so later the passes were shut with snow, and I don't think Stalky wanted to be found particularly just then.'

'He didn't,' said the fair and fat Abanazar. 'He didn't. Ho, ho!'

Dick Four threw up his thin, dry hand with the blue veins at the back of it. 'Hold on a minute, Pussy; I'll let you in at the proper time. I went down to my regiment, and that spring, five months later, I got off with a couple of companies on detachment: nominally to look after some friends of ours across the Border; actually, of course, to recruit. It was a bit unfortunate, because an ass of a young Naick* carried a frivolous blood-feud he'd inherited from his aunt into those hills, and the local gentry wouldn't volunteer into my corps. Of course, the Naick had taken short leave to manage the business; that was all regular enough; *but* he'd stalked my pet orderly's uncle. It was an infernal shame, because I knew Harris of the Ghuznees* would be covering that ground three months later, and he'd snaffle all the chaps I had my eyes on. Everybody was down on the Naick, because they felt he ought to have had the decency to postpone his—his disgustful amours till our companies were full strength.

'Still the beast had a certain amount of professional feeling left. He sent one of his aunt's clan by night to tell me that, if I'd take safeguard, he'd put on to a batch of beauties. I nipped over the Border like a shot, and about ten miles the other side, in a nullah,* my rapparee*-in-charge showed me about seventy men variously armed, but standing up like a Queen's company. Then one of 'em stepped out and lugged

round an old bugle, just like—who's the man?—Bancroft*,
ain't it?—feeling for his eyeglass in a farce, and played "Arrah,
Patsy, mind the baby. Arrah, Patsy, mind"—that was as far as
he could get.'

That also was as far as Dick Four could get, because we had
to sing the old song through twice, again and once more, and
subsequently, in order to repeat it.

'He explained that if I knew the rest of the song he had a
note for me from the man the song belonged to. Whereupon,
my children, I finished that old tune on that bugle, and *this*
is what I got. I knew you'd like to look at it. Don't grab.' (We
were all struggling for a sight of the well-known unformed
handwriting.) 'I'll read it aloud:

"FORT EVERETT, *February* 19.
"DEAR DICK, OR TERTIUS: The bearer of this is in charge of
seventy-five recruits, all pukka* devils, but desirous of leading new
lives. They have been slightly polished, and after being boiled may
shape well. I want you to give thirty of them to my adjutant, who,
though God's Own ass, will need men this spring. The rest you can
keep. You will be interested to learn that I have extended my road
to the end of the Malôt country. All headmen and priests concerned
in last September's affair worked one month each, supplying road-
metal from their own houses. Everett's grave is covered by a forty-
foot mound, which should serve well as a base for future
triangulations. Rutton Singh sends his best salaams. I am making
some treaties, and have given my prisoner—who also sends his
salaams—local rank of Khan Bahadur.*

"A. L. CORKRAN." '

'Well, that was all,' said Dick Four, when the roaring, the
shouting, the laughter, and, I think, the tears, had subsided.
'I chaperoned the gang across the Border as quick as I could.
They were rather homesick, but they cheered up when they
recognised some of my chaps, who had been in the Khye-
Kheen row, and they made a rippin' good lot. It's rather more
than three hundred miles from Fort Everett to where I picked
'em up. Now, Pussy, tell 'em the latter end o' Stalky as you
saw it.'

Abanazar laughed a little nervous, misleading, official
laugh.

'Oh, it wasn't much. I was at Simla in the spring, when our Stalky, out of his snows, began corresponding direct with the Government.'

'After the manner of a king,' suggested Dick Four.

'My turn now, Dick. He'd done a whole lot of things he shouldn't have done, and constructively pledged the Government to all sorts of action.'

'Pledged the State's ticker,* eh?' said M'Turk, with a nod to me.

'About that; but the embarrassin' part was that it was all so thunderin' convenient, so well reasoned, don't you know. Came in as pat as if he'd had access to all sorts of information—which he couldn't, of course.'

'Pooh!' said Tertius, 'I back Stalky against the Foreign Office any day.'

'He'd done pretty nearly everything he could think of, except strikin' coins in his own image and superscription*, all under cover of buildin' this infernal road and bein' blocked by the snow. His report was simply amazin'. Von Lennaert tore his hair over it at first, and then he gasped "Who the dooce is this unknown Warren Hastings?* He must be slain. He must be slain officially! The Viceroy'll never stand it. It's unheard of. He must be slain by His Excellency in person. Order him up here and pitch in a stinger." Well, I sent him no end of an official stinger, and I pitched in an unofficial telegram at the same time.'

'You!' This with amazement from the Infant, for Abanazar resembled nothing so much as a fluffy Persian cat.

'Yes—me,' said Abanazar. "Twasn't much, but after what you've said, Dicky, it was rather a coincidence, because I wired:

> "Aladdin now has got his wife,
>   Your Emperor is appeased.
> I think you'd better come to life:
>   We hope you've all been pleased."

Funny how that song came up in my head. That was fairly non-committal and encouragin'. The only flaw was that his Emperor wasn't appeased by very long chalks. Stalky extricated himself from his mountain fastnesses and loafed up to Simla at his leisure, to be offered up on the horns of the altar.*'

'But,' I began, 'surely the Commander-in-Chief is the proper——'

'His Excellency had an idea that if he blew up one single junior captain—same as King used to blow us up—he was holdin' the reins of Empire, and, of course, as long as he had that idea, Von Lennaert encouraged him. I'm not sure Von Lennaert didn't put that notion into his head.'

'They've changed the breed, then, since my time,' I said.

'P'r'aps. Stalky was sent up for his wiggin' like a bad little boy. I've reason to believe that His Excellency's hair stood on end. He walked into Stalky for one hour—Stalky at attention in the middle of the floor, and (so he vowed) Von Lennaert pretending to soothe down His Excellency's top-knot in dumb show in the background. Stalky didn't dare to look up, or he'd have laughed.'

'Now, wherefore was Stalky not broken publicly?' said the Infant, with a large and luminous leer.

'Ah, wherefore?' said Abanazar. 'To give him a chance to retrieve his blasted career, and not to break his father's heart. Stalky hadn't a father, but that didn't matter. He behaved like a—like the Sanawar Orphan Asylum, and His Excellency graciously spared him. Then he came round to my office and sat opposite me for ten minutes, puffing out his nostrils. Then he said, "Pussy, if I thought that basket-hanger*——" '

'Hah! He remembered *that*,' said M'Turk.

' "That two-anna basket-hanger governed India, I swear I'd become a naturalised Muscovite tomorrow. I'm a *femme incomprise*.* This thing's broken my heart. It'll take six months' shootin'-leave in India to mend it. Do you think I can get it, Pussy?" '

'He got it in about three minutes and a half, and seventeen days later he was back in the arms of Rutton Singh—horrid disgraced—with orders to hand over his command, etc., to Cathcart MacMonnie.'

'Observe!' said Dick Four. 'One Colonel of the Political Department in charge of thirty Sikhs on a hilltop. Observe, my children!'

'Naturally, Cathcart not being a fool, even if he *is* a Political, let Stalky do his shooting within fifteen miles of Fort Everett for the next six months; and I always understood they and Rutton Singh *and* the prisoner were as thick as thieves. Then Stalky loafed back to his regiment, I believe. I've never seen him since.'

'I have, though,' said M'Turk, swelling with pride.

We all turned as one man.

'It was at the beginning of this hot weather. I was in camp in the Jullunder doab* and stumbled slap on Stalky in a Sikh village; sitting on the one chair of state with half the population grovellin' before him, a dozen Sikh babies on his knees, an old harridan clappin' him on the shoulder, and a garland o' flowers round his neck. 'Told me he was recruitin'. We dined together that night, but he never said a word of the business of the Fort. 'Told me, though, that if I wanted any supplies I'd better say I was Koran Sahib's *bhai;** and I did, and the Sikhs wouldn't take my money.'

'Ah! That must have been one of Rutton Singh's villages,' said Dick Four; and we smoked for some time in silence.

'I say,' said M'Turk, casting back through the years. 'Did Stalky ever tell you *how* Rabbits-Eggs came to rock King that night?'

'No,' said Dick Four.

Then M'Turk told.

'I see,' said Dick Four, nodding. 'Practically he duplicated the trick over again. There's nobody like Stalky.'

'That's just where you make the mistake,' I said. 'India's full of Stalkies—Cheltenham and Haileybury and Marlborough chaps—that we don't know anything about, and the surprises will begin when there is really a big row on.'

'Who will be surprised?' said Dick Four.

'The other side. The gentlemen who go to the front in first-class carriages. Just imagine Stalky let loose on the south side of Europe with a sufficiency of Sikhs and a reasonable prospect of loot. Consider it quietly.'

'There's something in that, but you're too much of an optimist, Beetle,' said the Infant.

'Well, I've a right to be. Ain't I responsible for the whole thing? You needn't laugh. Who wrote "Aladdin now has got his wife"—eh?'

'What's that got to do with it?' said Tertius.

'Everything,' said I.

'Prove it,' said the Infant.

And I have!

THE END

EXPLANATORY NOTES

11 *spadger-hunt*: spadger is a dialect or colloquial word for sparrow.

   stalky: cf. p. 13: '"Stalky", in their school vocabulary, meant clever, well-considered and wily, as applied to plans of action; and "stalkiness" was the one virtue Corkran toiled after.'

   potwallopers: roughly speaking, it means householders, property owners, as opposed to labourers, vagrants, and people who own nothing. In the eighteenth century it meant someone who 'dressed his own victuals', i.e. 'boiled his own pot' in his own house, and in certain places was entitled to vote for a member of parliament. In the nineteenth century it went down in public esteem and from meaning, more or less, a respectable villager, it came to mean someone rough, rude, and clumsy.

12 *Corky*: Corkran's nickname until this episode gave him the name of Stalky.

13 *thrown out any pickets*: sent out anyone to keep a look-out. According to the *OED*, pickets are 'a small detached body of troops, sent out to watch for the approach of the enemy, or his scouts'. In the Army Regulations it is spelt 'piquets'.

15 *quickset*: hedge made of living plants set in the ground to grow, especially hawthorn.

18 *Tweakons*: let us tweak (schoolboy compound of English and French).

19 *A people sitting in darkness and the shadow . . .*: echo of Isaiah 9: 2: 'The people that walked in darkness . . . they that dwell in the land of the shadow of death.'

22 *swottin' dumb-bells*: working furiously hard; dumb-bells being clubs for exercising, with weights on each end.

24 *'Pon my Sam*: jocular asseveration, perhaps from "pon my sang' (blood).

26 *Sweeter than honey*: echo of Psalm 19: 10: 'sweeter than honey and the honeycomb'.

29 *pugs*: from the Hindustani word 'pag', the track of a beast.

30 *'Bother! Likewise blow!'*: Slightly misquoted from W. S. Gilbert, *The Bab Ballads*, 'The Bishop of Rum-ti-foo'. The original reads: ' "Bother!", also "Blow".'

His rebus infectis: not having accomplished these things.

destricto ense: with drawn sword.

31 *Pax*: literally 'peace'. Colloquially used to mean: 'Stop it, Let's make a truce'; even: 'I apologize'.

fags: in *Something of Myself* Kipling wrote (p. 29): 'Oddly enough, "fagging" did not exist, though the name "fag" was regularly used as a term of contempt and sign of subordination against the Lower School.'

Jorrocks: the sporting hero of R. S. Surtees's hunting stories, which first appeared in the *New Sporting Magazine* and were collected into a book in 1838 as *Jorrocks' Jaunts and Jollities*, followed by other books of Jorrocks stories. On p. 32 we learn that *Handley Cross* (1843) is the book Stalky has with him that day. Surtees is often quoted or referred to, especially by Stalky.

32 *you blind lunatic!*: this is one of several references to Beetle's poor sight, some kindly or at least friendly, because they come from friends, like this one; but in one case (in 'The Moral Reformers') rousing Beetle into one of his few powerful rages.

a tergo: from behind.

Handley Cross: see note to p. 31.

35 *the Castle*: Dublin Castle, the seat of government in Ireland.

deep calling to deep: echo of Psalm 42: 7: 'Deep calleth unto deep'.

36 *Out of the mouths of——*: Psalm 8: 2. Colonel Dabney omits 'babes and sucklings'.

37 *'Oh, Paddy dear . . .'*: first line of the Irish nationalist song 'The Wearin' o' the Green'.

young-eyed cherubim: *The Merchant of Venice*, V.i.

39 *the Pleasant Isle of Aves*: from Charles Kingsley's poem 'The Last Buccaneer', 1857:

And such a port for mariners I ne'er shall see again
As the pleasant Isle of Aves, beside the Spanish main.

Chingangook: sc. Chingachgook: a Red Indian chief, skilled in fieldcraft and stalking, who figures in Fenimore Cooper's novels *The Last of the Mohicans*, *The Path-Finder*, *The Deerslayer*, and *The Pioneer*.

40 *in loco parentis*: in the place of a parent; responsible for the boys.

cachuca: sc. cachucha: a Spanish dance.

40 *'But what's the odds, as long as you're 'appy?'*: there seems to be something of an anachronism here. George du Maurier quoted this line (origin unknown) in *Trilby*, which appeared in 1894. Thus, it was obviously too late for Stalky to quote it in the early 1880s, but not, of course, for Kipling, who wrote 'In Ambush' in 1898.

vice: in place of.

42 *flagrante delicto*: in the very act of crime.

43 *linhay*: a shed, open in front.

45 *'Quis custodiet ipsos custodes?'*: Juvenal, *Satires*, VI, 347–8: 'Who will guard the guards themselves?'

'. . . Zeal, all zeal, Mr Easy': a reference to one of their favourite books, Captain Marryat's *Mr Midshipman Easy*, 1836.

Hounds choppin' foxes . . . vice: quotation from *Handley Cross*.

46 *paddy-wack*: rage, fit of temper. The word 'paddy' is used in the same sense today.

47 *evil-speakers, liars, slow-bellies*: cf. Titus 1: 12.

'Thou hast appealed to Caesar: unto Caesar shalt thou go': Acts 25: 12.

48 *the Caudine Toasting-fork*: the Caudine Forks was a narrow pass in the mountains near Capua, where in the second Samnite war the Roman army was surrounded in 321 BC and made to pass under the yoke, the greatest humiliation that could be inflicted upon it. Stalky was obviously referring to the phrase 'We've got him on toast'.

'Too much ticklee, him bust': a reference to the Uncle Remus stories by Joel Chandler Harris, in which Mr Buzzard could not stand being tickled. Uncle Remus, once a slave, tells stories from Negro folklore to a little boy, the son of the house in which he is now a valued servant. *Uncle Remus and his Legends of the Old Plantation* and *Uncle Remus or Mr Fox, Mr Rabbit and Mr Terrapin* were published in England in 1881, and one of the Stalky stories, 'The United Idolators', is about the craze for the Uncle Remus stories which swept the school.

49 *'Wine is a mocker, strong drink is ragin' '*: Proverbs 20: 1.

quodded: imprisoned. First used about 1700, origin unknown. Quod means prison; to quod, to imprison.

Chingangook: see note to p. 39.

50 *'Take not out your 'ounds on a werry windy day'*: R. S. Surtees, *Handley Cross*, chapter 38. Surtees was quoting from Peter

Beckford's *Thoughts on Hunting*, 1781.

Heffy is my only joy: reference to 'Phyllis is my only joy' by Sir Charles Sedley (*c*.1639–1701).

53 *Monte Cristo*: *The Count of Monte Cristo* (1844–5) by Alexandre Dumas (*père*).

suppressio veri: suppression of the truth; *suggestio falsi*: suggestion of the false.

54 *Aladdin*: *Alladin, or the Wonderful Scamp*, by H. J. Byron, first acted 1861.

55 *Arrah, Patsy . . .*: music-hall song by Edward Harrigan, pub. 1878.

John Short: the College bell-ringer.

56 *A gray princess shirt*: a princess dress or petticoat is one without a seam at the waist, so a 'princess-skirt', presumably starting at the waist, seems a contradiction in terms; perhaps Kipling simply did not realize what 'princess' implied in dressmaking language.

imposition-paper: paper used for impositions, written tasks imposed as punishments, generally 'lines' by the hundred, often Latin. Colloquially called 'impots'; therefore, on pp. 61, 105, 235, and 237, impot-paper; and on p. 226, impot-basket, a basket in which impositions were placed and collected by the master.

Gigadibs: a reference to Browning's poem, 'Bishop Blougram's Apology'. 'So you despise me, Mr Gigadibs' comes early in the poem (line 13); King here changed it to 'Master Gigadibs', probably also echoing Kipling's school nickname of Gigger.

57 *Fors Clavigera*: a series of monthly pamphlets by John Ruskin in the form of letters, 96 in all, begun in 1871 and continued, not quite regularly, until 1884: 'Letters to the Workmen and Labourers of Great Britain'. 'Fors Clavigera is fortune bearing a club, a key and a nail,' Ruskin wrote, 'symbolising the deed of Hercules, the patience of Ulysses, and the law of Lycurgus.' Lycurgus was the legislator of Sparta in ancient Greece.

58 *I'll correct his caesuras for him*: I'll deal with him. The caesura, in Greek and Latin prosody, is the division of a metrical foot between two words, especially in certain recognized places near the middle of the line; and so it has come to mean, in English, a pause or break in the middle of a line. Here perhaps Kipling uses the word in a broader sense, to mean gaps, shortcomings.

you chaps are communists: in 'An English School' (*Land and Sea*

Tales), Kipling says that the three friends 'lived as communists and socialists hope to live one day, when everyone is good . . . their possessions were in common, absolutely'.

59 *his unlovely name*: see J. C. Dunsterville, *Stalky's Reminiscences* (London, 1928), p. 45: 'His nickname of "Rabbit's-Eggs" was due to his having offered for sale six partridge eggs which he stoutly maintained were "rabbut's aigs". He genuinely believed them to be so. He was passing a clump of bushes when a rabbit ran out of them, and for some reason or another he peered into the bushes, and there, sure enough, were the six eggs, obviously the produce of the rabbit!'

a fat, brown-backed volume of the late Sixties: obviously the poems of Robert Browning, as the reference to Gigadibs shows, and later the one to men and women. In 1855 Browning published two volumes of poems called *Men and Women*, the best known of which are the dramatic monologues ('Fra Lippo Lippi', 'Andrea del Sarto', etc.).

60 *the Opium-Eater*: Thomas de Quincey (1785–1859), who wrote *Confessions of an English Opium-Eater* (in book form, 1822 and 1823; reprinted in a longer form in 1856).

children of noble races trained by surrounding art: Ruskin, misquoted.

61 *beastliness*: homosexuality. This is the word generally used in school stories, where the subject is treated very obliquely.

à la Fagin: reference to the trainer of young pickpockets in *Oliver Twist*.

62 *Eric, or, Little by Little* (1858) and *St Winifred's; or The World of School* (1862): famous school stories by F. W. Farrar, much mocked by Stalky and Co for priggishness, exaggeration, and mawkishness.

strong, perseverin' man: see R. S. Surtees, *Mr Facey Romford's Hounds* (1865), chapter 19. Facey advertises for a 'strong, persevering man, to clean horses'.

privatim et seriatim: medieval Latin, meaning privately and one after another.

these ossifers of the Ninety-third, wot look like hairdressers: see R. S. Surtees, *Handley Cross*, chapter 51, where Jorrocks calls someone 'you hossifer in the ninety-fust regiment, who looks like an 'airdresser'.

Binjimin, we must make him cry 'Capivi!': we must make him admit his fault. Another quotation from *Handley Cross*. Jorrocks was presumably confusing *capivi* with *peccavi*, I have sinned.

a basket-hanger: the term basket-hanger is thereafter used as one of abuse by Stalky and Co. M'Turk explains what it means in the next paragraph: 'He [King] has a basket with blue ribbons and a pink kitten in it, hung up in his window to grow musk in.' See p. 295, where Stalky says to Abanazar: 'Pussy, if I thought that basket-hanger——' 'Hah! He remembered *that*,' said M'Turk. 'That two-anna basket-hanger governed India, I swear I'd become a Müscovite tomorrow.' M'Turk's exclamation makes it clear that the term 'basket-hanger' is taken from their private language, still remembered after fifteen years from King's basket with the kitten in it; a concrete example of the hold which school experiences and the memories and phrases they produced still had on the adults the boys grew into.

Down went M'Turk's inky thumb: as in a gladiatorial contest, when thumbs down was a signal for the *coup de grâce* to be given to the vanquished.

63 *Placetne*: literally, Does it please you? (i.e., do you agree?).

'*Or who in Moscow toward the Czar . . .*': from Robert Browning's poem 'Waring'.

bargees: originally bargee meant a barge-man, one who worked on a barge. It is used throughout the book as a term of abuse; for instance, on p. 216, Stalky uses it to describe the MP who comes to lecture on patriotism; and on p. 221 Beetle says of Stalky, 'he cursed me like a bargee'.

Actum est: [King's] done for.

'*There's a great text in Galatians . . .*': from Browning's 'Soliloquy of the Spanish Cloister'.

64 *Setebos . . .*: from Browning's 'Caliban upon Setebos'.

Strong, perseverin' man: see note to p. 62.

Capivi: see note to p. 62.

Beans: to give someone beans means to punish or to scold.

65 *It's a way we have in the Army*: song by J. B. Geoghegan (1863).

Habet!: literally: he has [it]. In other words, he's had it. Cry of the spectators when a gladiator received the fatal blow.

67 *Gibbon*: Edward Gibbon's *The Decline and Fall of the Roman Empire*.

Casabianca: at the battle of the Nile in 1798, Louis Casabianca, captain of the French flagship *l'Orient*, fought on to the end, though the Admiral had been killed. His son, aged thirteen, refused to leave him and died, too. Mrs Hemans's poem, 'Casabianca'—'The boy stood on the burning deck, Whence all but he had fled'—often mocked and embroidered, is about his fate.

67 *Number Five lavatory*: the word does not mean WC, as it does now, but 'washroom', which is closer to the Latin root. Here there were several baths, probably tin ones.

68 *'Shockin'!'* . . .: further mockery of Farrar's *St Winifred's*.

69 *It's an alibi, Samivel*: quotation from *The Pickwick Papers*.

   gallipots: small earthern glazed pots; probably called after galleys, as they were brought in galleys from the Mediterranean.

72 *hypothecation*: pawning; from a term used in Roman law.

73 *saloon-pistols*: pistols adapted for short-range practice.

   gig-lamps: spectacles.

74 *straw*: straw hat, boater.

76 *Jugurtha tamen*: Jugurtha, however. From the historian Sallust.

   Pas si je le connai[*s*]: not if I know it.

   Panurge: a companion of Pantagruel, in Rabelais' *Gargantua and Pantagruel*, who made grotesque faces.

77 *a terrace of twelve large houses*: a row of seaside boarding houses converted into a school. See the introductory poem with its reference to 'Twelve bleak houses by the shore', p. 5 above.

78 *keep cave*: keep a look-out, keep watch. *Cave* in Latin means beware (as in *cave canem*, beware of the dog), and until recently children used it as Stalky does.

79 *Violet somebody*: Eugène Emmanuel Viollet-le-Duc, 1814–79. French scholar and architect, more important as medievalist and restorer than as architect, whose ideas were (mainly) known through his *Dictionnaire raisonné de l'architecture française*, published between 1854 and 1868. First translated into English by Benjamin Bucknall, 1874.

80 *O Beadle*: quotation from Edward Lear's 'There was an old man of Quebec' ('But he cried, "With a needle/ I'll slay you, O beadle!"')

   doggaroo: writer of doggerel; a word probably invented by Kipling.

81 *Come to my arms, my beamish boy . . . Calloo, callay!*: from the Jabberwocky poem in Lewis Carroll's *Through the Looking Glass*, 1872.

82 *Big medicine—heap big medicine!*: from *Uncle Remus*.

83 *There's something about your pure, high, young forehead . . . innocent boyhood*: more mockery of Dean Farrar's books.

84 *spidgers*: a variant of spadgers, sparrows.

85 *a gaudy lot*: a fine lot. Here this word of many meanings is used just for emphasis.

'With one shout and with one cry': misquoted from Macaulay's 'The Armada', 1832: 'And with one start and with one cry, the royal city woke'.

86 *minute-gun*: gun fired at intervals of a minute.

''Tis but a little faded flower': song by Ellen Clementine Howarth, American writer, 1827–99.

87 *Lazarites*: lepers, from the name of Lazarus.

Hoplites: heavily armed infantry in ancient Greece (as opposed to 'skirmishers').

88 *a large cross, with 'Lord, have mercy upon us,' on the door*: in times of plague, especially during the Great Plague of 1665 in London, houses were identified as plague-stricken by a cross and 'Lord have mercy upon us' written on the door.

the learned Lipsius: Justus Lipsius, an eminent humanist, 1547–1606. His quality as an infant prodigy was also recalled by Laurence Sterne in *Tristram Shandy*: 'You forget the great Lipsius, quoth Yorick, who composed a work the day he was born.'

90 *Falling into the pit he has digged*: reference to Ecclesiastes 10: 8, and Psalms 57: 4.

91 *He 'nursed the pinion that impelled the steel'*: Byron, *English Bards and Scotch Reviewers*, line 841.

privatim et seriatim: see note to p. 62.

the fishpools of Heshbon: Song of Solomon 7: 4.

92 *certain lewd fellows of the baser sort*: Acts 17: 5.

Bring out your dead: cry of the carters who went about at night collecting corpses during the Great Plague of London in 1665.

glandered: suffering from contagious horse-disease.

93 *Cave*: see note to p. 78.

94 *ipso facto*: by that very fact.

98 *Summa*: to sum up, or: the main facts.

99 *pot-wallopers*: see note to p. 11.

99 *barbarous hexameters*: quotation from Tennyson's 'On Translations of Homer'.

100 *'Roman d'un Jeune Homme Pauvre'*: by Octave Feuillet, 1821–90. This, his best-known novel, was published in 1858.

to elegise the 'Elegy in a Churchyard': probably to put into Latin elegiacs Thomas Gray's 'Elegy in a Country Churchyard'.

to punt-about: to kick a football about for practice.

101 *'But by the yellow Tiber . . .'*: from Macaulay's 'Horatius' in *Lays of Ancient Rome*.

Belial somebody: see F. W. Farrar's *St Winifred's*: 'Master Wilton—Belial junior, as Henderson always called him'. This suggests Mammon and Lucifer, his companion fiends in *Paradise Lost*.

the B.O.P.: the *Boys Own Paper*, 1879–1967, an influential magazine for boys, published by the Religious Tract Society, launched to appear weekly but from 1913 appearing monthly. Many famous writers for boys contributed to it. Beetle mocks its school-story views on school behaviour.

103 *metagrobolised*: from the obsolete French verb *métagrobuliser*, used and probably invented by Rabelais, meaning 'to puzzle, mystify'.

106 *Shylocks*: usurers. The reference is of course to Shakespeare's *The Merchant of Venice*.

Head in a drain-pipe . . .: reference to one of Mr Jingle's stories in *Pickwick Papers*, chapter 2.

107 *Keyte's*: the school tuck-shop.

108 *Cave*: see note to p. 78.

111 *the baser-side-of-imagination business*: in *Something of Myself*, p. 23, Kipling wrote: 'It was clean with a cleanliness that I have never heard of in any other school.' He believed that 'if masters did not suspect them [cases of homosexuality, etc] and show that they suspected, there would not be quite so many elsewhere.'

114 *Mrs Oliphant's 'Beleaguered City'*: an 'occult' novel published in 1880. 'A Story of the Seen and the Unseen', it tells how the dead rise from their graves and take possession for a while of Sémur (in Haute Bourgogne), driving out the inhabitants and filling it with darkness and terror (*Readers' Guide to Rudyard Kipling's Work*, p. 445).

115 *giddy palladiums of public schools*: reference to Dean Farrar's books. See p. 72: ' "The Sixth," he says, "is the palladium of all public schools." '

They said it very loud and clear . . .: from 'I sent a message to the fish' in *Through the Looking Glass*, chapter 6, by Lewis Carroll.

shibbuwichee or tokonoma: supposedly ju-jitsu terms, but they seem to be M'Turk's invention.

117 *Et ego . . . in Arcadia vixi*: I too have lived in Arcadia; supposedly written on a tombstone; but here perhaps an indication that the Head, too, was young once, and remembers what he learnt then.

Prooshian: Cormell Price had acted as tutor to a nobleman's son in Russia: hence the soubriquet 'Rooshian', transmuted in *Stalky & Co* to 'Prooshian'.

119 *lictor*: officer attending ancient Roman consul (who had twelve lictors) or dictator (who had twenty-four), bearing fasces and carrying out sentences on offenders. Here, of course, meaning someone in authority.

he ain't in Orders, thank goodness: Cormell Price, Kipling's headmaster and family friend, and the model for Bates, was not in Holy Orders, nor was he a strong churchman, which was unusual in a headmaster at the time. In *An English School* Kipling writes: 'I think that one secret of his great hold over us was that he was not a clergyman, as so many headmasters are. As soon as a boy begins to think in the misty way that boys do, he is suspicious of a man who punishes him one day and preaches at him the next' (*Land and Sea Tales*, London, 1923, p. 257).

121 *A Daniel come to judgment!*: from Shakespeare's *The Merchant of Venice*, IV. i.

the world . . . is too much with you sometimes: a reference to Wordsworth's sonnet CCLXXVIII, 'The world is too much with us: late and soon'.

123 *Abana and Pharpar*: 2 Kings 5: 12. 'Are not Abana and Pharpar, rivers of Damascus, better than all the waters of Israel? May I not wash in them, and be clean?'

my own Tenth Legion: the Tenth was Caesar's favourite legion.

124 *we ain't goin' to have any beastly Erickin' . . . his neck*: another reference to *Eric*. 'D'you want to walk about with your arm round his neck?' refers to the sentimental behaviour scorned by Stalky and Co, and the warm friendships between older and younger boys, as described by Farrar in his books.

'*As beautiful Kitty . . . tripping——*': Irish song with traditional tune. The words in this version (there are others) are by E. Lysecht.

125 *oratio directa*: direct speech; *oratio obliqua*: indirect speech.

126 *Galton's 'Art of Travel'*: *The Art of Travel* by Sir Francis Galton, 1854, later reprinted with additions.

wipe: handkerchief.

130 *Isabella-coloured*: greyish yellow. Which particular Isabella inspired the name has not been established for certain.

133 *my giddy Narcissus . . . reflection!*: Narcissus was a beautiful youth in Greek mythology, who saw his image reflected in a pool and fell in love with it. Then, unable to approach it, he killed himself. According to Ovid, his blood was then turned into the flower which still bears his name.

134 *pax*: see note to p. 31.

136 *The only son of his mother . . . widow*: Luke, 7: 12.

137 *Augurs*: official predictors of events in ancient Rome.

139 *Venus and Liber*: the goddess of Love and the god of Wine.

Charon: the boatman who ferried the souls of the dead across the river Styx to Hades.

140 *a Major and his Minor*: an older and a younger brother. Boys at school were then addressed as Smith (or whatever) major, Smith minor, and, if there was a third, Smith minimus. At a school with many brothers or cousins with the same name they might be known as Smith 1, 2, 3, 4 (cf. 'Dick Four') or by Latin equivalents like Tertius.

141 *Look here, Har——Minor*: this shows how at school even brothers did not address each other by their Christian names. Har—presumably Harold or Harry—was unusable as a name at school, even when the two were alone together. The same sort of thing can be seen in P. G. Wodehouse's *A Prefect's Uncle*, in which uncle and nephew, very close in age, address each other by their surnames. It was not always so; the earlier school stories use Christian names between friends, and at certain schools, in certain periods, this continues. But around the 1880's it would have been usual to use surnames, indeed not to know the first name of most other boys. Kipling at school was able to pretend his name was John, since his first name was Joseph and he was thus J. R. Kipling.

quarter-decking: walking up and down, like a captain on his quarter deck.

143 *Loungin' round and sufferin'*: Uncle Remus, chapter XII: ' "Lounjun' roun' en suffer'n," sez Brer Terrypin, sezee.'

Blundells: a real public school, near Tiverton in Devon.

myall-wood: Australian acacia, with scented wood used for pipes.

segashuate: Uncle Remus, chapter II: ' "How duz yo' sym'tums seem ter segashuate?" sez Brer Rabbit, sezee.'

the Cri: the Criterion (theatre).

Turn me loose, or I'll knock the natal stuffin' out of you: Uncle Remus, chapter II: ' "Tu'n me loose, fo' I kick de natal stuffin' outen you," sez Brer Rabbit, sezee.'

Shotover: a filly which won the Derby and another major race in 1882.

Cetewayo: last King of Zululand, deposed after Zulu War (1879); arrived in England August, 1882.

Arabi Pasha: he headed a nationalist revolt in Egypt, which the Khedive was unable to deal with. After massacres at Alexandria, Britain intervened and Arabi Pasha was defeated at Tel-el-Kebir on 13 September 1882.

Spofforth: Frederick Robert Spofforth, known as the Demon Bowler, an Australian cricketer who took a record number of wickets in 1882.

144 *Ti-yi! Tungalee! . . . I pick um pea!*: from Uncle Remus, chapter XXIII, 'Mr Rabbit and Mr Bear', sung by Brer Rabbit to his children.

Ingle-go-jang, my joy, my joy! . . .: from Uncle Remus, chapter XXIV, 'Mr Bear catches old Mr Bullfrog', sung by Brer Bullfrog.

'Pinafore' and 'Patience': Gilbert and Sullivan's *H.M.S. Pinafore* (1878) and *Patience* (1881).

Mea culpa!: the fault is mine.

We: Stalky & Co.

145 *the worst*: i.e. homosexuality.

146 *Dont 'spute with de squinch-owl . . . fier*: from Uncle Remus. One of the 'Plantation Proverbs' that follow chapter XXXIV.

Dick's nose shone like Bardolph's: Bardolph is a character in Shakespeare's *Henry IV*, *Henry V*, and *The Merry Wives of Windsor*, one of Falstaff's gang. His red nose was much mocked.

or and sable: gold and black, in heraldic language.

147 *R.N.*: Royal Navy.

147 *Stinking Jim*: *Uncle Remus*, chapter X: ' "Brer Fox call Brer
Tarrypin Stinking Jim" sez she.'

Hypatia: novel by Charles Kingsley, 1853.

148 *the only begetter*: reference to Shakespeare's dedication of his
sonnets: 'To the Onlie Begetter of These Insuing Sonnets Mr
W. H. . . .'

Tar Baby: character in *Uncle Remus*, chapter II, 'The wonderful
Tar Baby story'.

149 *If you're anxious for to shine . . . line*: Bunthorne's song in
Patience, Act I, words by W. S. Gilbert.

heave-offerings: voluntary offerings lifted up before the Lord by
Jewish priests.

'Here I come a-bulgin' and a-bilin' ": *Uncle Remus*, chapter
XVIII. Two lines are combined here.

Miss Meadows: a character in *Uncle Remus*.

150 *Symmachus*: a convert from paganism who was Pope from
498–514.

151 *Bishop Odo*: Odo, Bishop of Bayeux, was brother of William the
Conqueror.

152 *pot-hunting*: to pot-hunt, academically, was to seek for rewards
and prizes; in this case, presumably, to get them.

153 *we must all bow down, more or less, in the House of Rimmon*: we
must all tamper with our consciences, and do what we know is
wrong in order to do our job. Rimmon was the Babylonian god
who presided over storms. Naamon got Elisha's permission to
worship the god when he was with his master (2 Kings, 5: 18).

not usually devout: see note to p. 119.

preter-pluperfect: echo of R. S. Surtees, *Handley Cross*, chapter
XXXVI, where Jorrocks says to Benjamin: 'Come hup, you
preter-plupfeetense of 'umbugs.'

154 *esprit-de-maisong*: ·joke-French for 'house-spirit'.

155 *Chiron*: a centaur, and teacher of young centaurs, famous for his
knowledge of shooting, medicine, and music; also teacher of the
great heroes of his age, Achilles, Jason, Aesculapius, Hercules,
Aeneas, etc. Kipling uses him as an image of Bates, the
headmaster, otherwise Cormell Price.

157 *Cras ingens iterabimus aequor*: Horace, *Odes*, 1, 7: 'Tomorrow we
set out over the vast sea.'

The only way to make clear what King and his class are up to
is to give the text of Horace's ode, and a translation:

Caelo tonantem credidimus Iovem
regnare; praesens divus habebitur
Augustus adiectis Britannis
imperio gravibusque Persis.

milesne Crassi coniuge barbara
turpis maritus vixit et hostium
(pro curia inversique mores!)
consenuit socerorum in armis

sub rege Medo, Marsus et Apulus
anciliorum et nominis et togae
oblitus aeternaeque Vestae,
incolumi Iove et urbe Roma?

hoc caverat mens provida Reguli
dissentientis condicionibus
foedis et exemplo trahentis
perniciem veniens in aevum,

si non periret immiserabilis
captiva pubes. 'signa ego Punicis
adfixa delubris et arma
militibus sine caede' dixit

'derepta vidi, vidi ego civium
retorta tergo bracchia libero
portasque non clausas et arva
Marte coli populata nostro.

auro repensus scilicet acrior
miles redibit. flagitio additis
damnum: neque amissos colores
lana refert medicata fuco,

nec vera virtus, cum semel excidit,
curat reponi deterioribus.
si pugnat extricata densis
cerva plagis, erit ille fortis

qui perfidis se credidit hostibus,
et Marte Poenos proteret altero,
qui lora restrictis lacertis
sensit iners timuitque mortem.

hic, unde vitam sumeret inscius,
pacem duello miscuit. O pudor!
o magna Carthago, probrosis
altior Italiae ruinis!'

fertur pudicae coniugis osculum
parvosque natos ut capitis minor
ab se removisse et virilem
torvus humi posuisse voltum,

We believe that Jove is king in heaven because we hear his thunder peal; Augustus shall be deemed a god on earth for adding to our empire the Britons and dread Parthians.

Did Crassus' troops live in base wedlock with barbarian wives and (alas, our sunken Senate and our altered ways!) grow old in service of the foes whose daughters they had wedded—Marsian and Apulian submissive to a Parthian king, forgetful of the sacred shields, the Roman name, the toga, and eternal Vesta, while Jove's temples and the city Rome remained unharmed? 'Twas against this the far-seeing mind of Regulus had guarded when he revolted from the shameful terms and from such precedent foresaw ruin extending to the coming ages, should not the captive youth perish without pity. 'With mine own eyes,' he said, 'have I seen our standards hung up in Punic shrines and weapons wrested from our soldiers without bloodshed; with mine own eyes have I seen the hands of freemen pinioned behind their backs, the gates [of Carthage] open wide, the fields once ravaged by our warfare tilled again. Redeemed by gold, forsooth, our soldiers will renew the strife with greater bravery! To shame ye are but adding loss; the wool with purple dyed never regains the hue it once has lost, nor does true manhood, when it once has vanished, care to be restored to degenerate breasts. If the doe gives fight when loosened from the close-meshed toils, then will *he* be brave who has trusted himself to perfidious foes, and *he*

donec labantis consilio patres
firmaret auctor numquam alias dato,
interque maerentes amicos
egregius properaret exsul.

atque sciebat quae sibi barbarus
tortor pararet. non aliter tamen
dimovit obstantes propinques
et populum reditus morantem,

quam si clientum longa negotia
diiundicata lite relinqueret,
tendens Venafranos in agros
aut Lacedaemonium Tarentum.

will crush the Carthaginians in a
second war who has tamely felt
the thongs upon his fettered arms
and has stood in fear of death.
Such a one, not knowing how to
make his life secure, has
confounded war with peace. Alas
the shame! O mighty Carthage,
raised higher on Italy's disgraceful
ruins.'
'Tis said he put away his chaste
wife's kisses and his little
children, as one bereft of civil
rights, and sternly bent his manly
gaze upon the ground, till he
should strengthen the Senate's
wavering purpose by advice ne'er
given before, and amid sorrowing
friends should hurry forth a
glorious exile. Full well he knew
what the barbarian torturer was
making ready for him; and yet he
pushed aside the kinsmen who
blocked his path and the people
who would stay his going, with
no less unconcern than if some
case in court had been decided,
and he were leaving the tedious
business of his clients, speeding to
Venafran fields, or to Lace-
daemonian Tarentum.

Andrew Lang wrote of it: 'That poem could only have been written
by a Roman! The strength, the tenderness, the noble and
monumental resolution and resignation—these are the gifts of the
lords of human things, the masters of the world.' And Maurice
Baring called Lang's translation of it 'more satisfactory than any of
the versions in verse which [he had] seen, as satisfactory as the
translation made by Mr King to his class in Kipling's *Stalky and*
[sic] *Co*.

158 *Thank God, I have done my duty*: almost Nelson's last words.

159 *Oblittus . . . Oh-blight-us*: Beetle uses a false quantity and then
corrects it.

signs affixed to Punic deluges: the translation should be 'standards
hung up in Punic temples'.

160 *Flagitio additis damnum*: you add injury to disgrace.

162 *Bœotian*: Boeotia in ancient Greece had a reputation for boorish ignorance.

probrosis: an adjective which Vernon had rendered as a verb.

163 *Conington*: verse translation of the *Odes* of Horace by John Conington (1825–1869), first published in 1863.

Wardour Street: at the time, Wardour Street in the west end of London was used mainly by dealers in antiques and imitation-antiques, and Wardour Street English was therefore a sort of pseudo-archaic English used by historical novelists, today known as 'Tushery' (from 'Tush!' as an exclamation).

164 *As though . . . Tarentum's bay*: from Conington's version.

167 *law . . . of the Medes and Persians*: unalterable law. Daniel 6: 8.

169 *'the sin I impute to each frustrate ghost'*: Browning, 'The Statue and the Bust'. King stresses *I*, meaning himself. Browning continues: 'Is—the unlit lamp and the ungirt loin.'

the Mantuan: Virgil, who came from Mantua.

Tu regere . . . superbos: in the translation by J. W. Mackail (1850–1945) this reads: 'Be thy charge, O Roman, to rule the nations in thine empire; this shall be thine art, to ordain the law of peace, to be merciful to the conquered and beat the haughty down.' Mackail was, incidentally, Kipling's cousin by marriage; his wife was Margaret Burne-Jones, daughter of the painter Edward Burne-Jones and Kipling's Aunt Georgiana.

174 *Hypatia*: seen note to p. 147.

177 *a quasi-lictor*: a half-lictor; see note to p. 119.

178 *Analects of Confucius*: religious treatise by Confucius (551–479 BC).

178 *K.C.B.*: Knight Commander of the Order of the Bath.

White sand and grey sand: words of a well-known 'round'.

180 *A TRANSLATION*: this is not in fact a translation—there is no Fifth Book of Horace's *Odes*—but an imitation or pastiche by Kipling himself.

181 *Qui procul hinc*: from Sir Henry Newbolt's 'Clifton Chapel'. The Latin means 'Who perished far away, before his time, but as a soldier and for his country'. The third line is on the plaque in Burwash church in Sussex, which commemorates Kipling's son John, who was killed at the age of 18 in 1915 at the Battle of Loos.

the Pavvy: the London Pavilion, then a famous music-hall.

King's 'whips an' scorpions': from 1 Kings 12: 11: 'my father hath chastised you with whips, but I will chastise you with scorpions'. Since King keeps mentioning them, and they appear in the Old Testament book of Kings, it is a double joke.

182 *cat*: vomit. From the late eighteenth century to the early twentieth it was used with this meaning.

Pomposo Stinkadore: echo of Surtees's Pomponius Ego, and Bombastes Furioso, hero of a burlesque opera parodying *Orlando Furioso*.

183 *Oh, you Prooshian brute!*: see note to p. 117.

184 *'Strange, how desire doth outrun performance'*: misquoted slightly from 2 Henry IV, II. iv.

186 *Board-school games*: board-school meant what is now called a state school. Games like marbles and hopscotch were supposed to be played by children at such schools and were therefore socially despised by masters like King.

we aren't a public school . . . a shareholder, too: these are among the most quoted sentences in *Stalky & Co*, often used to make points about the United Services College. See H. A. Tapp, *United Services College* (1933), p. 1: 'The need for a school where the sons of officers of the two services could be given a good education at a moderate fee, and whence their subsequent entry into Sandhurst or Woolwich could be ensured, led to the founding of the United Services Proprietory College Ltd. at Westward Ho! in September 1874. A Company was formed, consisting mostly of Army officers, and the purchase of fifty £1 shares enabled the holder to nominate one boy for education at reduced terms. This company was not formed for profit, and the name of the School was soon shortened to the United Services College.'

187 *the mute with the bow-string*: the Turkish executioner who was a mute and strangled his victims with a bow-string.

my pound of flesh: reference to *The Merchant of Venice*.

189 *the Shop*: Royal Military Academy, Woolwich, where officers were trained for specialist arms like the Artillery and Engineers, while Infantry and Cavalry officers were trained at the Royal Military College at Sandhurst.

Chiron: see note to p. 155.

190 *D.S.O.*: Distinguished Service Order.

194 *cleek*: cloth(?). From the late 1950s, in beatnik slang, cleek has meant a wet blanket at a party. The more usual sense is a metal hook or a special kind of golf club.

Kalabagh: in the North-West Frontier Province, south of Peshawar.

Afridis: Afghans.

Sepoys: native soldiers in Indian Army.

200 *Aaron and Moses*: an unidentified but presumably obscene song.

Desire don't outrun performance: see note to p. 184.

201 *It's a way we have in the Army*: cf. note to p. 65. This seems to have been a school adaptation of the song, which Kipling quotes again in 'An English School'.

203 *K.C.B.*: see note to p. 178.

204 *fly*: hired one-horse carriage.

205 *sassingers*: sausages.

206 *Sobraon*: battle in 1846, when the Sikhs were defeated in the First Sikh War (1845–6).

207 *cads*: the word cad was then used in public schools in describe anyone not of the public-school class. It was not meant to be rude or offensive, but must have seemed so to outsiders.

208 *Minhla Fort*: near Theebaw and Mandalay in Burma. The first officer killed in the Burma campaign of 1887 was R. A. T. Dury, who was at the UCS in 1878–81, and so seems likely to be the model for Hogan.

bimbashi: British officer in the Egyptian service. It also means a Turkish military captain or commander.

209 *Sandhurst or the Shop*: see note to p. 189 above.

210 *Catullus*: Roman poet, 87–54 BC.

Defence or Defiance: the motto of the Volunteer Movement of 1859 was 'Defence not Defiance'.

rot: chaff, tease, mock, talk ironically [of].

privatim et seriatim: see note to p. 62 above.

ergo: therefore; *propter hoc*: on account of this.

212 *They've tiled the lodge . . . complete*: reference to the secrecy of Masonic meetings.

215 *five years of Mr Gladstone's rule*: beginning with the defeat of the Conservatives in 1880.

without form and void: Genesis I: 1.

216 *bargee*: see note to p. 63.

217 *Bopper*: this may have been an invented word, referring to the *Boy's Own Paper*. See note to p. 101.

Jebusite: the Jebusites were the original inhabitants of Jerusalem and the land around it. David said: 'Whosoever smiteth the Jebusites first shall be chief and captain. So Joab the son of Zeruiah went first up, and was chief.' In the seventeenth century it was used as a nickname for Roman Catholics, particularly Jesuits, and in general as a term of abuse. The *Hivites* were another of the peoples inhabiting Palestine before the Jewish settlement there.

Gadarene Swine: Mark 5.

220 *bred in a Board-school*: see note to p. 186.

223 *pearls . . . cast before young swine*: reference to Matthew 7: 6.

ad hoc: for this purpose.

224 *epigonoi*: originally, the seven sons of the Argive chiefs who in Greek legend marched against the city of Thebes in Boeotia. The Greek word, meaning descendants, came to mean the less distinguished descendants of an earlier generation.

Harrison Ainsworth: (1805–82) a writer of historical novels, which were not intended particularly for the young but were very popular with children until recently; the best known are *The Tower of London* and *Old St Paul's*.

Marryat: Captain Frederick Marryat, 1792–1848, writer of adventure stories which were popular with schoolboys before Kipling's day (Tom Brown and his friends were reading them in the 1850s). His best-known books are *Peter Simple, Mr Midshipman Easy, Masterman Ready, The Settlers in Canada*, and *The Children of the New Forest*.

the dog of Scripture: 2 Peter 2:2.

Allow me to observe . . . Peter Simple: In his introduction to *Peter Simple*, David Hannay writes: 'Gentleman Chucks, who by common consent is Marryat's masterpiece . . . would of himself be enough to place the book high . . . In Marryat's hands he is one of the fellowship of brave, good men with a bee in his bonnet, a relation, humble but undoubted, of Don Quixote, my Uncle Toby, Lismahago and the Baron of Bradwardine. Not one of them would have seen anything absurd in Mr Chucks's aspiration to be a gentleman.'

Dr Johnson, as limned by Macaulay: see Macaulay's essay on Samuel Johnson in the *Edinburgh Review*, September 1831. Collected in his *Critical and Historical Essays*.

Admirable Crichton: someone distinguished by outstanding all-round talents. The original, who inspired the name, was James

Crichton (1560–85), a Scottish traveller, scholar, and swordsman, who was portrayed in Sir Thomas Urquhart's *The Exquisite Jewel*, which in turn inspired Harrison Ainsworth's novel *The Admirable Crichton*. J. M. Barrie's play of the same name, often performed, and the film made from it, have made it familiar in more modern times. The expression obviously never fell out of use, as it is used descriptively and in a familiar way in, for instance, Cuthbert Bede's *Adventures of Mr Verdant Green* and H. A. Vachell's school story, *The Hill*.

Du Maurier: George du Maurier, whose drawings in *Punch* and book illustrations made familiar, both then and even today, a certain style of (particularly female) looks.

225 *De tous ces défunts cockolores*: this, in *Punch*, was a limerick. Kipling leaves out the first line: 'Chaque époque a ses grands noms sonores.'

Fénélon: François de Salignac de la Mothe (1651–1715), known as Fénélon after his birthplace, French writer and ecclesiastic.

'Oh, won't you come up, come up?': traditional chorus sung after each solo when limericks are sung. The full chorus is:

> Oh, *won't* you come up, come up (twice)
> Oh, won't you come up,
> Come all the way up,
> Come all the way up to Limerick.

225 *Curiosities of Literature*: by Isaac D'Israeli, father of Lord Beaconsfield; a rag-bag of literary anecdotes and miscellaneous information which obviously appealed to the young Kipling.

not without dust and heat: quotation from Milton's *Areopagitica* (1644).

226 *impot-basket*: see note to p. 56.

Twelfth of the Third: the twelfth Ode in Horace's third book of *Odes*.

Ionicum a minore: the techical name of the metre used in this Ode, with feet consisting of two 'short' followed by two 'long' syllables.

Miserar' . . .: the opening lines of the Ode.

227 *Aubrey*: John Aubrey, 1626–97, antiquary whose biographical collections were published as *Brief Lives* after his death.

his Dikker: Johnson's *Dictionary of the English Language: in Which the Words are Deduced from Their Originals, and*

Illustrated in Their Different Significations by Examples from the Best Writers, 1755; last revised by him in 1775.

For a draw: as a leg-pull.

Philistine: Matthew Arnold's term for the English middle classes, first used in *Culture and Anarchy*, 1869, and much used in Kipling's day.

Picciolas: *Picciola*, a sentimental novel about a prisoner and a flower, by Joseph Saintine, 1836, often used in schools.

Sammivel, not Binjimin: Samuel (Johnson), not Ben (Jonson); also of course a reference to Dickens (*Pickwick Papers*) and Surtees (*Jorrocks*).

228 *della Cruscan*: a school of poetry started by some young Englishmen in Florence in the eighteenth century, which took its name from the Accademia della Crusca (Academy of Chaff) founded in Florence in 1582, hoping to sift the 'chaff' from the Italian language, and publishing a dictionary in 1611.

Ap-Howell: 'Ap' is a Welsh prefix to a surname, meaning 'son of'.

divvy: divide up.

229 *Claude Halcro in the 'Pirate'*: unstoppably verbose poet in *The Pirate* by Sir Walter Scott.

Nearly all the facts and names on this page and the next come from Isaac D'Israeli's *Curiosities of Literature*.

Hell Crow chap: mispronunciation of Halcro.

Mandeville: Robert de Mandeville (1670–1733), a Dutchman who came to England and wrote medical and other works, including *The Fable of the Bees* in 1714.

two girls: Swift's two loves, Vanessa and Stella (in real life, Esther Vanhomrigh and Esther Johnson).

Saw a tree an' said 'I shall die at the top': this is not in the *Curiosities of Literature* but is quoted by Sir Walter Scott in his *Memoirs of Swift* (1814): 'I shall be like that tree, I shall die at the top.'

ridiculous and trivial: from *Curiosities of Literature* but not a direct quotation; Isaac D'Israeli mentions 'ridiculous amusements' and 'perpetual trifles'.

Bags I: I claim, I'm having. Slang used by schoolchildren until recently; perhaps still used today.

230 *Diderot*: Denis Diderot, 1713–84, French philosopher and man of letters.

Sappers: nickname for Royal Engineers.

231 *Not much*: certainly not. Cf. 'not half'.

some Transatlantic abomination about Shakespeare and Bacon: the suggestion that Shakespeare did not write his plays but that they were written by Francis Bacon was first made by Herbert Lawrence in 1769. In 1857 books by William Henry Smith and Delia Bacon appeared on the subject, and by the end of the century there were many 'Baconians', mainly American. *The Great Cryptogram* by Ignatius Donnelly, published in 1887, tried to show that cryptograms in the plays showed Bacon as their author, but this was too late for *Stalky & Co*, of course.

Sutton: a fictitious Oxford college.

233 *hirpling*: hobbling and limping.

Lundy: the island, famous for its puffins, which is visible from this part of the north Devon coast.

234 *Elsie Venner*: novel by Oliver Wendell Holmes (1809–94), American physician and writer, about a woman whose mother was poisoned by a rattlesnake before her birth.

Nathaniel: Nathaniel Holmes, author of *The Authorship of Shakespeare*, New York, 1866.

Delia: *Philosophy of the Plays of Shakespeare Unfolded* by Delia Bacon (1811–59), with a preface by Nathaniel Holmes, published in London and Boston, 1866.

235 *seidlitz powder*: a laxative named after Seidlitz in Bohemia; a substitute for mineral water.

ushers: disparaging word for masters.

236 *Bonnie Dundee*: song with words by Sir Walter Scott.

237 *Virtue has gone out of me indeed*: Mark 5: 30 and Luke 8: 46.

ab initio: from the start.

'rustic' and 'sorry poetaster': Nathaniel Holmes described Shakespeare as 'the sorriest poetaster'.

lie in the soul: phrase used by Benjamin Jowett, 1817–93, in his introduction to his translation of Plato's *Republic*: 'The lie in the soul is a true lie.'

one Jowett: Jowett was Master of Balliol, 'where King came from'.

238 *'There lives more faith . . . creeds'*: from Tennyson's *In Memoriam*, XCVI.

spunging-house: a house kept by a bailiff or sheriff's officer, formerly used as a place of preliminary confinement for debtors.

nott: not a misprint but an attempt to give M'Turk's Irish accent.

viva voce: oral examination.

239 *gigs*: spectacles, from gig-lamps; Kipling's school nickname, from the spectacles he wore, was Gigger. See note to p. 56.

cushat dove: ring dove or wood pigeon.

240 *Don't—make—a—noise . . . Baby!*: from a popular song written and composed by G. W. Hunt, *c.*1875.

I bowed down in the House of Rimmon: see note to p. 153 above.

242 *Cyrano de Bergerac*: play, 1897, by Edmond Rostand, 1868–1918, on a seventeenth-century author famous for the largeness and redness of his nose.

fags: see note to p. 31.

'burning marl': Milton, *Paradise Lost*, I, 295–6; Satan's 'uneasy steps/Over the burning marle'.

coals of fire: Proverbs 25: 22.

blue-snouted Mandrill: large, hideous, and ferocious baboon.

243 *Royal Line of Ashantee*: King Prempahl of Coomassie then represented the royal line.

His naval uncle had fought in those parts: in the Ashantee War of 1873–4.

The Temple of Janus was opened: war was declared. Janus, the most ancient king in Italy, and according to some the son of Apollo, was shown with two faces because he knew the past and the future. The gates of his temples were opened in times of war, closed in peacetime.

Cartel: written challenge to a duel.

the Gaboon: a river in West Africa, which gave its name to the delta district.

Dahomey: a large country in the Gulf of Guinea, famous for its Customs, an annual festival in October at which human victims were put to death. Dick 'robed in a tablecloth' may have been imitating the way victims were dressed in white shirts and long white nightcaps.

Fantee: large tribe living south of Ashantee, whose language, also called Fantee, was used widely on the Gold Coast.

245 *The Lord's Anointed*: king by divine right; in other words, indescribably grand, don't touch him.

246 *'slugs in a saw-pit'*: from Marryat's *Peter Simple*. The midshipman challenges Peter to a duel: 'Then sir, as a gentleman, I demand satisfaction. Slugs in a saw-pit. Death before dishonour.'

sally: saloon pistol. See note to p. 73.

Plica Polonica . . . Polish plat: a matted, filthy condition of the hair, due to disease (Polish plait).

Marryat: see note to p. 224.

247 *Selah!*: Hebrew word of unknown origin, supposed to be a musical direction and used in the psalms.

248 *the King of Coomassie*: Dick Four. Coomassie was the capital of Ashantee.

249 *'I've drilled the Mandrill . . .'*: to drill was a slang term in duelling; see *Peter Simple*, chapter 4: 'Being winged implied being shot through the arm or leg, whereas being drilled was to be shot through the body.'

in absentia: in his absence.

250 *scrabbling, like King David*: when he pretended to be mad, fearing Achish the King of Gath. 1 Samuel 21: 13.

lousy Fenians: in this case, merely 'Irish'; strictly, members of the league founded in 1858 among the Irish in America to promote revolution and overthrow English rule in Ireland.

252 *nott*: see note to p. 238.

252 *Rabbit's Eggs*: see note to p. 59.

253 *nott*: see note to p. 238.

R.E.: Royal Engineers.

254 *he tipped like Croesus*: Croesus, 560–46 BC, was king of Lydia and immensely rich.

House of Rimmon: see note to p. 153.

in Abraham's bosom: dead. Luke 16: 22.

256 *Non omnis moriar*: I shall not altogether die. Horace, *Odes* III, 6.

257 *Cathay*: China. Dunsterville served there in 1900–2.

258 *Sinim*: Isaiah's name for the land at the back of the Orient, therefore usually taken to mean China. Isaiah 49: 12.

259 *the College paper which Beetle edited*: the *United Services College Chronicle*, Nos. 4–10, from June 1881–July 1882.

Swillingford Patriot: a reference to Surtees's *Mr Sponge's Sporting Tour*.

Hakluyt: Richard Hakluyt, 1553–1616, compiler of first-hand accounts of travels and explorations, published in 1589 as *The Principal Navigations, Voyages, Traffics and Discoveries of the English Nation*, now more familiarly known as 'Hakluyt's Voyages'.

Rubáiyát: Edward Fitzgerald, 1809–83, translated (freely) the *Rubáiyát* of Omar Khyyâm, the astronomer-poet of Persia (died c.1122). This was published in 1859, revised and enlarged in 1863, revised again in 1872 and revised finally and reprinted in 1879. It is still popular and much quoted.

Alexander Smith: poet, 1830–67.

L.E.L.: Letitia Elizabeth Landon, a mid-nineteenth-century poetess.

Lydia Sigourney: American poetess, born Lydia Howard Bentley, who wrote children's books, stories, moral pieces in prose and verse, and biographies.

Fletcher: Phineas Fletcher, 1582–1650, who wrote *The Purple Island* (1633), a long poem.

Ossian: Gaelic poet, translated very freely by James Macpherson, 1736–96, the authenticity of whose poems was challenged, especially by Dr Johnson.

The Earthly Paradise: a long poem by William Morris, published in 1863.

Atalanta in Calydon: a poetic drama by Algernon Charles Swinburne, published in 1865.

journals, long dead: the *Oxford and Cambridge Magazine* of 1856, which contained much early work by William Morris (prose and verse), and contributions from Burne-Jones, Rossetti, and Price himself. Also *The Germ*, a much earlier Pre-Raphaelite paper.

260 *high and disposedly*: a reference to Sir James Melville's description of Queen Elizabeth in his *Memoirs*.

Cooper's Hill: familiar name for the Royal Indian College of Civil Engineering.

262 *Ulpian serves your need*; *'Aha! Elucescebat, quoth our friend'*: both from Browning's 'The Bishop orders his tomb at St Praxed's church'.

266 *Confer orationes Regis furiosissimi*: Kipling's own Latin: Compare the speeches of the very furious King.

formes: the forme is a metal frame into which the type is locked after composition. Loose blocks of type are made into a single solid mass by hammering in wedges of wood, called quoins. Thus a forme can be moved about, stood on its side, etc.

267 *In Verrem: actio prima*: one of Cicero's *Orations*, delivered in 70 BC.

"Member what the considerate Bloomer did . . . Hounds?": a Bloomer was a follower of Mrs Bloomer's dress reforms of 1849, of which bloomers were a part. In R. S. Surtees's *Mr Sponge's Sporting Tour*, 1853, chapter XLII, a girl altered an account written by Spraggon about a hunt, making nonsense of it. Hence, 'we must sugar Mr King's milk for him'.

One of those scientific rests . . . celebrated: another reference to *Mr Sponge's Sporting Tour*.

268 *Quis multa gracilis*: Horace's *Ode*, I, 5, much translated and quoted.

'Let me from the bonded ware'ouse . . . knowledge' (and the following quotations): R. S. Surtees, *Handley Cross*, chapter XXXII.

269 *'Hellish dark and smells of cheese'*: *Handley Cross*, chapter LVII.

Pomponius Ego: a self-satisfied character in *Handley Cross*.

272 *Hakluyt*: see note on page 259.

273 *Tulkiss is an honourable man*: reference to Mark Anthony's speech after Caesar's murder, beginning 'Friends, Romans, countrymen', in Shakespeare's *Julius Caesar*, in which he says repeatedly that Brutus is an honourable man.

274 *Pretty lips . . .*: popular song of the 1870s.

gig-lamps: see note to p. 73.

Didn't I 'Eric' 'em?: didn't I use Farrar's sort of language and attitudes on them?

276 *par-ergon*: a by-work, any work subsidiary to another.

277 *Dolabella & Co.*: Dolabella was an associate of Verres whom Cicero was attacking in this speech.

278 *frabjously*: taken from the Jabberwocky poem in Lewis Carroll's *Through the Looking Glass*, and made into an adverb. See note to p. 81.

279 *Boh*: a chief of dacoits in Burma.

detrimentals: slang, meaning younger brothers of heirs, or unsuitable suitors.

cut the service: resign my commission.

Tamar: a troopship, used mainly to take soldiers to and from the UK on change of station or on leave.

280 *a lean Irishman*: M'Turk.

dak-bungalow: Indian rest-house.

princess-skirt: see note to p. 56.

281 *broke*: here means cashiered, dismissed from the army.

282 *Khye-Kheen Hills*: an invented name, not a real place, though the story is based in part on the defence of Chitral in 1895.

283 *summo ingenio*: with the greatest cleverness.

nucleused: possibly an invented word; it means 'made a nucleus of'.

D.A.Q.M.G.: Deputy Assistant Quartermaster General.

Umballa: Umbala or Ambala, city in the Punjab (now Pakistan).

Durbar Sahib at Amritzar: holy audience offered by Sikhs to the Golden Temple at Amritsar.

khud: a deep ravine or chasm; a precipitous cleft or descent in a hillside.

Old, old story: reference to the hymn 'Tell me the old, old story' by Katherine Hankey, 1834–1911.

284 *poshteen*: according to the *OED*, it should be 'posteen'. An Afghan leather pelisse, generally of sheepskin, with the fleece on it; a sheepskin coat worn with the wool inside.

whack: rations.

285 *sungars*: breastworks of stone.

promiscuous: in no special order or position.

Jullunder: a good recruiting area between Amritsar and Ludhiana.

286 *nullah*: riverbed.

287 *grabbed his boots*: made obeisance.

288 *Pushtu*: The language of the Afghans, intermediate between the Iranian and Sanskrit families of the Arian languages.

289 *Koran Sahib*: Indian pronunciation of Corkran Sahib.

'Kubbadar! Tumbleinga!': 'Careful, you'll fall!' 'Kubbadar' means 'news', 'tumbleinga' is a mixture of English and Urdu.

Dera Ismail: a large trading town in the Punjab.

Martinis: the service rifles of the Indian Army at the time.

brownin': firing into the mass without taking precise aim.

290 *à la pas de charge*: at the double.

Arrah, Patsy . . . Baby: see note to p. 55.

Sepoy: see note to p. 194.

291 *gram-bags*: bags containing horse-fodder.

a Brahmini bull: sacred bull of the Brahmin, which must not be interfered with in any way.

consilio et auxilio: with the advice and help [of].

292 *Engadine*: Swiss district of resorts, the main one St Moritz.

Naick: corporal in the Indian Army.

Ghuznees: there was no such regiment: this is an invented name.

nullah: see note to p. 286.

rapparree: originally an Irish pikeman or irregular soldier, hence Irish bandit, robber, or freebooter. Here it means a disreputable rascal.

293 *Bancroft*: Sir Squire Bancroft (1841–1926), a famous actor-manager who specialized in drawing-room comedy; at the Haymarket Theatre from 1880–5.

pukka: Anglo-Indian word meaning regular, good, sound, proper.

Bahadur: title of respect in India appended to a person's name; from a Hindi word meaning gallant.

294 *Pledged the State's ticker, eh?*: promised more than he was entitled to. 'Ticker' recalls the pawning of Beetle's watch at school.

image and superscription: Matthew 22: 20.

Warren Hastings: 1732–1818; Governor-General of Bengal, initiated many reforms. He was impeached after his retirement in 1783, his trial lasted for seven years (1788–95), and he was finally acquitted.

295 *horns of the altar*: 1 Kings 1: 50. The popular misconception is that (as Kipling obviously thought) victims could be offered up on the horns of the altar. In fact, they were to provide someone seeking sanctuary with a support to cling to.

basket-hanger: see note to p. 62.

femme incomprise: misunderstood woman; phrase possibly used by Sardou.

296 *doab*: tongue of land between two rivers.

bhai: brother.

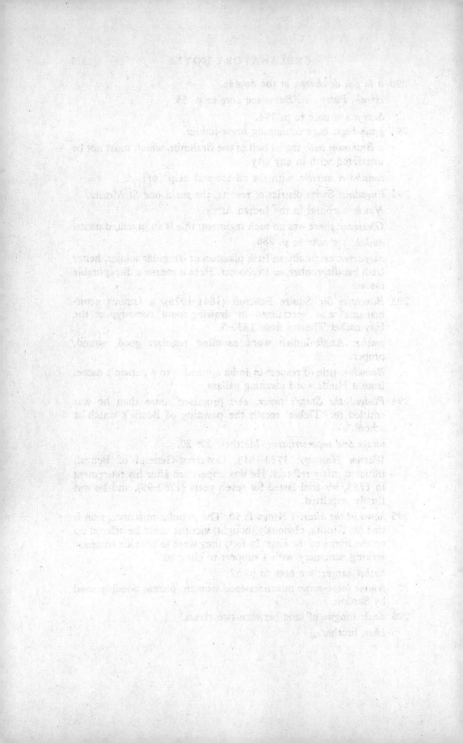

The Oxford World's Classics Website

www.worldsclassics.co.uk

- Browse the full range of Oxford World's Classics online

- Sign up for our monthly e-alert to receive information on new titles

- Read extracts from the Introductions

- Listen to our editors and translators talk about the world's greatest literature with our Oxford World's Classics audio guides

- Join the conversation, follow us on Twitter at OWC_Oxford

- Teachers and lecturers can order inspection copies quickly and simply via our website

www.worldsclassics.co.uk

American Literature

British and Irish Literature

Children's Literature

Classics and Ancient Literature

Colonial Literature

Eastern Literature

European Literature

Gothic Literature

History

Medieval Literature

Oxford English Drama

Philosophy

Poetry

Politics

Religion

The Oxford Shakespeare

A complete list of Oxford World's Classics, including Authors in Context, Oxford English Drama, and the Oxford Shakespeare, is available in the UK from the Marketing Services Department, Oxford University Press, Great Clarendon Street, Oxford OX2 6DP, or visit the website at www.oup.com/uk/worldsclassics.

In the USA, visit www.oup.com/us/owc for a complete title list.

Oxford World's Classics are available from all good bookshops. In case of difficulty, customers in the UK should contact Oxford University Press Bookshop, 116 High Street, Oxford OX1 4BR.